SAVAGE AND BARBARIC, the mighty SPACE Wolves are amongst the most ferocious of the Emperor's Space Marines. Many times has their feral fury been the deciding factor in key battles against the enemies of mankind.

Together with the other members of the Wolf-blade, Ragnar is sent to the planet Hyades, where the Space Wolves run into their ancient rivals, the Dark Angels. Can the two Space Marine Chapters put aside their ancient enmity and learn to work together before the dark forces of Chaos destroy them all?

A WARHAMMER 40,000 NOVEL

SONS OF FENRIS

By Lee Lightner

We'd like to dedicate this book to our families for their sacrifice and support, to all of our battle-brothers for their unending friendship and finally to the folks at Black Library for giving us this incredible opportunity.

A BLACK LIBRARY PUBLICATION

First published in Great Britain in 2007 by
BL Publishing,
Games Workshop Ltd.,
Willow Road, Nottingham,
NG7 2WS, UK

10 9 8 7 6 5 4 3

Cover illustration by Geoff Taylor.

A CIP record for this book is available from the British Library

ISBN 13: 978 1 84416 388 5

ISBN 10: 1 84416 388 1

Distributed in the US by Simon & Schuster
1230 Avenue of the Americas, New York, NY 10020, US.

See the Black Library on the Internet at
www.blacklibrary.com

Find out more about Games Workshop
and the world of Warhammer 40,000 at
www.games-workshop.com

IT IS THE 41st millennium. For more than a hundred centuries the Emperor has sat immobile on the Golden Throne of Earth. He is the master of mankind by the will of the gods, and master of a million worlds by the might of his inexhaustible armies. He is a rotting carcass writhing invisibly with power from the Dark Age of Technology. He is the Carrion Lord of the Imperium for whom a thousand souls are sacrificed every day, so that he may never truly die.

YET EVEN IN his deathless state, the Emperor continues his eternal vigilance. Mighty battlefleets cross the daemon-infested miasma of the warp, the only route between distant stars, their way lit by the Astronomican, the psychic manifestation of the Emperor's will. Vast armies give battle in his name on uncounted worlds. Greatest amongst his soldiers are the Adeptus Astartes, the Space Marines, bio-engineered super-warriors. Their comrades in arms are legion: the Imperial Guard and countless planetary defence forces, the ever-vigilant Inquisition and the tech-priests of the Adeptus Mechanicus to name only a few. But for all their multitudes, they are barely enough to hold off the ever-present threat from aliens, heretics, mutants – and worse.

TO BE A man in such times is to be one amongst untold billions. It is to live in the cruellest and most bloody regime imaginable. These are the tales of those times. Forget the power of technology and science, for so much has been forgotten, never to be re-learned. Forget the promise of progress and understanding, for in the grim dark future there is only war. There is no peace amongst the stars, only an eternity of carnage and slaughter, and the laughter of thirsting gods.

PROLOGUE

SPLASHES OF COLOUR painted the clouds with a swirl of reds, oranges and yellows, silhouetting the black and grey towers of Saint Harman, the once great capital city of Corinthus V. Wolf Lord Ragnar Blackmane found a sense of satisfaction in the ability of instruments of Imperial justice to duplicate the dawn of a new day in the middle of the night. Every explosion from the Imperial artillery, every bombardment from the fleet above, left its own mark on the tapestry of the sky.

Ragnar took an extra moment to commit this battle to memory. So many wars on countless worlds could make a Space Marine forget. The wars never ended for humanity's defenders. They constantly went forth to do the will of the Emperor of Mankind and battle the enemies of the Imperium. The Imperial Guard had fought the Chaos incursion for almost a year. After only a month, Ragnar and his great company of Space Wolves had turned the tide of the campaign.

Once Corinthus V had produced munitions and vehicles for the Imperium's vast armies, and the populace took pride in their work, too much pride in fact, looking to the glory of the machine instead of keeping their faith in the Emperor. While the citizens had performed their duties making ammunition for the Space Marine Chapters and the Imperial Guard, including Ragnar's own Space Wolves, the taint of Chaos had slipped onto Corinthus V. Every one of the Space Marines, the ultimate warriors of the Imperium, knew the dangers of Chaos. Daemons from the warp whispered twisted thoughts, corrupting even the most dedicated. Only faith in the Emperor could protect one from Chaos. When Corinthus V lost its faith, Chaos gained its hold. Now, the Space Wolves had almost reached victory.

Ragnar made a point of trying to remember each campaign before its end, and it was time for the end. The time was right for his Space Wolves to make their final assault. The treacherous enemy, rebels and worshippers of the ruinous powers of Chaos, were all but destroyed. One last strike and this campaign was won.

RAGNAR STOOD ALONE on top of the rocky heights overlooking the city. He enjoyed this time the most. Just before battle, the world seemed different, quiet and tranquil. Moments of quiet were rare in a lifetime of constant warfare. He knew that the moment would not last. His job was not yet done. He caught a familiar scent on the air, and knew it was time.

Powerful strides brought Ranulf, a member of the Wolf Guard, Ragnar's own elite bodyguard, to the top of the hill to stand next to his Wolf Lord. Ranulf was the largest Space Wolf that he had ever known, gifted by the spirit of Leman Russ, primarch of their Chapter, with unparalleled strength. Ragnar thought that if Leman Russ returned to lead the Space Wolves, this Wolf Guard might be able to look the ancient primarch in the eye. More important than his size, Ranulf was one of Ragnar's oldest and dearest friends and the most trusted of his Wolf Guard, holding the title of battle leader, giving him command if the Wolf Lord should fall.

'Are the men assembled?' Ragnar asked.

'Yes, Lord Ragnar, your Wolf Guard awaits you,' Ranulf replied.

Ragnar turned and clapped Ranulf's shoulder. 'As well they should. I'd hate to have them finish the war without me. Ranulf, let's finally be rid of this Chaos filth.'

'What's the current status?' asked Ragnar.

'For the most part, the heretics are scattered and disorganised, but some of them have fortified small strong points within Saint Harman. The Imperial Guard has kept them at bay, but they need us to break the final strongholds.'

'Good. The Imperial Guard commander remembered my instructions from the beginning of the campaign. He's saved the last for us to face in the assaults. Starting a war is easy, finishing it is hard.

We've got the hard part to do. These heretics have one last push in them.'

'M'lord?' asked Ranulf.

'My instincts tell me that they are luring us into a false sense of security. They haven't fought nearly as hard this time. We haven't even moved into the combat in Saint Harman. Our Space Wolves had to help the Imperial Guard to even gain a foothold in the other cities. On every other location on this planet, the Chaos worshippers fought tooth and nail, but here in the capital as their last stand, they are routed? I don't think so. They are in trouble, but a cornered animal is always dangerous. Of course, so are Wolves,' Ragnar grinned, exposing his long and sharpened canines. The gene-seed, which transformed Space Wolves from men to superhuman warriors, gave them many gifts. Besides their stature, standing half a metre taller than any man, the most outwardly visible sign was their extended canines. The older a Space Wolf was, the longer they grew. For a Wolf Lord, Ragnar was rather short in the tooth, but no one dared mention it to him.

The Wolf Guard stood ready. Three of Ragnar's finest warriors, Tor, Uller and Hrolf, awaited him. Unlike other packs, Ragnar's Wolf Guard each carried their own individual arms and weapons. The most experienced and reliable of all of his Space Wolves, they had proven themselves a hundred times over. Now, they would have to prove themselves once more, and each one relished the chance.

'You'll break up and go to the packs for this one. Each one of you will lead a pack. Ranulf, I want you and Tor to take Grey Hunter packs near my flanks.

Uller, you'll move your men parallel to Tor. I'll be with the Blood Claws.'

Ragnar preferred to fight alongside the Blood Claws, the youngest and most restless warriors, newly initiated Space Wolves. They possessed a wild abandon, a raw desire for victory that required strong guidance.

Ragnar unfolded a map. 'Tor, your pack will flank my right. You will enter the city here and move north towards the Administratum sector. Ranulf you'll flank my left, on the edge of the merchant sector. We'll be spread thin, so stay alert.'

Ranulf, Tor and Uller took command of their Grey Hunters, the Space Wolves' tried and true veterans. Ragnar watched them leave. He had fought alongside all three countless times. However, Ragnar had just granted Tor the honour of joining the Wolf Guard. Ragnar knew he was ready for it. He just wondered if Tor knew it.

'What would you like me to do, m'lord Ragnar?' The sarcasm in Hrolf's voice was so thick that a frostaxe could cut it.

'Hrolf, I'm sorry I thought you were dead,' Ragnar stated. The two men shared a long running joke, as Hrolf was by far the oldest member of the great company and Ragnar was the youngest of the Wolf Lords. Despite the difference in rank and age, Hrolf and Ragnar shared a strong bond of brotherhood.

'Haven't found the war big enough to kill me yet, Ragnar, and once I do, you'll have the Iron Priests wire me into the next available Dreadnought, because you hate going to war without me.' Both men burst into laughter.

One look at Hrolf's face said everything about the old Space Wolf. It was a map to his past, riddled with scars like landmarks from centuries of war, while his storm-grey eyes reminded Ragnar of the worst hurricanes on their home world of Fenris. Ragnar could see countless horrors and wonders reflected in those eyes. However, his huge smile stood out in contrast to his rough face.

Ragnar threw an arm around his oldest Wolf Guard. 'Old friend, once again I need you with your Long Fangs. Who else can best handle the heavy support? I'm assuming that you've scouted the best place to position your pack?'

'Aye sir, up on the ridge where you spent the morning admiring Saint Harman, and the ruins of the old spaceport shuttle pad there.' Hrolf pointed to the south-east ridge, which jutted from the tree canopy, and then to the south-west.

'Looks perfect, Hrolf, in fact you're in luck, someone positioned my Long Fangs at both locations.' Ragnar admired Hrolf's initiative. 'Should anything unexpected arise you'll have enough firepower to shift the balance back in our favour.'

THE SPACE WOLVES moved into the city on foot, making their way first through the burning industrial sector. The air held the scents of blood, decay, smoke and death, along with burning toxins from destroyed machinery. Beneath it all, Ragnar could separate one scent from the others: the sickly sweet taint of Chaos. The enemy was here. The hairs on his neck rose.

The Space Wolves spent the next few hours in silence, communicating through hand gestures and body language. The packs knew each other and each individual covered his battle-brothers. There was no resistance, even though the Imperial Guard had reported fire from several of the buildings that the Space Wolves cleared. Ragnar found access tunnels and entrances to sewer pipes large enough for a man. The enemy was moving. He suppressed a low growl. Stories of Commissar Yarrick's defeat of the orks on Armageddon came to mind. Surrounded and left for dead, the commissar had rallied a hive to hold out against the ork horde using pipes and tunnels to ambush the greenskins. If the heretics intended to defeat Ragnar that way, they'd learn that he was a wolf, not an ork.

The packs had spread out, seeking resistance. Ragnar worried that they had moved out too far. His Space Wolves had a little of their Wolf Lord in them, and confidence was not something he lacked. He activated his comm.

'Ranulf, report your position and situation.'

'We've moved along the merchant sector and entered what looks from the ruins to be the workers' housing area. We're just to the north of you. Everything is quiet, Wolf Lord… too quiet.'

'Agreed. Stay cautious and hungry. We're in a bombed-out intersection on the western edge of the Administratum sector, near the library. If they are going to strike, it will be soon. Pass the word,' Ragnar replied.

The Administratum sector of Saint Harman was once the heart of the city. Holding elements of the vast bureaucracy meant to enforce the Emperor's will, the area dictated the ebb and flow of Corinthus V. Reports flowed freely on every aspect of the citizens' life. Like many worlds in the Imperium, freedoms were strictly controlled to protect humanity from outside influences. Administration buildings, mediator precincts, and Imperial chapels were everywhere, all designed in the architectural style of the same structures on Holy Terra, home of the Golden Throne, eternal resting place for the Holy Emperor. They served as a constant reminder that it was from Terra that the Emperor of Mankind launched his holy crusade to reunite humanity in the hopes of protecting them. They hoped to protect them from exactly what had happened on Corinthus V.

Ragnar turned to the Blood Claws around him. The pack was restless. Arik, one of the youngest, kept activating his chainsword, causing the blade to growl like a hungry beast. Ragnar shook his head. 'Steady lads. Keep your senses keen and your minds focused,' he said quietly.

Suddenly, Ragnar heard a crash from inside the ground floor of the Imperial library to the east. It was a tall monolithic building, which put Ragnar in mind of a colossal crypt. Before the war, servitors and aged scholars would have moved quietly through stacks of scrolls, books and datapads within its walls. The tall windows of the library were dark, giving no signs of life, but Ragnar and his pack had definitely heard a crash.

Arik broke into a run, waving his chainsword, and howling his desire for combat. 'There, Wolf Lord, in th–'

Those were the last words that Arik would ever speak. A bolter shell tore through the Blood Claw's head, spreading fragments of his skull in front of his body. To Ragnar's surprise, the shot had come from behind. It was an ambush.

A barrage of fire echoed from behind the pack, and Ragnar felt a bolter shell ricochet off his power armour.

'Ranulf, ambush, we're pinned in crossfire! Hold your ground and be ready for a rapid fire drill.' Ragnar growled in anticipation, feeling more like a Blood Claw than the Wolf Lord he was. 'It should be a full-scale counter-attack.'

Suddenly shards of reinforced rockcrete and ceramite exploded all around the pack. The hot wind of plasma fire vaporised stone and reinforcing steel. The Blood Claws howled, more like wolves than trained Space Marines, circling for a target, looking for someone to attack. 'Find cover,' ordered Ragnar, but the violent explosions drowned his words. The air was rank with smells, so much so that it was hard to isolate and identify them. They were surrounded. Quick glimpses of targets were all they could see, like smoke in a strong wind, almost visible for a second and then gone.

Then Ulrik, Bori and three others stopped. Ragnar knew they had a target, he also knew...

'Ulrik, Bori, stop,' Ragnar shouted. It was too late. They had committed themselves in the direction of the library. He had lost control and his pack was going to charge into that dark vault. Ragnar had no choice. 'In the Emperor's name...' he cursed.

'*Charge!*' Ragnar howled, drawing his frostblade and charging at the library.

The Blood Claws all heard their leader's command. Charging replaced confusion, as the rest of the pack joined Ragnar, screaming out their battle cries as one, 'For Fenris, for Russ, for the Emperor!'

The Space Wolves unleashed a hailstorm of bolt pistol shots into the library as they charged. Chainswords growled to life, and power weapons flashed with energy, hungering for the blood of their unseen foes. The huge Space Marines raced each other, each one hoping for the first strike.

Before the Blood Claws could reach the enemy the ground rippled and exploded as a missile strike stopped them short, shredding two of their number and sending Ragnar flying. Melta guns lashed out into the pack, instantly incinerating even the Space Marines' ancient power armour. Ragnar watched his own symbol melt away with the arm of one of his Blood Claws, and realised that he and his Wolf brothers were not facing a mere group of Imperial citizens corrupted by the foul powers of Chaos. Their hidden enemies were too well equipped and far too accurate. The Space Wolves were in trouble. Ragnar had only seconds to regain control. He moved through the cover, trying to get a better view. Taking up a position against a large section of collapsed wall, a cold chill enveloped Ragnar's hearts as he realised who they faced – Chaos Space Marines!

TEN THOUSAND years ago, a terrible civil war nearly destroyed the Imperium. After the fall of the rebels' leader, Horus, the traitors fled into the warp, the nightmare realm beyond space and time. Living in a realm of daemons for ten thousand years, they had honed their skills and fuelled their hatred. Their armour and weapons had changed, fusing with the daemonic energies of Chaos. In all ways, they were better warriors than the Space Wolves, with age-old experience empowered by millennia-old hatred.

Chaos Space Marines lacked only one thing that the Space Wolves possessed; faith in the Emperor. For Ragnar's Space Wolves, they would have to hope that their belief in the Emperor was greater than the Chaos Space Marines' desire for revenge. That was their only advantage.

Ragnar saw one of the Chaos Marines stride forth from the swirling smoke of battle. The giant figure wore glittering dark armour that reflected the light as if it was wet with slime – a Night Lord. A halo of burning fire leapt between the traitor's mutant horns. He swung a black flail that howled like the winter winds of Fenris in one hand, while a skull covered bolter spat death from his other hand.

Ragnar felt the wave of hatred and anger lash out as the servant of Chaos fired his bolter, each shot striking a Space Wolf as if the ancient warrior willed his shells into his victims.

The Wolf Lord raised his gun to return fire, but the Night Lord stepped to the side, avoiding the shots instinctively. For a second, Ragnar thought the smoke of battle poured from the Chaos Marine's armour. If it did, then it served the traitor well. The veil enshrouded him once more. When it cleared a second later, Ragnar's giant enemy had moved. He felt the beast howl in rage within, eager to give chase and destroy his treacherous enemy.

Glancing around, he saw that not all of the buildings held enemies. 'Blood Claws to me,' Ragnar commanded as he leapt and rolled to the nearest shelter. The former Administratum building had never seen much excitement. Now, it might witness the last stand of a Wolf Lord. Nine Blood Claws joined him. Better numbers than he had expected.

They entered what looked like an office complex. The room spanned the length and depth of the entire building. Large rockcrete columns were spaced evenly throughout. Sections of the walls and floor had been destroyed, and remnants of desks and other furniture were strewn about. At the far end of the room was what looked like an old elevator shaft, filled with debris from the floors above. Next to it was a stairwell. It looked severely damaged, but it was intact.

'Sons of Russ, follow me. Our destiny awaits!' Ragnar crossed the room and vaulted up the stairs. They had to reach higher ground and get above the fray. He hoped that whatever spirits held old buildings together they'd keep this one from collapsing.

It was time for Ragnar to stop playing Blood Claw and be the Wolf Lord. He activated his comm.

'Hrolf, bring your Long Fangs to bear. Target the Imperial library and whatever building nearby has Chaos Havocs shooting from it. We've got real enemies.'

'Havocs? They're mine. You'll have new drinking vessels from their helms, if my men leave enough of their horns.'

The stairway shook as explosions rocked the building's foundations. Ragnar looked behind to check on his pack. Despite his concerns, the Blood Claws kept their balance as they clambered across rubble and broken stairs, moving ever higher. More tremors struck and Ragnar saw a bright orange flash through one of the cracks in the walls. This was what being a Space Wolf was all about, he thought. Ragnar and his Wolves were in their element, outnumbered and outgunned, but not outmatched. It was good to be a Wolf Lord.

Ragnar's comm crackled into life. 'Wolf Lord, this is Tor. I'm not going to let the enemy assassinate you. You have the only action, centred around the Imperial library. My Grey Hunters have not met resistance. I'm bringing my pack and having the others coordinate as well. Just give me the word.'

Ragnar didn't like this. He responded, 'Tor, hold your position,' but his only reply was a high-pitched buzz. They were being jammed. It wasn't a trap for Ragnar, he was the bait, and loyal Tor was about to put his foot in it.

Ragnar reached a reinforced metal door, sealing off the roof. Despite the seal, he could smell the stench of Chaos on the other side, a sickly odour somewhere between sulphur and rotting meat. This building wasn't abandoned. The enemy were waiting on the other side of the door, ready to cut Ragnar and his Blood Claws to ribbons the minute it opened. They had set another trap for him. If they smashed the door, they'd step out into a firing squad. Fortunately, the pack wasn't going through the door. Ragnar hoped that a Havoc squad held this roof, just to get them before Hrolf did.

Ragnar gestured to his Blood Claws. They had the scent as well. Stepping away from the door, Ragnar turned towards the right wall. Made of solid rockcrete, it still appeared less reinforced than the metal door. Years of experience had taught Ragnar that engineers often made their doors stronger than their walls. He took a couple of steps back from the wall, signalled and readied his Blood Claws. Lunging forwards into the wall, the force of Ragnar's impact reduced the rockcrete to micro-particles. Ragnar and his Space Wolves poured through the opening to find nothing. All that remained was the scent of the Chaos taint. The Chaos Marines had passed this way, but they weren't here any longer. Like spiders, they had lurked on the rooftops, and then lowered themselves down into positions near the library square for the ambush. Ragnar chided himself for a moment, but he knew that he couldn't take chances against these foes.

TOR AND HIS Grey Hunters closed the distance to the Imperial library. There had been no response from Wolf Lord Ragnar, so it was up to him as a Wolf Guard to make a decision. He needed to protect Ragnar. If the Wolf Lord was all right, he would have responded, and if something had happened to Ragnar, Tor would make sure that the heretics got to see their Chaos masters when they went screaming to hell.

The pack of Space Wolves came to a large pile of debris, where the upper floors of an unrecognisable building had come to rest at its foundations. The ruins provided a strong defensible position for Tor to get his bearings and formulate a strategy.

'Tor, are you sure about this?' asked the voice of Uller, one of the other Wolf Guard over the comm.

'I have no response from Ragnar. We need to get as many Space Wolves to his side as we can, right now! It's my decision,' answered Tor. 'Bring as many of the others as possible, and keep moving.'

'Tor, this is Ranulf. My last orders were to hold and stand ready for attack.'

'Ranulf, you're too far away to help. You should hold, but the rest of us need to be there.'

'You should wait for Lord Ragnar.'

'He may not have time.' Tor clicked off his comm.

Tor led his men out of cover and ran fast through the empty streets. Tall office buildings loomed all around them. Each one could contain dozens of enemies. The Grey Hunters were the only living things running through a deserted rockcrete canyon. The dark empty streets could become a kill zone at any second. For Tor, caution was no longer a concern. The pack would save their Wolf Lord, or their spirits would go back to Fenris covered in glory. They reached the library square, coming beneath the long shadow of the vaulted Imperial library. Across the square, Tor spied Uller's Grey Hunters hugging the edge of an Administratum building. The air was quiet. Tor scanned the rubble, catching glimpses of blue-grey ceramite, fragments of Space Wolf power armour, scattered among the debris. He moved his Grey Hunters forwards.

Night Lords burst from hiding places behind the Grey Hunters, leaving the Space Wolves pinned against the cover. Space Wolves were known across the galaxy for their superior senses, a fact the Chaos

Marines were obviously aware of. Establishing their point of ambush down wind, they had been able to hide their presence from the Space Wolves.

Unlike Tor, the traitors did not hesitate. They fired their weapons with brutal accuracy. Nearly every shot found the armour of a Space Wolf. Tor caught a glimpse of the skulls and bones hanging as trophies from their belts, along with the heads of Imperial Guardsmen and even a Space Wolf helm. The young Wolf Guard looked to Uller's men, hoping for support. He saw three of Uller's Grey Hunters drop to their knees as blood poured from their armour. The Night Lords had got in behind Uller's pack as well.

Tor realised his mistake. The enemy had used the Wolf Lord as bait, and not only had Tor led his own pack into the deathtrap, he had led the others as well. Mere moments before, he had seen the square as the perfect cover to approach the large grey doors of the Imperial library. Now, it was a maze of debris, trapping his men. The Night Lords had closed off their exit routes and left them pinned. They were surrounded and outnumbered. They were going to die.

He tried the comm but it was jammed.

Bolter rounds came from all sides, but unlike normal bolter shells, these shrieked and exploded with burning flames. Inhuman laughter echoed across the library square as if the buildings themselves mocked the dying Space Wolves. A dark-armoured Chaos Marine stood up in the middle of the debris, less than three metres from Tor. With a war cry akin to the howl of a banshee, he raised a writhing metal gun, and fired a burst of blue-white plasma, not at Tor, but at a cluster of Grey

Hunters, engulfing two, and leaving them melted piles of flesh and ceramite. An incendiary ignited within the debris all around the Grey Hunters. Even if the Space Wolves had found cover in the plaza, they were in danger of roasting alive.

There was only one chance. Tor's Space Wolves had to assault the enemy and break out. He yelled at Uller, while his men fell around him. 'We've got to charge.'

Uller nodded, although Tor could see the glare in his eyes. Uller blamed Tor for this disaster, and rightly so.

'For Russ!' howled Tor as he charged the Chaos forces. The Space Wolves had to break free and regroup. The inhuman laughter grew louder. The enemy wanted the packs to come closer. The Night Lords never hesitated in firing. A Grey Hunter twisted to the ground as a bolter round tore through his armour and his intestines. Tor felt the bolter rounds crunch on his armour, each a hammer-blow. He prayed to the Emperor that his armour would hold, even as he watched the Chaos Marines draw their spiked and rune-covered weapons, continuing to fire their bolters one-handed.

Tor swung his axe at a Night Lord, who hissed like a serpent. The Chaos Marine parried with a tendril coiled around the hilt of a chainsword, sending blue sparks flying from the frostaxe as the blade's teeth shattered one by one. The traitor's bolter slammed a round into Tor's chest plate.

Tor gritted his teeth and fired his plasma pistol, all the while trying to keep his eyes off the enemy's armour.

The plasma enveloped the chest plate of the Night Lord, burning its way through the ancient ceramite. The intense heat melted everything it came in contact with including the chest of the Marine encased within. Liquid remains oozed out of the opening as he collapsed to the ground.

There was no time to celebrate the death of his enemy. A black-clad giant, its armour covered in writhing green runes, drove a spiked blade into the joint of Tor's armour above the thigh. The Wolf Guard felt the end of the blade twist back and forth inside him as if it was alive. Another Night Lord, with horns twisting out through his armour like weeds through broken rockcrete, delivered a hard blow with a double-bladed axe, cracking Tor's helm.

'Tooorrr,' cried out one of the Grey Hunters as he dived to protect his Wolf Guard. A third Chaos Marine moved to intercept with preternatural speed, catching the Grey Hunter on a chainaxe in mid-air. The Grey Hunter's heroic dive proved his undoing, as the chainaxe carved through him, splattering Tor with his comrade's blood and insides. The Night Lord raised his chainaxe in triumph and inhuman laughter echoed round the square.

RAGNAR COULD SEE everything from the roof's edge. Chaos Space Marines surrounded his packs of Grey Hunters. Ragnar's insides curled in knots. He could make out Tor and Uller. Tor was on the ground, but still struggling. Uller swung his large power fist around in a deadly arc, heroically keeping three Night Lords at bay as he tried to force his way to Tor. A Grey

Hunter sliced off the arm of a Chaos Marine, yet his inhuman foe didn't falter, redoubling his attacks with his remaining arm and thrusting a burning crimson power sword through the Space Wolf's chest. One Night Lord tore the helmet off another Grey Hunter, and spat acid across the Fenrisian's face. The Night Lords were more than a match for the Space Wolves, and they had the advantage of terrain and numbers. The enemy was toying with the Space Wolves, enjoying the slaughter of the Emperor's finest.

Ragnar wanted to leap down into the fray. The fall would kill any normal man, but he knew he could survive. However, it would only drop him into the trap. Even he wouldn't last long in the middle of the melee. He had to come from the side, from somewhere unexpected.

He spotted a neighbouring building that was leaning threateningly towards the one they stood on. Weeks of fighting had damaged it badly but somehow it hadn't completely fallen. However, it was close enough to their building to give Ragnar and his men a way out. 'Follow me,' he ordered then backed up and ran as fast as he could, leaping at the last moment. He flew across the chasm between the buildings, and for a moment, he wondered if Logan Grimnar, the Old Wolf and greatest of the Wolf Lords, would have tried this. He crashed into the roof of the other building, smashing through the rockcrete. He had made it, and his power armour had kept him going. The other Blood Claws landed around him, like a volley of missiles. 'Let's move,' Ragnar snarled.

They raced through the oddly angled building, running. crawling, and even jumping at times to reach the far side. If Ragnar needed evidence of Chaos infestation here in Saint Harman, he had found it. The facades of the buildings looked normal, but the insides held architectural madness. The builders had fallen away from Imperial standards and walked the edge of sanity. Corners jutted out into hallways, and strange rounded floors bulged upwards. Discoloured ceiling tiles seemed to form alien glyphs, and the height of the ceiling changed, sometimes reaching over three metres and other times forcing them to crouch.

Ragnar hoped that by travelling through the building his pack had crossed the Chaos lines. Now was the time to find out. There was no time for stairs. Ragnar tore his way out of the building through the wall and dropped, reaching out against the side of the building to slow his fall. He landed heavily in a shower of debris, followed by his loyal Blood Claws. They showed no hesitation. Power armour and myomer muscle had absorbed the impact, micro-servos contracting and releasing, transferring the energy of the landing. Ragnar's gambit had worked.

Ragnar leapt to his feet and broke into a run. He knew where Tor was trying his breakout, and knew they had little time. The sounds of warfare clearly guided them to the assault.

'This is Ragnar, if you aren't near the library, hold your positions and brace for possible attack,' he growled over the comm.

'Hold here,' he ordered the Blood Claws, raising a fist in the air and pointing to a ruined building that looked as if it might provide decent cover. 'Ulrik, take the four other Blood Claws with you, move through that building and take up firing positions on the other side. Wait for my command before you act. Is that clear?'

'Yes, Wolf Lord,' Ulrik replied. The Blood Claw showed signs of control. Perhaps he was on his way to being a Grey Hunter.

'The rest of you, come with me.' Ragnar waved them forwards.

Ragnar manoeuvred closer through the debris and rubble, keeping cover. He could see Chaos Space Marines surrounding Tor and his remaining Grey Hunters. The Night Lords were firing into the fray without regard for their own, killing Space Wolf and Chaos Marine alike. One of the Night Lords clutched a standard bearing the icon of their wretched god of Chaos, a mystical item not uncommon to their ilk. Laughter echoed from below, centring on the icon itself. The essences of daemons were often bound to such standards, allowing horrors from the warp to manifest and claim victims for the Dark Powers. However depraved the enemy's attacks seemed so far, daemons would do worse. As Ragnar watched, a ghostly green mist formed around the icon bearer. His heart pounded in his chest, the enemy was about to summon their daemonic allies. He had to destroy that icon.

'When I break cover shoot everything you have into the traitors.'

Ragnar tried his comm again, only to receive an earful of high pitched static. He'd have to do it on his own. He hurled himself over the wall and sprinted towards the cultists. Behind him, the Blood Claws unleashed the wrath of Fenris with their bolt pistols. Ragnar heard Ulrik's force following their lead. The traitors turned their attention away from the Grey Hunters, searching for their new attackers.

Ragnar crashed into the melee, snapping the neck of a Night Lord by twisting its horned helm. Bile, ichor and goo shot forth instead of the flesh and bone of a man.

The suddenness of the Wolf Lord's attack threw the Chaos Space Marines into confusion. Ragnar put his blade through the twisted faceplate of another traitor. Their enemies had let themselves become overconfident.

A gigantic Chaos Marine, nearly the size of Ranulf, threw Tor to the ground, and stood over him, gloating and carving through the Imperial eagle on his armour, trying to reach his heart. Ragnar could hear him speaking a strange chant as he prepared to sacrifice the Wolf Guard to the gods of Chaos. The traitor's depravity was his undoing, as Ragnar shot him point blank, never giving him a chance. Only Tor and two Grey Hunters were left alive, and one of the Space Marines was too wounded to fight on. Without hesitation, Ragnar hoisted the wounded Space Wolf over his shoulder and ran back towards the ruins where his Blood Claws continued firing. A bolter shell crashed into Ragnar's backpack. The attack had startled the Chaos Marines, but they recovered quickly. 'Don't stop,' he shouted.

Behind Ragnar, the world exploded in a bright fireball. Then, a second blast erupted, and a third. The

Night Lord holding the icon fell as a lascannon shot instantly vaporised him. The greenish mist dissolved with a high-pitched wail, and the laughter was cut short.

'Wolf Lord, didn't you promise me some Havocs?' came Hrolf's voice from the comm.

Thank Russ for that grizzled old warrior. The Long Fangs were giving them cover fire. They would escape.

The rest was a blur of smoke, debris and confusion as the Long Fangs pounded the Chaos position. A few more Grey Hunters found their way out of the trap, but they were too few, far too few.

WITHIN THE HOUR, Ragnar stood at the clamshell hatch of his Land Raider Crusader. He had established a command outpost just below the ridge in the industrial section of Saint Harman, where his men had entered the city hours before. The Chaos forces had forced the Space Wolves to withdraw and regroup. Fortunately the casualties were not as heavy as they could have been. Heaviest hit was his Blood Claws pack, and Tor and Uller's Grey Hunters.

Ragnar had no time for thoughts of remorse. His battle-brothers had met a worthy end in the service of Russ. He had to focus on how the enemy forces had reinforced on such a level. He had underestimated them.

Ranulf ran up to the Crusader, just ahead of two Space Wolf scouts. 'The scouts have returned, Lord Ragnar. They bring news.'

Scouts of the Space Wolf Chapter were an odd sort, shunning the standard organisational doctrine of the

Space Wolves, serving Russ in a more solitary and isolated way. Like the Priests of Iron, the Great Wolf himself controlled them, dispatching and deploying them wherever he saw a need. In fact, it was the Wolf scouts who had identified the first signs of Chaos on Corinthus V. Ragnar was aware of their presence and had been receiving intelligence from them.

Two grizzled Wolf scouts walked up slowly, as if they were saving their energy for combat. The taller of the two looked to be several centuries old. Wolf pelts hung around his waist and over his right shoulder. He wore wolf teeth, more than could be counted, on a leather cord around his neck. His face was weathered, a scar running across it, starting just above his left eye and spreading down across his nose and through his lip, ending on his right lower jaw. The wound was so deep that when it had healed it had separated his lip, exposing his canines, making him appear to be constantly snarling. He was armed with a bolter, but there was nothing simple about the ice-blue edge of the axe that was strapped across his back. Ragnar knew his name was Hoskuld.

The second scout seemed more subdued, wearing a hooded wolf pelt that almost completely enveloped him. The hood hid his face so that Ragnar could only see the glow of a bionic eye. Across his back, he carried a sniper rifle.

Ragnar nodded to them both.

'Hoskuld, it is good to see you again. What have you discovered?' he asked.

'M'lord, as instructed we made our way deep into the city. It is as you feared. The traitors have significantly reinforced their numbers,' the scout reported. 'The enemy has a sorcerer who opened a portal to bring reinforcements through. We overheard them talking–'

'You overheard them talking?' Ranulf interrupted. 'Just how close were you?'

'Close enough to hear them talking,' replied Hoskuld, dryly.

'Ranulf!' Ragnar held a hand up to silence his battle-brother. 'Please continue.'

'They are too few to open a portal big enough to bring anything very large through, but they did say that by tomorrow night they would be strong enough to open a larger gate,' the scout concluded.

'We have to go in tonight, Ranulf,' said Ragnar.

Ragnar turned back to the scouts. 'Could you lead a small force back to the position where you witnessed this ritual?'

'A small force, yes m'lord,' the scout replied.

'Good. Ranulf, gather the Wolf Guard, and find Tor. I will need him for this.'

'M'lord, are you certain that you want Tor?' Ranulf inquired.

'He's going to lead the force,' stated Ragnar.

'Lead it?' Ranulf growled with surprise.

'Yes Ranulf, Tor will lead the incursion force to destroy the portal. We will launch our own attack to distract them.'

'But m'lord, Tor–'

'Needs an opportunity to redeem himself, Ranulf. Redemption requires two things, desire and opportunity. I know this better than most. Tor will get his chance for redemption.'

ONE
Service to Belisarius

WITH A QUICK strike, Ragnar splattered a large beetle. A yellow smear on his blue-grey power armour marked its passing, and finally he could focus and listen. He needed the full use of his ears, many times sharper than those of ordinary men. The jungle scents confused his acute sense of smell after he had spent so long on the industrialised surface of Terra, and his vision couldn't penetrate far in this endless thicket of greenery.

Hyades was a lush planet, many sectors from the Imperial capital of Holy Terra on the fringes of Space Wolf territory. Life had taken root on this world in quantity and variety at the high end of Imperial surveys. Colonists had quickly established strongholds on the planet, and although it was not a deathworld, the native fauna and flora did fight against the colonists. On Hyades, the men and women of the Imperium had turned the planet's promethium deposits to good use. The planetary law of survival was simple: if it moved, it burned. The first colonists had established their cities near promethium mines and burned the jungle to expand their territory. Citizens of Hyades destroyed the environment rather than adapting to it.

After years of political manoeuvrings, the Celestarch of House Belisarius had been granted custodianship of Hyades. Ragnar wondered what types of closed-door dealings had resulted in the acquisition of a planet but he had spent enough time on Terra not to let politics surprise him.

The Navigators of House Belisarius kept their power through their abilities to guide ships safely through the warp. The value of their gift to the Imperium could not be understated. Without Navigators to guide them safely through the immaterium, Imperial spaceships could never travel long distances between the stars. Even the custody of a planet was a side business interest compared to the House's true asset of Navigation.

Promethium production was one of House Belisarius's many benefits to the Imperium. Promethium, the white-hot fuel used in Imperial flame weapons, was found naturally in only a few places, including Hyades. In the last three years, production on the planet had fallen dramatically. The excuses given for the drop in production bordered on the ludicrous: reports of unusual equipment failure, coupled with narratives describing attacks from native predators unafraid of Imperial lasguns. The bureaucrats even blamed the weather for problems, claiming that they had faced an abundance of storms. Ragnar was all too familiar with bureaucrats from his time on Terra. They were spineless men who would blame anything for their failure. These people took the coward's path for their failures, instead of facing them with the responsibility of a true warrior.

The Celestarch had ordered Lady Gabriella to review the situation. She was one of the most promising of the young Navigators and it was generally agreed that she would rise to take the reins of leadership in House Belisarius. In addition, she had spent time on Fenris, homeworld of the Space Wolves, continuing to cement the centuries-old alliance between the Space Marine Chapter and her House. She had brought with her to Hyades living proof of this alliance, the House's most trusted defenders: the Wolfblade. Ragnar would have volunteered to escort her, but luckily Gabriella had selected him to accompany her anyway.

Ragnar wanted, as much as he wanted anything, to leave Terra and return to a galaxy where he could easily tell friend from foe instead of confronting the conspiracies and verbal sparring of the Imperial capital. Despite his desires, he accepted his duty and his responsibility. Once, he had served as a Blood Claw, a young hot-blooded member of the Space Wolves. Ragnar had battled on the front lines against the Imperium's deadliest enemies: the bloodthirsty orks, the enigmatic eldar and the heretical followers of Chaos. However, he had been responsible for the loss of a precious artifact, the Spear of Russ, a weapon that had belonged to his Chapter's primarch, the legendary Leman Russ. The cost of his failing had been his exile to the Wolfblade, in honour of an ancient pact to defend House Belisarius from its enemies.

And he had done his duty well, saving the Celestarch from an assassin, back on holy Terra. Still, he longed to return to the endless wars on the frontiers of Imperial space.

Gabriella's shuttle had arrived on Hyades, in its capital city of Lethe, earlier that day. She had been received with a formal celebration in the city's central palace, where she had met with the governor and dozens of other local dignitaries and functionaries.

Once Gabriella had been settled in, Ragnar had requested permission for the Wolfblade to inspect the city and review its defences, taking the opportunity to investigate the fall in promethium production. Gabriella had suggested the Space Wolves also search out the creatures that the locals were claiming were attacking them.

Ragnar's fellow Wolfblade members, especially Torin, a veteran of the civilised life on Terra, seemed less than pleased. Haegr had wanted to go, probably just to annoy Torin, Ragnar suspected.

Gabriella had assigned eight of the twelve Wolfblade escorting her to the patrol. Ragnar thought she sensed that he needed the adventure. The team was organised into a single pack of eight men, even though the Wolfblade was accustomed to smaller units. The unit was organised more for actual warfare than the skirmishing that the Wolfblade commonly participated in as the bodyguards of House Belisarius.

The members of the Wolfblade had quickly reviewed the city and its defences, although in truth, after spending so much time on Terra, Ragnar had had enough of cities. When they left the city walls to explore the surrounding wilderness, he could feel the excitement creeping in his blood.

The jungle was thick with closely placed trees coiling their roots together just below the soil and their branches together far above to create a dense canopy. Creeper vines hung between the tree trunks and bushes and ferns pushed through any spot of soil left by the roots. Little light penetrated to the jungle floor, and Ragnar wondered how so much life could survive without sunlight. He wondered if the heat of the promethium below the surface somehow sustained the jungle life.

The jungle wasn't uniformly dense. In places, spaces opened up beneath the canopy. The entire environment made Ragnar feel more like he was moving underground or through a cluttered building than outside. The jungle also held a constant hum from the beetles that the Space Wolves found everywhere. The team had remained silent and on alert but in the first four hours of their patrol, they had found nothing larger than a fist-sized crawling insect.

Finally, the silence was broken by the grumbles of Ragnar's fellow Space Wolves. 'Great idea Ragnar, coming out here,' said Haegr. Although his friend's girth made him seem unfit, Ragnar had seen the speed and power that his massive comrade possessed. Haegr was probably half as dangerous as he boasted, and since he was a master at boasting, that made him formidable indeed.

'Come on, Haegr, don't you feel better now that we're away from civilisation?' replied Ragnar.

'Well, of course I do, but I would have chosen somewhere less hot and buggy.' Haegr flicked a beetle from the end of his boltgun.

Ragnar's ears picked a strange noise out of the buzz of the jungle's insects: a faint scratching sound, and then a click, coming from off to his left. A reptilian scent brushed against his nostrils. Another click answered to the right. Ragnar's blood warmed as he braced himself and held up a hand to his compatriots. To their credit, the other members of the Wolfblade kept up their bickering as they readied their weapons.

The attack came with a torrent of leaves, as the creatures tore through the jungle overgrowth. One of the beasts hurtled itself into Ragnar hard enough to send him sprawling. Ragnar's blade glowed with power as he fell back against a solid tree trunk. The sharp edge of the weapon sliced its way into the tree behind Ragnar as if it was paper, not wood. The tree tilted down, trapping the sword for the moment as it teetered on the verge of falling.

Ragnar's assailant reared over him. Covered in emerald scales, the alien creature blended perfectly into the jungle. Three rows of serrated teeth gnashed in its mouth, while its yellow eyes fixed on Ragnar and black diamond pupils narrowed. The creature's arms and legs reminded Ragnar more of an ape than a lizard, but the triangle-shaped head, forked tongue, lashing tail and reptile smell suggested it was mostly lizard.

Ragnar put three shells from his bolt pistol into the lizard thing's chest. Blood spurted out of its tattered torso and it twisted forwards, trying to attack, before something in its primitive brain realised that it was dead. It fell in a heap, and Ragnar moved on to his next foe.

A lizard-ape tore at Haegr in a frenzy, claws sparking as they failed again and again to penetrate the Space Wolf's ceramite armour. The creature increased its efforts, and the strength of the blows kept Ragnar's fellow Space Wolf pinned on the ground. Haegr was not hurt, but he was off-balance against the assault.

Ragnar hit the beast in the back of the head with his bolt pistol before putting a shot through its skull. With a roar, Haegr clambered to his feet, and leaving his weapons behind, he grabbed two lizard things by their necks and slammed them together with bone-crushing force. Ragnar thought of grenades exploding as their skulls burst.

The entire attack was over in less than a minute. The corpses of the beasts lay strewn around the blackened jungle. They certainly matched the description of the predators reported by the local people.

'Ragnar to Lady Gabriella, we've encountered some of the alien life forms,' he relayed on the comm.

'This is Gabriella. What is your status?'

'We're fine. They're dead. We'll find their trail and track it back to their lair. Ragnar out.'

The rush of excitement was intoxicating. Ragnar had missed it. He yanked his blade out of the jungle tree. 'Let's go,' he said, as he hacked his way along one of the creature's trails.

The team found a worn path in the dirt leading away from Lethe to the east. From the size of it, the Space Wolves agreed that it seemed to have been left by the lizard-ape life forms. The team couldn't be more than a few kilometres from the city itself, although Ragnar had lost exact track of their exact location. He suspected that his armour's locators needed some recalibration.

The slope of the ground indicated that the team had found a valley beneath the thick canopy of Hyades. Ragnar recalled from one of the briefings before arrival that in places the jungle canopy could reach over two hundred metres. As they continued, the sunlight faded. Ragnar was reminded of nothing so much as swimming into the depths of the sea.

After another quarter of an hour of travel, Ragnar caught the sickly smell of death and rot in his throat. He swallowed and shook his head. The stink was strong enough to make his eyes water. Considering a Space Wolf's superhuman resistance to toxins, Ragnar was impressed.

Just in front of the team, the tree trunks spread out, leaving a large clear space beneath the canopy. The space was big enough for the canopy above to be broken, and the size of it was comparable to the sanctuary hall in a cathedral. Sunlight filtered down from far above, shining down on the huge carcass of an enormous reptilian creature. The life form stretched almost twenty metres from tip to tail. Behind the dead beast, the far side of the clearing appeared to be a vine-covered rock face.

Ragnar quickly gestured for some of his team to secure the clearing, while he went to examine the corpse more closely. The men carefully readied their weapons and spread out to the edges of the clearing, checking for signs of movement or another ambush.

Ragnar deduced that the massive monster had fallen off the cliff to its doom, crushing trees and destroying vegetation on its way down. He could imagine that it had fallen in stages, catching on trees until its weight snapped them, sending it hurtling again until its final impact.

On further examination, Ragnar realised that his initial deduction might have been wrong. Cuts and tears marred the creature's mottled skin and long stakes jutted from its sides. Dried blood covered the beast. It appeared that the monster had been driven off the cliff to fall into a clearing filled with stakes. By the positioning of the stakes, the monster must have survived the fall and tried to stand, pulling up the stakes meant to impale it. Then, it had been attacked again.

A smashed emerald lizard-ape lay beneath the corpse's jaw. Three other bodies lay shattered near its tree trunk-sized tail. Ragnar wondered how many more might be underneath the corpse. He guessed the lizard creatures had driven the monster off the cliff, and then ambushed it.

'Those things killed this,' said Ragnar, voicing the thoughts of his fellow Space Wolves. In order to take down this behemoth, the lizard-apes must have hunted with patience and cunning. It appeared that they had stalked and wounded the beast using spears, and then driven it off the edge of the cliff. A group of them had lain in wait to finish it off once it landed. They had coordinated their efforts to kill the rotting leviathan. Odd, then, that they had attacked the squad like frenzied animals.

Ragnar activated his comm. A healthy amount of static blared back at him. One of the complaints about production stated that something about Hyades caused problems with communications.

'At least they had hefty appetites,' remarked Haegr, 'a sure sign of deadly warriors.' Bite-sized holes showed in the behemoth's skin. Haegr looked like he was considering a taste.

Despite Haegr's jocularity, Ragnar stayed serious. 'Did any of the briefings say anything about intelligent alien creatures on this planet?' asked Ragnar.

The Space Wolves looked back and forth. They all knew that no one had reported intelligent native life on Hyades.

'Over here,' said Haegr, 'there's something that can't escape my keen senses.'

'Is it food?' asked Ragnar, trying to collect his sense of humour. Haegr's appetite was legendary.

Haegr shook his head. 'Just remember who saved you from that Imperial assassin.'

'All I remember is the way you fell down when he shot you,' said Ragnar.

Cautiously, he pushed through the foliage in the direction Haegr pointed. A faint path between the trees marked the way. Haegr had found a path well traversed by the native fauna. Only a few hundred metres from the rotting corpse, a second immense space opened beneath the canopy.

The new space was extremely large, reaching a height of perhaps twenty-five metres and possibly having a diameter of ninety metres. This new opening looked unnatural, with an arched ceiling created by the twisting vines and trees, almost as if some alien gardener had created a cave out of plants. Strange flora shone with phosphorescence giving the setting an eerie blue and green glow. A large stone structure, wider than it was tall, sat shadowed in the centre of the space, perhaps half the height to the canopy, but at least thirty metres wide. It reminded Ragnar of a great toad lying in ambush for unwary insects.

Magni, a recent addition to the Wolfblade, pushed his way closer. The others followed, scanning for guards, feeling both compelled to investigate and an uneasy sense of horror. Ragnar was reminded of the feeling he had on a silent battlefield, covered with the wounded and the dying. It was that same sense of not wanting to see the carnage visited upon your battle-brothers, and yet having an inability to tear your eyes away.

Magni moved as if drawn by an invisible magnet. Ragnar felt his fellow Space Wolves' unease as they checked their weapons and scanned their surroundings. When Magni reached the base of the hidden structure, he activated his armour's illuminators. The bright light revealed far more than the flora's phosphorescence.

The stones formed a great, tiered ziggurat. Ragnar couldn't tell if it was a great rock that had been carved into the shape of a ziggurat or if it was a carefully built structure. Faces leered out from the stone, grinning and laughing, some human, some insect, some animal and some completely unrecognisable.

Ragnar felt that this was the home of evil, an ancient evil. Though he had no reasons other than his old tribal superstitions, Ragnar suspected that this place was somehow tied to the gods of Chaos. Ragnar always suspected Chaos.

Other members of the team activated their illuminators, combatting the dark and quiet atmosphere of the temple with bright light. Slowly, the Space Wolves circled the ziggurat, studying it, looking for openings and signs of age and use. Stone stairs led up the tiers while sculptures of flame marked the way. Ragnar thought the symbols were appropriate for a planet that produced so much promethium. He led a few members of his team in a climb of the stairs, while the others stood guard at the base of the structure.

On the third tier, the team found an opening. The outside of the passage was carved in the shape of a single eye. The hair rose on Ragnar's neck. He didn't like this, but he knew that if it was dangerous there was only one course of action.

'We should go inside,' proclaimed Ragnar.

'I agree,' said Magni. For a moment, Ragnar felt as if he was looking into a mirror of his past. Young Magni had all the fire of a new Blood Claw.

'Ho,' Haegr shouted up from below. The heavy Space Wolf had stayed on the ground to guard the stairs. Haegr directed his illuminators to a section of soil.

Ragnar could make out tread marks. Alien creatures didn't use tracked vehicles. He gestured and took the team members who had made the climb back down with him to investigate.

The tracks that Haegr had seen were recent, but the Space Wolves soon found signs of older tracks beneath the fresh ones. The tracks belonged to a vehicle, probably a Chimera. The trail went off in the direction of the jungle back towards the east. Ragnar could make out where the trees parted, leaving only a sea of vines to cover the hole used by the vehicle.

Imperial troops had been here, and from the freshness of the tracks, within the last few days. They might even have been here just hours before Gabriella's shuttle had arrived. Why in the Emperor's name had they let such a foul place stand?

'Chimera tracks,' stated Magni, voicing the conclusion Ragnar had already reached. The Chimera was the standard transport vehicle of the Imperial Guard. Although troop carriers, Chimeras boasted an impressive amount of firepower. It could have easily burnt its way through the forest and survived the twists and turns of the hills beneath the canopy.

Ragnar said what the other members of the team were thinking. 'If they knew about this place, someone should have told us.'

Haegr clapped Ragnar on the shoulder with his meaty hand. 'Then why are we still standing here? Let's go.'

Ragnar paused, glancing back at the temple. 'I agree. We can study this place later,' he said, but he wondered if he'd regret not continuing their exploration. Besides, what if there were traitors in Lethe, possibly inciting these beasts to cover their own sabotage? Ragnar shook his head. It was best not to engage in unfounded speculation.

The squad moved as one, following the tracks through the undergrowth. The Chimera was a versatile vehicle, but even with terrain modifications, Ragnar found it surprising that one would force its way here to the temple. A tank driver couldn't have followed one of the narrow paths used by the reptile things, so they must have known where they were driving.

Unlike the slow hacking of before, the Chimera had burnt a hole through the jungle easily large enough for the Wolfblade squad. Insects smacked into the eye plates on Ragnar's helm as he took the lead over the others. Few Space Wolves could match Ragnar's speed, especially when his duty was at stake. He couldn't fail House Belisarius.

As his armoured boots crushed the remnants of foliage beneath them, he thought back. It wasn't House Belisarius he didn't want to fail, it was Logan Grimnar. He recalled that day on the Fang, standing in front of the Great Wolf himself, the leader of all the Space Wolves, when he had been assigned to the Wolfblade. He had seen it as a punishment. He was an exile from the Space Wolves. Since then, he had learned from Haegr, Torin and others about the glories of the Wolfblade, but still, he longed to return home to the Fang. He wanted to be back on Fenris, as a Space Wolf. Then, if he volunteered for the Wolfblade, that would be his choice, not something he had been forced to do. All he needed was a chance.

More light filtered through the jungle as the trail twisted and turned. The squad was surfacing from the jungle depths. Surprisingly, the further along the path they ran, the more the jungle had grown back. The entire jungle seemed accursed. The tracks couldn't have been more than a few hours old, yet vines crossed the trail and new saplings almost half a metre high thrust out of the ground.

Plants couldn't stop Ragnar. With his enhanced strength and the servo-motors in his armour, he tore the vines and snapped saplings. A group of blood thorn trees flung their deadly poison spines at the Space Wolf as he passed. An unprotected man would have died in seconds from the barrage, but the volley provided only a moment's distraction as it clattered off his power armour.

The team ran for over half an hour following the tracks. With their enhanced muscles, each Space Wolf moved faster than an ordinary man despite their armour. The pace was relentless. They were on the hunt.

Magni reached Ragnar and then passed him. The young Space Wolf gave the victorious howl of a Blood Claw. Ragnar remembered that Magni had been sent to the Wolfblade for disobeying orders in his zeal to fight. Although all Blood Claws were hard to control, when battle lust and excitement gripped Magni, he lost his head and had trouble regaining it. Ragnar considered ordering him back in line, but decided that he would simply meet the young one's challenge.

Ragnar saw the trees thinning and he knew that they were coming close to the capital. The city's defenders worked to keep a swathe of clear ground around the walls and would kill anything that ventured out of the jungle. The kill zone wasn't far away. He pushed himself to pass Magni, although he knew that such a breakneck pace was dangerous. Ragnar wasn't going to let anyone beat him.

The city of Lethe was a walled fortress in the jungle. Massive walls, reaching twenty metres high, loomed over a several hundred-metre kill zone. The citizens had poisoned the earth and kept the jungle away from the city with flame. Several gates allowed transports to move in and out to the mines along guarded roads maintained with more flame. Planetary defence force Sentinels with armoured cockpits patrolled the kill zone, armed with Hyades's signature heavy flamers and chainblades to fight the ever-encroaching vegetation. Hellhound tanks stayed ready to emerge and unleash their Inferno cannons on anything that threatened their city. The planetary defence force manned the walls with large twin- and quad-linked heavy bolter turrets.

The amount of emphasis placed on defending Lethe from its surroundings seemed suspicious to Ragnar, but he had been around the galaxy enough to know that war would find the unprepared. Now, he wondered exactly who had done the preparing.

Ragnar dropped his pace as he reached the kill zone. The other Space Wolves behind him started catching up, although it appeared that giant Haegr was lagging a little behind the others. Magni surged forwards as Ragnar slowed.

Ragnar activated his comm. 'Magni, stop,' he ordered, but there was no stopping the young Space Wolf.

Magni looked up at the walls, and Ragnar knew that he could see the gun turrets. The men on the wall were trained to fire at anything entering the kill zone from the jungle. Still, the defenders knew that the Space Wolves were on patrol and surely, they would recognise power armour.

Ragnar heard the retort of the turrets from the wall. Heavy bolter shells pounded Magni. Dirt sprayed into the air as the blasts gouged holes in the earth. The large shells knocked Magni from his feet, cracking his power armour.

Ragnar watched in horror. He was in charge, and Magni was one of his men. The turrets had targeted the young Space Wolf, and Ragnar wasn't sure if the wall's defenders had recognised his fellow Space Marine as an ally.

Magni twisted backwards as another blast threw him into the air, instinctively seeking the shelter of the jungle. He came to rest at Ragnar's feet in a broken heap of blue-grey armour.

Ragnar shook with rage as he knelt to check Magni. Taking a deep breath to control his anger, he activated his comm. 'This is the Wolfblade, we've arrived on the southern edge of the city. Stop firing the guns.'

No one answered. Were the city's defenders fools? Bolter shells ripped through the trees, tearing through bark and wood. They were still firing. Ragnar was furious, and the other Space Wolves started yelling. Despite the noise, Ragnar's ears caught the whirr of large servo-motors. The Sentinels were coming.

'We're under fire from our own side. Go defensive. Let's show them that we're Space Wolves, not animals,' Ragnar said, but in his heart, he wanted to teach the men a lesson.

'Ragnar, native predators attacking from the rear,' said one of the Space Wolves.

Ragnar heard Haegr yell a war cry, using the sound of snapping bones to punctuate his statement. The alien creatures had attacked the rear of the patrol. In his zeal, Ragnar had strung out his squad, and the creatures had ambushed them.

'Pull back and regroup,' Ragnar shouted to his men. 'If something comes at us from the jungle, kill it.'

Again, he tried to contact Lethe. 'By the tendrils of the kraken, someone answer this comm. We're on your side.' More bolter shells tore through the jungle canopy. Ragnar realised that the comm wasn't working. The men on the wall probably didn't know that they were firing on their own side.

The ground shook, and acidic sap sprayed from the side of the path as a chainblade ripped the jungle asunder. Like a giant of legend, a Sentinel towered over the Space Marines. The two-legged walker was armed with a chainblade mounted on a mechanical arm, and it had a heavy flamer attached on its side, just beneath the pilot's compartment.

Without even hesitating long enough to identify his targets, the pilot activated the Sentinel's heavy flamer. A bright fireball of promethium blew through the jungle, turning everything in its path to ash.

Ragnar's superhuman reflexes barely saved him as he dived towards the walker. He knew from countless battles that the flames spread outwards in a cone, meaning that the safest place was right next to the Sentinel. Of course, most Sentinels weren't armed with chainblades.

The blade pivoted downwards, slicing towards Ragnar in a deadly arc. The blades blurred as they cried out for his head. Ragnar raised his glowing sword in an attempt to parry. The large chainblade struck the sword with enough force to make the Space Wolf's arm go numb. Gritting his teeth and straining his enhanced muscles, Ragnar kept his grip on the sword. The runes on the ancient blade glowed as it held against the Sentinel's chain-weapon. The teeth of the chainblade snapped, flying in all directions. Then Ragnar's sword cut through the mechanism, sending sparks flying after the blade's teeth.

Ragnar could hear the rest of the squad fighting off their alien attackers. From the sounds of blades, bolters and breaking bones, he suspected that his men had the best of the enemy. One of them fired a bolter at the Sentinel, but the rounds bounced off its armour.

Not wanting his squad to endure another blast from the heavy flamer, Ragnar gripped his sword with both hands and swung it around at the two-legged walker's knee joint. The sword ripped through the servos and maimed the mechanical beast. The walker balanced on its sole remaining leg for a moment, and then fell forwards, driving the nozzle of the heavy flamer into the soil.

Haegr flung the body of an ape-lizard into the upper branches of the jungle. Bolter fire echoed as the other members of the Wolfblade dispatched the hissing lizard things. Even in an ambush, the creatures were no match for the Space Wolves.

The guns stopped. The ground shook. Another Sentinel was approaching. Then, Ragnar felt the earth vibrate. Years of warfare had taught the Space Wolf what an approaching tank felt like. From the engine noise, Ragnar could identify the vehicle. Lethe's planetary defence force was sending a Hellhound to roast the entire section of jungle.

Several members of the squad shook themselves while their armour smoked from the heat. The Sentinel's heavy flamer had whitened the ceramite and discoloured the heraldry on every Space Marine caught in the blast. Besides Magni, two other members of the Wolfblade were down.

'Ragnar, what's going on?' yelled Haegr.

'No comms. They think we're the enemy and they are shooting at us.'

'Give me a moment, I'll do something,' said Haegr.

Ragnar looked out of the jungle to the kill zone. He had to think of something. The Space Wolves might be among the best warriors in the Imperium but they weren't ready to fight the defences of an entire city.

Haegr grabbed the hatch on the fallen Sentinel. In an impressive display of strength, the giant Space Marine ripped open the hatch to reveal the frightened man inside.

'Get out,' ordered the Space Wolf.

The pilot said something and leapt out of the hatch. Haegr reached inside with substantial effort and grunted before pulling out a comm. The vibration grew louder. 'Hurry,' said Ragnar.

'By the frozen hells of Fenris, this comm is jammed as well,' shouted Haegr, shaking his prize.

Ragnar knew what he had to do. 'Brothers, stay here.'

Ragnar charged out into the kill zone. The heavy bolters on the walls opened fire immediately, ripping gouts of soil from the earth. He changed direction, evading the shells, uttering a swift prayer to the Emperor that his armour would hold.

Bolter rounds clanged off Ragnar's shoulder pad, breaking his stride. To his left, another Sentinel charged forwards, although only armed with a heavy flamer, the walker remained out of range. To his right, he saw the source of the bolter fire, a Hellhound. He had hoped that the defenders would realise that a giant man in grey power armour wasn't a jungle beast.

The Sentinel slowed its advance. Perhaps the driver had some brains after all. The gunners on the wall kept firing, but fortunately their aim lacked accuracy. The Hellhound revved its engines and the front end of the tank leapt towards the Space Wolf.

Ragnar took in the situation and did the only thing that he knew the driver wouldn't expect: he charged. The turret of the tank's Inferno cannon swivelled in Ragnar's direction. This was going to hurt. Ragnar let out a howl and as the promethium flames splashed out of the Hellhound, he leapt at the tank, straining his legs and his armour's servo-motors. He only had one chance.

Flames sizzled against his leg guards as he flew through the air. The heat was overwhelming. Alarms screamed in his armour. He hoped that he had pushed himself enough. He wanted to land on the tank. If only the members of his original Claw could see him. The next time that he saw his old friend,

Sven, from his Blood Claw days, he'd have to tell him about this, assuming that he lived.

Ragnar crashed heavily against the top of the Hellhound and pulled himself onto the turret of the Inferno cannon. His plan had worked. The guns had stopped firing. Lethe's defenders didn't want to risk blowing up their own tank.

A moment of silence and indecision followed from the walls and the lone Sentinel. Ragnar took a deep breath. His hearts felt like they wanted to pound out of his flesh. He stood and pulled off his helmet, letting it bounce off the Hellhound's armour.

'We're on your side,' he shouted. 'The comms aren't working.'

A flurry of activity broke out on the wall. Amid the shapes of defenders, Ragnar saw the familiar blue-grey of Space Wolf armour. He hoped that it might be Torin, his friend and Wolfblade veteran.

Ragnar's comm crackled to life. 'What do you mean your comms aren't working?' asked Torin. The grey-armoured figure on the wall waved down to Ragnar.

'I mean that this place isn't as different from Terra as I'd hoped. We've got a problem,' answered Ragnar on the comm, 'and we're at least one man down. Magni was wounded.'

'We wouldn't be Wolfblade if we didn't have problems, lad. Now, stop wrecking the paint on that Hellhound and get inside the city.'

Haegr came out of the jungle, leading the others. Two of the Space Wolves carried Magni. Haegr dragged part of the Sentinel's leg behind him. The large Space Wolf made an announcement to anyone who could hear.

'Let the planetary defence force know that they need to repair one of their Sentinels,' said Haegr with a note of disgust in his voice.

The massive gates leading into Lethe shuddered open, and the squad shed one wilderness for another. Ragnar knew that he had felt safer with the beetles. At least in the jungle, he had known that everything was an enemy.

TWO
Unknown Enemies

AFTER ENTERING LETHE, Ragnar and his team had
quickly made their way to the central palace complex and the med labs with Magni. Although he was
a Space Marine, Magni had suffered serious injuries
and had lost consciousness. Lady Gabriella had
joined Ragnar after the medics and chirurgeons had
begun their examination. She sent the other members of the Wolfblade off to continue their duties,
but she had let Ragnar wait for a time to make sure
Magni recovered.

Ragnar stood watching as the medical servitors
and medics worked on Magni. The lab was up to
Imperial standards with prosthetics, augmetics and
surgical tables. Like all labs, it was a place of anti-
septic smells mixed with blood and waste,
unnatural scents that irritated Ragnar's inner beast.

Despite their knowledge, the strange anatomy of a genetically enhanced Space Marine defied the medics. They had cleaned Magni up and performed some healing rituals but in the end, Magni would have to heal himself naturally.

The young Space Wolf began to stir, starting to regain consciousness.

One of the medics left their patient to speak to Gabriella. 'Your servant should recover, my lady. We are unfamiliar with Space Marine physiognomy, but we have done our best.' The grey-haired man shook his head. 'I've heard of the Astartes' regenerative abilities but I was a sceptic until witnessing it myself, today. May the Emperor be praised.'

Gabriella nodded as she stood beside Ragnar. She was a tall, slender woman, more angled and severe than beautiful, yet in her black dress uniform she made a striking figure. A black scarf stayed tied over her forehead, covering her Navigator's third eye, and her long black hair flowed out below it.

One look at her pale skin made it apparent that she wasn't from Hyades. The natives of the planet all had a reddish tinge to their skin. Ragnar wondered if it was something in the air, an effect of exposure to the sun or a result of vapours from promethium leaking from the soil. Whatever it was, it made it easy to distinguish those who lived on the planet from most of its visitors.

Ragnar kept his eyes on Magni. Ragnar felt guilty about the young Blood Claw's wounds. He knew that he should have kept better control and not let Magni race him to the city. The young warrior lay across two tables, since one wasn't large enough to support the massive frame of a Space Marine. Magni grumbled and complained as the medics continued to examine him.

The sheer number of mechanical limbs in the room impressed Ragnar. Prosthetics of all sorts, some utilitarian and others covered in attachments, such as electro-blades and fusion torches, hung all along the walls. The men of Hyades apparently lost limbs on a regular basis.

Gabriella turned to look up at Ragnar. 'He's out of danger.'

'I wanted to make sure. We need to talk.'

'Come.' Gabriella walked out of the infirmary into a quiet hallway outside the examination room and sighed. 'Tell me why you think what happened outside the walls was not a mistake.'

Ragnar had given Gabriella a full briefing upon his arrival inside the city gates and she knew him well enough to tell that he sensed that something was wrong. 'We should talk somewhere more secluded.' Ragnar glanced up and down the hallway. He couldn't see anyone and yet he felt as if its walls might hold listeners.

Would you prefer we talk like this? Gabriella's voice echoed in Ragnar's mind.

The Space Wolf shuddered. He trusted Gabriella, indeed he was pledged to her protection and service, but there was something that bothered him about her psyker abilities. Although the Rune Priests of the Space Wolves had similar gifts, Ragnar still kept something of the superstitious warrior in his heart, and he clung to his old instincts.

'Let's go to the shuttle,' said Ragnar. 'It's shielded and secure.'

If you insist, but it's a good walk to the hangar. Gabriella's voice echoed in Ragnar's mind.

The Space Wolf shuddered ever so slightly, and Gabriella smiled, enjoying Ragnar's discomfort.

As THEY WALKED through the upper floors of the palace, Ragnar gazed out at the city. From above, it looked more like a series of mining structures and service buildings than a city. Since Lethe had been constructed atop tunnels connected to the mines and underground refineries, the architecture made sense, although it held all the style of a series of rockcrete bunkers. Many of the buildings were solidly constructed and were a constant reminder of the potential danger of explosions from storage tanks filled with the precious promethium.

The one exception to the uninspiring city was the palace, where the Wolfblade were getting settled alongside the dignitaries of Hyades. The building conveyed a regal image with architecture that included finely crafted columns, wooden floors, arched ceilings and courtyards with gardens of imported flora. The entire palace made Ragnar uneasy, as if the imposed sense of civilisation was a blasphemy against the constant struggles of the people of Hyades and the natural power of the jungle.

Where the rest of Lethe was built for function, the palace was built as a symbol. It felt out of place to Ragnar, but the citizens of Lethe respected and admired it. For them, the building represented the promise of wealth and luxury, a future in which humanity would tame Hyades.

As Ragnar and Gabriella walked down the carpeted corridors, they were joined by Torin. 'Ragnar, my lady, we need to talk,' he said.

'Join us, Torin. I think we all need to talk,' said Gabriella.

Torin was more at ease in these civilised surroundings than Ragnar, who preferred battlefields. A long-standing member of the Wolfblade, Torin had spent decades assigned to Holy Terra. He was the best-groomed Space Wolf that Ragnar had ever met. His hair was neat, unlike Ragnar's wild mane, and he wore a moustache that would be the envy of most overly powdered Imperial nobles. Torin wore jewelled amulets and medals from many worlds, rather than the typical wolf teeth and runes of his Chapter. He constantly smelled of perfumes and cologne, which to Ragnar carried the stench of civilisation.

Torin had mentored Ragnar upon his arrival on Terra as he adjusted to the Wolfblade, and had continued to do so, because despite his time in the Wolfblade, Ragnar still had to make necessary adjustments. The Wolfblade could take him off Fenris, but no one could take Fenris out of his heart.

Despite his friend's foppish tendencies, Ragnar respected Torin's skill as a warrior and a diplomat.

Gabriella led the two giant armoured warriors to the hangar and they escorted her inside the shuttle. There, she led them to a private cabin covered in the heraldry of House Belisarius. She crossed to a large chair and sat down, then pushed a button, and the door slid shut. 'We can talk safely now,' she said.

Torin started. 'I spoke with Cadmus, the planet's military commander, immediately after Ragnar returned from the jungle. He told me that sometimes promethium beneath the surface interferes with communications. The city guards were trying to maintain that kill zone. They've been working extra shifts to keep the entire area around the city clear, but with the increased activity in the jungle, they've only been able to protect about half of the walls. In the other places, the trees and vines come right to the city.

'They detected the movement before our men even broke cover and someone was trigger-happy. Once one of the men fired, the rest did as well. The officers on the walls were ordering everyone to stand down when Ragnar performed his acrobatics on the Hellhound. The planetary commander apologised for the incident.' Torin smiled as a thought crossed his mind. 'Although, I think he was a little disappointed. With all the guns on the wall, two Sentinels and a Hellhound, his men didn't manage to kill a single Space Wolf.' He looked at Ragnar. 'You should have seen yourself leap onto that Hellhound while it was firing. What made you think of that?'

'I just knew what I had to do. I thought the comms were being jammed,' said Ragnar. 'We found something out there in the jungle, a large ancient structure. The native life-forms killed some large behemoth near there, and there were Chimera tracks leading away from the temple.'

Gabriella raised her hand as she spoke. 'Perhaps Commander Cadmus and the governor are aware of this temple. The commander asked to speak to all of the Wolfblade after you returned from your excursion. These people are part of House Belisarius and they have asked for help. That is why we are here, to help them.'

'She's right,' said Torin. 'Let's go find Commander Cadmus, and see what you think, Ragnar.'

'I'm not going to like him,' said Ragnar.

'One day, Ragnar, I'm going to teach you how to act like something besides a barbarian,' said Torin.

'At least you can trust barbarians,' commented Ragnar.

THE TRIO FOUND Governor Pelias and Commander Cadmus sitting in a large stateroom, with windows open to the sun, and the colours of Hyades and House Belisarius prominently displayed. A tech-priest stood facing their chairs, unable to sit with his extensive cybernetics and appearing remarkably out of place in the elegant chamber.

Governor Pelias was the least imposing of the three. A slight man with the burnished glow that marked him as native of Hyades, he had a thin ring of silver hair around a bare scalp. His dress uniform included a clasped cape, a number of medallions weighing heavily on the front, and polished long leather gloves and boots. He looked uncomfortable, even lounging, as if he was the sort of man who had

had the burden of leadership thrust upon him, rather than desiring it.

The tech-priest wore a crimson hooded cloak, as was their custom. Ragnar's nostrils burned with the acrid scent of oils and smoke that clung to him. Faint whirring noises accompanied the priest's breathing.

At least one of his eyes was false, replaced by a red light burning within his skull. He had a massive musculature, and Ragnar could not tell how much of the man was flesh and how much machinery. A large bundle of wires and gears clung to his back, like a giant mechanical insect hiding under the cloak. The six appendages on the man's back were thick and short, suggesting that they weren't fully extended.

'Governor Pelias, Commander Cadmus, Tech-Priest Varnus, allow me to present my Wolfblade. I know you've met Torin, and this is Ragnar, who along with his men, was a victim of the friendly fire incident this morning,' said Gabriella.

The governor and commander stood to greet Gabriella.

Ragnar met Commander Cadmus's gaze. Something was missing. When Ragnar looked upon most men, he saw fear, no matter how well they hid it, but Cadmus showed no such emotion.

The commander was a massive man, although not quite the size of the towering Space Wolves. His eyes struck Ragnar: pale blue and very calm, watching everything. Ragnar felt the hair on his neck rise. Cadmus didn't have the typical Hyades skin colour, marking him as an offworlder. The commander wore a uniform jacket over mesh armour and his sidearm was a plasma pistol.

'My apologies for the earlier incident, Ragnar,' said Cadmus, returning to his seat. 'My guardsmen are trained to react to anything coming out of the jungle as if it were a threat. I must admit, I'm surprised that your men escaped the initial volley with so little damage. I hope Magni – that is his name, isn't it? – is recovering?'

'Wolves don't die easily.'

'Evidently,' said Cadmus.

'Lady Gabriella,' said the governor. 'I hope that you and the Wolfblade realise that the earlier incident was exactly what the commander said, an accident. I'm ordering a review of the defence procedures immediately, so nothing like this will ever happen again.'

'Sir,' said Cadmus, 'is that wise? It was a foolish error to be sure, and I'm already disciplining the men involved. If I have my men slow down operations to review the defences the jungle will reclaim sections of the kill zone. We've almost completely cleared it from around the city. If we don't, something might find a weakness in the wall and make its way inside.'

'By the way, commander, what sort of threat are you preparing for?' asked Torin.

'The ape-lizard creatures are the greatest danger. We call them the reptos, although I'm not sure that the Imperium has approved our choice of name,' said Cadmus, 'but I believe in being ready for anything. I've travelled from one end of this sector to the other, and I've seen a lot of fighting. An invasion could come at any moment. We need to be eternally vigilant.'

Cadmus nodded. 'I have security concerns. There are strange structures out in the jungle, buried deep under the canopy. We think that the reptos built them, but they could be remnants of a lost colony or, well, anything. I'm sure you can understand and respect that, as members of the Wolfblade.'

'Indeed, we can, commander,' said Torin.

'Has anyone contacted the Inquisition about these structures? What does the local Ecclesiarch have to say?' asked Gabriella.

The governor answered. 'Centuries ago, the Inquisition declared the structures abandoned and safe. We've been busy mining as opposed to worrying about such things, and I'm afraid the priesthood is poorly represented here on Hyades. It's a harsh world and we do dangerous work mining the promethium.'

'We ensure the wellbeing of the workers,' said Tech-Priest Varnus, his metallic voice hollow and echoing. 'If the Ecclesiarchy wishes to send representatives, we will do our best to accommodate them.'

Ragnar bristled. Before he had been part of the Wolfblade, he had learnt that the Space Wolves didn't trust outsiders, even members of the Inquisition. Some could be trusted, but others had their own agendas. He had learned on Terra that not all servants of the Imperium were on the same side.

'I want to know more about the structures and the behaviour of the reptos. I believe that such investigations may uncover the truth about the attacks and why the flora and fauna of this planet have decided to remove humans from their soil,' said Gabriella.

'Lady Gabriella, have you sensed any disturbances with your Navigator's gifts?' asked Cadmus.

Ragnar thought the question was unusual. Although it was no secret, indeed quite the opposite, that House Belisarius was a Navigators' House, and the abilities of the Navigators to guide ships through the horrors of the warp were the key to Belisarius's wealth, such a frank question seemed strange. It would not have been asked in mixed company on Terra. He reminded himself that everyone in the room was supposed to be supporting House Belisarius.

'No. I would have let the governor and you know if I had. Governor Pelias, I'd like Commander Cadmus to consult with my Wolfblade on the progress of the investigation of these structures and the activities of the reptos.'

'Of course, Lady Gabriella,' responded the governor.

'If you'll excuse us, governor, commander, I wish to check on the drop in production and review your records,' said Gabriella. She rose, as they did, and exited, flanked by Torin and Ragnar.

Haegr stood outside the doorway. 'My lady, mighty Haegr stands ready to protect you.'

'Thank you, Haegr.'

'Lady Gabriella, Ragnar and I will go and check on the shuttle,' said Torin. 'I want to make sure that the crews have resupplied it and the proper litanies have been chanted over its engines,'

'You have my leave. I'll be safe enough with Haegr,' she replied. 'We may go and inspect the promethium refining facilities. I'll contact you if I need you.'

'I assure you, you won't need them with me around,' said Haegr.

Torin guided Ragnar down a wood-floored hallway covered in tapestries depicting the history of House Belisarius. One of them showed Leman Russ holding his spear. It was a scene with which Ragnar was familiar, but it always painfully reminded him why he was a Wolfblade.

'Torin, why do we need to check the shuttle?' asked Ragnar.

Torin gave Ragnar a look that made him feel like an ignorant Blood Claw before realising that his friend simply wanted to talk to him in private.

'Brother,' started Torin, in a tone that was a sure sign that the older Space Wolf was irritated with him. 'Do you remember the lessons you learned on Terra, or has traipsing through the jungles of Hyades purged them from your mind?'

Ragnar sighed. 'Of course, I remember.'

'Well then,' said Torin, 'let me remind you of what I told you there. On Terra, you never have the whole picture. It's true here in Lethe as well. Be cautious.'

'I don't trust Cadmus and I'm not sure why,' replied Ragnar. 'He's dangerous. He carries himself like a man who isn't afraid of Space Marines. Outside of the Inquisition, I've never met a man who wasn't a little intimidated by us.'

'Brother, of course he's dangerous, he's the commander of the planetary defences. If he wasn't dangerous, we'd be standing in a jungle or dealing with a rebellion. The people here mine promethium. There are as many servitors as men in those mines. The citizens here have more in common with Terra than they do with other people from frontier worlds. They are a soft people. Cadmus is a hard man.'

'Torin, he's not from here. Why don't they have a leader from their own world commanding their military?'

'It should be obvious even to a young pup like you that he's seen his share of combat. Be careful about making assumptions about who your enemies are and who your friends are. If he wanted to harm Gabriella, then he threw away a fantastic opportunity to eliminate some of the Wolfblade this morning,' said Torin.

'He's not afraid of us, Torin,' stated Ragnar.

'I know, brother, but I also know that he's afraid of something,' said Torin, rubbing his moustache in thought. 'No one emphasises preparedness as much as he did without fearing something. It's probably his previous battle experiences. You'd be the best person to find out,' said Torin.

'Why me?'

'Because he knows you don't trust him,' said Torin.

'Do you trust him?' asked Ragnar.

'This isn't about me,' answered Torin. 'We'll talk more later. Go check back on Magni. I better make sure that the food supplies are stocked in our quarters. After all, Haegr will be looking for a good meal when Gabriella finishes with him.'

Ragnar tried to think of a reply as Torin walked away. He couldn't come up with anything worth saying, so he walked towards the infirmary.

Torin was right. Even though the planet of Hyades bore little resemblance to Holy Terra, the city of Lethe itself tried to emulate Terra and mask the fact that it was a frontier colony. The people stayed away from the world around them and insulated themselves, instead of learning how to survive in the jungles.

Ragnar had made it halfway back to the infirmary, when a voice came over his comm. 'Wolfblade Ragnar, please meet me at Tower 4 on the city's north wall.'

It was Cadmus.

Ragnar considered saying no, but he was sure Torin would tell him to meet with the commander. The summons was close enough to a request for Ragnar to decide to go along with it, despite his instincts.

'I'll be there,' was Ragnar's reply.

A CHIMERA MET Ragnar at the main entrance to the palace. He thought having an armoured vehicle drive him through the city seemed extreme, but Cadmus was in charge of the military. He sat alone in the back of the tank as it rumbled to the mighty wall protecting Lethe. Ragnar took note of the way, committing it to memory as a tactical lesson.

The tank stopped by the outer wall. Ragnar got out the tank and looked around. On one side, he could see nothing but the city wall and the buildings, mostly barracks and command centres built into its base. Back towards the centre of Lethe he saw nothing but uniform blocky rockcrete buildings. A few soldiers and a servitor with a bionic claw walked around atop the wall. The wall stretched skywards and given the choice between the lift and a set of rungs set into the wall in case of emergency, Ragnar chose to climb the rungs. He wasn't in that much of a hurry to see Cadmus and besides, it just felt right.

He paused mid-climb to look out over the city. The banners of House Belisarius flew from a number of buildings. Far off, he could see the gleaming palace rising from the centre of the city. The palace complex was at the heart of Lethe, where shuttles launched for the heavens, monuments rose to the glories of the people, and the only bit of green within the city wall was there. Despite the dramatic view, Ragnar felt unsettled, as if something was not right.

Cadmus was waiting for Ragnar at the top of the wall, staring out at the kill zone. Behind him, servitors and military men ran drills, checking and rechecking reports. Cadmus had his people ready, as if they were expecting a full-scale invasion. Ragnar thought they'd spend their time better worrying about the jungle.

The commander's uniform was immaculate: well-pressed, his boots polished to a reflective shine. He smiled as Ragnar walked over.

The Space Wolf took a moment to catch the commander's scent. He hoped that somehow he'd detect the taint of Chaos, anything to have an excuse to deal with this man he distrusted.

'Ragnar, once again, I want to offer my apologies for the earlier incident,' Cadmus said.

Ragnar nodded. 'Why did you want to see me?'

'I want us to understand one another, Ragnar. We seem to be very much alike, you and I. I've heard rumours that most of the Wolfblade receive their assignments due to some issue during their service as Space Wolves,' said Cadmus.

'How do you know about that?' asked Ragnar, surprised by the statement.

Cadmus nodded. 'I've studied the history of House Belisarius, and I understand a bit about how the Wolfblade are selected. Many great men do things that others don't understand. I have many such men with me. They serve in positions of authority here, helping ready the people of Hyades in case of attack.'

'Why did you need to bring your own men here? Why did they select you to lead them?' asked Ragnar.

'I lead these men because they know my skills. I've fought in many battles across the Imperium. The people of Hyades need protection from the wilderness of their own planet. They strive to change their world for the better. However, they do not have practical experience in dealing with the threats this galaxy has to offer. I do. They look inward, and I can see much more.'

Ragnar shook his head. This amount of talk was never to his liking, unless heavy amounts of Fenrisian ale and good stories were involved.

'Ragnar, I'm glad that you and your Wolfblade are here, and I want to make sure that you are ready to defend House Belisarius against all threats.'

'Commander, I'm ready.'

'Good. I'm glad to have you. What you did today against the Hellhound was remarkable, and I'll have some of my best men ready to go with you into the jungle in the morning. One reason that I've held off investigating those ruins more fully is because I didn't see them as a threat. Ages ago, the Inquisition declared them safe.'

Ragnar said nothing, not really knowing what to say. An uneasy moment passed. He wanted to make sure that he didn't insult Cadmus with his tone or his words. 'Tell me what you know about the ruins. I discovered signs of activity there, and I know that a Chimera made its way there recently.'

'I'll find the reports and have them sent to Lady Gabriella as soon as I can. I'll let you get back to your duties, Wolfblade,' said Cadmus.

'You can be sure of that,' said Ragnar.

Far below, Ragnar could see one of the Hellhounds belching promethium into a section of jungle. It looked as if Commander Cadmus had his men working hard.

'Are you able to maintain the integrity of the kill zone?' asked Ragnar.

'We have it encircling about seventy per cent of the city at the moment. Of course, it changes, but luckily we have an unlimited amount of promethium. All of the gates are constantly monitored and reinforced in the areas where the jungle touches the wall. Are you concerned about the reptos breaching the wall, Space Wolf?' asked Cadmus.

'No, but I do think the security of Lethe is important,' said Ragnar.

'Good, on that we agree.'

Ragnar walked over to the rungs and began his descent down the wall. Ragnar still didn't like Cadmus, but he didn't know why. His instincts told him that something was wrong. The Chimera was waiting for him at the bottom of the wall. He climbed in, ready for the ride back to the palace complex.

COMMANDER CADMUS watched Ragnar climb down the wall, admiring the power of the superhuman warrior. 'The Space Wolves will serve their purpose,' he whispered to himself, 'and wrongs will be made right.'

THREE
To Kill a Kill Team

HIGH ABOVE THE planet of Hyades dozens of transports, cargo barges and cruisers of various designs and sizes were going about their business, transporting supplies and promethium to and from the planet. The amount of activity within the orbital corridors above Hyades made it easy for a light cruiser to enter into high orbit without attracting any attention. Following the standard merchant flight path the cruiser slowly crossed the terminus into the night skies of the planet. To standard scans the ship's configuration was that of a light cruiser, no different from any other used by merchants to transport goods and cargo. However, the cargo on board this vessel was very different.

A solitary figure stood at the observation port watching as the transport slid into orbit around Hyades, his dark green power armour appearing black in the low light. His clean-shaven, almost youthful face hid his years well, however his deep piercing blue eyes did not. They reflected centuries of wisdom in service to his Chapter and the Imperium.

Watching as the transport took its place within the controlled orbital lanes he could not help but be concerned. His purpose on Hyades was of such importance that every detail must be conducted with flawless precision. Recognising his concern over the flight path of the transport he smiled inwardly, realising that he had much greater concerns to occupy his mind than that of piloting the transport into a stationary orbit.

However, Captain Jeremiah Gieyus was not just a Dark Angel, he was a member of the Deathwing, the elite Dark Angels First Company. He had reached this level of authority by controlling every detail of his assignments. It was with meticulous care that he inspected every weapon and each grenade, and supervised the Techmarines as they prepared the armour that his battle-brothers wore.

Jeremiah crossed the corridor and entered a large cargo bay, at the centre of which stood a teleport chamber. Cables ran across the floor to this structure, connecting it to ship's power, sensor and internal computer terminals. Servitors, cybernetic caretakers, moved around the outside of the device, confirming that everything was properly anointed, and that all the proper chants had been evoked, preparing the teleportation chamber for activation. As Jeremiah watched these servants of the Machine-God perform their rituals he could not help but feel a sense of profound pride.

Within moments Jeremiah was joined by five of his fellow Dark Angels. He watched as they entered the chamber, taking their assigned positions inside. Thirteen pillars circled the interior of the chamber, each covered with inscriptions of faith and devotion to the Emperor. Servitors made final anointings to the interior systems, couplings, conduits and power emitters. Everything had to be in order to ensure that no harm would come to the Sons of the Lion this day.

Jeremiah joined the rest of the kill team within the chamber. The Dark Angels green armour appeared almost black in the low light, and their weapons were in hand and at the ready. Combat deployment was needed, even though Jeremiah had picked a secluded position for the insertion, making detection almost impossible. However, when dealing with an objective of this nature one could never be too careful. Jeremiah did not intend to lead his brothers into a trap.

Several weeks ago the Dark Angels had received intelligence that a member of the Fallen had been detected on Lethe, capital city of Hyades. The information was vague and limited on details. All they knew was that one of their ancient brothers was in a position of authority within the governor's inner circle.

Jeremiah and his kill team had been sent to reconnoitre the situation and, if possible, capture and detain the member of the Fallen until an interrogator-chaplain and reinforcements could be dispatched.

Only the Dark Angels' most senior officers and the Deathwing were aware of the terrible shame the Chapter carried. For ten thousand years they had hunted down the Fallen, rooting them out wherever they hid and thrusting them into the cleansing light of the Emperor. So it would be with this new report of one of the Fallen being present on Hyades. He and his kill team would confirm his presence and then capture him, turning him over to the interrogator-chaplains. Then, if need be, reinforcements would descend and remove any additional Fallen and the contamination they may have left behind.

As the other members of the kill team were not aware of the existence of the Fallen, they had been told their mission was to locate and capture a heretic commander who had thrown in his lot with the Dark Powers.

Their preparations complete, Jeremiah finally signalled the Techmarine to begin the litanies of transport. Slowly the pillars began to glow until a searing white light filled the chamber.

THERE WAS A flash of light in the jungle as the Dark Angels kill team materialised on the surface. At night a flash of this nature would be visible several kilometres away, however Hyades's thick jungle canopy restricted the flash's visibility considerably.

Slowly, the kill team began to move, each member taking his position to secure the drop area, their dark green power armour virtually invisible against the night. Five of the Space Marines moved out from the teleport site enlarging the circle while one remained at its centre.

Releasing the auspex from its belt restraints, Elijah made several adjustments to the controls. Its screen blinked in and out, revealing only quick glimpses of what it detected in the area. He studied what information it did reveal very closely to ensure that his report would be as accurate as possible.

'Brother-Captain, there is some kind of interference that is diminishing the auspex's effectiveness. However, I believe we have deployed approximately fifty metres off our original target point, which places us 1.5 kilometres from Lethe.' Elijah pointed in the direction of the city.

'Understood,' Jeremiah responded. 'Also Elijah, we all share the same risk and fate this night, so normal protocols are not required. Please refer to me as Jeremiah.'

'Yes, Jeremiah,' Elijah responded.

'Besides, my brother, it will hide from our foe the chain of command. Plus Jeremiah knows his rank, so we do not need to remind him.' Nathaniel's humour made the entire team chuckle.

Jeremiah looked at each member of his kill team in turn, then spoke.

'The Lion watches over us, his guiding hand leads us this day. Praise the Lion.' His words made a physical impact on his team. Evoking the name of their primarch sent a ripple of pride through his men, reminding them all of the importance of their mission.

'Who are we?'

'We are Sons of the Lion! We are Dark Angels.' Their response was in unison, a testament of their honour, an oath to right the sins of their brothers. Each in turn fell into line, taking up the position that he had been assigned.

Elijah was the most recent addition to Jeremiah's team, having proven himself on several campaigns before finally earning the honour of this placement. Although the youngest in age, his experience was equal to that of any of his battle-brothers, and his keen eye and attention to detail made him the perfect choice. Nathaniel was next, being the oldest and most experienced as indicated by the grey that gathered at the temples of his short-cropped black hair. He and Jeremiah had served together the longest and he felt it his duty to look after the younger Elijah. However, his constant reference to Elijah as 'young one' at times visibly annoyed his battle-brother.

Marius was always third. His plasma gun was best suited to supporting Nathaniel and Elijah should they run into unexpected trouble. As always, Jeremiah took the fourth spot, allowing him a tactical position should the need arise. He was followed very closely by Gilead, with Sebastian bringing up the rear.

Once again Elijah attempted to scan their surroundings. The soft almost imperceptible hum of static was the only reading that he could obtain. With ritualistic precision Elijah made a series of adjustments. A slight change in the hum's pitch was the only result.

'The interference seems to have worsened, Brother-Cap… Jeremiah. I'm uncertain as to the exact cause,' Elijah explained as he brushed away a large beetle that was crawling across his helmet visor.

'We could be picking up some kind of feedback or impulse from the promethium mines,' Nathaniel theorised. 'Intelligence reports indicated that the entire area was honeycombed with mine shafts and pipelines that feed to the many refineries on Hyades.'

Jeremiah nodded his acknowledgement and signalled that they keep moving. As the team moved through the dense brush the jungle seemed to engulf each member. It became so dense at times that Jeremiah would momentarily lose sight of his battle-brothers.

The foliage of Hyades was of a type that he had never seen before. Its shapes and colours all appeared similar, but it was dramatically different. Leaves like small combat knives scraped and scratched as they tore across Jeremiah's armour, and the vines and branches seemed to voluntarily constrict and contract around his arms and legs as if trying to capture or restrain him for some purpose. This feeling was reinforced by the many sounds that swirled around them. Most were similar to sounds he'd heard on other worlds, others however, seemed to be calling out to one another. Jeremiah was certain that they were being observed. His only concern was whether they were being stalked as well.

The team continued to make its way through the jungle. As they proceeded, Jeremiah noticed skeletal remains of small creatures ensnared in ivy-like foliage around the base of several trees. They continued to trudge through the thick jungle, receiving momentary respite from the native fauna of Hyades when the occasional clearing would appear. The jungle ceiling was not as generous. There were no breaks or openings, with the canopy allowing no light to penetrate its shielding of the jungle floor. The visual enhancements of their helmets coupled with the Lion's gift of genetically enhanced vision were all that allowed them to see.

They were moving through one of the few clearings when a fury of sound and movement erupted from beneath a thicket of tangled vine to Jeremiah's right. He unleashed his sword ready to meet whatever was coming for them. A small, fur- and feather-covered creature leapt up onto the exposed gnarled root of one of the trees. It turned, hissed and spat at Jeremiah, spraying the right flank of his helmet. The ceramite underneath the creature's spittle began to blister. The poisonous phlegm was not strong enough to actually penetrate his armour, but Jeremiah did consider that if the creatures were bigger they could pose a serious threat.

The rodent-like thing hissed again in defiance and leapt from the root. It had made two hops deeper into the woods when suddenly the ivy-like growth ensnared it. The creature instantly began to convulse and blue-white tendrils of electricity danced across the ivy and its now stunned victim.

'Stay vigilant brothers. It would appear that Hyades's reputation is well deserved.'

'I think we may have discovered where some of the interference is coming from,' Elijah stated.

'Small rodent things, electrically charged, carnivorous ivy; I think this place's reputation may be an understatement,' Nathaniel added.

'That may be,' said Jeremiah. 'However it will not deter us from our objective. Let's keep moving.'

* * *

THE DARK ANGELS had been travelling for almost two hours when Elijah's voice broke through the comm. 'I see light ahead.'

The team slowly began to spread out, taking great care to move quietly: detection at this point would be disastrous. Jeremiah crouched and crept up behind Elijah. Then he raised his right hand, making a closed fist, and the team stopped instantly, frozen in place like ancient statues.

A beam of light began to strike the leaves and trunks of the trees as it moved slowly across the jungle. The searchlight indicated that they had finally reached the capital city. Using hand signals, Jeremiah instructed Nathaniel to move forwards to the very edge of the jungle to retrieve better information on their current situation. Nathaniel slowly moved through the foliage while the other members of the team remained perfectly still awaiting his return.

'I would estimate the kill zone to be one hundred to one hundred and fifty metres across,' reported Nathaniel. 'Looks like a manned weapon emplacement every thirty metres, and two squads of Sentinels patrolling the kill zone in thirty-minute intervals.'

Jeremiah pulled the entire team back into the seclusion of the canopy, with the exception of Nathaniel, Gilead and Sebastian. Nathaniel was left to observe and report the activity of the planetary defence forces while Gilead and Sebastian were dispatched to reconnoitre along the perimeter and report back any weakness or opportunity that the team could exploit. Upon his return Sebastian's report echoed Nathaniel's. Jeremiah awaited the final report. If

Gilead's report mirrored the others then he would need to formulate a new insertion plan.

Prior to their departure, Jeremiah had been given a fairly detailed intelligence report of Hyades and its capital city of Lethe. Included in that report were troop strengths, defensive capabilities and a fairly detailed map of the city as well as a layout of the governor's palace and control compound.

Initially the plan was to reach the city walls, scale them and move through the city under the cover of night until they reached the compound. According to the reports, there was no known conflict or crisis in this area of space so Hyades's defences would be minimal. Something must have changed to cause this level of fortification. This heightened level of defence was not a coincidence, for in Jeremiah's experience coincidence did not exist. His thoughts were broken when Gilead's voice broke through the comm.

'Jerem… hssssst… the jungle I… Hsst…' The rest of the transmission was lost to static.

Jeremiah looked at the rest of the team, confirming that they had received the partial comm transmission as well. With a quick nod of his head he sent his battle-brothers into action. He had no idea of Gilead's location or condition; he only knew his direction. The team formed a skirmish line, moving as quickly and as quietly as possible. Stealth was not a skill that most Marines possessed, their sheer bulk making that difficult, but fortunately the jungle provided them with enough cover and background noise to make things a little easier.

'Gilead, respond please. Report your location and situation,' Elijah requested.

'Tra…. brea… p… Kil… alls,' was the only response.

The team had travelled through the jungle for three hundred metres when Jeremiah ordered them to stop. He then signalled to Elijah to try to make contact again.

'Gilead, respond please. Report your location and situation,' Elijah repeated.

Gilead did not respond. The Dark Angels waited, but there was no response.

Jeremiah's frustration grew. One of his team was lost, and he wanted know why, but he could not jeopardise the mission by sending more men out to look for the missing Marine. He scanned the jungle in front of him looking for a sign, any indication at all of what could have happened to Gilead. The plants and trees here were not as dense as the area they had come from, and the strange electric ivy, which the team called the shocker vines, was much more prominent. That might account for the increased difficulty with the comm. He wondered just how large the ivy would grow and if it could become a threat to him or his battle-brothers.

'Transmission breakin… Ha… ound end to kill zon… making way back…' Gilead's voice broke through the comm.

'Understood Gilead. We have moved closer to your position. We will await your arrival,' Elijah responded.

Within minutes Gilead broke through the jungle, rejoining the team.

'What have you found out?' Jeremiah asked.

'There is a large section of the jungle that has not yet been cleared away,' said Gilead. 'And it goes right up to the city wall.'

'How wide is this area of jungle?' Jeremiah asked.

'At least one hundred and seventy-five metres, brother, if not wider,' Gilead responded. 'I managed to scout into it about one hundred and fifty metres before I realised that I had lost comms, and turned back to report.'

'Excellent work, Gilead.' Jeremiah stroked his chin while turning away from Gilead.

'You seem troubled, Jeremiah,' Elijah said.

'Our leader is curious as to why the details of the kill zone were not in our intelligence reports,' Nathaniel speculated.

'Exactly. What has occurred on Hyades that would require this heightened defensive posture? And why now?' Jeremiah's words silenced the team.

'The time for speculation is over brothers, whatever the cause it will not deter us from our holy mission. We move on.'

THE TEAM HAD moved to a point they estimated was the centre of the uncleared jungle area. Determining their position was now easier. The noise from the flamers and patrolling vehicles dominated the jungle orchestra, giving them a permanent reference point, as well as allowing them to travel more quickly, as they no longer needed to conceal their movement so much.

All that remained for Jeremiah was to determine how to gain entry to the city. Using charges to burn through the wall was out of the question. He considered scaling the wall, a task the Space Marines could accomplish with ease, but with the increased patrols and heightened security measures they would risk detection, and although the Hyades defence forces that manned the wall would be no match for them they could not take on the entire city, nor could they risk alerting the target to their presence. However, the latter was becoming less of a concern for Jeremiah, who was certain that their presence was already known to the Fallen.

Elijah looked up from his auspex, turning towards the others. 'Interference is still too intense. I cannot penetrate it.'

It had taken the team about three and a half hours to reach this point. Based on Hyades's rotation cycle, they had about eight more hours to breach the city walls and reach their objective. Although time was always a factor when on a mission of this nature, it was becoming increasingly more important. Their final obstacle was finding a way to gain entry.

Jeremiah had ordered the team to pause for a moment, allowing them a little rest. He was once again pondering the events of the last few hours when Nathaniel placed his hand on his forearm. Jeremiah looked up to see what his brother required, noticing that Nathaniel was not looking at him, but past him. He turned, slowly.

'We are not alone, brother,' Nathaniel stated. 'Something is moving through the jungle.' He pointed in the direction of the city wall.

At first Jeremiah did not see anything, but finally he caught a glimpse of something moving through the jungle past them. With the rest of the team alert and ready, he nodded and they all moved towards the disturbance. Each member of the team had slung his weapons and was wielding his combat knife. Even with the cover from the noise made by the clearing teams a firefight was not an option this close to the city's defence forces. Whatever this threat was it had to be dealt with by hand to hand means.

A hissing noise was the only warning any of them received as the jungle seemed to come to life around them. Several creatures erupted from the foliage. Jeremiah, raising his knife to ward off the unknown assailants' attack, suddenly found himself falling backwards as something entangled his legs and pulled them out from underneath him. Landing on his back his mind leapt back to the shocker vines and his thoughts of how large they could grow and whether they could attack a creature as large as a Space Marine. Before he could discover the answers, the real enemy landed squarely on his chest.

His genetically enhanced vision augmented by the helm of his cherished armour revealed a large creature that looked like an unholy combination of lizard and ape. Jeremiah struck the creature with his closed fist, in its ribs just under its arm, knocking the creature off him.

Rolling onto his side and bringing himself to one knee, he was ready for the next attack. The creature squared itself with the Space Marine, when its elongated tail lashed out wrapping itself around his arm at the wrist. The strength of the creature was staggering, catching him momentarily by surprise and almost pulling him off his feet once again. Jeremiah stepped in the direction of the creature stabilising himself while raising his arm and pulling the creature towards him. Then in one quick motion he brought his combat knife down in a circular strike, slicing completely through the tail severing it, while the creature tumbled backwards into the jungle.

Blood sprayed from the severed appendage as the tail whipped back and forth and the creature screamed in pain as it clambered to its feet. Fear and panic ruled its primitive mind as it turned, leaping into the jungle, fleeing from the cause of its pain. Jeremiah leapt up and gave chase, realising that the creature was heading towards the clearing teams. He did not want the creature to be found. The clean cut of his combat knife would reveal that the wounded tail was not the result of a fight with another animal. He had to catch the thing before it reached the edge of the jungle.

Crashing through the jungle he realised that whatever this thing was it was fast, moving through the jungle with unbelievable agility. He could no longer see the creature, only the visible signs of where it had been. It was escaping.

Suddenly, several metres in front of him the jungle became engulfed in fire as flames roared amongst the trees. Rising above the roar of the flame came a horrific screaming. The clearing team had found the creature, or more correctly, it had found them. Jeremiah dived for the ground, coming to rest underneath several thickets of razor leaf bushes. He was in no danger from the flames. He was more concerned that he would be detected. As the screaming and the flames began to subside he could hear the sounds of a Chimera engine as well as several defence force personnel as they moved around the area of the burnt remains.

'Looks like one of those damn reptos again,' a man stated.

'That's just great! See any more?' another man responded.

The Chimera's engine roared and Jeremiah heard it begin to move, the sound of small trees snapping as they gave way to the greater strength of the transport. Slowly reaching down to his belt he retrieved a grenade, preparing for the coming engagement. Then the Chimera stopped and Jeremiah could see a searchlight piercing the jungle, silhouetting the trees as the light moved slowly over his position.

'I don't see any more,' the voice said, rising to overcome the noise of the Chimera.

'All right then, let's get back to work. We've got a lot of jungle to clear.'

Jeremiah sighed with relief. He waited for a few moments to ensure that the men had returned to their work before he slowly crawled away. Once clear he rose to his feet and moved towards his team.

WHEN JEREMIAH REJOINED the rest of the team he learned that the attack was short-lived, and there were seven of the lizard-ape creatures lying dead on the jungle floor.

'Everyone all right, no one injured?' he asked.

'We are all intact and unharmed, sir,' Nathaniel responded. 'We've found something of interest, though. After the attack had been dealt with, I dispatched Elijah and Sebastian to reconnoitre the area that these things had come from to determine if there were any more there and they've found something we should check out.'

Jeremiah followed as Elijah and Sebastian led him and the rest of the team through the jungle. Within just a few short minutes they reached the point where the jungle met with the city wall. Jeremiah could not believe what he saw before him. These ape creatures, which they had thought were mindless animals, had been removing chunks of the city wall. The area around the opening was strewn with chunks of rockcrete and primitive tools made from bones and tusks of other animals.

'They were creating a tunnel into the city,' Jeremiah stated in amazement.

'Not exactly,' Sebastian replied.

Elijah and Sebastian stepped towards the opening. Reaching in, they removed several pieces of foliage and rock, placed there by the ape creatures to conceal their work.

Behind the makeshift screen was what appeared to be an old metal maintenance hatch.

'Looks like these creatures discovered an area of the wall where they had sealed off an old maintenance hatch,' Elijah said.

'They were almost finished I would say. We must have gotten close enough to interrupt their work,' Sebastian added.

'It would appear brothers that we have found our access point. Praise the Lion!'

JEREMIAH STOOD IN an alley at the edge of the entrance to the street. Since gaining access to the maintenance hatch he and the team had crawled their way through several maintenance tunnels until finally reaching what appeared to be an abandoned sewage system. Then they had followed the sewers until they found a service shaft that would allow them to exit undetected. They had found other shafts, but upon inspection they opened up into areas that were not secluded enough to conceal their presence.

Once they were free of the sewers they were able to conceal their movements by using back alleys and side streets. The few citizens they encountered were either attempting to avoid detection themselves or were too intoxicated to care who was there.

At one point they passed a large vid panel mounted on the side of one of the buildings. A thin, pinch-faced woman was elaborating on the events of the day: production quotas from the mines, scores for athletic events, local magistrate activities, and how the curfew was a popular and necessary edict from the governor.

Now they were at the entrance to a light-filled street, illumination panels spaced along either side of the street ensured that. Personal ground craft were parked at various points along the street. Movement through the alleys had been fairly easy and the time of night made the streets of Lethe all but deserted. Six large men moving along a city street at night would be fairly easy to conceal, however six of the Emperor's Space Marines would be a much more difficult prospect. Jeremiah scanned each and every alcove looking for any sign of activity, or anything that could give away their presence.

'Spectral rotation scan.' Jeremiah sub-vocalised this command.

The optics in his helmet responded, switching through each wavelength of the light spectrum, giving Jeremiah a clear picture of what was on the street. However, Jeremiah was also aware that whatever the divine technology of the Emperor would allow him to see could also be thwarted by the insidious technologies of the Emperor's enemies.

Like all of his team, Jeremiah wore dark-coloured robes that covered most of his armour, but the sheer size of a Space Marine was hard to hide regardless of the time of day. They would have to risk moving down the street.

Jeremiah removed his helmet and clipped it to his belt. He indicated to his team that they follow suit. Should they be spotted, they had a slight chance to explain away their size, but their helmets were another matter. His curly blond hair was matted by sweat against his forehead, but his blue eyes held within them wisdom that belied his youthful appearance.

'Elijah, find the best path to approach the palace compound,' Jeremiah instructed.

Elijah silently activated the auspex and uploaded the city maps to the display. Even though the interference had played havoc with its sensors, it could still display the city maps they had acquired.

'The south-eastern entrance of the palace is the least protected,' he said. 'Only a few lightly armed palace guards are standing sentry, and it's the farthest away from any reinforcements that could be summoned should we be detected.'

'Good! Take the point and get us there. Remember we want to get in, locate and capture our target and then get out. We do not want to alert the entire city to our presence,' Jeremiah warned.

Once again Elijah took the point position and began moving through the shadows, followed by Jeremiah and the rest of the kill team.

As THE TEAM made its way down the street, a figure watched from the shadows atop one of the tall residential buildings that lined the streets. As if by sheer force of will he held the light at bay, hiding his features in the shadows, shrouded in an unnatural darkness. Once the team rounded the street corner he began to move, bringing his hand up to his mouth.

'The bait has been taken. They've arrived. They'll be at the palace in about ten minutes. Make sure everything is set. Let's be certain that we have a greeting befitting guests of their stature. I'll be joining you soon.' Having sent his message, the mysterious watcher turned and disappeared into the darkness.

THE SERVICE KITCHEN was efficient, making the best use of space. Three large refrigeration units stood to one side, while cabinets occupied the opposite wall. Although compact, there was room enough for several kitchen staff to work within its confines quite easily. The large bulk of the Space Marine on all fours with his head in a refrigeration unit made the room look abnormally small. Haegr made a growling sound as he looked through the chilled drawers. Actually, it was the massive Space Wolf's stomach that was making the noise at that moment.

He was searching through frozen concentrated food packs looking for something, anything, that was fit to eat. He had not had a decent meal since they had left Holy Terra; in fact it had been so long that earlier today while they were scouting outside the walls, he had considered eating one of the many beetles. It would not have been very satisfying, and it would have tasted fairly awful, but it would still have been better than the frozen food packs. This was the second refrigeration unit he had looked through, and so far his luck had not been good.

'How do these people live on this? I'm going to starve. Wait, that's it, that's been their plan all along!' Haegr was fond of talking to himself.

'Torin and Ragnar cannot take me in a fair fight so they brought me along on this mission knowing that food would be in short supply, weakening me.' Haegr began to put the pieces together.

'Well, there is food here. I can smell it. If it wasn't for this accursed planet with all its wildlife! I'm lucky to breathe.'

In frustration Haegr stood up, forgetting that he was halfway in the refrigeration unit. The upper two shelves came crashing down, spilling food packs all over the floor and making enough noise to wake the entire palace. Haegr was oblivious. He was on the hunt, and nothing could deter a wolf in search of food.

'What in the name of Russ is going on in here?' a voice asked.

Ragnar stood in the doorway, holding the leg of a large cooked bird, his other hand hidden behind his back. Taking another bite from the leg he asked again.

'Haegr, what are you doing?'

Haegr answered without even turning around. Nothing would stop him from reaching the third refrigeration unit.

'I'm onto your little scheme, Ragnar! You and Torin have your little laugh. I will find what I'm looking for, and then you will both pay.'

Ragnar swallowed. 'Hmm… What is it you are looking for my friend? Maybe I can help,' he said, taking another bite.

'Don't distract me, Ragnar, the scent is stronger now. I've nearly found it. It's so close I can almost taste it.'

Haegr finally made it to the door of the refrigeration unit. Grabbing the handle he yanked the door open, gazing inside to see more shelves full of food packs. Howling in frustration he slammed the door shut with so much force that his footing gave way and he spun and crashed to the floor. Haegr came to rest sitting on the floor with his back against the door of the refrigeration unit and his legs sprawled out in front of him.

'See what you've done, Ragnar. See what you and Torin have reduced me to,' said Haegr with frustration.

'Well, my old friend, I came here to ask your help with something,' Ragnar said as he walked across the room, bringing his other hand from behind his back, revealing a platter containing the rest of the roasted fowl.

'I seem to have found this meat and I can't possibly eat it all myself,' Ragnar finished.

Haegr looked up to see the huge roasted bird, and a smile stretched across his face. He grabbed the platter with one hand while ripping off the remaining leg with the other.

'You… *chomp*… and Torin… *gulp*… both have a… *chomp*… severe beating coming when I'm done here,' Haegr said.

'Well then you'd better take this as well,' Torin said, entering the room with a flagon of what appeared to be ale.

'I'd hate to see you smash both of us while you were parched and dehydrated,' Torin teased as Haegr grabbed the flagon.

'You show wisdom beyond your years, Torin,' Haegr said.

'Well, before you administer that beating, please be sure that you clean up in here. Let's not be too much trouble to our hosts,' Torin instructed.

Both Ragnar and Torin turned and left the kitchen.

'We'll be enjoying more of that fine ale on the atrium balcony. Why don't you join us when you've finished here,' Ragnar shouted over his shoulder. Haegr did not reply, at least not in a way that Ragnar could understand.

RAGNAR AND TORIN stood on the balcony overlooking the palace atrium. The hour was late. In fact it had rolled over into early morning. Maintenance personnel scurried around, watering the many plants that lined the space and cleaning and polishing the floors. These were tasks that were to be done in the late and early hours of the day. Ragnar had learned on Holy Terra that those who did the everyday drudgeries were not to be seen in the light of day where the palace or political officials could observe them at their work.

Ragnar was glad to be off Terra and back in the galaxy again. He had hoped that by getting away from Terra he would have seen an end to all the cloak and dagger mischief they always had to contend with. He longed for the black and white of the battlefield, the clear view of who the enemy was, but considering all he had witnessed he was beginning to believe that political intrigue was simply a part of life. Even his assignment, or one might say exile, to the Wolfblade was politically motivated. Perhaps it was just the way of things and Ragnar could no longer afford to view the galaxy through the eyes of an immature Blood Claw. Perhaps it was time that he grew up and stopped longing for how he wanted things to be and started accepting things the way they were.

'Ragnar!' Torin raised his voice to get Ragnar's attention.

'I swear sometimes you are the most brooding sort I've ever seen,' scolded Torin.

Ragnar looked up from his drink to see that Magni had joined them. Magni still had not regained his colour, and he appeared to have a slight limp, but other than that he seemed fine. His armour also showed signs of recent repair. The young Space Wolf could thank Russ that his armour had absorbed the brunt of the explosive rounds.

'My apologies, brother, I did not see you enter the balcony.' Ragnar still bore the guilt of Magni's wounds. Getting up from his seat he retrieved a chair for Magni and allowed him to sit before retaking his own seat.

'Yes, Magni, you'll have to forgive our honoured friend, he is sometimes a brooding sort,' Torin continued. 'However, tonight I decree will be a night of song and story, and of daring deeds and warriors of Fenris overcoming insurmountable odds. It will not be a night of brooding and analytical debate,' Torin concluded.

'Perhaps I should start with the story of how I defeated Torin in hand to hand combat back on Terra,' Haegr stated as he entered the balcony. He was carrying a new flagon of ale and there were enough particles of roast meat in his beard to feed a platoon of palace guards for a week.

The three Space Wolves lifted their tankards in salute of their battle-brother as he approached.

'Yes, yes, or perhaps we could discuss the time you were bested by a tankard that attached itself to your foot,' retorted Torin. Ragnar laughed so hard he almost snorted ale out his nostrils as he recalled his first day at house Belisarius. Magni was laughing as well, but it was an uncomfortable laugh. Noticing this, Ragnar elaborated on the story, only embellishing occasionally and only enough to make the story funnier.

'I would have loved to have seen that,' Magni continued, 'but what I would really like to hear is the story of Ragnar and the Spear of Russ.'

Silence instantly fell over the four Space Wolves as all eyes fell upon Ragnar.

'Why would you want to hear that story, pup?' queried Ragnar. 'Why would you want to hear about a young Blood Claw's foolish mistake?'

'I meant no offence, Ragnar, really, and it was not told to us as the mistake of a Blood Claw at all. Lord Ranek tells the story quite differently in fact. He tells of how you used Russ's own spear to thwart Magnus the Red, preventing his entry through the portal and saving the lives of your battle-brothers with quick decisiveness and courage,' Magni stated proudly.

'So the old man tells that story, eh?' Ragnar never realised how much he missed the council of Ranek until that moment. 'Perhaps some day I'll grace you with the tale, but not this night. There are far better things to talk about than that.' Ragnar looked at Torin who gave Ragnar a wink.

Torin knew all too well the anguish in Ragnar's heart and his desire to return to Fenris.

'Besides, why would we want to talk about that when I'm here? I've got much more entertaining stories,' Haegr began to elaborate.

Ragnar walked to the edge of the balcony and looked out over the atrium, its cathedral-like pillars, rising up into a vaulted ceiling. The ground level was clear glass all across the front and down both sides, so that passers-by could see in and enjoy the astounding collection of plant life, and a fine collection it was. Exotic offworld plants were painstakingly cared for and displayed here. Ragnar thought it was odd that anyone felt the need to transplant plant life onto a planet like Hyades. Just above the ground level several large stained glass windows lined both sides of the atrium, each one depicting some glorious part of Hyades's rich history: soldiers fighting back unspeakable creatures, and heroes protecting the masses from certain death. Ragnar understood these images. He, like all his Wolf brothers, was dedicated to the same calling, destined to defend those who could not defend themselves.

Laughter from behind Ragnar caused him to turn. Haegr had picked up the small table and was wielding it like a shield, no doubt acting out one of his greatest adventures. Ragnar knew that even here among the Wolfblade their calling was the same, it was no different here than on Fenris, within the Fang. The mission was the same, and he knew that it was here that he belonged.

Ragnar turned once again, but this time it was Haegr dropping the table that had caught his attention. As usual Haegr's story skills were no match for his imagination. Ragnar was heading back to rescue his out-matched comrade when a scent caught his attention. It was subtle, almost undetectable but it was a scent that should not be there. During the maintenance of a Space Marine's armour, the Iron Priests were very careful during the rituals to utter every incantation exactly, and to anoint every part with the sacred oils. It was this attention to detail that allowed these ancient artefacts to serve the Emperor. The scent of anointing oil was on the air this night, and it was not coming from the Wolfblade.

It was Torin who noticed the change in Ragnar first. All Space Wolves were gifted with an enhanced sense of smell, it was one of the many gifts from Russ, but Ragnar's was the sharpest Torin had ever known. If Ragnar had a scent then there was something out there.

Torin crossed the balcony to stand beside his friend.

'What's got your attention, little brother?' Torin asked, referring more to their comparative ages than their sizes.

'As I've told you before, Torin, you've been on Terra too long,' Ragnar replied. 'The scent should not be here, and I definitely can't explain it, but there are Space Marines on the palace grounds.'

'Other than the Wolfblade there should be no other Marines here, Ragnar. Are you certain?' Torin asked.

'There are definitely other Space Marines here,' said Ragnar, trying to locate the direction of the scent so he could pick up the trail.

Haegr and Magni had noticed their two companions' movement and had joined them. Ragnar opened the exterior door that went outside onto a mezzanine outside the atrium. He was locked on the scent; it was strong and unmistakable. He held up his open hand, placed it in the air horizontally and slowly pulled it down. This signalled the others to slow their pace and move with stealth. Slowly, Ragnar moved along the mezzanine, following the olfactory trail.

Quietly, the Space Wolves readied their weapons, prepared for whatever they might encounter.

It was not common for servants of the Imperium to exchange fire, but it had been known to happen, so the Wolfblade could not afford to take any chances. Whoever the intruders were, they did not belong here, and he needed to know why they doing on Hyades.

As Ragnar approached the end of the mezzanine, he spotted six large cloaked figures moving along the opposite side of the garden, heading towards the parade ground. As one of the cloaked figures turned the wind pulled the edge of the cloak from his shoulder, revealing the shoulder pad of power armour. They were definitely Space Marines and Ragnar recognised the winged sword immediately, but why were there Dark Angels here on Hyades?

FOUR
Firefight

WHEN JEREMIAH WAS assigned the mission on Hyades he pored through every document on humanity's colonisation of the world that he could locate. The more he knew about the planet and its capital the better prepared he and his team would be. Unfortunately, as with most planetary histories, time and neglect made finding information difficult at best. However, while searching through the technical data from the Adeptus Mechanicus he found several historical schematics of the city of Lethe. This, combined with the other historical data, enabled him to piece together a basic construction record of the city.

Lethe was the capital city of Hyades, but it was also the original point of mankind's first presence in this harsh realm. Lethe was the location of the first promethium mines on the planet, mines that from every piece of information Jeremiah could find were still intact. Some were still in operation, while others were exhausted and no longer in use. In addition, the area of the city that was referred to as the governor's palace was in fact Hyades's first human settlement. The walls that surrounded the palace grounds were the walls of the original city.

Due to the hostile environment of the planet, as the settlement began to expand, the inhabitants left the original walls in place and built the new city around the old. Once complete, the citizens left the old city in favour of the new. Rather than destroy the old structures, subsequent governors had simply refurbished the original core of the city, using it to house the Administratum, the defence forces and any other offices they deemed important.

Jeremiah found the basic common sense of the city's previous governors fascinating and impressive. The palace compound was completely separate from the new city in almost every way: it was self-contained for power, waste reclamation, as well as water and food storage. This meant that during a siege the palace could hold out for an extended period of time.

JEREMIAH AND HIS men found themselves standing just outside the ancient city wall. From his vantage point in the alleyway, Jeremiah could see the main entrance. The palace compound was completely surrounded by a rockcrete wall about ten metres in height. Its facing had been modelled to appear like an ancient brick and mortar structure, giving it more of an artisan-built feel than most walls. This made it aesthetically pleasing to look at, but easy to breach. Surveillance skulls were placed at each corner and at the midpoints of the wall. Each skull panned back and forth scanning the conveyance road and pedestrian walkways that surrounded the compound, roads and walkways that were now clear due to the newly imposed curfew. Squads of sentries were posted at each of the four gates and at least a dozen two-man patrol teams moved along the top of the walkway. These teams patrolled in thirty-second spreads in counter rotating patterns. This made an undetected entry difficult, but not impossible.

Using hand gestures, Jeremiah signalled the team, and each man acknowledged with the all clear. With that the team went into action. Synchronising their actions with the patrols and surveillance skulls, each, at the appropriate time, crossed the street and scaled the palace wall. Using the seams and cracks of the decorated wall as foot- and hand-holds, the Dark Angels successfully traversed the wall and gained access to the palace in no time. Jeremiah was last to cross, waiting to ensure that each member of his team was safely over before he followed them.

Jeremiah quickly broke from cover and ran to the compound wall, as his team had done before him, and scaled the wall with relative ease. Grabbing the top, he swung his legs over and crouched on the surface walkway. From here, he could see the interior of the compound for the first time.

The governor's palace rose from the centre of the city. It was a beautiful structure of glass and ceramite steel, with stained glass windows depicting many aspects of the city's history. Fantastically lush gardens and small stands of trees populated the grounds surrounding the palace. It was surrounded by rows of buildings that all had a purpose in the day-to-day operation of the city, including the defence force's billets just behind the palace. The Dark Angels' intelligence reports were unclear on exactly where their target would be, however it was a good bet that the palace compound was the best place to start. Jeremiah quickly made a rough mental map of the area then dropped off the other side of the wall to join the rest of his team.

Once on the ground and in the cover of shadows, Jeremiah spoke.

'How does it look, Elijah?'

Elijah was focused on the auspex, studying the maps and intelligence reports of the palace compound.

'The interference is not as strong here, but the signal is still sporadic. According to the maps, we need to move in that direction,' Elijah explained.

Slowly, and with precision, the Dark Angels moved through the shadows towards their objective.

The parade ground was nestled in the centre of the palace grounds, where the planetary governor could inspect his troops. Over one hundred and fifty metres in length and nearly seventy-five metres wide, its flat grassy surface was used for the governor's military ceremonies. The entire grounds were bordered by a paved walkway, which was often used by palace guards as an exercise area or training track.

From the centre of the palace, a large two-storey stained glass atrium jutted out into the grounds. From here the governor could stand in the centre mezzanine as his troops passed by for his inspection. The outer edge of the parade ground was spotted with small areas of trees and shrubs landscaped around manmade brooks and streams with benches and tables positioned so that guests could enjoy the tranquillity of the gardens away from the hustle and bustle of the palace.

It was this tranquil environment that concealed the kill team. They would proceed from here without the use of the auspex as it was rendered useless, apparently by the palace's own internal defence systems.

Their optical scans revealed nothing in the vicinity. Jeremiah signalled the team to begin moving through the parade ground using the foliage for cover. Staying on the opposite side of the grounds from the atrium they should be able to move through undetected.

Elijah took point with Jeremiah bringing up the rear. They moved quickly, stopping occasionally to scan ahead to ensure that there were no visible threats. They were approaching the centre of the grounds.

'Elijah, do you see anything within the atrium itself?' Jeremiah asked.

'Full spectrum scan,' Elijah sub-vocalised the command. The optics within his helmet began to cycle through the visual spectrum. To his surprise the visual sensors were unable to penetrate the glass of the atrium.

'The atrium is shielded from my optical scan, my lord.' Elijah's voice came through the comm. 'I'm unable to detect anything within.'

'Very well, keep moving,' said Jeremiah. 'The living quarters are located on the other side of the grounds, we should locate our target there.'

The Space Marines spaced themselves out as they moved from shadow to shadow. Elijah led the way while Jeremiah assumed the rearguard position. They met no resistance at all. One by one they reached the opposite edge of the grounds, moving across the open area between the grounds and the palace. From there it was a mere fifty metres to the planetary defence force barracks.

Jeremiah was the last one to cross. Using the foliage for cover he surveyed the area behind them one last time to ensure that they weren't being followed. There was no visible movement. He slowly broke cover and made his way across the opening to the corner of the palace. As he crossed, something caught his eye, and he turned to see four figures moving along the mezzanine of the upper floors of the palace. Judging by their size and bulk, they could not possibly be normal humans. There could only be one explanation, there were other Space Marines on Hyades.

THE SPACE WOLVES and the Dark Angels had a turbulent history that dated back to the time when Leman Russ the Space Wolves primarch and Lion El'Johnson, the primarch of the Dark Angels, still walked among the stars. The exact reason for the animosity between the two Chapters had long since been forgotten. All that was known was that a great rift grew between the brother primarchs over events that occurred during the Horus Heresy, events so great that Russ challenged

Johnson to single combat. Ten thousand years later the Sons of Russ still bore this old grudge from those events and although they were not considered outright enemies, the Dark Angels were not to be trusted.

Ragnar knew that in the Spaces Wolves' long history there were times when the Great Wolf of the time refused to aid or assist the Dark Angels and there were even limited engagements between the Chapters.

He was not sure why there were Dark Angels on Hyades but he knew the Wolfblade had to act.

'Magni, I want you to alert Commander Cadmus. Inform him that we have uninvited guests in the grounds, let him know that Haegr, Torin and I are moving to engage,' Ragnar instructed.

'But Ragnar you're outnumbered you'll need my–' Magni pleaded.

'Do as you've been instructed, pup,' Haegr interrupted. 'There are only six of them, that's barely enough for me,' he boasted.

Magni knew not to argue any further, more from the look he was receiving from Ragnar than from Haegr's barking. He turned and ran back into the atrium.

Ragnar grabbed the handrail and leapt, swinging his legs over the railing and landing on the asphalt of the track, barely noticing the four-metre drop. Torin and Haegr followed immediately. Before they had hit the ground Ragnar was already at a full run across the parade ground.

The three Wolfblade crossed the parade ground in no time. Ragnar and Torin leapt over the foliage that a mere moment ago the Dark Angels intruders had been using for concealment.

Ragnar paused for an instant and took in the scent. From here it was no longer a faint hint, but a fully-fledged trail: one that he could easily follow. As Ragnar turned to Torin the foliage behind them erupted and Haegr crashed through.

'What are you standing here for? Let's get moving,' Haegr said.

Ragnar and Torin exchanged a grin and moved to the corner of the palace that the Dark Angels had just gone around. Slowly Torin looked around the corner, but seeing nothing he turned and signalled the all clear. As he and Ragnar stepped out onto the walkway, the side of the palace wall exploded as bolter rounds peppered the corner. Torin took a hit to his arm, which spun him around and back. Seeing where the shots had come from, Haegr instantly opened fire. Although the target was well out of his pistol's range, it gave Ragnar enough time to leap back behind the corner.

Torin was getting up from the ground.

'Are you all right, my friend?' Ragnar inquired.

'Armour stopped it cold, just caught me off guard. I won't make that mistake again,' Torin answered.

Haegr continued shooting at their unseen adversaries. As he leaned out to fire another burst, Ragnar and Torin broke from cover and ran across the small courtyard to the large statue of a former governor of Hyades. There was no return fire. Haegr quickly joined his fellow Wolfblade battle-brothers.

Ragnar wasted no time. He rounded the base of the statue and sprinted towards the corner of the barracks. Flattening himself against the building wall, he quickly glanced around the corner just in time to see their Dark Angel assailant. Ragnar and the Dark Angel's eyes locked, and in that quick glance more information was exchanged between the two warriors than could be exchanged in hours of conversation.

Ragnar knew that giving chase would lead them into an ambush. He had to find a way to gain the advantage. Turning, he ran back along the Administratum building's wall, leapt up the entrance steps and crashed through the double doors. Torin and Haegr who were just behind him instantly adapted to the change in tactics and ran into the building after him.

Ragnar was in full combat mode. The Dark Angels should not be here. If they were here for legitimate reasons they would have observed standard Astartes protocol. The Chapter-wide distrust and hatred of these so-called Space Marines was proven. They had fired upon him and his brothers with no provocation. They were not the enemy, but they were not supposed to be here. They would live to regret their deceit.

Ragnar ran past the reception desk into a maze of corridors and hallways that had statues of long-dead city officials placed throughout. Using his genetically enhanced memory and intellect, he manoeuvred down several long corridors until he reached a door to a room that from his best estimate would lead to the opposite wall of the building. If he had got this right the Dark Angels would be on the other side.

Ragnar stopped at the door, grabbed the handle, and cautiously entered the room, trying to avoid being seen through the widows should the Dark Angels be where he suspected they were. Ragnar looked in upon what appeared to be a large conference room. A large table lined with high-backed chairs sat in the centre. There were three windows on the opposite wall, grand paintings adorning the walls between them. A large tapestry of the Holy Emperor hung from the wall at the end of the room. Skulls of previous adepts were stacked on shelves like books, while candles burned brightly from their corner holders, sending a wavering glow across the room. Ragnar spotted his adversaries through the middle window. They appeared to be setting up for an ambush.

Ragnar wasted no time. He leapt onto the table, took one additional step and then dived through the centre window. Glass and wood showered down onto the nearest Dark Angel. Landing on the Marine, Ragnar grappled him around the shoulders. Using Ragnar's momentum, the Dark Angel threw Ragnar from his back and then tumbled across the ground and came up on one knee. Ragnar landed on all fours, crouching low, ready to strike.

Ragnar sized up his opponent. He had recovered nicely from his initial attack. The Dark Angel, now on one knee, glared at him, flung his cloak aside and drew his sword. The remaining five members of the Dark Angels squad were spread out behind his current prey, scrabbling to support their apparent leader. His attack had taken them all by surprise.

Now that he had accounted for them all, Ragnar once again returned his focus to his original foe. This Dark Angel appeared younger than he'd expected, but the service studs he wore indicated otherwise. The moment seemed like a lifetime as the two Astartes sized each other up, waiting for the right moment to strike. Tension built, stronger and stronger, and myomer muscles and tendons tightened and released. Finally the time came.

Thumbing the activation rune on his sword the Space Wolf leapt forward, his battle cry echoing through the courtyard. Raising his weapon high above his head, Ragnar brought it down in a swift killing blow towards the Dark Angel's neck. His adversary had barely enough time to bring his own weapon up to parry the blow. The two swords crashed together and locked. The warriors struggled against each other, and their weapons sparked as each man tried to gain the advantage. The blades were crossed and locked at the hilts.

Ragnar leaned in, trying to force his blade down, while the Dark Angel kneeling below pushed up with all his might trying to keep Ragnar's sword at bay. Ragnar knew that his opponent was determined and would not yield.

Torin leapt from the window that Ragnar had broken, followed closely by Haegr who made his own contribution to the remains of the wall as he forced his large frame through the makeshift opening.

Torin immediately assessed the situation. Ragnar had proven time and time again that he could take care of himself. However, there were at least five other Marines that needed to be dealt with.

Torin and Haegr flanked Ragnar on either side, protecting him should any of the Dark Angels try to overrun him. They would have to get through them first. Torin could make out five figures in the shadows.

Suddenly one of the Dark Angels was bathed in a faint bluish green glow. Torin immediately leapt to his right, barely evading the ball of plasma flame. The wall of the Administratum building burst into flames as the plasma erupted against it.

Torin watched as the Dark Angel stepped closer, ensuring that he would not miss a second time. The Dark Angel raised the plasma gun for a second shot. Suddenly the plasma gun began to glow first red and then white hot. Waves of electrical energy danced across the surface of the weapon and up the arms of the Marine, who began to convulse from the sudden surge of energy that the plasma weapon was discharging.

The technology behind plasma weapons was ancient and their devastating power made them highly effective in combat. However, that effectiveness came at a price. Sometimes the massive energy was too much for the weapon to contain, and it would short circuit, overheat and then explode, sometimes taking the wielder with it.

This was not one of those times. The weapon exploded, engulfing its wielder in the blue-green flame of plasma fire and throwing him back and to the ground. His armour was scorched and melted in spots, but it was intact.

Haegr squared off against the remaining three Dark Angels, bolt pistol and sword ready.

'You should feel honoured, for it is Haegr you face and it will be Haegr who ends your days,' the Space Wolf bragged as he closed on the three Dark Angels.

Suddenly the entire courtyard was flooded with light, and the roar of military transports was deafening as several squads of the planetary defence forces surrounded the Astartes warriors.

'This is Commander Cadmus of the Hyades planetary defence forces. You are hereby ordered to lay down your weapons and surrender.' Cadmus's voice echoed around the courtyard.

Ragnar was distracted for only an instant, but an instant was all that his opponent needed. With a surge of strength, he pushed Ragnar away, rolling to one side and onto his feet.

The six Dark Angels stood together, their backs to the wall surrounded by dozens of the planetary defence troops and three members of the Wolfblade.

Ragnar stood up and walked over to join Torin and Haegr. It was over.

'It's time for some answers,' Ragnar stated as he walked towards the surrounded Dark Angels.

Suddenly the Wolfblade and the defence forces found themselves blinded by an intense white light. Then the ground shook so hard that Ragnar was knocked down, confused and disoriented.

'What in the name of the krakens of Fenris was that?' Ragnar heard Haegr shout.

'Blind grenades,' Torin shouted.

Blind grenades exploded with a blinding visible white flash. While the explosion did no physical damage, the bright burst of light could cause momentary or even permanent blindness to the unprotected eye. However, they also emitted an electronic pulse, designed to disrupt electrical and even neurological systems. This would cause even the optic in an Astartes helmet to temporarily cease to function.

It TOOK SEVERAL minutes for the effects of the Blind grenade to wear off, and Ragnar could see again. He stood up and looked around. Even though the Wolf-blade were not wearing their helmets for protection, they were Space Marines, and their genetic gifts allowed them to recover their faculties quickly. Unfortunately the defence forces were not quite as lucky and even those with eye protection were affected. Several had fallen to their knees, sobbing, succumbing to the panic of the loss of their sight. Many walked around, arms stretched out in front of them, trying in vain to find their friends. Ragnar knew that the effects would wear off soon, and he turned his attention back to the matter at hand.

Cadmus walked past Ragnar towards where the Dark Angels had been standing. All three of the Space Wolves turned and followed. As they approached the area, the smoke began to clear, and they discovered what had caused the ground to tremble with such force. There was a two metre-wide hole in the ground where the Dark Angels had been standing.

'Where are they? Where did they go?' Haegr asked.

'Down there it would appear,' Torin replied, pointing to the large hole.

'Lethe was the site of the first promethium mines on Hyades, and although the ones below the city are exhausted and no longer in use, they still exist, and as the city grew they built right on top of those old mines. It would appear that our intruders made their own escape route,' Cadmus explained.

Ragnar knelt down to examine the makeshift escape route. The dirt was scattered around the outside of the hole in a circular pattern, with most of it gathered around the hole's edge. Smoke still hung heavily in the air. The sick stench of promethium residue assaulted Ragnar's senses.

'This looks more like something erupted out of the ground,' Ragnar stated.

'I would imagine that some sort of directional explosive, possibly a melta-bomb charge was placed on the ground, it burnt through the dirt and bedrock until it reached the abandoned mine, igniting the promethium fumes,' Cadmus explained.

'You seem to know a lot about how these intruders were able to escape, commander.' Torin's tone was more interrogatory than curious.

'Not really, Space Wolf, it's merely what I would have done.'

'It doesn't matter how they got there, that's where they went and that's where we're going,' Ragnar stated.

'I think not, Wolfblade Ragnar. My men will handle this from here,' Cadmus countered.

'Fortunately we don't take our orders from you Commander Cadmus,' Ragnar retorted.

'Of course, I would never dream of giving you or any of your fellow Wolfblade orders. I was merely assuming that you would wish to search the palace to ensure that no other kill teams were present to endanger the life of Lady Gabriella. She was undoubtedly their target. However, my men will endeavour to fill your shoes in your absence.'

Ragnar wanted nothing more than to simply reach out and remove the arrogant smirk from the commander's face, but the point he made was undeniable. The Wolfblade were honour-bound to serve House Belisarius, which only made the situation that much more frustrating.

'Of course commander, you are correct,' Ragnar agreed. 'The Wolfblade's place is beside Lady Gabriella.'

'We can't just let them go, Ragnar, we must follow them,' Haegr stated.

'My blood is up as well, my friend, and I too long to finish this fight, but our first duty is to see to Lady Gabriella's safety,' Ragnar replied.

Torin nodded his head in agreement. Haegr merely snorted his compliance.

Ragnar turned, looking back towards the defence forces, several of whom had started to recover and were leading those still affected to medical personnel. The Administratum building that had been set alight by the plasma fire raged on, fire teams working to bring the blaze under control. It was quite apparent that the Wolfblade was not needed here. Their duty was to locate Gabriella and to ensure that she was safe.

Ragnar moved to leave, heading in the direction of the palace. Torin walked beside him.

'You'll make a fine politician Ragnar,' Torin said with a grin.

'Great, now I've got to take your insults as well.'

'Well, that was a good bit of exercise,' Haegr commented.

'I'm glad you enjoyed yourself, Haegr,' Torin replied.

'Did you see how those Dark Angels ran when they realised that they faced the mighty Haegr of the Wolfblade?' Haegr continued.

'Yes, I did. You should be most proud of yourself,' Torin quipped.

'I've never driven a foe underground before! That's a first even for me. I can't wait to tell Magni.'

Ragnar stopped in his tracks. He had sent Magni to alert Commander Cadmus, but he had not been with the defence forces. Where was he?

'Torin...?'

'I'm thinking the same thing, Ragnar,' Torin replied.

Ragnar and Torin broke into a run, heading straight for the palace, both worried that the presence of the Dark Angels was just a distraction.

Ragnar activated his comm.

'Magni. Magni, respond!' There was no reply.

Earlier, Ragnar had felt as if he and the Wolfblade were being manipulated. What if he was right? The role of the Wolfblade was to serve and protect the members of House Belisarius. Although Ragnar always said he was in exile, he knew it was more than that. He knew that Logan Grimnar himself had sent him here. If he had been manipulated he would not only have failed the Wolfblade, he would be failing Logan Grimnar too.

Ragnar's stomach tightened as they entered the atrium, reaching the steps to the second level instantly. In two bounding leaps he had cleared the stairs, moving to the hall that led to the main conference chambers.

Just as they were about to reach the entrance to the hallway Magni and Gabriella emerged, bringing the trio to an abrupt halt.

'Magni, we sent you to alert Commander Cadmus. We expected you to come with him,' Ragnar scolded.

'The comms were down so I went to the command centre but he wasn't there. He was apparently on a night training mission with his elite regiment,' Magni replied. 'I was on my way back, when I ran into Lady Gabriella.'

'Once he had informed me of the situation, I instructed him to assist me,' Gabriella explained.

'Now, why don't you fill me in on the details to this point?'

Ragnar took a moment to gather his thoughts.

'As you are aware, we discovered a small team of Astartes attempting to move through the palace compound.'

'Dark Angels, Lady Gabriella,' Haegr interrupted.

Torin placed his hand on Haegr's shoulder.

'Sorry, Ragnar,' Haegr apologised.

Ragnar nodded his acceptance and continued.

'We began to stalk the Dark Angels through the parade ground when they fired upon us.'

'They opened fire on you!' Gabriella's shock was undeniable.

'Yes, it was after that that we moved to engage them. During this engagement Cadmus and the planetary defence forces were able to surround our position, cutting off their escape route, or so we believed.' Ragnar paused.

'So they managed to escape?' Gabriella asked.

'Yes, Lady Gabriella. Using Blind grenades, giving them just enough time to blow open an access point into the abandoned mines below the city,' Torin replied.

'That's one of the things I find odd about this whole situation,' Ragnar added.

'They ran away like the cowards they are,' Haegr scoffed.

'No, Ragnar is right,' said Torin. 'I'm puzzled by that and by the fact that they fired upon us without any provocation. The history between our Chapters is well-known; neither trusts the other. However, they are Astartes and nothing in that history justifies their actions tonight.'

Lady Gabriella stepped forwards, hands clasped behind her back as she mulled these events over in her mind. 'I agree. There is something bigger going on here, something beyond a simple production slow-down. I sense that the events of this evening are bigger than just promethium production. I'll inform the governor of the situation. Perhaps you should ensure that the palace is secure and then assist the commander in his search,' Gabriella instructed.

'Very good, my lady,' Ragnar replied.

'Magni, let me tell you about the time that my mere presence alone drove six Dark Angels into hiding underground,' said Haegr.

FIVE
Escalation

THE DARK ANGELS kill team had been moving through the abandoned mines since their escape from the Space Wolves and the Hyades defence forces. Jeremiah had kept them moving to ensure that their escape had been secured, in case there was anyone following them. He had also kept them going to give him time to prepare for the inevitable discussion that would take place. He and his brothers were Dark Angels, Adeptus Astartes, Space Marines. They had just retreated from a fight, and if that was not enough, their retreat had been from a pack of Space Wolves, ancient enemies of the Dark Angels Chapter. His brothers did not take kindly to retreat, and since he encouraged and valued their opinions he knew that they would have some thoughts on the recent events, thoughts that would need to be addressed.

A room off one of the tunnels provided a convenient stopping place.

'We'll stop here, brothers, and assess our next move,' said Jeremiah to his team. 'Elijah, Marius, stand watch at the door.'

The rest of the team took positions throughout the chamber. Empty barrels and crates were strewn about, and ancient lighting systems hung from the walls. Their internal power source was still intact, and generated minute amounts of light, casting the chamber in an eerie twilight glow.

Jeremiah watched as Sebastian paced back and forth across the room, a mix of anger and disappointment etched onto his face, looking up occasionally as if ready to speak, but changing his mind at the last minute. Nathaniel was standing next to a large metal vat against the opposite wall from Jeremiah, arms folded across his chest as he leaned back against the wall. His expression was one of composure and control. Jeremiah knew that he would never openly speak against him.

However, he also knew that he had some concerns. The rest looked at the other three, and feeling the tension that was building, they waited the inevitable confrontation.

'Sebastian, you wish to speak?' Jeremiah inquired.

'With respect, no,' Sebastian stated.

'Sebastian, we all have an equal voice within Lion's Pride. You know that. Jeremiah will hear your words,' Nathaniel prompted.

'I'm uncomfortable with retreating, regardless of the reason. There is no honour in such an action,' Sebastian stated.

'Do you share Sebastian's concerns, brothers?' Jeremiah made eye contact with each member of his team, and they all nodded their agreement until he reached Nathaniel.

'And you, Nathaniel?' Jeremiah asked.

'Let's just say I understand it, brother,' Nathaniel replied.

'As do I, Nathaniel, as do I. However, there are more important things than personal honour, Sebastian.' Jeremiah's words drew the air from the room. He again scanned the room gauging their reaction. 'Yes, we retreated, but we did not retreat in fear of defeat. We retreated to protect what we could not afford to lose.'

Jeremiah watched as his words began to take hold. Sebastian lifted his eyes from the floor and looked him squarely in the face. Nathaniel stood, unfolding his arms, looking like the warrior that he remembered.

'We sacrificed nothing. The honour was ours because we had to protect something much greater than ourselves: the honour of our Chapter. The success of our mission is paramount. We gain honour by keeping that oath, my brothers.'

With those words the team was whole again, ready to continue its mission. Jeremiah looked to Nathaniel his oldest and dearest friend. Nathaniel simply nodded his head, assuring him that he was right.

* * *

A DAGGER OF LIGHT ripped through the black canvas of stars, leaving a jagged tear in the fabric of space and time. Imperceptibly the tear expanded, until it became a hole filled with light. Time stood still, making mere moments last an eternity, until something emerged from the light.

The bow launch bay of the starship entered normal space first. A robed winged figure thrusting a sword upwards stood above the bay opening, challenging all that lay in her path. With a ripple, the remainder of the Space Marine battle-barge cleared the tear and completed its entry into real space. The hole of light shuddered to a close in the vessel's wake.

The starship's dark green colour made it almost invisible against the blackness of space. After a moment, running lights flickered on and off, outlining this monster of Imperial technology. Along its bow, the words 'Vinco Redemptor' became visible. The winged sword emblem of the Dark Angels was clearly displayed above them.

INTERROGATOR-CHAPLAIN Vargas dominated the bridge of the battle-barge. His mere presence seemed to control every function of the vessel. His gaze panned from control station to control station, ensuring that all was in order. Any variance would be unacceptable. He was the master of all things aboard his vessel.

'Lord-chaplain, we have successfully transferred from warp space into real space. We have now entered the Hyades system.' The adept's voice revealed his relief.

Vargas caressed the large tome that hung from his belt: an ancient book with a gold binding, on its cover the symbol of his Chapter. Its contents were for his eyes only. A gold rosarius hung from a gold chain around his neck. His robes covered almost all of his dark green power armour, partially obscuring the Imperial eagle emblazoned on his armour's chest plate. Although the hood of his robe shadowed his face, his bionic eye gave off a gentle red glow beneath it. His crozius arcanum, the ancient weapon of his order, hung from the left side of his belt.

The Chapter Master had dispatched Vargas to Hyades to retrieve one of the Fallen. He had inserted a kill team in secret, hoping to avoid unnecessary conflict and retrieve the traitor without incident. The kill team had instructions not only to capture their target, but also to assess the extent of the contamination.

Vargas studied the comms podium confirming that there-had been no word from the kill team since insertion. His men could find no signal from the Thunderhawk that had been left for emergency withdrawal of the team. Vargas could only surmise that the kill team had been compromised or destroyed outright. Their fate would be determined in time.

Vargas turned, walking the length of the bridge until he stood just behind the helm station. The adept quickly glanced towards the interrogator-chaplain in an effort to acknowledge his presence before turning his attention back to guiding the *Redemptor*.

'Distance to Hyades?' the interrogator-chaplain asked. His raspy voice had a metallic quality to it.

'Approximately twenty-five million kilometres, lord-chaplain,' replied the helmsmen.

Vargas nodded. 'Comms, contact our kill team on Hyades. See if they respond.'

Vargas strode over to the comms console. 'We have high levels of interference, lord-chaplain, but I think, yes, we have a signal,' the relieved communications officer stated.

Vargas took the main comm. 'Captain Jeremiah, this is Interrogator-Chaplain Vargas aboard the *Vinco Redemptor*. Respond.' Vargas paused for a moment.

'Captain Jeremiah Gieyus of Interrogator Kill Team Lion's Pride, respond.' Vargas's impatience was apparent through his metallic tones.

Static answered him.

'Comms, are you certain we have enough signal strength to get through?' asked Vargas.

'Yes, lord-chaplain we–' He was cut short by the response of the kill team.

'This is Captain Gieyus of the Kill Team Lion's Pride, reporting, Interrogator-Chaplain Vargas.' Jeremiah's voice burst through the comm speakers.

'Captain Gieyus, may I assume that you have subdued your target and are awaiting extraction?'

'Negative, lord-chaplain, we encountered unexpected obstacles in our mission,' Jeremiah stated.

'I am confused, Captain Gieyus. What "unexpected obstacles"?'

'We gained access to the governor's palace when we were engaged by a small force of Space Wolves.

To avoid capture we escaped into the mines below the city,' Jeremiah explained.

'Space Wolves?'

'The Space Wolves are in the service of House Belisarius, administrators of Hyades. Their presence was unexpected,' Jeremiah said.

'The presence of the Space Wolves is unexpected but not a cause for great concern, considering the area of space we are in. Have you located the target?' Vargas tried to hide his frustration.

'No, lord-chaplain,' Jeremiah replied.

'Well then as with my original plan I will deploy several squads of Dark Angels to secure the city and we will root out our objective, street by street, building by building.'

Vargas sounded almost pleased. The interrogator was well known within the ranks of the Dark Angels. He had never failed when hunting down the Fallen. He ran them to ground each and every time. He was also known for using any and all means at his disposal to accomplish his task. The ancient secret of the Dark Angels could never be revealed. This above all else was his goal.

'The target must be captured and brought to justice, captain; everything else is secondary.' Vargas attempted to hide the annoyance in his voice.

'I understand that, my lord, but once again I respectfully submit that we do not need to secure the entire city for one heretic, no matter how dangerous. Lion's Pride will locate and subdue the Fallen. We simply need more time,' pleaded Jeremiah.

'Captain Gieyus, you have already failed in your mission. However, let it not be said that I am not a fair man. How much longer will you require?'

'We will only need another twelve hours to locate and secure our objective, Lord Vargas. We will not fail again,' Jeremiah replied.

'See to it that you do not, captain. You've had ample time. Another failure will not reflect well on you in my report.' Vargas's statement was clear.

'My lord chap–' Jeremiah's reply was cut short as a high pitched whine broke through the comms, forcing several adepts to quickly cup their hands over their ears.

'Things are dramatically different with the Sons of the Lion than I remember.' The strange augmented voice burst through. 'In my day failure such as this would not have been tolerated.'

'This is Interrogator-Chaplain Vargas of the Dark Angels. Identify yourself,' Vargas commanded.

'So I am addressing the great Interrogator-Chaplain Vargas. I am honoured, your reputation precedes you. However, you have disappointed me, Vargas, disappointed me greatly.' The unknown voice laughed.

'I say again, identify yourself,' Vargas repeated.

'I thought that would have been obvious to one of your reputation, again I am disappointed. Very well if I must: I am the one you seek.' Laughter once again filled the bridge.

'I will not bandy words with the likes of you! I will simply offer you this one chance to surrender to receive just punishment, or we will use ultimate force.' Vargas's voice was strained with anger and disdain.

'As I said, Vargas, you have disappointed me. Sending down a simple six-man kill team, delegating subordinates to do your job, I mean really Vargas, I had hoped for better from you.' Venom dripped from the voice of their persecutor.

'You have an expanded perception of your own importance. A simple kill team is more than sufficient to apprehend you.' Anger grew to rage in Vargas's voice.

'Do you think I am some terrified refugee cowering in a corner?' The voice laughed. 'I am prepared for you and your fellow Astartes, but I do not think that you are prepared for me.' Again laughter filled the bridge.

Suddenly defensive alarms sounded throughout the ship drowning out the hideous laughter. Vargas quickly turned to the tactical screen. Adepts and servitors reacted furiously to identify the new threat.

'Lord-chaplain, several orbital defence platforms just went active. I'm detecting laser batteries and torpedo bays.' The adept was shouting to overcome the alarm sirens.

'Lord-chaplain, I'm detecting launch. We have an inbound torpedo salvo!'

'You see Vargas! Do you finally see what a great disappointment you are to me?' With its final assault the voice cut off.

Vargas felt his anger growing, but he was too experienced to allow that anger to completely take over.

It was time to bring this to an end, to bring it to an
end his way. He turned to give his instructions
when a single voice came from the comm. It was the
voice of Jeremiah Gieyus.

'Lord Vargas–' Vargas cut off Jeremiah in mid sen-
tence.

'The target must be located, captured and brought
to justice, captain. All other concerns are secondary.
Do what you must to secure him. The threat of
contamination is too great, and the time for covert
operations is over. I will be sorting this my way.'
Vargas gestured to the communications officer to
close the channel.

'Guidance, bring us within assault range. Activate
shields and all weapons batteries,' his metallic voice
commanded.

Weapon and defensive system adepts repeated
Vargas's words back to him as they accomplished
each command with lightning precision. The bridge
access doors sprang open as two Dark Angels
entered the bridge, taking positions on either side
of the door. Should the ship be boarded they along
with the adepts, servitors and Vargas would defend
the bridge.

Activating the inter-ship comms, Vargas contin-
ued, 'Forward launch bay prepare and launch
Thunderhawk Squad Alpha for defensive cover.
Drop-pods prepare for immediate launch.'

Returning his attention the bridge, he continued
his commands, 'Tactical control, display the current
position of the *Redemptor* and all other vessels in
the system,'

Vargas turned to the tactical screen. A holographic image sprang to life. The planet Hyades was at the centre. Several ships floated at various orbits above the planet. The orbiters were mostly transports and cargo vessels in standard docking orbits. These ships posed no threat to the *Vinco Redemptor*. The defence platforms however were another matter.

'How is it you missed the platforms on your initial scans?' Vargas demanded, clenching his gauntleted hands.

'Their power grids must have been down as we approached, Lord Vargas, and we were too far away for visual confirmation,' the tactical officer replied, failing to hide the stress in his voice.

Vargas was troubled by the fact that the defence platforms were left powered down. Not to mention that these defences had not been included in the intelligence reports. It wasn't uncommon for planets like Hyades to have planetary defence platforms, but to leave them powered down to hide their presence was unheard of. Was it possible that the Fallen had set a trap for them? Well if it was a trap, the fools were about to catch far more than they could have imagined.

'It would appear that we are in for a bigger fight than we expected. So much the better,' said Vargas, the anticipation in his voice coming through the metallic tone.

Vargas stroked his rosarius and let his hand rest on the two black pearls hanging there. An interrogator-chaplain earned one black pearl for each Fallen who confessed his sins and sought redemption before his death. Today, he was determined to capture the Fallen that would bring him his third pearl.

The interrogator-chaplain stormed across to the bridge's observation deck. From his vantage point, the massive ship stretched out before him. He could see its weapon batteries spring to life, powerful weapons capable of punching through a ship's hull with ease. Planetary bombardment cannons rose from their enclosed bays, primarily used to soften a target prior to Space Marine deployment by orbital bombardment. However, that would not be their purpose this day, since there was no need to lay waste to the capital city... yet.

Doors covering the massive torpedo bays retracted in preparation of their impending salvo. Vargas knew that within his ship's hull, her crew moved to their assigned combat stations. Cybernetic servitors, half-man and half-machine, lumbered through their programmed duties, moving within areas of the ship where radiation, heat and the harsh bite of vacuum would not allow others to venture.

The Dark Angels commander looked out from the pulpit on the observation deck as the battle-barge closed on Hyades. Small pinholes of light flashed through space towards the great vessel. The incoming torpedo salvo was almost upon them. Subconsciously he grabbed either side of his pulpit, preparing for the inevitable engagement.

'It begins,' Vargas said to himself.

'Lord-chaplain, impact with inbound torpedo salvo in twenty seconds,' the tactical adept declared.

Twenty-four torpedoes cut across the void on a collision course with the *Redemptor*. The civilian transports and cargo ships between the torpedoes and their target banked and turned, making dramatic course changes and showing manoeuvring abilities more akin to warships in avoiding the oncoming wall of destruction. Weapons turrets aboard the battle-barge vomited a hail of defensive fire against the unexpected onslaught. Several torpedoes unable to alter course exploded while others fell horribly off course as they passed through the *Redemptor's* defensive salvo. Four passed through the hail of defensive fire unscathed. Onboard klaxons trumpeted the impending collision.

'Four torpedoes remain inbound,' the adept shouted, attempting to be heard over the alarm klaxons.

'Launch torpedoes... brace for collision.' The chaplain's voice remained calm and precise.

Torpedoes erupted from their launch tubes on course for the defence platforms. The *Vinco Redemptor* banked hard to her port side in a sluggish attempt to position her heavier armoured side to the enemy torpedoes, protecting the open launch bays from the destructive force careening in her direction. Not designed for manoeuvrability, the *Redemptor* resisted the unnatural movement, but slowly she brought her bow around.

The first of the torpedoes struck amidships. Ripples of blue energy radiated in waves out from the point of impact as the *Redemptor's* defensive shielding absorbed most of the weapons' energy. The next two torpedoes sent waves of blue energy rippling across the ship as they also wasted themselves on the defensive shielding. The fourth torpedo struck home just outside the forward launch bay. The defensive shield, already strained by the previous strikes, was not able to withstand another direct hit.

The explosion ripped through the weaker sections of the armoured hull and flames engulfed the launch bay. Shards of metal, fragments of ceramite plating and other debris ripped through crewmen manning the launch craft. Secondary explosions from ammo lifts and fuel carriers enhanced the destruction. Automated fire suppression systems activated, working to extinguish the flames and contain the damage.

Servitors moved into the damaged bay, clearing debris and rubble. Techmarines took their places near the wounded deck, beginning the ritual anointing ceremonies, which would allow them to reroute damaged systems and control functions.

'Damage control reports minor damage to forward launch bay, lord-chaplain,' reported the tactical officer.

The *Vinco Redemptor* returned to her course. She was almost in range to launch the landing force. The transport and cargo ships appeared as small green images on the tactical display, scattering as they attempted to avoid the coming conflict.

Vargas turned his attention away from the observation deck, back to the tactical display. As Vargas watched, he noticed something odd. Though the civilian ships were in disarray, one of them was following an escape course dangerously close to the Dark Angels battle-barge.

Collision alarms sounded.

Vargas spun back to the observation deck. 'Report?' Vargas asked already knowing the answer.

'Proximity alarm, lord-chaplain. One of the transports is on a collision course with us.'

'I want that transport out of our flight path,' commanded Vargas.

'Lord-chaplain?' asked the fire control officer.

'All port weapons, bombardment cannons two and four, target that ship and fire.'

The transport ship rocked as the *Redemptor* obeyed its master. Laser and plasma fire sliced through the transport's hull, cutting through the craft's bridge. Then, the dreaded bombardment cannons struck the transport's cargo bay. The ship listed, drifting lifelessly. Fire and electrical residue danced across her hull. Unexpectedly, the transport exploded.

The force of the blast was not like anything that the engines of a transport of her size should be capable of producing. The blast shot outwards, as if in dying, the ship had become a small star. The bridge of the *Vinco Redemptor* rocked violently as the shockwave crashed into the ship's port side. Flame and debris peppered the ship like shrapnel, causing secondary explosions to erupt across the ship.

JEREMIAH DEACTIVATED HIS comm and took a deep breath. His mind flew back to the moment when the intelligence report for this mission had been presented. Commander Azrael, Supreme Grand Master of the Dark Angels, had been there for its presentation. After its reading, a debate among several of the interrogator-chaplains had begun about who would pursue this member of the Fallen, and how his apprehension would be effected. After several days of deliberation Lord Vargas had been nominated and approved. He remembered this quite clearly because after the chaplains had agreed they had turned to Commander Azrael who simply nodded his approval.

Vargas very quickly began to discuss his plans for securing the Fallen.

'My plan is quite simple: I will dispatch a kill team to Hyades to locate and secure the Fallen. Once our objective has been achieved, the *Vinco Redemptor* will arrive to extract the team. Should something go wrong or the team fails in its mission then I will deploy troops to search and subdue the city until he is found.'

There were no objections to Vargas's plans, only a question from Commander Azrael. 'Hyades is in a sector that falls under the protection of the Space Wolves. How can we explain such action on one of their protectorate worlds?'

There was a long pause before Vargas spoke. 'Grand Master, the entire operation will not take long at all. In fact we should be in and out before they even know we are there. However, to ensure the highest possibility for success, I will deploy Kill Team Lion's Pride, led by Captain Jeremiah Gieyus.'

* * *

JEREMIAH KNEW THAT Chaplain Vargas had just absolved himself of any responsibility of failure. Everything rested squarely on the shoulders of him and his team.

He looked into the eyes of the members of his team. None of them knew the real reason why they had been assigned to this hunt. The path they were on would require more from them than he had ever asked before.

'My brothers, you are all aware of what's about to happen. Chaplain Vargas will be launching the assault force in a matter of minutes. Our target has infiltrated the Hyades defence forces. That means they will be used as cannon fodder so he can make good his escape. We cannot allow this to happen. It is imperative we locate him and bring this matter to a swift conclusion.' The passion in Jeremiah's voice rose.

'We are all with you Brother-Captain Gieyus. You have but to lead.' Nathaniel spoke for the entire team.

Jeremiah drew his sword and held it out in front of him. Each Dark Angel in turn placed his mighty gauntleted hand on the blade and they spoke in unison.

'Repent! For tomorrow you die.'

VARGAS REACHED UP and grabbed the pulpit, pulling himself back up to his feet. As the bridge lighting returned, he checked the bridge and the crew for damage. Adepts and servitors were pulling themselves up and doing their best to assume their duty. Some lay still and twisted on the floor; these would not rise again.

Vargas had seen many ships burn in space. He'd witnessed reactor explosions, but this was different. The explosion was much more powerful than a ship of that size should have made. Had the transport been any closer, it could have severely damaged the *Redemptor*.

'What caused that explosion? It was too big to be a reactor overload,' Vargas asked.

'Lord-chaplain, I've conducted a focused scan of the remaining transports. Most of them are empty, but four of them are loaded top to bottom with promethium fuel cells.' The tactical adept transferred the sensor information to the tactical screen. The holo images of the loaded transports glowed red to demonstrate their threat potential.

'Treacherous bastards! Damage report! How badly are we damaged?'

'Reports are coming in now, sir. We've lost our port weapons batteries, gravity generators on decks twelve through fifteen port side are down, and the port shields have been depleted to thirty per cent,' reported the tactical officer.

Vargas scanned the restored tactical display. The *Vinco Redemptor's* initial torpedo salvo had severely damaged several of the planetary defence platforms, but they still posed a threat. It was time to bring this to an end. Vargas activated his armour's internal comm system and patched directly into the ship's speakers.

'Brethren, prepare for ground assault. The Lion will be with us on this day. All drop-pods prepare for immediate launch.' Vargas resumed his place on the observation deck.

Dark Angels from the Fifth Company along with support equipment reported to their assigned drop-pods. Marines passed by the Thunderhawks towards the drop-pod launch tubes. Each drop-pod could deliver a single squad of Marines amongst the enemy, hurtling through the atmosphere with incredible velocity, making them virtually impossible for enemy weapons teams to target. Just before impact, powerful engines would ignite, bringing the pod to a safe touch-down. Only the toughened bodies of the Astartes could survive the pressures involved in such a descent.

The *Redemptor* closed on Hyades. Starboard and forward weapons batteries opened fire. Torpedoes and missiles raced from their launch tubes. Wave after wave of Thunderhawks burst from the forward launch bay, forming a shield in front of the *Redemptor*. Smaller and more manoeuvrable than their mother ship, they provided the perfect screen for the much larger battle-barge.

Hyades's remaining defence platforms opened fire with everything they had, using torpedoes and lance batteries. Thunderhawks engaged the torpedoes, protecting the *Redemptor* until she was in range to launch her drop-pods.

Lasers from the defence platforms' lance batteries sliced through the Dark Angels Thunderhawk shield. A few Thunderhawks broke off to conduct strafing runs on the slower and less manoeuvrable suicide transports, destroying them far from the *Vinco Redemptor*.

The *Redemptor* turned slightly, attempting to protect her weaker port side. With the bombardment cannons in range, she opened fire on the defence platforms. Massive projectiles ripped through the remaining platforms, turning them into clouds of metal fragments. With the sky clear of enemy fire the drop-pods were clear to launch. In moments, the Dark Angels would be on the planet.

Vargas stood on the bridge observation deck, watching as his battle-brothers entered the atmosphere.

'The Fallen will be redeemed,' he murmured.

WITH THE ASSISTANCE of the governor's guard, the Wolfblade had just completed a search of the palace grounds. Ragnar and Torin had considered entering the mines to continue their search for the Dark Angels when they received a message from Gabriella.

'My Wolfblade, a Space Marine battle-barge has engaged Hyades's orbital defence forces. Report to me immediately at the governor's command centre,' she ordered.

Ragnar and the others were stunned by the news. Their encounter with a squad of Dark Angels in the capital was strange enough, but now a battle-barge had not only entered the system, but had actually begun an assault of the orbital defences. The foursome quickly broke into a run.

IT TOOK THE four Space Wolves several minutes to reach the command centre, but upon their arrival they found themselves in the middle of a torrent of activity. Two large circular tactical screens filled the far wall. Control podiums and communication pulpits stood directly in front of the tactical screens, where a number of adepts delicately ran their fingers across runes, constantly feeding new data to the screens. Several of them glanced towards the Space Marines. Many had never seen a warrior of the Astartes before, let alone a Space Wolf, and they were afraid. Ragnar could smell their fear, it hung on them like a cloud, but even filled with fear they were not distracted from their duties, which impressed him.

Governor Pelias stood next to the consoles surrounded by advisors, all of whom seemed to be talking at once. Gabriella stood beside the governor listening as the reports came in. Upon noticing the Wolfblade, she immediately made for them.

'My lady, we've detected no signs of any other forces within the palace grounds,' Ragnar reported.

Gabriella swept her hand towards the tactical display. 'We have. Our uninvited guest is a Dark Angels battle-barge.'

'They brought a battle-barge?' Torin said, shaking his head. 'But why? Are they planning a planetary assault?'

'That appears to be their intent. What we don't know is why they are attacking. The governor has made several attempts to make contact with them, but they refuse to answer,' Gabriella responded.

Ragnar searched his memory for some grain of information, some insight into why the Dark Angels were here. Why were they invading Hyades? What could they possibly want?

He replayed the fight with the Dark Angels over and over again in his mind. He must have missed some detail. He had first spotted them moving through the parade grounds, but where had they been heading? Ragnar pictured the palace grounds, trying to map out where the Dark Angels might have been going.

Ragnar scanned the command centre, podium to pulpit, looking for the adept that could provide him with what he was searching for. Finally he saw what he needed: a young pale technician who looked confused.

Ragnar walked over to the man. 'I need you, now,' he said. The man nearly fell out of his chair as he stared up at the armoured Space Wolf. 'Can you bring up a map of the palace grounds?'

'Yes, sir, Lord Wolf, sir, I mean...' With a few simple keystrokes, his screen came to life with a topographical view of the palace grounds. Ragnar traced the path of the Dark Angels through the parade ground. Torin and Gabriella leaned over, flanking Ragnar on either side.

Haegr tried to push through to see for himself, but there wasn't enough room.

'Haegr, old friend,' said Torin, 'why don't you take Magni and gather the rest of the Wolfblade, I've a feeling that we are going to have need of our wolf brothers shortly.'

Haegr looked as if he wanted to protest, but he knew that planning and calculating were not among his strengths.

'Come, lad,' said Haegr, 'Torin's right, we'll be around for the fighting, don't worry.' Haegr realised what Torin was doing. There was a fight coming, and they needed to be ready for it. He and Magni would collect their brothers, and the Emperor help them when they met up with him.

Torin quietly asked Ragnar, 'Care to share with us what you're looking for, my friend?'

'A reason, something, anything that we may have missed during our engagement with the Dark Angels, anything that will give us some insight into why Hyades is so important to them. If we discover why they are here, we may be able to bring this conflict to a quick end.' Ragnar continued to analyse the map.

'You think that the answer is on this map?' Gabriella asked.

'I'm trying to work out where they were going before we engaged them,' replied Ragnar. 'We've assumed that it was somewhere in the palace, that they were trying to assassinate you, Gabriella, or maybe Governor Pelias.'

Ragnar stepped in closer to the display and continued. 'We detected them right here,' he said, pointing to the relative position on the map. 'They moved along the parade ground, beside the Administratum building, on the opposite side of the atrium, leaving the parade ground here.'

'Yes, but then they moved around to the front of the Administratum building,' said Torin. Circling the area with his finger, he continued, 'So you think they were searching for someone or something in the Administratum building?'

Gabriella leaned back, folding her arms across her chest. 'I cannot imagine what they could have been looking for there. Information on trade or weapons, possibly, although it would take weeks to work out what.'

Ragnar travelled back in his mind to the moment when he and his companions had encountered the Dark Angels. He remembered making eye contact with the leader of the kill team. 'They altered their path to engage us,' Ragnar said softly, not realising that he was speaking aloud.

'What's that, Ragnar?' Torin asked.

'The Administratum building had nothing to do with what they were looking for. They altered their plan to engage us. They realised that they had been detected and they reacted to that threat,' Ragnar concluded.

Gabriella folded her hands, obviously aware of more activity and shouts. 'So, if not to the Administratum building, then where were they heading?'

Torin turned back to the map. 'We can assume that if we had not detected them, they would have continued along in this direction.' Torin traced his finger along the map. 'So what lies in that direction?'

Gabriella stopped pacing. 'The armoury, the physical training facility, and the barracks for the elite palace guard,' she said.

'Maybe they were hoping for a decapitation strike before the invasion began.'

'I don't know,' Ragnar said, but he was certain there was something more.

The command centre suddenly exploded with a flurry of action, as alarms sounded. 'Excuse me for a moment,' Gabriella said, leaving to confer with Governor Pelias, who was speaking to someone on the comm; Ragnar guessed it was probably Cadmus.

Gabriella touched the governor reassuringly on the shoulder, and then left him to rejoin Ragnar and Torin.

'Come with me,' she said.

The Wolfblade joined her, flanking her on either side as she moved to the opposite side of the room and entered a lift. The doors closed behind them. Gabriella pressed a button on the control panel and the lift ascended.

'The time for speculation is over, my trusted Wolf-blade. The Dark Angels have refused all our hails. They've destroyed our defence satellites, and right now several drop-pods are on course for Lethe.'

The doors slid open. Gabriella and the Wolfblade stepped out of the lift into a large, well-furnished office. Ragnar guessed it might belong to the gover-nor or one of his aides. Gabriella walked over to a balcony on the far side of the room that overlooked the city.

The Space Wolves stood and watched the smoke trails from the drop-pods as they burned their way through the atmosphere. All three shared a moment of silence; this entire situation had rapidly spiralled out of control.

Gabriella placed both hands on the balcony rail. She leaned forwards, and for the first time, Ragnar could see the tremendous stress she was under. She was trembling ever so slightly. 'The answer we seek lies with the Dark Angels in the mines. The Dark

Angels sent a kill team to infiltrate the palace looking for something or someone. You somehow stopped them from achieving their objective. I should have let you go after them when you wanted to, but I thought we should secure the palace grounds first.'

'Your decision was the correct one, Lady Gabriella. We needed to make sure that your and the governor's immediate safety were assured,' Torin explained.

Ragnar had never seen Gabriella like this before. She was afraid. Even in the most serious of situations on Terra, she had kept her composure. He remembered when they had come upon the dead elder Navigators of House Belisarius. She had wept, but stayed firm. He needed no other measure of the seriousness of this situation, although he wondered if she knew something more than she had told them. Had she seen some psychic vision?

'Ragnar, Torin, go into the mines and locate the Dark Angels. Find out what is going on. We have no other options at this point,' Gabriella sighed.

'Lady Gabriella, we cannot leave you unprotected,' protested Ragnar.

'Whatever is happening here is bigger than my safety, Ragnar. Warriors of the Astartes have engaged in combat. We must know why so that we can bring this to a halt before it expands beyond Hyades.' Gabriella's voice quivered as she spoke.

'Then I will remain by your side while the rest enter the mines,' Ragnar replied.

'A compromise then and I will speak no more of it, Ragnar. Torin and Haegr will need you, so you will go with them. Magni is still not fully recovered from his injuries so he will remain here with me.'

Ragnar knew that the time for debate was over and Lady Gabriella's wishes must be carried out. He and Torin straightened and bowed their heads in acknowledgment, then turned to leave the balcony. As Ragnar walked away he felt Gabriella touch his mind.

Ragnar, I cannot express how imperative it is for the Wolfblade to succeed. I feel that everything rests on you.

Ragnar made no acknowledgement of the words. They would find the Dark Angels, and they would tell him what they knew.

SIX
Capture

RAGNAR KNEW THAT he could never live in a city like
Lethe. As the Wolfblade moved through the darkened
tunnels and refinery that still existed beneath the city,
he had a new appreciation of how tenuous human
existence was on this planet. All around him, promethium flowed through cooled pipes to keep it from
exploding in the hot air of Hyades. Though he trusted
in the tech-priests, still it seemed to Ragnar that the
danger of this underground complex dwarfed that of
the jungle surrounding the city. He wondered just
how much promethium flowed through those pipes.

Underground, Ragnar had hoped the temperature
would fall, but the servants of the Machine-God had
made minimal use of fans and vents. Keeping the oxygen content of this complex low probably made the
promethium safer, Ragnar thought.

The corridors and tunnels were cramped and narrow, meant to be only large enough for the workforce to run the refinery and maintain the pipes. The walls were alternately reinforced with ceramite and rockcrete or left as bare rock. Everywhere, servitors meticulously performed their duties. They smelled more of oil and unguents than sweat as they ignored the Space Wolves stalking past them. Whirrs and whines of machinery accompanied by a low rumble from the pipes echoed through the tunnels. The refining equipment and gauges provided the only light sources, giving what little could be seen an artificial blood-red cast.

They had been searching for hours. Haegr panted as Ragnar led the Space Wolves as quickly as caution and stealth would allow through one of the bare rock sections of tunnel. He didn't want to fall into an ambush. The other Wolfblade followed, constantly scanning the area for signs of the Dark Angels. Ten men from the planetary defence force trailed behind them.

They all had to be careful how they reacted to a sudden strike by the enemy. Ragnar was sure that a wrong move or weapon discharge could burst a pipe and set off large quantities of promethium, cooking all of them in their armour. Ragnar hoped that the Dark Angels would fight as true Space Marines and not resort to shooting a pipe to end things for both groups. Still, while the Space Wolves conducted themselves with honour, the Dark Angels had a reputation as fanatics in their pursuit of their own interpretation of the Emperor's will.

Despite his protests, Magni had stayed to protect Gabriella, along with two other Wolfblade. The young Space Wolf had recovered quickly from his wounds, and Ragnar recognised his potential and prowess. Torin had told him that Magni was one of the best young recruits he'd met, despite the offence that had led him to the Wolfblade. Magni had disobeyed orders in his zeal to defeat the enemy, a sentiment that Ragnar found understandable. However, Ragnar could see that Magni still hadn't learnt his lesson from the kill zone incident.

Ragnar still had trouble believing that the Wolfblade hunted fellow Space Marines. Like all Space Wolves, he was well-versed in the rivalry between the primarchs Leman Russ and Lion El'Jonson. Yet, like his initial experiences with the Wolfblade, he had never expected servants of the Emperor to battle each other on Holy Terra. Now, two groups of Space Marines would engage in combat for the second time on Hyades. Perhaps in battling the Dark Angels, Ragnar might gain a better understanding of his primarch. In his heart he believed that Leman Russ would have ordered him to use the Spear of Russ to defend the Imperium.

The mines shook, sending streams of rock down on the Wolfblade, making Ragnar suspect that a battle raged above their heads. He could imagine the PDF fighting the Dark Angels in the streets. He knew that Lethe's defenders didn't have much chance. Lasguns would be useless against the Dark Angels' power armour, while the human troops would be mown down by the Space Marines' bolter fire.

Despite their superior troops, the Dark Angels wouldn't have it easy. The city centre would hold out the longest with its strong defences and numbers of men, and the rest of Lethe was basically a series of rockcrete bunkers. He guessed Cadmus would have his troopers armed with flamers and heavy flamers. If the men stayed loyal to Cadmus and didn't lose their heart, the Dark Angels would have to fight building by building to defeat the men of Lethe. He hoped that the troopers of House Belisarius could continue to hold out long enough for reinforcements to arrive.

Though he distrusted the commander, Ragnar liked the leader of the PDF unit ordered to search with them. The man, an offworlder named Markham, had learned to fight in a unit of deathworld veterans. Ragnar's instincts and observations told him that Markham was a tested warrior who commanded respect from his men. He hadn't questioned the Wolf-blade and had managed to keep pace, even though the stifling heat of the tunnels and the sounds of warfare from above weren't making it easy on his men.

The members of Markham's team were from Hyades, wearing carapace armour and rebreathers. They were some of the best-armed and armoured troops Ragnar had seen, virtually the equal of elite Imperial Guard storm troopers in regard to their equipment. Ragnar had asked Torin to keep an eye on the man who carried the flamer, and had given orders for its tanks to be disconnected while they were underground. Ragnar knew that if the Dark Angels escaped into the city above or the jungle, then the weapon would be invaluable, but the sheer madness of anyone having a flamer in these tunnels made his guts churn.

The Wolfblade kept their assault weapons in hand. With the twists and turns of the tunnels, any corner could hide an enemy ambush, and they had to be ready to initiate hand-to-hand combat at a moment's notice. At extreme close quarters, the Space Wolves might not have a chance to shoot, even if the pipes would allow it. Ragnar gripped the hilt of his personal sword, his Wolfblade. It had been a gift for saving the Celestarch of House Belisarius, and it was at least the equal of a frostblade, a weapon only given to the greatest Space Wolves. Torin had his sword out, and Haegr hefted his hammer. They were ready.

Ragnar had an idea. He checked his comm, just as a precaution. He wouldn't take chances with communications on Hyades any longer. His armour's systems all appeared fully functional. He raised his hand, stopping the Wolfblade behind him and activated his comm. 'Markham, take your men and continue the search. The rest of you, go with them and give them support worthy of the Wolfblade. Torin and Haegr, stay here with me.'

'Wolfblade Ragnar, I have orders to assist you,' stated Markham. Even in the bad light, Ragnar could read enough of Markham's expression to know that the man wanted to make sure he had the opportunity to battle the Dark Angels.

'The best assistance you can give us is to press on with the search. I want to try something. If it doesn't work, we'll rejoin you. Go,' said Ragnar.

Markham saluted, 'Yes, sir.' He signalled his men and moved forwards along with the other members of the Wolfblade. They turned down an intersection of tunnels ten metres past Ragnar.

Torin and Haegr both gave Ragnar a hard look. 'Little brother, what kind of scheme have you come up with?' asked Haegr.

'Indeed, lad, what are you thinking?' asked Torin.

'By the bones of Russ, don't you trust my instincts yet, old friends?' asked Ragnar.

'I'm still thinking you haven't had a good thrashing in some time to keep the sense in you,' said Haegr.

'I'm thinking like our prey. They are hunters and Space Marines. They don't intend to go back as failures.' Ragnar activated his comm, pleased that it still worked. 'Tech-Priest Varnus, this is Ragnar of the Wolfblade.'

JEREMIAH'S KILL TEAM had outmanoeuvred the city militia. A planetary defence force, even trained by one of the Fallen, was no match for the Dark Angels. He had not anticipated Space Wolves. Vaguely, he remembered some information about one of the Navigator Houses having an alliance with Space Wolves. Now, events had escalated to a full-scale assault on the city.

Of all the Chapters of Space Marines, none had the rivalry that existed between the Dark Angels and the Space Wolves. Jeremiah knew that the Space Wolves had a reputation as savage berserkers, relying on brute force and animal cunning to defeat their foes. Their devotion to their primarch and their homeworld of Fenris was legendary. Few foes could survive the fury unleashed by the Space Wolves.

For their part, Jeremiah believed that no Chapter inspired as much loyalty among its members as the Dark Angels. For thousands of years, the Dark Angels had kept their secrets, hunting down the Fallen and working to redeem themselves. They had an unwavering faith in the Emperor and in their primarch, Lion El'Jonson. Just as their primarch had before them, they used intelligence as well as power to defeat their foes. The mere presence of the Dark Angels was enough to send most enemies fleeing in terror.

Reputation would not defeat the Space Wolves. Furthermore, they were the Wolfblade. Unlike their brethren, nay, Wolf Brothers, they had experience on Terra. They would be cautious, balancing the wild tendencies of their Chapter with the acumen needed to survive the politics of mankind's homeworld.

When Jeremiah had fled to the mines, he had hoped to find a way out into the jungle, through another maintenance hatch or engineering tunnel. While parts of the refinery were well marked beneath the main city complex, the outer sections had fallen into disrepair. The servitors might not need signs or markers to navigate these corridors, but men certainly would.

Many of the tunnels appeared abandoned and in other places, the original engineers had made use of natural caverns. Jeremiah was accustomed to standard design patterns from Imperial engineers, but as his team passed through sections of the mines that curved back on themselves, he found himself disoriented. As yet, they hadn't found a way out, just endless underground facilities containing mindless servitors working the promethium. Originally, they had merely dropped down four metres to the tunnels, but now Jeremiah suspected they were much deeper. Elijah had few readings on his auspex.

What disturbed Jeremiah most was that the Fallen had known the attack was coming and had been able to prepare for it. The presence of the Space Wolves had to be his doing. The Fallen were clever and resourceful foes, with the skills to match the most dangerous members of his Chapter. Nonetheless, if the Fallen had known about the battle-barge in orbit and suspected the possibility of a planetary assault, then Jeremiah would have expected him to do his damage and make his escape. The Fallen had to have a contingency plan to deal with the assault, and it had to be something completely, incredibly dangerous. Their target had to have allies.

Could the Space Wolves be more involved than Jeremiah suspected? What if the Fallen had made a deal with the Space Wolves to expose the Dark Angels to the Imperium in exchange for their aid?

But from what Jeremiah knew of the barbaric Space Wolves, a deal with the Fallen made no sense. The Fallen would manipulate the Space Wolves, but he would have his own allies and his own resources. The Fallen's allies would have to be extremely powerful for him to risk being trapped in a city filled with the Dark Angels.

Ultimately, Jeremiah knew it made no difference. His faith told him that the Fallen would be redeemed. The Dark Angel shuddered when he thought of the redemption process. Few dared to gaze upon the interrogator-chaplains and they would stop at nothing to restore honour to the Fallen's soul.

'Jeremiah, the auspex is no longer functioning,' said Elijah. 'I do not know where the Space Wolves are.'

'The radiation of the machinery and promethium flows must be causing problems. Our adversaries will suffer the same difficulties. Even now, our brethren above attack, seeking to make certain our target does not escape. The time for flight has ended. The Sons of the Lion do not flee from wolves. Elijah, find a way back to the surface. Our target may send his dogs to hunt us, but we are the hunters. We have not failed in our mission. We will not return to our battle-barge without our prey,' said Jeremiah.

Jeremiah's battle-brothers nodded in unison.

A DARK ANGELS Thunderhawk roared between the rockcrete buildings of Lethe, using them to evade the anti-aircraft rounds of the city's Hydra platforms. From the ground and the upper floors of buildings, individual defenders targeted the low-flying landing craft with small-arms fire.

Dozens of lasgun shots glanced off the Thunderhawk's armoured hull, as ineffective as fireworks. As the Thunderhawk landed on a building halfway between the wall and the palace complex, its ramp was already lowered, and a squad of ten Space Marines opened fire on their unseen assailants in the surrounding buildings.

The men of Hyades kept a constant stream of fire against the invaders, but to little avail. The power armour of the Space Marines rendered their defensive fire virtually useless. One Marine stumbled, but the rest forced their way through the roof of the Administratum building where they had landed with a combination of krak grenades and melta-bombs. The Thunderhawk was already gone, dispatching more troops on another rooftop.

The same scene was being repeated throughout Lethe. To this point, the air defences of Lethe had only slowed the Dark Angels, but nothing Hyades had to offer appeared able to stop them.

As more Space Marines landed, the planetary defence force took action, turning their Earthshaker cannons from their positions aiming at the jungle to target their own city. A terrible explosion shattered the night as the first shell smashed into one of the Administratum buildings, just as a Thunderhawk lowered its ramp to discharge more Dark Angels.

The destruction of the building sent rockcrete in all directions, catching the evasive Thunderhawk in a shower of debris. The squad on its roof fell down into the rubble of the former building. Despite the blast, the power armour of the Emperor's finest still allowed some of them to survive. The remaining Space Marines inside the Thunderhawk blew their way free of their wounded vessel and started to make their way through the rubble and smoke that was all that was left of the Administratum building.

Cadmus had been watching everything from his command centre, assessing the enemy's tactics and guiding the battle to the best of his ability. As he watched the Thunderhawk's crash, he activated his vox. 'Now,' was his only command.

At that command, four Hellhound tanks emerged from hangars beneath separate buildings and raced towards the scene of the collapse. The tanks would incinerate the remaining squads of Dark Angels trapped in the rubble. Lethe would send the Space Marines to their own hells in promethium fires.

Cadmus didn't wait to watch the drama unfold from his command bunker. He had every confidence in the crews of his Hellhounds. And besides, he had other matters to attend to.

'Commander, how goes the battle?' crackled his comm. The voice was hushed, barely a whisper.

Cadmus paused for a moment before answering. 'As I told you, I will be able to hold out against the Dark Angels for a short while. Everything will depend on the Space Wolves,' he said, keeping his own voice low.

'Exactly, don't be concerned. Wolves will be wolves,' came the reply.

'I hope so. Now, with your leave, I have a battle to survive,' responded Cadmus.

'Of course. Remember, with every moment, we come closer to winning the war,' said the voice.

Cadmus clicked off the comm. He checked back on the scene of the Thunderhawk crash and building collapse. He could barely make out suits of power armour glowing from the heat of the Inferno cannons within the smoke. Three Hellhounds sprayed white-hot death into the rubble. With his tactical experience, he spotted the wreckage of the fourth Hellhound. A Dark Angels Dreadnought was moving away from the destroyed vehicle: a walking mechanical monstrosity containing the half-alive remains of a mortally wounded member of the brethren. It turned and levelled a twin-linked lascannon at another Hellhound which erupted into a fireball.

'The Lion still has its pride,' he remarked. 'Varnus, launch the suicide freighters filled with promethium. I want to give those Thunderhawks and the Dark Angels fleet something to think about.'

Cadmus wiped his brow and smiled. The Dark Angels had arrived. Phase one was complete.

Everything depended on the Space Wolf fleet arriving to patrol on schedule. It was all about timing and sequence.

THE DARK ANGELS kill team had begun its tactical withdrawal over two and a half hours ago. Jeremiah had decided that it was time for the withdrawal to become a redeployment. They had made the most of their head start on their pursuers, but with the enhanced senses of the Space Wolves, he knew that they would be found by their scent. He had hoped to get back to the jungle before things escalated, regroup and make another attempt to enter the city. That was not to be, however, and now Jeremiah had decided upon a new course of action.

'Marius, Sebastian and Gilead,' said Jeremiah. 'You will seek our brethren and support them. Report to the interrogator-chaplain on our progress.'

'Will you seek out the heretic yourself, captain?' asked Sebastian.

Jeremiah drew his blade. The reddish light of the mining machinery reflected off the polished weapon. 'By the winged blades, our mission has not failed. Elijah, Nathaniel and I will find our target. Further, if he commands the defences of this city, then we will decapitate the defenders, completing our victory. You have one final task, before rejoining the Brethren, a dangerous task, but essential to capturing our target. Engage the Space Wolves. Draw them after you as you retreat and lead them as far away from the city centre as you can. We three will find our way to the target.'

The three Dark Angels nodded their assent. 'The honour of the Lion shall be ours,' they chanted in unison.

Jeremiah said, 'I expect our adversaries will be in the tunnels to the north. They will find you if you do not find them. Engage and disengage, making your way to the surface swiftly.'

'Brother Jeremiah, what route will you take back to penetrate their defences?' asked Gilead.

'Our target is intelligent and understands that he fights a war with us, not just a battle. Though not a coward, he will be relentless in finding a way to continue his quarrel with us, and he will have planned a way to escape from our Chapter's holy strength. The best method of passing out of this city unnoticed and undetected would be these tunnels. We will find his escape route and follow it back to his lair. I have one idea of where to go. We passed a corridor built up like the rest of the refinery, but it was devoid of servitors and had few lights. I suspect that may be the path. If that proves false, we will find another. Do not underestimate the skills of the Space Wolves, and remember, the hand of evil guides our enemies. Your faith in the Emperor will be your shield and the pride of the Lion your strength. Go,' said Jeremiah.

The appointed three disappeared into the tunnels, moving quickly and quietly, guns drawn. Jeremiah knew they would fulfil their duty. The Space Wolves would not stop his team.

IT HAD BEEN several hours by Ragnar's reckoning since the Dark Angels had escaped from the Imperial palace complex in the city centre. Along with Torin and Haegr, he crouched quietly in a tight maintenance shaft, hoping that his plan worked.

If Ragnar was right, the Dark Angels would make their move at any moment. He hoped that he had anticipated things correctly. If he was wrong, then he, Torin and Haegr had just abandoned the rest of the search team.

An eternity passed with each second. Then, Ragnar caught the scent of anointing oils and heard the scrape of power armour against rock coupled with the swish of robes. The Dark Angels had taken Ragnar's bait. He had known that with their fanaticism, the Dark Angels kill team would not give up while there was any hope of completing their mission. With the help of the tech-priest, Ragnar had moved the servitors out of this tunnel and ordered the lights to be shut down. Ragnar had wanted to make this passage conspicuous with its lack of activity. He hoped that the Dark Angels might decide it would make a good place to hide, set an ambush or try to make their way back to the palace complex. It had all worked. The hardest part, besides waiting, had been fitting Haegr into the maintenance shaft.

Hidden behind the doors, Ragnar, Torin and Haegr couldn't see the Dark Angels, but with their well-trained senses, they could hear and smell them. Ragnar held himself in check, while his blood burned with anticipation of the fight to come.

'Here,' said the voice of one of the Dark Angels. He was undoubtedly the leader, as his tone wasn't muffled by his helm. 'We are blessed by the Emperor, my brethren. Nathaniel, remove the maintenance hatch.'

With a savage howl, Ragnar kicked the maintenance door from its hinges. The door struck the Dark Angel full in the chest, knocking him backwards and leaving him without his weapon drawn. From Ragnar's right, another Dark Angel whipped out a blade and drew his pistol with a speed worthy of a Blood Claw, although he paused before firing his bolt pistol, apparently rattled by Ragnar's howl. Torin engaged the quick one, because Ragnar had already chosen his target. There were only three of the enemy and the Wolfblade had the element of surprise in the darkened tunnel.

The helmetless Dark Angel had handsome, classical features, the sort sewn into tapestries to represent angels. Despite his youthful appearance, Ragnar could tell from his stance that he was a formidable fighter. Ragnar slashed at him. The Dark Angel just managed to parry the sudden attack. Ragnar's runed blade drove into the metal of the Dark Angel's sword. Ragnar heard the sounds of battle behind him as Torin pressed his foe. Something was missing.

'Let them know that mighty Haegr comes,' bellowed Haegr. Ragnar heard armour grate against metal. Haegr was having trouble getting through the maintenance hatch. 'Ragnar, Torin, leave some for me or I'll give you both a good thrashing.'

Ragnar kicked his foe as their blades locked. The Dark Angel fell backwards. Ragnar lunged forwards, nearly skewering his enemy with the blade gifted to him by House Belisarius.

The Dark Angel's eyes widened. 'You fight with a daemon weapon, wolf,' he spat, 'but it will avail you nothing against the Sons of the Lion. Just as Lion El'Jonson defeated Leman Russ, so I will defeat you.'

Ragnar looked at the Dark Angels. 'I am Ragnar of the Space Wolves, and I won't be defeated by a Dark Angel any more than Leman Russ was. If you wish to prove your strength against me, throw down your weapon, Dark Angel, and let us fight unarmed.'

Ragnar could hear Nathaniel extricating himself from the maintenance hatch, and was worried about an attack from behind.

With an echoing roar, Haegr burst free. The Dark Angel would have to get past the massive Space Wolf to reach Ragnar's back. From Torin's fight, Ragnar heard the distinctive clatter of bolter rounds ricocheting off ceramite.

'I, Jeremiah of the Dark Angels, accept your challenge, Ragnar of the Space Wolves.'

To Ragnar's surprise, the Dark Angel threw down his blade. Ragnar grinned and sheathed his own sword. The Dark Angel had undeniably realised that Ragnar had the better weapon, but if he thought he'd have a better chance in unarmed combat, Ragnar would prove him wrong.

'Brother Elijah, I'll help you with that one, once I've dispatched this giant,' said Nathaniel.

'Ho, the little Dark Angel thinks he can do something that no man can do. He thinks he can dispatch mighty Haegr of the Wolfblade!' Haegr laughed, swinging his mighty hammer. Nathaniel brought a chainsword up to defend himself, but against Haegr's onslaught, it was too little. Each blow echoed through the tunnels, booming like thunder. The Dark Angel was pushed back and smashed into a rock wall. Despite the pounding, he refused to fall. Haegr grabbed him and crushed him hard. The servos in the Dark Angel's power armour smoked as Haegr threatened to pop him like an overripe fruit.

Torin kept up his assault on his spirited foe, Elijah. The young Dark Angel lacked Torin's skills, but he made up for it with superhuman reflexes, arguably rivalling those of Ragnar. Still, little by little, Torin dissected the youth's defences, wearing him down with his finesse. Elijah caught Torin with his bolt pistol, but the shells bounced off the Wolfblade's chest plate. Torin realised that he had to end the fight quickly. The Dark Angel couldn't last, but he might get lucky.

Torin waited until Elijah managed to fire off another volley, then staggered, hoping that he had read his foe correctly. He had. Elijah rushed in with the sort of enthusiasm Torin would have expected from an untested Blood Claw. The feint worked. Torin thrust his blade up unexpectedly, catching it etween his foe's helm and shoulder, right against the neck. Elijah's life was in Torin's hands, and they both knew it.

Ragnar grappled with Jeremiah. By Space Wolf standards, he was strong, but the Dark Angel's strength startled him. Jeremiah was a match for him.

Ragnar pushed and shoved, trying to gain an advantage, but every move he made, the Dark Angel countered.

Ragnar felt his anger grow. Jeremiah had insulted Leman Russ. While Ragnar may have lost the Spear of Russ, he would not fail his primarch in this challenge. He felt the rage of the wolf within him, giving him strength and enhancing his senses.

For a moment, Jeremiah appeared to have the advantage. As Ragnar struggled with the beast inside, Jeremiah hammered blows against him. Then with a howl, Ragnar found the strength he needed.

In a rage, he grabbed Jeremiah and hefted him off his feet, ramming him against the wall. The world went blood-red and Ragnar could no longer hear the battle around him. He smashed Jeremiah's head against the wall then smashed it again. Then, it seemed to shift to resemble the helm of the Thousand Sons, the traitor Chaos Marines who were the eternal enemies of the Space Wolves. He could no longer think about anything but the honour of the Space Wolves and Leman Russ.

'For Russ!' he screamed and smashed his head into Jeremiah's, drawing blood.

'Lad, that's enough. We want them alive for questioning,' Haegr said, grabbing Ragnar and pulling him off Jeremiah. Ragnar looked at Haegr, taking a moment to recognise his old friend. Finally, the anger subsided.

Jeremiah lay unconscious, his handsome face covered in blood. Nathaniel groaned on the ground. His power armour had not yielded to Haegr's strength, but his bones had not fared as well. Torin's blade remained at Elijah's throat, and the young Dark Angel had lost his weapons.

'You're the only one awake, so I guess it's up to you to surrender,' offered Torin.

'Dark Angels don't surrender to Space Wolves,' snarled Elijah.

Haegr smashed the young Dark Angel on the head, dropping him instantly.

'So that would make this case a special exception,' remarked Torin.

Ragnar retrieved his weapons and tried the comm. 'Markham, do you read me?'

The comm crackled with static before coming to life. 'We've suffered some casualties among the men, Wolfblade Ragnar, but we've got them on the run. They are making their way to the surface. I'm broadcasting the location to Commander Cadmus. I believe we have them. The rest of the Wolfblade are giving chase,' said Markham.

'Good work. You are a tribute to House Belisarius. Ragnar out.' He clicked off his comm.

Ragnar was impressed. The Dark Angels had split up to try and draw his men away. In some ways, the members of this kill team thought like Space Wolves.

'Are you all right, brother?' asked Torin.

Ragnar nodded. He had come close to losing control and letting the wolf come out. Within every Space Wolf lived a beast, a primal savage. They all had to work to control it, to constantly keep the beast in check. Now that the adrenaline had died, Ragnar was starting to feel aches and bruises. Jeremiah had given him a good bout.

'Let's take these prisoners back up to the surface and see how the defences are holding. We need to know why they are here. Perhaps they know something we don't,' said Ragnar.

'Perhaps they think they know something we don't,' offered Torin.

'I suspect that they all needed a good sound thrashing, and once they heard that Haegr was here, well, they knew they'd found the most solid thrashings in the galaxy. What say you to that?' Haegr kicked Nathaniel.

The Dark Angel groaned.

'I'd say he agrees,' said Ragnar.

An explosion rocked the mines. The scent of the anointing oils intensified heavily. More Dark Angels were coming, most likely from the surface. Some of them had penetrated the mine, and it was bad luck that they had entered near the Space Wolves' location.

'They better be careful. Too many more explosions like that and they'll puncture one of the pipes and set the promethium ablaze,' said Torin.

'This whole place, the refinery and the mines, could turn into an inferno!' said Haegr.

'I hope not,' said Torin. 'I believe that the machine-spirits would shut down parts of the pipes where any explosions took place. This whole set of tunnels is convoluted simply because they have an array of pipe systems in case a section malfunctions… Maybe if someone intentionally sabotaged the system.'

'What?' asked Ragnar. 'You mean that if one of us shot one of the pipes it wouldn't cause all of these tunnels to erupt?'

'Exactly,' said Torin. 'Ragnar, did you think… That's why you looked so nervous about the man with the flamer.' Torin chuckled. 'If the whole place was likely to erupt, Lethe would have been destroyed a long time ago. Even the servants of the Machine-God aren't flawless. You'd start a large fire, Ragnar in one section of tunnel, like this one, roughly like getting roasted by a heavy flamer point-blank or an Inferno cannon. Hardly healthy, but that's why we are Space Marines in power armour.'

'So, it's not much more than using a heavy flamer?' asked Ragnar.

'No,' said Torin. 'Believe me if it was, I'm sure one of the Dark Angels would have shot that promethium pipe during our hand-to-hand combat. I know I would have if I was sure that we'd die on an espionage mission rather than be captured by the enemy. However, I think, rather than debate the explosiveness of the tunnels, we need to consider getting out of here. I smell more Dark Angels.'

The tunnel where the Wolfblade stood connected the abandoned mines to the working refinery. The sound of bolter fire came from the direction of the refinery. Ragnar could smell Space Marines from both ends of the tunnel. It was hard to tell just how far away they were. 'Don't worry,' said Ragnar, 'Varnus told me that the maintenance shaft we hid in leads to an old command centre for the unused sections of the mines.'

'What?' asked Haegr. 'Tell me that I didn't hear that right?'

'He's right old friend. We may have to leave you behind. Too many pies, roast meat and barrels of ale.' Torin paused to sigh. 'I doubt you'll fit in the shaft, so you won't make the climb.'

'That's only because Haegr has so much power that he needs food worthy of his stature,' said Haegr.

They heard more bolter fire from the direction of the refinery, and the explosions of grenades. A flash of light came from that direction as well, along with a blast of heat.

'See, they detonated part of the promethium,' said Torin.

In a strangely serious tone, Haegr said, 'Don't worry, I'll fit in the maintenance shaft, even holding one or two of these Dark Angels. I'll bring up the rear.' Then he added, 'Besides, that way I can best protect you two in case the enemy comes down this tunnel and decides to check the maintenance shaft.'

'I'll go last. I'm going to discourage any pursuit,' said Ragnar.

'Fine, I'm not going to waste time debating.' Torin grabbed Elijah and pulled him into the maintenance shaft.

'Are you sure about bringing up the rear, Ragnar?' asked Haegr.

'I'm sure, but I may need your help with Jeremiah.'

The giant heaved Nathaniel and Jeremiah, laying one over each shoulder. The large Space Marines looked like children on Haegr's shoulders. 'Even if I have to go on my knees,' Haegr said ducking down and entering the shaft.

Ragnar was torn. He had decided to turn this tunnel into a flaming ruin. On one hand, maybe he should wait until the last moment to see if he could catch any Dark Angels in the blast. He still felt that it was dishonourable, even if it was no worse than using a heavy flamer. These were the hated Dark Angels, but they were Space Marines as well.

Once again, he had to make a choice: to remain loyal to House Belisarius and to his oath of duty, or to listen to his heart and trust in the Emperor.

He missed life on Fenris.

The Dark Angels, whatever their motives, were the enemy, and had to be treated as such. In their place, he doubted the Space Wolves would have behaved any differently.

Hearing enemy approaching, Ragnar clicked his belt and a grenade came free. With one hand, he set the charge and threw it towards the large refrigerated promethium pipe in the centre of the tunnel. Without waiting, Ragnar leapt as far as he could into the shaft. Behind him, the grenade went off.

The initial blast was a simple burst. Then, there was a rush of flame and a great roaring, as the promethium ignited and split the pipe, spilling its deadly contents into the tunnel. Ragnar reached a ladder at the end of the shaft and began climbing up it. Below him the shaft filled with light as the fireball flew into it.

'By the Fire Wolf itself,' said Haegr, reaching down and grabbing Ragnar's arm, 'you managed not to kill yourself, lad.'

'That should discourage them from entering the tunnel, and I suspect the lower part of the ladder melted,' said Ragnar.

'Do you think you got any of them?' asked Haegr.

'No, I was trying to stop them pursuing us,' said Ragnar.

They had climbed up the ladder into an empty corridor, fitting Varnus's description of the unused mine monitoring station. In Imperial Gothic, a sign on a metal door at the hall's end declared it to be a security station. The three Space Wolves exchanged glances, gathered their prisoners, one each, and made their way forwards.

Haegr placed his Dark Angel on the ground, roared, and threw himself against the security door. The door groaned, but didn't budge.

'Haegr…' said Torin.

But there was no stopping the massive Space Wolf. He took his hammer and pounded the door, again and again. The booming strikes resounded in the hall. After several blows, Haegr threw down his hammer and charged the door once more. This time the enormous girth of the Space Wolf was too much for the door and it collapsed beneath Haegr, falling into the room.

'There,' declared Haegr. 'Now Torin, what were you going to say?'

Torin clapped his large battle-brother on the shoulder. 'I was going to say something unimportant about knowing the House Belisarius security override codes.'

Ragnar laughed and then his battle-brothers joined him. 'It was much more impressive Haegr's way.'

'Indeed,' said Torin, 'and after that clamour, we know that our enemies are truly unconscious, but, perhaps I can use the security codes on these vid-screens.'

Haegr and Ragnar carried their unconscious prisoners into the room, laying them apart and keeping a watchful eye on them, while Torin worked on the command centre's controls.

The security station had several vid-screens, but based on the signs and indicators, Ragnar could tell that it was more for monitoring the unused sections of the mines than for city security. Still, Torin stood in front of one of the vid-screens and gave the codes, performing the required ritual to activate the machine-spirits within the security monitors.

Amazingly, half of the screens flickered to life. At first, they showed only darkened images of the mines. Then, with a few gestures, Torin moved dials and changed indicators and views of the city filled the screens.

'Torin, you did it,' said Ragnar. 'Are you sure you aren't part Iron Priest?'

Torin didn't answer, pointing to the screens instead.

The activated vid-screens showed the ongoing battle. On one large screen, a dramatic encounter drew the attention of the Space Wolves. A Dark Angels Dreadnought strode through the streets of Lethe. Three Imperial Guard Sentinels closed on it, each one carrying deadly saws and blades, designed for cutting through the jungles of Hyades, but now put to deadly use on the battlefield. A twin-linked lascannon from the Dreadnought made short work of one Sentinel, while the others covered the Dark Angels war machine in promethium fire. The Dreadnought disappeared in a cloud of smoke for only a moment, before striding out to smash one of the Sentinels with its massive power fist, shattering it as if it was a child's toy.

Other screens showed the defence guns firing at Thunderhawk gunships and drop-pods. Ragnar also saw the people of Hyades fighting back as best they could. The entire populace used makeshift weapons, along with flamers, grenades and lasguns to defend themselves. Ragnar was impressed with the raw courage, and he saw that the Dark Angels were not unscathed.

'People fight hardest protecting their homes. It's true even here,' said Ragnar.

'One of the smartest things you've ever said,' said Torin. 'We need to find out why the Dark Angels attacked, and that means waking these men up.'

'They won't tell us willingly. Maybe they think we're Chaos-tainted,' said Ragnar.

'What is this bunker?' he asked Torin. 'It seems more to be than an old mine security room.'

'It appears to be a secondary command post. Commander Cadmus probably has a couple of backups hidden throughout Lethe.'

Ragnar found a communications station. Messages flashed across the screen. One in particular caught his attention. It read 'Dark Angels escaping, Wolfblade in pursuit on the street. Quadrant three, sector five north, target on Markham'.

'Can we see quadrant three, sector five?' asked Ragnar.

'Give me a moment.' Torin fiddled with the dials and levers. 'Yes, this screen,' he said.

A message flashed across the screen: 'Bombardment imminent'.

Cadmus was going to kill both sets of Space Marines.

SEVEN
Betrayal

THE DARK ANGELS had surprised Lieutenant Markham and the Space Wolves with their sudden attack and withdrawal. Markham's team had given pursuit, only to be ambushed a second time. They suffered three casualties, but the lieutenant didn't have time to tend to them, as the enemy was close. He and his men had followed the Dark Angels through an access hatch back into the streets of Lethe.

The city of Lethe was in a state of pure carnage. Down the street, a squad of men fired their lasguns at an unseen foe in the ruins of a habitation complex. The night breezes had a caustic tinge and particles of ash floated in the air. Explosions punctuated the night, bright flashes of light followed by booming sounds as if a hundred storms were competing to make the loudest thunder.

In the light from burning buildings, Markham saw three Dark Angels crossing the street, seeking cover provided by the sparking rubble of what might have been a manufactorum due to its many wires and bits of twisted machinery. The Wolfblades accompanying him howled. 'We'll take care of this,' one of them ordered. 'Head to the wall.'

Just as the Space Wolves charged, Markham's vox buzzed. 'This is Commander Cadmus. Belay that order. Stay with the Space Wolves and keep your vox ready for further orders.'

'Yes, sir,' replied Markham, leading his men after the Space Wolves.

The lieutenant was a hard man, a veteran of countless wars. In his time, he had seen massive green-skinned orks tear the guts out of living men with their teeth. He had seen violent act upon violent act, and he had committed more than his fair share of them too, but he knew that he and the PDF would be no match for the Dark Angels and little help to the Space Wolves in a fight. Nevertheless, he would perform his duty.

The Space Wolves engaged the Dark Angels in the middle of a cratered street, 'Wait for a clear shot,' Markham ordered his men as he watched the genetically altered warriors attack each other with chainswords and bolt pistols.

'Lieutenant, I thank you for your fine service,' said Cadmus over the vox.

Markham felt his heart leap into his throat. Both groups of Space Marines fought hard, exchanging bolter fire and blows that would have left squads of guardsmen dead. 'Disengage,' Markham yelled to the Space Wolves and the men around him.

If the Wolfblade heard him, they paid him no heed. They were lost in battle. Markham heard an eerie whistling noise. He dived towards a shallow crater in the street, even as his brain told him that he, the Space Wolves, the Dark Angels, and his men were all about to die.

RAGNAR, TORIN AND Haegr watched the vid-screen in the old command post, while the message 'Bombardment imminent' scrolled across the screen. The Dark Angels still lay unmoving on the ground. Ragnar kept a close eye on them; they were Space Marines and would recover soon. On the grainy vid-screen, Space Wolves were fighting Dark Angels in the city streets, guard units close behind them.

'It's the rest of the Wolfblade,' said Haegr as a Space Wolf knocked a Dark Angel to the ground. 'And isn't that Markham?'

Ragnar felt his blood quicken. The Space Wolves had the Dark Angels outnumbered, but the outcome was by no means certain. He tried to raise the other members of the Wolfblade on the comm, but all he received was interference.

'Torin, do you think the PDF will fire on them?' asked Ragnar.

'Doubtful, it probably means that they expect the Dark Angels to bombard that area. Keep trying to establish contact with them. We need to let them know they are in danger,' he answered.

Markham's men still had not engaged or retreated for cover. Perhaps the message was wrong, because surely someone would have informed the PDF. Then, Lieutenant Markham looked skywards, shouted, and dived towards a crater. For the briefest moment, Ragnar saw the blurred outline of a massive shell hurtle towards the battle scene, then there was a blinding white flash.

Bodies of Space Wolves, Dark Angels and planetary defence forces flew into the air.

'They've used Earthshakers,' Torin gasped.

The Earthshaker was a ground-based artillery piece, and the Wolfblade knew that Cadmus had several of them in the city. Unlike the encounter at the kill zone, Hyades's planetary defence force wasn't taking any chance with killing Space Marines.

The scrolling message changed from 'Bombardment successful' to 'Targets destroyed'.

'No...' gasped Jeremiah, sitting up from where he lay on the floor. He lunged towards the monitor and fell, obviously still groggy from the fight. His companions remained motionless.

Ragnar didn't even care that the Dark Angel had been faking his unconsciousness, as he, Torin, Haegr and Jeremiah all watched their companions die. They were stunned and shocked. Of the nine Wolfblade who had come to Hyades, only the three of them and perhaps Magni survived.

Ragnar decided to try Magni. The younger Space Wolf was supposed to be with Lady Gabriella, guarding her, and he was due for some luck with the comms.

Torin and Haegr turned their attention to their prisoners. Both of them looked more than ready for another fight.

'Magni,' shouted Ragnar into his comm unit.

Surprisingly, he received an answer. 'Ragnar? No need to shout! I can still hear. My ears weren't damaged. I'm still holding out with Lady Gabriella and Governor Pelias. The house guard is here as well. We're secure in a bunker beneath the Imperial palace,' answered Magni. 'Do they need me out on the streets to help fight off the Dark Angels?'

'Which house guard? The ones we brought from Terra or the ones here on Hyades?'

'Terra, why? What's wrong, Ragnar?' asked Magni.

'I'm not sure.' Ragnar looked around at the consoles, hoping he could figure out the situation. 'We may have just lost every member of the Wolfblade except for Torin, Haegr, you and me. Stay with Gabriella, and trust no one. I'll report back when I know more, Ragnar out.'

Ragnar's comm buzzed immediately.

'Ragnar, this is Commander Cadmus, I'm surprised that you answered. Was your mission a success? I'm afraid that you lost several of your men, according to my information.'

'You bastard! You ordered those strikes against the Wolfblade! I knew that I couldn't trust you,' growled Ragnar. 'I'm sure that Markham didn't survive that close to four Earthshaker blasts, and he was one of your own men.'

'I'm impressed that you found a way to stay aware of the situation,' said Cadmus. 'Unfortunately, you survived, Ragnar. I'm afraid that although I need Space Marines, they don't have to be alive. Thanks to this little communication, I've located your position. Don't worry, Space Wolf, I won't underestimate you again. Oh, and you do have my admiration. You and the Wolfblade are worthy of your reputation. This is your last communication, so give my regards to Leman Russ when you see him.'

The power went off through the room. All of the monitors died at once. Ragnar suspected that the commander had cut the power to the entire building. As if to demonstrate Cadmus's authority, Ragnar's comm went dead with a burst of static as well.

Haegr and Ragnar activated the torches at their belts in unison.

Torin stood over Jeremiah with his thin blade at the Dark Angel's throat. He hadn't given Jeremiah an opportunity to take advantage of the darkness. Without glancing over at Ragnar, he clicked his comm. 'My comm is dead too, brother.'

'They have even jammed the communicator of mighty Haegr. They will not escape Haegr's vengeance,' growled the largest Space Wolf.

'We should kill our prisoners,' pronounced Torin in a flat tone.

Jeremiah looked over at Ragnar. Dark Angel or not, Jeremiah was an honourable opponent, and had fought well. He had also lost his men in that salvo.

'What is going on? Why are you here? Who is Cadmus? Is he the reason that you are here?' asked Ragnar, going from question to question without pausing to let the Dark Angel answer.

'He will kill us all if you let him. I need a weapon,' answered Jeremiah. 'Can my brethren, Nathaniel or Elijah, be revived?'

'I don't know,' said Haegr, 'both received a mighty thrashing at my hands.'

'We should kill them,' said Torin. 'Their Chapter is destroying the holdings of House Belisarius, and I don't think we can break them, brother.'

'Ragnar, I pledge to you by my faith in Lion El'Jonson and the Emperor, that my men and I will remain your prisoners, unless the time comes when our brethren free us or you release us. Give us weapons. We are Space Marines, just as you are, and we share a common enemy, this Commander Cadmus,' said Jeremiah.

Something about the sincerity with which Jeremiah made his pledge made Ragnar believe him. Furthermore, he knew the Dark Angel was an enemy of Cadmus, and Cadmus had proven his treason by threatening the Space Wolves. He decided they had to trust the Dark Angels. 'Torin, give the Dark Angel a weapon. We can trust him.'

'Lad, have you gone mad?' asked Haegr. 'These are Dark Angels. We *can't* trust them.'

'Haegr, Torin, old friends, we *need* to trust them. They know something about Cadmus. You both heard him threaten us and we all know that he ordered the Earthshakers to bombard the other members of the Wolfblade,' said Ragnar. 'They came here to remove Cadmus. We share a common enemy.'

'You have good instincts, Ragnar of the Space Wolves,' said Jeremiah. 'I will handle my men.'

Torin reluctantly handed Jeremiah his sword. 'I try to keep good weapons, even if they are slightly damaged.'

Jeremiah nodded, and raised his sword skywards. 'In the name of the Lion, I swear upon my soul that the lives of my brethren: Gilead, Sebastian and Marius, will be avenged.' He then sheathed his blade and wiped the caked blood from his face.

Ragnar found a medkit under a console and gave it to Jeremiah who went over to Elijah first.

'Hurry, we don't have much time,' said Ragnar. 'Cadmus killed our electricity and he knows where we are. If he thinks we are still a threat to him, then he'll send troops to kill us.'

Jeremiah nodded and injected Elijah with a stimulant. 'We won't surrender,' gasped Elijah as he woke. The young Dark Angel swung his fist wildly in the air.

'Stop,' commanded Jeremiah. 'We did surrender, Brother Elijah; we are prisoners of the Wolfblade, and we will fight alongside them and not attempt to escape. They know we have a common enemy. Say nothing more. Our mission has not failed.'

Elijah nodded and moved slowly. Distrust filled his eyes. 'I will obey,' he said, reluctantly.

Jeremiah helped Nathaniel up and woke him using the same litanies that he had used on Elijah. 'Brother, we triumphed?' asked Nathaniel before his eyes focused on the Space Wolves.

'No, but we've come to an understanding. How bad are your wounds?' Jeremiah asked.

'I can fight.' Nathaniel stood, determined not to fall.

Seeing the Dark Angels this way reminded Ragnar of life with the Space Wolves. The Dark Angels made him think of a Claw of young Space Wolves, a group bound together in fellowship, even friendship in some cases. Although Torin and Haegr were truly Ragnar's battle-brothers, the feeling was different. These Dark Angels were men who had become accustomed to working together in a battle zone. They had a bond stronger than words, a constant sense of shared purpose.

'We need to find a way out, besides the main doors to this section of the building or the mines below,' said Torin.

Ragnar knew he was right. The seldom-used corridor they had used to enter this monitor room was just a maintenance corridor and access route to the mines and refinery below. Ragnar could see that the large sliding double doors were made of plasteel and marked with the double-headed Imperial eagle. Cadmus's forces would come through those doors and there were probably more Dark Angels in the tunnels below.

'The walls are reinforced,' said Haegr, 'but we can burn through with melta-bombs.'

'Good thing that our prisoners brought some with them.' Torin produced a pair of melta-bombs, confiscated from the Dark Angels and set them against what Ragnar hoped was the outer wall.

'What are you doing?' Jeremiah asked Torin. 'What's behind that wall?'

'We aren't sure,' answered Ragnar, 'but if the Emperor smiles on us, it will be the outside world and even if he doesn't, it'll be a new exit that Cadmus's men won't expect to be there.'

'Why don't we run out of the main entrance?' asked Jeremiah. 'Surely, the enemy isn't waiting for us.'

'Cadmus had men throughout the city. If they aren't there now, it won't be long,' said Torin.

'I can smell the stench of something foul behind those doors,' said Haegr. 'Someone's there.'

A gentle tapping started at the plasteel doors, and they could hear muffled voices. Someone was behind them, probably trying to get inside. It was time to go.

Ragnar and the others pulled back and put their heads down. The melta-bombs flashed and the wall crackled as they detonated. The rockcrete vaporised under the tremendous power of the blast. The hole they left was a decent sized door. Ragnar couldn't help but wonder if Haegr would fit through it, but he didn't have much time to worry about it.

The main doors flew open and gunfire blasted through the room, destroying consoles and vid-screens and pelting the power armour of the Space Marines. Giant hulking shapes shambled in. For a moment, Ragnar thought someone had cloned Haegr and ripped off his power armour.

'Ogryns,' said Jeremiah.

The ogryns were huge mutants, one of the few altered humans allowed in Imperial forces. Imposing figures, they dwarfed the Space Marines, standing a full head higher than even Haegr. Ragnar had heard stories of ogryns strong enough to lift tanks.

The massive creatures were pure muscle and stupid as rocks, with no mind except for killing. Unfortunately, that meant that their brains took longer to realise when they were wounded or even dead. Ragnar had once seen an ogryn fighting with a large hole in his chest, until a medic had pointed the wound out to him and he fell over.

The ogryns wore a mishmash of armour and were armed with ripper guns. The solid weapons had such a kick that only the large mutants could keep them steady, but they unleashed a massive barrage of fire, so much so, that each ogryn wore belts of ammo around their arms and chests. Moreover, each gun was at least as deadly as a club in hand-to-hand combat.

'We never received word of ogryns,' said Torin.

'They must be part of Cadmus's special forces, the ones he brought with him,' said Ragnar.

'Raaarhh!' Haegr charged, as quickly as Ragnar had ever seen him move. He crashed solidly into the first ogryn that entered the room. The monstrous creature didn't move its feet but swung its arms back into its fellows, spraying the foot of one with its ripper gun.

'Go, Torin, get the others out,' yelled Ragnar. 'I'll cover for Haegr.'

'Elijah, Nathaniel, go with Torin. Remember what I told you and stay true to our pledge. Do not betray him. I'll follow in a moment,' said Jeremiah.

'Jeremiah, we must first deal with these abominations. We cannot allow these mutants to live,' Elijah responded.

'You will follow my orders, Elijah. Now go!' Jeremiah's order was reluctantly obeyed.

Ragnar exchanged glances with Jeremiah. The Dark Angel looked like he had something to prove. Ragnar grinned. So did he.

'Armour man, get off,' shouted the ogryn as Haegr literally hammered him, striking him with blow after blow. The size of Haegr and the size of the ogryns was buying everyone else precious time. The door was completely blocked.

'Haegr, move!' Ragnar said.

'Ha! You've gone mad, little brother,' said Haegr, turning his head. 'I'm winning.'

It appeared that Haegr was right for the moment. Then an ogryn with a metal plate for a forehead brought the stock of his ripper gun around, striking Haegr on his backswing, hard enough to crack the ceramite of his power armour. The Space Wolf fell backwards into the ruins of the command consoles.

Jeremiah took advantage of the moment to put a bolter round into the ogryn's skull, directly under the metal plate. The Dark Angel put a second bolter round into one of the beast's large yellow teeth, shattering the tooth and spraying blood and bone into the air. Ragnar was impressed with Jeremiah's precision, but he wasn't about to be outdone by a Dark Angel.

He charged into the mass of ogryns, leaping over fallen Haegr. His runeblade took the knee off one ogryn, although it felt to Ragnar as if he had sliced through a tree trunk. Instinctively, he fired off several shots from his bolter pistol into another, blowing off most of its arm in the process. Behind the ogryns, Ragnar could see troopers from the planetary defence force.

An ogryn kicked Ragnar with its large steel-shod boot, knocking him back from the fray. He rolled with the blow, and between his reflexes and his armour, managed to ignore most of the impact. He brought his sword up to defend himself, only to find that Jeremiah's precision bolter fire had eliminated his enemy.

This seemed a perfect time to escape before the sheer weight of numbers took them down.

'Let's go,' said Ragnar.

For once, Haegr didn't argue. Instead, he thrust himself through the hole in the wall. Thankfully, he fit.

'Wolf, hand me a melta-bomb,' said Jeremiah.

Ragnar hesitated for only a fraction of a second before tossing a melta-bomb to Jeremiah.

The Dark Angel leapt onto a ruined console and attached the bomb to the ceiling. Ragnar covered him, firing bolter shots one-handed into the oncoming ogryns. Almost without thinking, Ragnar stopped firing the moment Jeremiah finished setting the charge. The Dark Angel dived through the hole with Ragnar immediately behind him, as if the two of them had practised the manoeuvre a hundred times before.

The melta-bomb detonated with a deafening noise. The ogryns howled in agony, then fell silent. A low rumble indicated that the ceiling in the room had given way, crushing everything beneath it.

The others had moved a few dozen metres down an unmarked rockcrete passage.

'Where are we?' asked Ragnar.

'I don't know,' said Torin and Elijah simultaneously.

'We need to find Cadmus,' said Jeremiah.

'No,' said Ragnar, 'first we find Lady Gabriella and Magni. Then, we'll both go after Commander Cadmus.'

'I have men to avenge,' said Jeremiah.

'And I have an oath to keep and my last battle-brother to keep alive against a world full of potential enemies and the invasion of you Dark Angels. If you want to give me the truth about what's going on maybe you can convince me, otherwise, we make sure Lady Gabriella of House Belisarius is safe, first and foremost. Do we still have an understanding?' asked Ragnar.

Jeremiah stared directly at Ragnar. 'I gave you my word. I do not break oaths.'

'Good, then you understand,' said Ragnar.

'Let's keep moving,' suggested Torin. 'She'll be at the palace. We just need to get out of here.'

'Ah, what a great day for battle,' said Haegr.

The six Space Marines made their way down to the end of the passage where a reinforced door was marked 'Lethe defence forces only'. The security lock on the door looked intact and everything about the door gave the impression that short of a lascannon, nothing was going to get through it.

Nathaniel was having trouble keeping up with the rest, wheezing and limping. Haegr's bone-crushing grip had hurt him badly. As if sensing what the others were thinking, Nathaniel spoke, 'My faith in the Emperor will sustain me.'

A squad of the planetary defence force appeared at the other end of the passage, while the Space Marines were inspecting the door. Now they were trapped at the end of the passage.

'They've found us,' snarled Torin.

The defence forces fired their lasguns down the passage at the Space Marines. Although none of the shots pierced their power armour, Ragnar knew that they could not remain in their position long.

Slowly, the door grated open.

'It's open, let's move,' said Jeremiah.

Torin and Nathaniel fired their bolters down the passage to deter the oncoming troopers, while Jeremiah, Elijah, Ragnar and Haegr went through the door, quickly checking for enemies in the room beyond.

They stood in the hangar of a large vehicle pool. The outer doors stood open, giving them a view of the city. Ragnar could only see smoke and rubble, punctuated by flashes from lascannons and exploding munitions. A few servitors tended to wires and consoles on the edges of the room. The large hangar was mostly deserted with the exception of a single Chimera.

'We may have found a way to get to Gabriella,' said Haegr.

'But who opened the door?' asked Ragnar.

'This must be a trap,' said Jeremiah.

'No, it's not. We have a friend on the inside,' said Torin as he and Nathaniel stepped inside the room between bolter shots.

Torin hit a control, sealing the door once again, now ironically, holding the Lethe defence forces on the far side. He put a bolter round into the control in the hope of shorting it. 'I contacted Tech-Priest Varnus after I activated the vid-screens and told him to do his best to monitor us. I suspect we would have had more help if the power had stayed on, but there's power here, probably from an independent back-up generator.'

Ragnar was pleased that Tech-Priest Varnus was still on their side. Just as he had helped the Space Wolves ambush the Dark Angels, he was helping them now. Faith in the Emperor was rewarded in the strangest ways.

'It's not a trap. Into the Chimera, we're heading to the palace,' announced Ragnar.

'I'll drive,' said Torin.

Torin opened the front hatch and got in. The rear hatch opened to reveal a small cramped space, complete with gun ports for the exterior lasguns. Elijah was the first in the rear, Ragnar second, and then Jeremiah.

Haegr paused. 'You want me to get in there?'

'Yes,' said Ragnar, gesturing Haegr over to the bench. The massive Space Wolf managed to climb in, but Ragnar could tell that the space made for Imperial Guardsmen was tightly cramped for the large Space Wolf in power armour. Torin started the engine. Nathaniel made it to the ramp, but barely, shooting off covering fire as the planetary defence forces entered the hangar.

Ragnar heard the planetary defence force outside even over the roar of the Chimera's tracks. The men hadn't taken long to breach the security door. One of them must have had the proper security codes and Torin's bolter shot probably hadn't done much to the doors controls on the opposite side. The men showed no hesitation in firing, but their guns couldn't penetrate the armour of the Chimera. Elijah returned fire with the Chimera's built-in lasguns.

Ragnar gestured for him to stop. 'These men are following orders, trying to defend their home. They aren't enemies of the Imperium. They don't know what is happening.'

Jeremiah nodded in reluctant agreement, but Ragnar knew what he was thinking. The men of Hyades would fight against the Dark Angels' own battle-brothers.

The Chimera roared out into the city, which had become a battlezone. Rubble and debris were strewn everywhere. Ragnar could hear the big guns of Lethe booming and smell the familiar scent of burning promethium. From the hatches, he saw the blackened bones of Lethe's defenders. Broken tanks lay in the streets, and although the Chimera was an all-terrain vehicle, it shook violently as it ran over the craters and through the rubble left in the streets. A few civilians staggered through the smoke, some screaming for help, while others did their best to run to cover. Ragnar estimated that they were about halfway between the outer walls of the city and the central complex with the Imperial palace.

'We won't make it to the palace,' said Nathaniel. 'Our brethren will take out any transport they see, just in case.'

'In case what?' asked Ragnar.

Jeremiah placed a hand on Nathaniel's shoulder. 'Ragnar, we have our own Chapter's secrets and honour to keep. I'm sure you respect that.'

Ragnar was getting tired of these conversations. 'I just hope that whatever your Chapter is doing it's worth destroying an Imperial planet for.'

* * *

GABRIELLA PACED ABOUT within the governor's bunker below the palace. It had been hours since the Dark Angels had first entered the Imperial palace complex. The governor had requested she come to the bunker with him for her own safety. Gabriella had brought a few of her House Belisarius guard and Magni of the Wolfblade with her. She had ordered the rest to join in defending Lethe from the Dark Angels. Since Magni had given her the news about the possible deaths of five of her Wolfblade, she was worried and the communication systems from inside the bunker were only receiving interference.

The interior of the main room in the bunker was lavishly decorated with portraits of ancient leaders of Hyades, thick carpets and hand-carved wood furniture. It seemed more like a formal stateroom than a bunker. Commander Cadmus had informed her that this was the safest place on Hyades, with reinforced plasteel and rockcrete walls behind the inlaid wood panelling.

Gabriella looked at Magni. 'This is terribly wrong. Space Marines shouldn't be attacking us.'

'I'll protect you, m'lady,' Magni said. 'I'm sure that the defence forces will hold out against the Dark Angels.'

Gabriella looked around the room. Even within the bunker, they could feel explosions rocking the city. Suddenly, she shook her head. A glow came from her forehead, shining through her black scarf.

'Lady Gabriella, what sorcery is this?' asked Magni. 'Are you all right?'

Gabriella moaned, collapsing to her knees. 'There's a disturbance in the warp, I can feel it. Something's coming.'

'Excuse me, everyone,' said Commander Cadmus, entering the room with an entourage of heavily armed men in carapace armour. These soldiers appeared to Magni to be the elite of Lethe's defences, armed and equipped like Imperial Guard storm troopers. 'Thank you, governor, for staying put and keeping Lady Gabriella with you as I requested. I'm afraid that we've had to make some changes due to the current invasion.'

'Changes? What sort of changes?' asked Governor Pelias.

'Changes in leadership, sir,' Cadmus said, drawing his plasma pistol nearly as fast as Magni's eyes could track him. A blue-green fireball engulfed the governor's head, killing him instantly. His second shot took Magni in the knee, burning straight through the Space Wolf's power armour and dissolving the knee, severing his left leg.

Cadmus's elite troops opened fire on the House Belisarius guard. Taken completely by surprise, Gabriella's defenders stood no chance and the fight was over in seconds. Cadmus and his men stood in the centre of the room; only Magni and Gabriella remained alive.

Magni writhed in pain and shock from the betrayal. Cadmus walked close to the fallen Space Wolf, careful to stay just out of arm's reach. 'I have a message for you to relay to your fellow Wolfblade. Tell them that I have Gabriella, and that the only way they'll see her again is for them to kill every Dark Angel on Hyades. Am I clear?'

Magni shook his head.

'I'll take that as a yes. This woman is now my prisoner.'

The commander aimed his pistol at Gabriella while one of his men took her and pinned her arms behind her. Still weakened by her vision, she was unable to resist. A set of binders locked her wrists together. Cadmus roughly pulled her to her feet by her left arm. 'Come.'

Gabriella tried to shake him off, but her captor held her with an iron grip. Magni was dimly aware that he was hurting her.

Cadmus's men had fanned out, securing all entrances and exits. In a strange moment of compassion, one threw a rug over the headless governor's body. There would be no statue in the courtyard for Pelias.

Despite the pain, Magni was a Space Wolf, and he would fight to the end. Slowly, carefully, he slipped his bolt pistol out of its holster. While Cadmus was half-leading and half-dragging Gabriella out of the room, Magni took aim at the commander's back.

Cadmus spun without warning, placing a perfect shot with his plasma pistol. The Space Wolf's hand was consumed instantly in blue-green fire. Magni screamed involuntarily. He had never felt pain so intense.

'I can't believe how hard you Space Wolves fight. It's quite remarkable. You should know when you are outmatched and defeated, and just die. Do you understand? Now, Fenrisian, I hope there's enough left of you to deliver my message. Gabriella is depending on it.'

The shock of his action roused Gabriella. She had no doubt that if she tried to struggle, he'd gladly shoot her, but she was determined to make her feelings known. 'Let me go. You're committing treason, commander,' said Gabriella. 'Have you gone mad?'

'Hardly; this is simply the act of a rational mind in an irrational situation, my dear Navigator,' said Cadmus. 'Now, let me take you away from the screams of this young Space Wolf. It's not proper for a member of a noble house to be surrounded by such violence. You are my prisoner, and I hold all the cards. The Dark Angels aren't going to spare you either. Every breath you take is at my whim. Please don't displease me. You are only alive because it amuses me to torture Ragnar. To think I apologised to him.'

'You are a walking dead man. I felt a disturbance in the warp and that can only mean one thing, the Space Wolves are here,' said Gabriella.

'You did? How amusing. You are quite a potent Navigator then. I'm sure if your father were alive, he'd be pleased,' answered Cadmus.

'I recognised the warp signs. The Space Wolves' patrol of the sector must have just arrived. Within hours, you won't have to worry about Dark Angels. The Great Wolf has an alliance with Belisarius. The Space Wolves will be here in untold numbers.'

Cadmus stopped. When he looked at her, all she could see was a malicious gleam in his eyes. When he spoke, he did so in a very soft voice.

'My dear Lady Gabriella, not only did I know that the Space Wolves were coming, that's exactly what I'm counting on. Everything depends on the Space Wolves getting here, everything. It's good to know that I won't be disappointed.'

Gabriella's blood turned cold.

EIGHT
The Space Wolves arrive

Wolf Lord Berek Thunderfist strode through the corridors of the *Fist of Russ*. He hated long patrols, too much time onboard ship made him uneasy. He stroked his beard as he walked, unconsciously flexing his power gauntlet. His mind wandered back to the battle in which he had lost his natural arm and smiled slightly. In that battle, he had squared off with Kharn the Betrayer, the legendary berserker of Khorne, a Chaos Marine whose name brought fear to even his own side. Now that was a battle, Berek thought to himself.

Berek entered the bridge, two of his Wolf Guard flanking either side of the entrance. Berek took inventory of the bridge, ensuring all was how it should be. The warriors of Fenris who worked here were proud men, selected for lifelong service to the

Space Wolves. They dressed as warriors, complete with weapons and whatever honours they had earned during their service, such as bits of fur or runes. Symbols of Fenris adorned the room, from shields mounted on rune-covered pillars, to the wolf pelts used as carpets. Indeed, many of the control gauges rested in the jaws of sculpted wolves and the consoles were made to appear as worked stone or even ice. Banners hung from the vaulted ceiling, and the command chair was set as a throne. The impression of the bridge was more one of a lord's great hall, than the nexus of machine spirits.

Berek held the crew of the *Fist of Russ* in high regard, and he clapped many of them on the shoulder or nodded to them as he passed. The men who served aboard this ship were here by choice, free men devoted to the Chapter, unlike other ships of the Imperium who enlisted the use of thralls and convicted criminals or mindless servitors to crew their vessels.

The *Fist of Russ* had finished its patrol of the Euphrates system, a star and its worlds considered insignificant by most within the Imperium. However, it was a place that fell under the watchful and protective eye of the Sons of Russ. For that reason alone, it was given the same consideration as any other system under the protection of the Space Wolves. Everything was in order, so they had executed a warp jump and proceeded to Hyades, the next stop on their patrol route to fulfil the Space Wolves' ancient pact with House Belisarius. As the stop was a recent addition to the patrol, Berek wondered if House Belisarius and the Wolfblade even knew they were coming.

As Berek thought about House Belisarius, he couldn't help but recall the young Blood Claw, Ragnar, now part of the Wolfblade. That reckless and honourable youth had left an impression on the Wolf Lord during his time with his company. Ragnar had served well, and then, he had lost the sacred Spear on the planet Garm. The Blood Claw had halted a Chaos invasion by throwing the holy Spear into a Chaos portal, collapsing it, and saving him and his great company. In Berek's mind, it was a deed worthy of song, even if one of the Space Wolves' greatest relics had been lost and a Chaos invasion had been stopped.

Had Ragnar been rewarded for his heroic action? No. In fact, Ragnar was immersed in the political infighting between the Chapter's Wolf Lords. In an effort to discredit Berek, his rivals lobbied the Great Wolf to exile Ragnar. So it was that the young Space Wolf had been exiled to Holy Terra to serve in the Wolfblade, a cadre of loyal Space Wolves serving House Belisarius. One day, Berek hoped that he would once again see Ragnar walking the halls of the Fang.

A warning alarm sounded, interrupting the Wolf Lord's reverie. 'Jump to normal space will commence in one minute,' the herald announced ship-wide. Berek, having been brought back to the here and now, gave one last look around the bridge. His crew was prepared for the jump back to normal space, attending their stations, saying the proper blessings, and performing the proper rituals. His Wolf Guard departed the bridge to secure themselves in their acceleration couches.

A warning alarm preceded the next countdown announcement, 'Jump to normal space will commence in thirty seconds.'

Even though Berek had made more warp jumps than he could remember, he still had moments of uneasiness. The warp was not devoid of entities, indeed it was a place where unspeakable horrors dwelled, horrors that one had to pass through when travelling amongst the stars in service of the Emperor. Deep in the Wolf Lord's heart, he was still a superstitious warrior from Fenris with a healthy distrust of magic, or anything that smelled like it.

'Jump to normal space will commence in fifteen seconds.'

Slowly, the bridge seemed to stretch and lengthen. Light danced across the ship's interior, emanating from no apparent source. A low rhythmic hum grew in Berek's ear. The process had already begun. Even now, the ship was trying to escape the warp.

'Jump to normal space will commence in ten seconds.'

The hum transformed into murmuring, sickly, twisted voices speaking in an unintelligible tongue. Every surface within the ship began to glow. Bulkheads screamed as if they were buckling under a terrible strain.

'Jump to normal space will commence in five seconds.'

Suddenly sound, light and motion blended together in a collage of horrors.

'Jump.'

In that instant, there was everything and nothing.

The jump to normal space was complete. Berek gave quick, silent prayers to the Emperor, Leman Russ and the old gods of Fenris.

The Wolf Lord checked the bridge and his crew. Everyone was removing their restraints and moving back to their positions. Berek took his time, making sure each member of the crew had survived the passage unscathed. The dangers of warp travel could never be underestimated. Having confirmed that all was in order, he slapped the restraining harness release.

As he stood, he turned to his men. 'Begin system scan. Comms, announce our presence and extend my compliments to Governor Pelias. Let's see if they have some hospitality to offer.'

'Wolf Lord!' said Hroth. 'Scans show a battle-barge in low orbit over the planet. Civilian ships are scattered throughout the system, fleeing the planet. There's an orbital defence platform in a decaying orbit, and I think she's scrap. I'm also reading weapons fire on the surface. It appears that the capital city of Lethe is under attack.'

Hroth was a warrior upon whom Berek had bestowed the title of ship's guide. Though not a Space Marine, Hroth had proven to Berek his ability to quickly assess tactical situations. Had he remained on Fenris, his tribe may well have slaughtered krakens due to his skill in suggesting ship movements.

'I'm unable to contact Lethe, Lord Berek. Their comms appear to be jammed,' the herald added.

A slight grin emerged on Berek's face. 'It would appear that our routine patrol has proven to be most timely.'

Berek did not believe in random chance. If he and the *Fist of Russ* were here at this place and time, it was destiny, providence. Berek was here to bring this conflict to an end, and that was exactly what he would do.

He crossed the bridge to the tactical console. 'Let's find out what we're up against.'

The tactical display sprang to life, showing a hologram of Hyades and all orbiting vessels. The unknown battle-barge was indeed in a low orbit over Hyades. Thunderhawks flew back and forth from the battle-barge to the planet's surface.

Berek was confused. These were ships of the Adeptus Astartes. What were they doing here and why by the frozen wastes of Fenris were they attacking a planet under the protection of the Space Wolves?

'We are receiving a transmission on gold priority Imperium frequency 7590.4.' Confusion was apparent in the herald's voice.

Berek waved his hand, indicating that the herald should put the transmission through to the speakers. The Wolf Lord's curiosity had turned to frustration. Berek had had many dealings with other factions within the Imperium. None of them had yet proven worthy of his trust, but he had never witnessed anything like this blatant violation of Imperial law.

'Unidentified vessel, this is the *Vinco Redemptor* of the Dark Angels. You are hereby ordered to leave Hyades's orbital space. This planet is under Imperial quarantine. Do not approach or attempt to enter orbit.'

Berek clenched his power gauntlet into a fist tight enough to make its servos whine in protest. He had dealt with the Dark Angels before. They were worthy of only one thing: their untrustworthy reputation. Although no Terran official would label them traitors to the Imperium, Berek had always known that one day the true nature of that self-serving Chapter would be revealed.

'This is the *Fist of Russ*, flag ship of Berek Thunderfist, Wolf Lord of the Space Wolves. You have moved against an Imperial world under the protection of the great Wolf Logan Grimnar and the Space Wolves. What do you mean by "quarantine"?'

'*Fist of Russ*, this is the *Vinco Redemptor* of the Dark Angels. This planet is under Imperial quarantine. Do not approach,' the metallic-sounding transmission from the battle-barge replied.

'Who gave the order to quarantine Hyades?' asked Berek.

'The quarantine order comes from Interrogator-Chaplain Vargas. Do not approach any closer,' came the response.

'Why is Hyades under quarantine? If I were to be made aware of the circumstances perhaps I could aid my brother Astartes.' Berek's patience was wearing dangerously thin.

The Space Wolf crew remained silent waiting for the answer to the offer of assistance. Moments passed and then the answer finally came.

'Wolf Lord, their weapons are tracking us,' Hroth said.

Although the Chapters had a strong rivalry, both the Space Wolves and the Dark Angels had a glorious history of service to the Emperor. The Imperium would not take kindly to a conflict between two of their own Chapters, and although both organisations were formidable, neither could hold out against the fury of the Imperium. The endless numbers of Imperial Guard, coupled with dozens of Chapters of Space Marines, could spell the end for the Dark Angels or the Space Wolves. Berek had made every effort to avoid an engagement with the Dark Angels, but enough was enough. Berek smashed his fist onto the comms activation rune.

'Withdraw your forces immediately or you will face the fury of the Sons of Russ! So you understand, that means we will remove your forces for you.' Berek waited for a reply, certain that the Dark Angels would back down.

'Their weapons are still tracking us, Lord Berek.'

'My lord, shall we move her back?' asked the helmsman.

'No, we won't back down,' said Berek. 'We're in the right and they know it. They wouldn't dare fire on us, warning shots or not.'

A barrage of shots came from the *Vinco Redemptor* towards the *Fist of Russ*, missing high. The Space Wolf ship continued to approach Hyades, undeterred.

'Get away from our planet... Now!' barked Berek. 'I don't care for your Chapter's tactics and I can fire off warning shots myself.'

'We will fire another barrage. This will be your last warning,' came the response.

Berek looked over at the ship's guide. 'Hroth, fire a volley at them. Make sure you come close. I want them to understand that Space Marines or no Space Marines, we will defend our own.'

'Ready, fire,' ordered Hroth, but just then, another barrage erupted from the *Vinco Redemptor*. The laser batteries struck the *Fist of Russ*. Just as the Space Wolf vessel fired her guns, a Dark Angels torpedo salvo was detected.

The explosion shook the vessel. 'We've been hit, Wolf Lord,' cried Hroth.

Berek clenched his fist. The Wolf Lord knew this was an accident. The Dark Angels were fanatics, but they wouldn't have the guts to fire on the Space Wolves first.

'You have attacked us, you barbaric idiots! Now, feel the wrath of the Dark Angels.' The *Vinco Redemptor* began rising from low orbit. 'You will suffer from our next volley.'

'My lord, the battle-barge is departing orbit, moving to engage, weapon batteries are charging,' Hroth announced.

Berek hated the Dark Angels. The Space Wolves were in the right and he was tired of being threatened. They had shot his ship and tried to make it look as if he shot them first. That was the conniving underhanded backstabbing way of the Dark Angels. If they wanted a fight, then so be it. He'd find a way to explain once he'd exposed whatever convoluted rationale the Dark Angels had for attacking a Space Wolf planet. 'I warned them,' he said under his breath.

The Wolf Lord triggered the comms activation rune on his console. 'Wolf brothers, Russ be praised, for he has brought us here to Hyades in their time of need.' Berek could feel the electricity building aboard ship. His Space Wolves had hungered for conflict for far too long. Soon, there would be a feeding frenzy.

'Prepare for battle, my brothers! We launch as soon as we are in range.' Berek deactivated the comm unit. 'Helmsman, bring us within lance battery range. Herald, keep trying to reach the Hyades command centre. We'll need to coordinate our efforts with them.' The crew rushed to execute Berek's commands. The Wolf Lord could see the pride in each of them.

The *Fist of Russ* was smaller than the Dark Angels battle-barge. Berek knew that in a close range ship-to-ship engagement, the Dark Angels had the advantage. Their bombardment cannons would rip the Space Wolves to shreds. The *Fist of Russ*, however, was not without teeth. Her lance batteries had much greater range than the bombardment cannons. Using the longer range, Berek would bring the *Fist of Russ* close enough to launch his Thunder-hawks and drop-pods, and carefully deploy his smaller ships. Using their speed and manoeuvrability, he could avoid a direct exchange of fire. The Space Wolves would win this battle on the surface of Hyades.

The *Fist of Russ* moved into position, entering Hyades space above the opposite hemisphere to the Dark Angels ship. Berek moved his ship into a low orbit to deploy the Thunderhawks. Drop-pods would be an entirely different matter to launch.

Unlike Thunderhawks, which could manoeuvre themselves into position once they were free of the launch bays, drop-pods operated exactly as they were named. Berek would need to risk a quick pass of the *Vinco Redemptor*, bringing the *Fist of Russ* within range of the bombardment cannons.

Many songs would be written this day. Berek longed to join his brothers on the surface, but he knew that his place was on board the *Fist of Russ*. This was one case where rank did not have its privileges.

Mikal, Captain of the Wolf Guard, Berek's personal bodyguard and most trusted warrior, confidently took the bridge. He was shorter than Berek by half a helm, but much broader across the shoulders. A full beard covered his face.

Berek greeted his friend. 'The fortune of Russ does not smile on us this day, my old friend. I have a grave mission for you.' His concern was etched across his face.

'You know you have but to ask, my lord, and it is my honour to attend to it.' Mikal's words brought the faintest of smiles to Berek's face.

Berek clasped his hand. 'Mikal, I need you to lead the ground forces on Hyades. I need you to discover why the Dark Angels have chosen to fire upon us.'

'Then it's true – the Dark Angels have attacked us?' Mikal replied.

Berek tapped a rune on the display console. An expanded map of Hyades appeared, the capital city highlighted on its surface.

'Take your Thunderhawk and establish contact with the governor here in Lethe. Find out what's going on.

Coordinate with his planetary defence forces, establishing a command post for our forces. If attacked, by all means defend yourselves, but I must have answers, Mikal.'

'As you wish, Wolf Lord! When we see each other again we will tap a keg of the Fang's finest, and I will tell you of our heroic deeds,' said Mikal slapping Berek on the shoulder as he left.

'Good hunting, my friend.'

Mikal had served with Berek for a long time and was Berek's most trusted Wolf Guard and his most trusted friend. They had saved each other's lives more times than either of them could remember. They had fought side-by-side against some of the most horrific creatures mankind had ever encountered and celebrated victories over insurmountable odds. There was no one Berek would rather have leading this assault, no one more qualified.

But before Mikal could lead the assault, Berek had to get him to Lethe and to do that, he had to get the *Fist of Russ* past the Dark Angels battle-barge. Berek looked at the power gauntlet that replaced his natural hand and grinned. It should be one hell of a battle.

The *Fist of Russ* lunged forwards, engines at full burn. As soon as they made range, laser batteries lanced out, striking the *Vinco Redemptor*. Blue energy sparked as the defensive shields absorbed the initial barrage. A volley of torpedoes surged from their tubes, rocketing towards their target. Space Wolf Thunderhawks launched from the *Fist of Russ* and fanned out behind the torpedoes' makeshift skirmish line, using the salvo to shield their approach.

The *Vinco Redemptor* came about, going head to head with the attacking ship. Weapons batteries swung into action, unleashing their firepower at the incoming torpedoes. One torpedo after another collided with the protective umbrella opened by the weapon turrets. Using the wall of exploding torpedoes for cover, the first flight of Thunderhawks dived on the battle-barge. Their speed, size and manoeuvrability made them virtually impossible for the turrets to track at such close range. The Thunderhawks strafed the battle-barge in unison, targeting the *Redemptor's* bombardment cannons. Missiles and battle cannon fire rained down, pounding the hull of the Dark Angels ship. Explosions erupted across the battle-barge.

While the first flight attacked, the second flight of Thunderhawks dived hard, entering the atmosphere at such an angle that friction fire blazed across the leading edges of their noses and wings. If the crews had not been Space Marines, their bodies would have been turned to bloody pulp by the forces involved. Once deep into the atmosphere, the Thunderhawks levelled off, on course for Lethe.

The first flight had strafed up the central axis of the barge until they reached the command centre superstructure. At that point, they split up. Circling around the superstructure, they regrouped and strafed down the central axis once again. A Thunderhawk disintegrated from the turrets' defensive fire. Realising the Dark Angels turret crews had analysed their flight path, the Thunderhawks broke off, peeling off the central axis in opposite directions, diving down below the firing plane of the weapons turrets and accelerating towards the planet. Another Thunderhawk erupted in flame before the rest escaped into the atmospheric shield of Hyades.

Meanwhile, the *Fist of Russ* closed on the *Vinco Redemptor*. Both vessels exchanged torpedo fire. Weapon battery rounds streaked across the void between the two vessels. Ripples of blue energy ran across both hulls as shields absorbed the weapons fire that splashed into them. As the defensive shields overloaded from the strain, secondary explosions blossomed on the hulls of both vessels.

The ships raced towards each other. It was time for battle to be joined in earnest. In their zeal, both vessels accelerated, closing the void between them faster than either anticipated. Simultaneously, the command on both ships realised the potential danger of collision. The *Vinco Redemptor* cut to starboard and the *Fist of Russ* did the same. Port Dark Angels weapons and port Space Wolf weapons erupted in violent broadsides. The ships tore into each other.

Finally, the *Vinco Redemptor's* bombardment cannons pivoted to port. The strafing run of the Space Wolf Thunderhawks had concentrated its fire on the bombardment cannons. Now, Berek would find out if their gambit had paid off.

Two of the four cannons were unable to bring themselves to bear upon the smaller cruiser. The

Space Wolf vessel shuddered from the salvo of the remaining two as wide holes appeared in the cruiser's hull.

The *Fist of Russ* was severely damaged, as was the *Vinco Redemptor*, but the vessels had finished their pass. As the starships widened the gap between them, each looked to distance itself from the other to repair and regroup. The *Fist of Russ* had succeeded. Space Wolf drop-pods accelerated down towards Lethe. Berek's radical strategy had worked, the battle would indeed be decided on the ground.

MIKAL'S THUNDERHAWK raced across the sky, flanked on both sides by several others. The Wolf Guard captain sat at the tactical station in the control den of the aircraft, just behind the pilots' chairs. He analysed the current deployment of the Dark Angels and sent attack plans to his battle-brothers. The other Thunderhawks peeled off, vectoring towards their assigned deployment coordinates. Mikal continued directly towards Lethe.

The ordered city blocks and streets of the city were gone, buried in rubble and debris and obscured by smoke. Planetary defence forces scrambled to establish a perimeter, but the Dark Angels drop-pods made it impossible. Space Marines did not fight by their opponents' rules. Drop-pod tactics were specifically random. They fell behind enemy lines, causing havoc.

The planetary defence forces were faring better than Mikal had expected. They appeared to have highly effective defence strategies against the Space Marine invasion, and several buildings in the capital had become redoubts for the defending troops. The defences of Lethe were set up so each group acted under its own command and control. The Dark Angels wanted to decapitate the Hyades defence forces, but they couldn't find a head.

LIEUTENANT PAULINUS AND his platoon paused as he checked his map, barely able to keep up with the events that were unfolding. He kept asking himself if it was true: were the Dark Angels attacking the city? He could not believe it. They moved through the streets with orders to reinforce the southern city entrance, reporting any activity along the way.

His hands shook as he held the map. His nervousness was impossible to hide. He'd been with the planetary defence force for just under a year, and most of that time he had been stationed in observation outposts, monitoring orbital traffic. He had requested a transfer to Lethe in hopes of gaining some recognition that might help his post-military career. Now, he wished he was still tracking transports instead of down here in the streets of Lethe, acting as bait.

They had been moving through the streets for a while and had not come across any Dark Angels, just explosions from unseen artillery, and rubble. He could hear fighting, but the platoon couldn't find the sources. The streets were a maze and every new street looked like the last. All Paulinus knew was that they were in the workers' section of the city.

Paulinus was from a rather prominent family on Hyades, and normally lived a lifestyle befitting his family's wealth and prestige. The seedier section of the city was a place that he had seldom ventured into before. Carnal pleasure rooms and gambling dens lined the streets, marking this area of town as the sort of place where human filth could acquire contraband and explore their secret vices. Paulinus was disturbed that it seemed relatively unscathed.

The men carefully stepped out into an intersection where three streets converged. Every street still looked like the last. Lieutenant Paulinus thought they were lost. He tried to think back to his younger days when he and his friends would drive down into these areas of the city. They had been callow youths looking for some cheap thrills. He had tried to distance himself from those days, but now, he needed his memories. He looked for familiar signs, for anything that would give him a clue to where they were. He saw nothing.

They approached a building that less than a day ago had been a gambling den; now it was simply another abandoned building. Paulinus raised his hand as a signal to his men to stop. He pulled out a map as he tried once again to determine where they were. He could call in, but he didn't want the humiliation. If his men found out, then they might lose morale.

Using the map, he managed to orientate himself using the street layout and nearby buildings as his guide. If they headed north, they should be able to find their way back to their checkpoint. The lieutenant gestured, instructing his men to move out.

None of them saw the Dark Angels until they opened up with their bolters. A red spray of blood

splashed across Paulinus's face and drenched his
map as his sergeant was ripped in half by bolter fire.
The lieutenant watched in horror as men all around
him twisted and fell before the Dark Angels' attack.

Lieutenant Paulinus ran to find cover from the hailstorm of rounds. He couldn't focus on his men, they
were dying and he needed to live. After all, he had to
give orders and he just didn't want to die, not here,
not like this. Paulinus looked back at the gambling
den, the source of the shooting, only to see another
man die on the ground behind him with his chest
ripped open by a bolter round.

Five Dark Angels strode from the gambling den,
mowing down troopers as they came. Their dark
green and black armour added to their aura of menace. Paulinus's remaining men made a vain attempt
to return fire, but their intense fear made their shots
worthless. All of the men, including Paulinus, were
shaking with shock. The Dark Angels holstered their
bolters, drew their close combat weapons and
charged.

It was clear to all of them how this engagement
would end. The Space Marines would slaughter them.

The street was instantly bathed in light and a searing wind struck everyone in the street as the gambling
den imploded. A cloud of dust and debris obscured
everything. The defence forces clutched at their
breather masks as the dust and rockcrete particles
clogged their lungs and scratched their eyes. The Dark
Angels continued to close.

Lieutenant Paulinus raised his sabre, making a
feeble attempt to defend himself. The Dark Angel

advancing on him easily countered his weak thrust. The lieutenant's arm felt numb as the Dark Angel knocked his sword away.

Paulinus screamed, 'I don't want to die!'

Then, the Space Marine's arm exploded. The Dark Angel's chainsword clattered to the ground. The explosive whirring of an assault cannon drowned out Paulinus's screams.

Five more figures emerged from the building just abandoned by the Dark Angels. They were Space Marines, but their armour was different, making them appear larger. They did not wear the dark green colour of the Dark Angels, but the icy bluish grey of the Space Wolves.

Paulinus didn't know what to think or hope. The newcomers moved surprisingly quickly, unleashing a volley of rounds into the Dark Angels. Taken by surprise, the Dark Angels tried to change tactics and engage the new threat, but the twin advantages of surprise and firepower made this a futile gesture. A few rounds from storm bolters and the spray of the assault cannon reduced the Dark Angels to piles of broken armour. Paulinus could not believe his eyes. He couldn't believe how quickly the new Space Marines had killed his attackers.

The Space Wolves wore armour adorned with the totems of wolf pelts, tails, and teeth strung on leather necklaces. The ground vibrated with each of their footfalls as they moved protectively around the defence forces.

One of the Space Wolves approached Paulinus, 'Lieutenant, we are here to assist in the defence of

Hyades. Berek Thunderfist sends his greetings and respects. We are his Wolfguard.'

'Lieu-Lieu-Lieutenant Paulinus, Hyades defence forces, I th-th-thank you for your assistance,' Paulinus stuttered.

FIERY CONTRAILS STREAKED across the sky as drop-pod after drop-pod plummeted towards Lethe. Thunderhawks touched down, pouring Space Wolves onto the streets. Dreadnoughts lumbered through the carnage laying waste to all who opposed them. Throughout the city, Space Wolves engaged the Dark Angels.

MIKAL'S THUNDERHAWK CIRCLED the city while the Space Wolves reconnoitred the battle zone. Mikal knew that the best plans only lasted up to contact with the enemy. His fellow Wolf Guard were on the ground with orders to protect the citizens of Lethe and to obtain any information as to the cause of this so-called quarantine. He needed to contact the governor, but so far radio contact had been unsuccessful.

'Sigurd, bring us about. Set course for the governor's palace. Put us down on the parade ground,' said Mikal, addressing the pilot.

After a Space Wolf was initiated and the canis helix implanted, he truly become one of the Sons of Russ. However, it took time for all the physical changes to manifest within the Marine. These new Space Marines were designated Blood Claws. During this time of service, they learned and grew.

Once they learned to control the wolf within and proved themselves in battle, they were promoted to the status of Grey Hunters. During this period, some Space Wolves showed an aptitude for specific skills. The Grey Hunters then trained to pilot aircraft, crew tanks and handle other attack craft.

Sigurd was one such Grey Hunter and Mikal had grown to trust Sigurd's instincts and respect his skills.

The Thunderhawk banked hard, changing course as instructed, flying low over the city. Wing-mounted weapons turrets spun rapidly, firing short controlled bursts. Small-arms fire from below bounced harmlessly off its fuselage.

Alarm sirens blared in the cockpit as anti-air defence missiles leapt into the sky, vectoring towards the Thunderhawk. Sigurd's hands darted across the panels, tapping activation runes for defensive system counter measures. Then, pulling the control arm back hard and turning the control wheel, the Thunderhawk executed evasive manoeuvres. Sigurd evaded three of the pursuing missiles. Unfortunately, the last one was proving to be persistent.

'This one's like a pack of Fenrisian wolves on the hunt,' Sigurd continued, executing evasive manoeuvres. 'Brace for impact, brothers.'

The missile struck the starboard wing, sheering off two-thirds of it. The severed section of wing struck the vertical stabiliser as it passed over the main fuselage. Sigurd struggled with the controls as the heavily armoured craft plunged towards Lethe. The force of the dive pushed the Space Wolf passengers against their restraints.

Sigurd desperately attempted to regain control over his wounded craft. Fire alarms activated as the fuel escaping from the severed wing ignited. Sigurd and his flight crew could have ejected to safety, but there were three packs of Grey Hunters and an ancient one in the transport hold. He had to bring this craft down safely, his crew would not abandon their passengers.

Mikal heard Sigurd curse under his breath, 'By Russ, Mikal will owe us a barrel of ale when this is all over, and not that swill he usually gets! I want the good stuff.' Sigurd's co-pilot laughed, as did Mikal.

The Thunderhawk shook and shuddered, as if trying to tear itself apart. Sigurd levelled the aircraft out as it raced on its crash course; he had done everything he could. The Thunderhawk was too badly damaged. They would crash, hard and fast. There was only one last tactic he could try.

Something caught Mikal's ear. Among all the clutter of noises, he heard singing. He swung his seat around and looked into the cockpit to see Sigurd and his crew belting out an old Fenrisian song about heroic deeds, courage and friendship. He simply grinned and joined them. Soon every passenger on board did the same.

They were still singing when the nose of the Thunderhawk ploughed into the ground. Mikal heard the impact and the sound of metal shearing away before the force of the crash rendered him unconscious.

* * *

MIKAL AWOKE, STILL strapped into his seat. The walls and ceiling of the Thunderhawk were misshapen. He saw several of his battle-brothers slumped in their restraints. His head was spinning, and he could feel where the straps had held him in place. He wasn't sure exactly what had happened after the initial impact.

Slapping the quick release, he unbuckled his restraints and attempted to stand. He rose to his feet, reeled and stumbled forwards. He had survived the crash with only minor bumps and scratches, the worst of which was on his forehead. Touching his fingers to his injury, he felt blood, but he was alive.

The emergency security door completely blocked the cockpit. The door was designed to protect the crew from fire or debris. It must have activated on impact. Mikal tried to force the door open, but it wouldn't budge. He looked for something to use to pry the door open, but saw nothing. Suddenly, the shrieking sound of metal on metal pierced his ears. The sound was so intense Mikal had to cover his ears. Turning towards the source of the noise, he saw a claw protrude through the bulkhead of the Thunderhawk, and then the bulkhead wall simply ripped open. Standing outside the newly formed exit was the massive form of Dreadnought Gymir.

Mikal shook his head to help clear his senses. The once proud ship lay atop a pile of rockcrete and glass rubble, twisted and broken, like an animal with a snapped neck. Mikal could see plumes of smoke rising in the early light of dawn, and rubble in all directions.

'Mikal, it is good to see that you are alive,' said Gymir the Dreadnought. Mikal thought that the electronically generated voice sounded relieved.

'Yes, ancient one, I am alive,' Mikal said as he clambered out of the makeshift opening.

On its descent, Mikal could see that the Thunderhawk had struck the top of a building, knocking apart the upper floors before crashing into the street, creating a trench as it gouged itself to a halt. The nose of the ship was completely buried in rubble and debris. Several Grey Hunters had set up a perimeter around the crash site, while others searched the wreckage for fallen battle-brothers. Mikal searched for Sigurd, but his comrade wasn't among the living. He glanced at the cockpit canopy where a large plasteel support beam jutted through the framework. Mikal bent his knee and mourned the loss of his old friend.

NINE
Dilemma of Belisarius

Smoke hung heavily in the air rank with the stench of burning flesh, machine fuel and the residue of promethium. Buildings that had stood for decades were nothing more than burned-out shells. Craters riddled the ground from repeated artillery bombardments. Pieces of bodies lay scattered throughout the ruins, all that was left of victims who were unable to get to the bunkers in time to avoid the shelling. Water from ruptured underground lines flowed freely through the streets, winding its way through the rubble and debris, filling craters and turning the newly exposed dirt to mud.

Impact tremors created ripple effects on the surface of the standing water, first one, followed by another, then another, the intensity increasing with

each one. A large beetle, disturbed by the vibrations, scurried out of one piece of debris in a mad
dash for the protection of another.

A mechanical footpad crushed the beetle and the
rubble beneath it. The Dreadnought Gymir the Ice-
Fisted surveyed the landscape. He'd seen bombed
out streets before, having served the Imperium for
centuries. He had been recruited from some forgotten battlefield on Fenris, and served as a Space
Marine for hundreds of years until he was so badly
injured that even the Wolf Priests were unable to
mend his wounds. However, they were not willing to
risk the loss of Gymir's decades of experience and
knowledge, so the honour of eternal service was
bestowed upon him with the privilege of entomb-
ment within one of the ancient Dreadnought
sarcophagi. From within his metal shell, Gymir was
a living keeper of the Space Wolf lineage. He spent
his time resting deep within the Fang until called
upon to serve once more.

Gymir slowly traversed the rubble. His visual sensors, much more efficient than genetically enhanced
eyes, swept the debris field as he advanced. The holy
assault cannon that formed his arm tracked first left
and then right. His power claw opened and closed
instinctively, in anticipation of impending conflict.

His heavy footfalls sent vibrations through the
ground. Dreadnoughts were not known for their
ability to sneak up on the enemy. Gymir did not hide
his presence. His visual sensors allowed him to separate organic heat signatures from artificial ones and
identify them. He sensed a potential threat hiding

behind the rubble twenty metres straight ahead. Locking his assault cannon on the possible threat, he continued forwards, stopping fifteen metres from the target.

The signal was too small to be a Space Marine. Dark Angels were treacherous, but not cowardly. His quarry would not be able to hide from him for long.

'Stand and be recognised,' Gymir's mechanical voice commanded.

A solitary figure slowly rose from behind the debris, his empty hands raised above his head. Gymir recognised the uniform of a planetary defence force officer, although the cloth was tattered, torn and blood-soaked from the soldier's numerous injuries. The man's face was badly burnt, and his left cheek was swollen enough for his eye to be forced shut. Blood trickled from both of his ears.

'Don't fire. I'm not armed,' the officer stated.

From this closer vantage point, Gymir detected eight other heat signatures, hidden throughout the debris. Gymir advanced towards the officer. 'Identify yourself,' he said, his deep mechanical voice leaving no doubts as to his intentions. The officer limped slightly as he stepped further from cover, moving slowly so as not to appear threatening.

'My name is Lieutenant Paulinus of the Hyades defence forces.'

THE CHIMERA CRASHED through the palace gate. Electrical sparks bounced off the hull of the transport as wires were severed and torn from wall conduits. The bent and twisted gate gave way to the war transport, wrapping itself around the nose of the Chimera until it was dragged under the tank's persistent treads. Leaving its metal victim behind, the Chimera careened across the circular entrance road, tearing across the flower garden in the centre. A wave of dirt and vegetation flowed out of the garden splashing onto the pavement. The vehicle erupted from the opposite edge of the garden, losing speed before finally coming to rest on the front steps of the palace entrance.

The rumble of the drive system of the transport roared and then suddenly went silent, as if accepting that it had travelled as far as it could. Pressure seals gave way, sending jets of trapped dust and dirt from the hatch's seam as the internal atmosphere equalised pressure with the exterior environment. Hydraulic cylinders hissed as the rear hatch began to lower. The sound of metal against metal screeched in defiance, as if announcing that a long awaited dignitary had finally arrived. Slowly Ragnar and Jeremiah stepped from the vehicle, taking up positions on either side of the rear door, covering the deployment of the rest of the passengers. Haegr, Nathaniel and Elijah followed closely by Torin fanned out as they leapt from the Chimera.

The palace grounds appeared abandoned but untouched thus far by the conflict that surrounded them. The city outside the old walls was a different story entirely. Columns of smoke rose into the sky in the city surrounding the palace compound. The air was filled with the sounds and the scents of combat. The streets were devoid of activity, and paper and other rubbish rolled across the ground, pushed along by the warm breezes. Grave concern crossed their faces as the sights and sounds reinforced their determination to bring this conflict to a quick end.

The Space Marines bounded up the steps towards the main palace doors. Torin and Nathaniel took the rear, watching for signs of trouble. As they entered the palace foyer, they discovered that the palace had been evacuated. Tables and chairs were overturned and papers lay strewn about the floor. The main power was out. Emergency lights dimly lit the rooms and corridors.

Ragnar directed the others swiftly through the palace. Gabriella should be in the command centre in the lower levels. When they had left the palace Magni had been with her and he could only hope that in the confusion that was still the case. So far however, attempts to contact him had been unsuccessful. Ragnar hoped it was just Cadmus's electronic jamming or promethium interference.

When the Wolfblade had first arrived, Ragnar had reconnoitred as much of the palace as he could, attempting to commit as much of its configuration to memory as he was able. He felt more comfortable and in control when he knew his surroundings. The hallways seemed longer and more maze-like than he remembered, but he knew it was just a trick of his mind.

His concern for Gabriella was distorting his perception. He needed to regain his focus, control his emotions. Ragnar cursed under his breath – he should never have left Gabriella's side.

The mixed squad of Space Marines had almost reached the command centre elevator when Ragnar scented blood. As he rounded the last corner before the elevators, Ragnar found the source of the scent. Bodies of the House Belisarius Guard were sprawled out on either side of the elevator doors. The stench of blood and burnt flesh hung heavily in the air. Ragnar summoned the elevator as the rest of the group examined the bodies.

'They were caught by surprise,' said Torin.

'How can you tell?' Elijah asked.

The elevator doors opened, and the group entered the lift. 'They never drew their weapons,' Ragnar answered.

Torin and Haegr nodded. 'If it was their trusted commander, why would they?' Torin replied.

Elijah, Nathaniel and Jeremiah exchanged quick glances. Jeremiah subtly shook his head, not wanting to be noticed. He could not tell the Space Wolves their secret. Until this night, Jeremiah's perception of the Space Wolves was that they were barbaric, more interested in their next tankard than concepts like duty and honour. Ragnar and the others were proving that his beliefs may not have been wholly accurate.

THE ELEVATOR CAME to a stop as the door slid open. Ragnar's senses were instantly assaulted by the overwhelming array of olfactory stimulus present in the command centre. The six Space Marines entered the room. Static danced across every display console, bodies of the House Belisarius Guard were everywhere, and another corpse lay in the midst of them. Ragnar did not need the scent to know that it was Governor Pelias.

Ragnar continued to scan the room. His relief grew when he did not see Gabriella's body amongst the carnage. That relief fled from him as his eyes crossed to the body at the far side of the room.

'Magni!' Haegr shouted as he ran across the room.

Their young colleague was slumped against a wall. A trail of smeared blood stretched across the floor from where he had dragged himself. Haegr fell to one knee, sliding to Magni's side. Magni was clutching the burnt, curled remnants of his right hand to his chest. The plasma fire had cauterised the wound, slowing his blood loss. The stump that was now his left leg was an entirely different matter. Plasma had burned completely through his leg melting away power armour, flesh and bone. Severed arteries, strips of muscle and tendons hung from where the knee and lower half of Magni's leg were once attached. Blood had pooled around him where he rested.

'Magni, come on lad! Say something,' Haegr pleaded.

Magni's voice was weak and raspy. 'By Russ, please don't let the last thing I hear be your whining, Haegr.'

Magni slowly raised his head. His skin was ash-grey and dark circles surrounded his eyes, giving him a deathly appearance. 'Cadmus is a traitor. He took Gabriella. I failed the Wolfblade! I failed her!'

'Try not to talk about it, lad. Save your strength,' Torin said.

Torin looked at Ragnar, and his eyes spoke for him. Ragnar knew that Magni would not survive. Torin turned to the other bodies, unwilling to watch as his fellow Wolfblade passed on. Ragnar saw anger and rage in Torin's normally calm eyes.

Ragnar felt the same way. To die in the service of Russ and the Emperor was how every Space Wolf expected to meet his end: on his feet facing the enemy. To be betrayed in this way was a death almost beyond a Space Wolf's comprehension.

Ragnar knelt next to the young Blood Claw. He saw that Magni was in great pain. Ragnar wished he could ease the lad's suffering.

Magni slowly raised his eyes to meet Ragnar's. 'Ragnar, Cadmus had a message for the Wolfblade.' He paused, labouring to get his breath. 'He took Gabriella, and he will kill her... kill her if we... don't...' Magni took another deep painful breath.

'Take your time, Magni. What does he want from us?' Ragnar wanted him to stop and save his breath and to rest, but they had to have every detail, everything that Magni knew.

Magni fought to carry on speaking. 'I'm sorry... Ragnar... the Dark Angels... He said he'll kill her if we don't... eliminate... every Dark Angel on Hyades... must kill... them all.' Relief crossed Magni's face as he finished.

Ragnar leaned in closer. 'Where was he taking her, Magni?'

Magni shook his head slowly. 'I... don't know... but... he knew... Space Wolves... were coming... counting... on it, killed everyone... evil.'

Ragnar wiped blood from Magni's face. The youngest Wolfblade struggled to stay conscious. He looked up at Ragnar, fighting to keep his eyes focused.

His body was failing. Space Marine bodies were designed to withstand almost any injury, to survive poisons and toxins, and they were immune to virtually any disease. Their respiratory systems allowed them to survive without oxygen for extended periods of time. Special organs were implanted to change the composition of their blood. This normally enabled their blood to coagulate almost instantly. Even with all these genetic manipulations Space Marines were not indestructible. Sometimes, in cases like Magni's, without immediate medical treatment, the enhancements weren't enough.

'Ragnar... you did... the right thing! I just... wanted you to know that...' Magni's body slumped to the floor as his life drained away.

Ragnar reached out and brushed Magni's hair off his face. Slowly sorrow grew to anger in the hearts of the Space Wolves. Their battle-brother was gone.

Ragnar rose and turned from Magni's body, reaching out and placing his hand on Haegr's shoulder.

'Cadmus has Gabriella. We must find her and bring her to safety.' Grim determination filled Ragnar's voice.

Haegr crossed the room towards Jeremiah. 'Sounds simple enough, we just have to eliminate all the Dark Angels,' he said, raising his boltgun at the Dark Angels captain. 'And we might as well start right here.'

GYMIR THE ICE-Fisted, ancient warrior of Fenris, stood in the centre of the street, his hulking mechanical form towering over the officer of the Hyades defence forces. The officer's platoon had scattered amongst the ruins, in an attempt to hide from the Dreadnought. On his command, Lieutenant Markham's troops emerged from their hiding places. Gymir's targeting system locked on each one in turn. Should the need arise, they would be quickly cut down.

'Mikal, I've encountered and secured planetary forces,' Gymir's voice came over the comm system.

Mikal and his Grey Hunters quickened their pace through the city streets. Reaching Gymir's position in under sixty seconds, they surrounded Lieutenant Markham's forces. Mikal approached the lieutenant. He needed to coordinate with the defence forces, but this officer was not what he'd expected. There were many unanswered questions here on Hyades.

'Lieutenant Markham, My name is Mikal, Wolf Guard to Berek Thunderfist.' Mikal extended his hand, engulfing Markham's.

'We were attempting to coordinate defensive efforts with the commander of the planetary forces. We were en route to the palace when our Thunderhawk was shot down.'

Mikal caught the scent of fear coming from Markham. Normally this reaction was not unexpected when dealing with forces from the Imperial ranks. However, Markham's reaction was different. Markham's demeanour changed when he mentioned the planetary commander.

The lieutenant met Mikal's gaze. 'Commander Cadmus is a traitor,' he said, rage and betrayal dripping from his words.

'The commander of the planetary defences a traitor? Explain yourself, lieutenant,' Mikal said.

'Cadmus intentionally fired an artillery barrage on our position. He was trying to kill the Space Marines. He would have killed us all were it not for them,' Markham explained.

'The Space Marines saved you?' asked Mikal.

'Yes, sir. Just before the barrage hit, some of the Space Marines managed to throw several of my men to cover. The others attempted to shield them from the blasts with their own bodies,' Markham answered.

'Please, lieutenant, start from the beginning.' Mikal gestured for Markham to follow him out of earshot of the defence forces.

The lieutenant walked beside Mikal. 'The Dark Angels dispatched a kill team to infiltrate the palace prior to the invasion.'

'Have we established what the kill team's objective was?' Mikal asked.

'We all assumed that Lady Gabriella was their target.' Markham was growing more comfortable as he answered Mikal's questions.

'Lady Gabriella is on Hyades?' Mikal was familiar with House Belisarius, Lady Gabriella and the ancient pact between Belisarius and the Space Wolves.

'Yes! She arrived only a few days ago with a contingent of Wolfblade from Holy Terra.'

'Please go on.' The lieutenant continued to relay his tale of treachery to Mikal as they moved through the streets towards an abandoned Administratum building. As it was still relatively intact, Mikal decided that this would be the best location to establish a command post.

He dispatched two battle packs of Grey Hunters to locate and establish communications with their Wolf Brothers. When completed he would be able to create a command and control centre from which he could direct his forces in the defence of Hyades. Once the Space Wolf forces were organised he would ask for Lieutenant Markham's assistance in identifying and locating the loyal planetary troops, giving him overall command of all the Hyades defence forces.

Across the city Space Wolves and Hyades defensive forces linked up to establish a definitive perimeter. The tide was turning.

RAGNAR LEAPT TO his feet, grabbed Haegr's boltgun, and forced it up. Craters created by boltgun rounds trailed across the ceiling. Jeremiah, Elijah and Nathaniel drew their weapons. Torin growled and drew his sidearm. Dark Angel squared off against Space Wolf. Ragnar stood between the two groups, arms raised, trying to exert his will on a situation that was fast spiralling out of control.

Eyes darted from friend to foe, each one trying to ascertain the next move. Fingers tensed on triggers. The standoff between the Wolfblade and the Dark Angels seemed to last forever. Ragnar looked from Jeremiah to Haegr. Everything would be decided by the actions taken in the next few seconds.

'Haegr, Torin, drop your weapons,' Ragnar ordered.

'Magni is dead because of their treachery, Ragnar,' Haegr roared. Ragnar could hear the beast in his giant friend. The wolf was dangerously close the surface.

'Cadmus is the enemy here, Haegr. It was his treachery that killed Magni.' Ragnar fought his own rage at Magni's death but it was not Jeremiah and his team who had killed their battle-brother.

Torin was the most controlled Space Wolf that Ragnar had ever known, never allowing even the slightest hint of the beast within. The brother he had always relied on to be the voice of reason and calm held his bolter on Elijah and Nathaniel. He could see the rage in his eyes, almost as a reflection of the madness that was all around them. He could not believe that after everything this was where they had ended up: at each other's throats. He gestured for Torin to lower his weapon. Torin looked blankly at him, as if he didn't know who he was. Then Ragnar could see rationality returning to his eyes. Slowly, Torin lowered his boltgun and Ragnar knew that his friend was back.

'Ragnar speaks truthfully, Haegr. I mourn Magni's passing as well. Cadmus will pay for his treachery. This, I swear by all the frozen hells of Fenris.' Torin walked over to Haegr and placed a hand on top of Haegr's weapon. 'We don't do what Cadmus demands.'

Haegr turned in disgust from his brothers. 'The decision rests with you Ragnar, just be certain it's the right one.'

In a very short time, Ragnar had learned that Jeremiah was a man of his word and held honour above all else, in direct contradiction to what he thought he knew about the Dark Angels. Treachery and deceit were the ways of the Dark Angels, or at least that was what most Space Wolves believed. Jeremiah's actions thus far indicated otherwise, but he had not been completely forthcoming with Ragnar on the subject of Cadmus. He had told Ragnar that he was unable to discuss the details

of his mission because of loyalty to his brethren. That
was something that Ragnar himself would do if the roles
were reversed.

Things were different now. It was no longer the Wolfblade versus a Dark Angels kill team. From the Chimera,
they had seen the assault landing of the Space Wolves.
Recognising the symbol emblazoned on the side of the
landing craft, Ragnar knew that the great company of
Berek Thunderfist was planet-side. Here on Hyades, two
of the Adeptus Astartes' greatest Chapters were at war.

Ragnar raised his hand, pointing a finger towards Jeremiah. 'It's time for answers, Dark Angel. If we are to
survive this, you must tell us the truth.'

'I've told you all I can, Ragnar.'

'No! You've told me all you've chosen to,' Ragnar corrected the Dark Angel.

Jeremiah knew Ragnar was right. There was more to
Cadmus than he was saying, but his hands were tied. He
could not divulge the commander's true nature.

Two Chapters of Space Marines waging war meant
nothing compared to what would happen if the terrible secrets of the Dark Angels were revealed. Ragnar
had proven himself to be a man of conviction and
courage, a far cry from the barbarian that he expected
a Space Wolf to be.

Jeremiah weighed the situation up in his mind.

He could not reveal to Ragnar the whole truth. Perhaps
however, he did not need to. He might be able to tell
some of what he and the Dark Angels knew without
betraying his Chapter.

'You are correct; I have chosen to withhold some of
our information in regards to Cadmus.'

'Jeremiah, do not betray the honour of our Chapter!' Nathaniel protested.

Jeremiah held up his hand to silence Nathaniel. 'The history of distrust between our Chapters is long. In a very short time, I've discovered that the mutual distrust we share for each other may be unwarranted.' Jeremiah stepped towards Ragnar. 'I will tell you what I can and nothing more.'

'Well, get on with it, then,' Haegr shouted at Jeremiah.

'Haegr,' Torin warned, realising that Haegr wasn't helping the situation.

'All this cloak and dagger makes my head hurt.' Haegr walked towards the elevator shaft. 'I don't know why Ragnar was so excited about getting back into the galaxy anyway! Doesn't seem any different than Holy Terra! Everyone has a secret.'

Torin followed Haegr to the elevator. 'Ragnar, I'll take Nathaniel and Elijah and maybe we'll reconnoitre the rest of the palace.' Ragnar nodded in agreement.

'Nathaniel, you and Elijah should go with Haegr and Torin.' Jeremiah's words were more a request than an order. Nathaniel looked concerned as his gaze passed from Jeremiah to Ragnar and back. Jeremiah crossed the floor to stand next to his oldest warrior.

'Do you trust me?' he asked.

'I always have,' responded Nathaniel.

'Then trust me now, brother,' said Jeremiah.

Nathaniel nodded and walked towards the Wolfblade.

'Come on, little one, let's help these Space Wolves. At least that way we can all keep an eye on each other.' Elijah looked annoyed as he stepped into line with the others.

As the four of them reached the elevator doors, Torin gave Ragnar a last look. Ragnar nodded. Torin returned the affirmation and entered the elevator.

'We'll meet up in thirty minutes or less, Torin,' Ragnar said as the elevator doors slid closed.

Jeremiah turned his back to Ragnar. Dropping his gaze to the floor, he began, 'Cadmus and the Dark Angels have a history. My team was dispatched here to confirm our suspicions, capture him and if possible deliver him to my superiors for questioning.'

Ragnar judged Jeremiah not only by his words, but if the Dark Angel wasn't telling the truth, his scent gave no indication of it. His body language was another matter: he was holding something back.

'What do the Dark Angels need with the commander of a planetary defence force?'

'We believe that he has been conspiring with the dark powers of Chaos,' Jeremiah explained.

'Chaos?'

Ragnar's mind travelled back to the Chaos temple and the sacrificial altar that the Wolfblade had discovered. He had distrusted Cadmus from the start. Now all the pieces of the puzzle started to fit together. When he and the Wolfblade had made the discovery of the Chaos temple and entered the kill zone, the planetary defence forces had instantly engaged them. The attack was not an accident as Cadmus had claimed, but must have been an attempt to destroy the Wolfblade as he had suspected.

Jeremiah turned to face Ragnar. 'I believe that Cadmus lured my team here intentionally, and allowed us to gain entry to the city wall and reach the palace unhindered.'

This caused Ragnar a momentary pause. 'Why would he lure you to Hyades when he knew that there were Wolfblade here, and that the Space Wolves would be conducting a patrol of the system?'

'I believe he has orchestrated this conflict from the beginning, using the Space Wolves and Dark Angels' ancient distrust to spark this conflict,' Jeremiah continued. 'Perhaps he intended to create a full-scale war between our Chapters.'

Ragnar pondered Jeremiah's words, trying to fathom what Cadmus could possibly gain by setting such events into motion. What could be gained by a conflict between two of the Emperor's greatest servants? Ragnar had learned enough about the forces of Chaos to know that if what Jeremiah was saying were true then there had to be a reason. Ironically, the forces of Chaos did nothing random. There was always a plan, always a reason. The same had to be true here. If Cadmus had set these events into motion, there had to be something to benefit him. The difficulty would be determining what that was.

'If what you are saying is true then we must no longer allow ourselves to be manipulated,' Ragnar said.

'Yes, but blood has been spilled on both sides. How can you and I bring this to an end?' Jeremiah's question was valid. How would they achieve this?

'Your team and the Wolfblade have managed to set aside our differences and forge an alliance, fragile as it is. If we can do it, then so can our Chapters. We must find and defeat the true enemy. We must succeed, Jeremiah. We must.'

Ragnar headed for the elevator. They had to move and move quickly. Each moment that the battle raged would make ending it even harder. Reaching the control panel to summon the elevator, Ragnar realised that Jeremiah had not followed. He turned to face his new Dark Angel ally.

'Ragnar, there is one more thing I must ask of you. Cadmus is an enemy of the Dark Angels and I must complete my mission,' Jeremiah said with guarded confidence.

'Cadmus killed Magni and abducted Gabriella, his life ends at the point of my blade.'

'I understand how you feel, Ragnar, but you must understand that I am a Son of the Lion, and Cadmus is mine.' Jeremiah's voice was unwavering and firm. He could see the anger cross Ragnar's face. His eyes were filled with rage.

He made one last attempt to gain the Space Wolf's understanding.

'You just told me that we must get our brothers to set aside their ancient distrust and bring this conflict to an end. We're not even out of this room and already we're back to this.' Jeremiah continued. 'I, like you, have made an oath to serve, an oath of loyalty! I cannot – will not – set that aside. I pledge to you that I will stand by your side and do anything we need to bring this conflict to an end, but I personally must deal with Cadmus.'

Ragnar considered what the Dark Angel had just said. Evaluating the events of the last few days, he put himself into Jeremiah's position. Again, he asked himself what he would do if things were reversed. He would not allow anything to deter him from his goal. Jeremiah was not what he would have expected from a Dark Angel. In fact, he was surprised at how alike they actually were, and if this was about redemption... He wondered what he would do to make up for the Spear of Russ.

Ragnar extended his hand to Jeremiah. Jeremiah accepted his gesture of friendship and trust.

'I know that there is more between the Dark Angels and Cadmus than you have told me,' said Ragnar. 'I also know that you've risked much in sharing with me what you already have. I understand what it means to risk something for the greater good, and that I cannot ignore. Cadmus will be yours to deal with as you see fit. You have my word as a Space Wolf.'

TEN
A Thousand Pains

CADMUS STOOD AMONG servitors wired into the monitor systems, in one of Lethe's command bunkers. These former criminals served out their sentences for cowardice, heresy and their other crimes by helping to power the many surveillance systems of Lethe's defences. They were more machines than men and as such, they were beneath Cadmus's notice. As far as he was concerned, he was alone, surveying the carnage throughout the city. Watching the battle unfold gave Cadmus a sense of power. He had orchestrated everything that had happened.

The door behind Cadmus opened, and Lieutenant Carson of the Hyades planetary defence force hurried inside. Carson was a young man who had risen quickly through the ranks, a tall charismatic man who had earned his rank. Carson's bravery and calm command were legend among the rank and file, but Cadmus could tell that his officer's vaunted courage was wavering as the Space Marines assault continued.

'We don't have much time, commander. The Dark Angels have breached many of our defences, and the Space Wolves...' the lieutenant swallowed. 'Sir, why are we attacking the Space Wolves?'

Cadmus fixed the lieutenant with his gaze. Faint beads of perspiration showed on the man's forehead. Cadmus sighed. It wouldn't do to have the other men see Carson afraid. It was a pity. Carson had been the type of tool that Cadmus would have forged into a legend on other worlds in times long gone.

'Come with me, Carson.' Cadmus led the lieutenant out of the monitor chamber. None of the servitors even registered the fact the two men had departed.

'Sir, where are we going?' asked Carson.

Cadmus raised his hand in answer and led the young officer down the hall to a large plasteel door.

'This is the most secure chamber in the city. I even had the servitors eliminated after its completion to maintain the security. Once we are inside, I'll explain the plan.'

Cadmus pressed the correct runes to activate the security door. With a rumble, the massive door slowly opened.

The lieutenant strained his eyes to see inside, but the room was pitch black.

'Go in,' ordered Cadmus. The commander followed the lieutenant inside. The door slid closed quickly, surprising the lieutenant as it slammed shut. The room was cold as well as dark. Carson felt as if they had entered a tomb. The two men stood in near darkness.

'Lieutenant, you were born and raised here on Hyades, were you not?' asked Cadmus.

'Yes, sir.'

'Did you know that the people of Hyades, particularly Lethe, are some of the most defence-minded that I've ever met? Your people adamantly refuse to give in to the wilderness and you refuse to adapt to the world. Instead, you try and force the world to adapt to you, an admirable quality. Unfortunately, you don't seem to realise that your world only exists at the whim of the Emperor, or should I say, the Imperial bureaucrats.'

'What?'

Cadmus smiled. 'Surely, you know that the Emperor is dead in that Golden Throne of his. He's been dead for ten thousand years. The Imperium is a lie, and the greatest liars are those devout Dark Angels come to butcher you. So, lieutenant, I'm going to give you a bit of honesty.'

'Sir?' The lieutenant took a step backwards. 'I don't understand,' he said.

'Lieutenant, I don't care about you or anyone else on this planet. I only care about my brothers and myself. To secure my safety and defeat my enemies, I'm afraid that I've had to make a deal and I'm going to sacrifice Lethe to my new allies,' Cadmus said.

The commander swept his arm out in front of him. As he did, an arcane circle sparked to life in the centre of the room. A bloody red light emanated from its twisting runes. Smoke swirled within the circle, and the lieutenant thought he could see something translucent moving inside it. Whatever it was, it was fascinating, and merely gazing on it made the lieutenant's blood freeze with terror.

'The power of the Lord of Change flows there,' whispered Cadmus. 'I can tell you are intrigued. The flames mesmerise even the strongest willed men. It's even more impressive when fully activated.'

'Why would you…? What does this…?' The lieutenant struggled with his words and emotions.

'Blood sacrifice activates it,' said Cadmus in a tone as cold as ice. His sword flashed through the air, slicing neatly through the lieutenant's throat. Cadmus carefully caught the soldier's body with his free hand, pushing it into the circle. The smoke turned a deep red, and a hissing sound filled the room.

Cadmus paused for a moment and wiped his sword clean as he watched the lieutenant's blood pulsing into the circle.

'The time is now,' said Cadmus, addressing the circle of power. 'I have done everything you requested. The bodies of Space Wolves and Dark Angels litter Hyades. I even have the Wolfblade here as you wanted.'

A moment of silence followed. Then a commanding voice boomed from beyond space and time.

'You have done well, Fallen. As promised, your enemies will be destroyed. Vengeance shall belong to both of us, for though you hate the Dark Angels, there is nothing that can compare to the hatred for the Space Wolves that belongs to the Thousand Sons! As for me, soon I shall personally end the life of one who has ever proven himself to be a thorn in the side of my master.'

'Surely you speak of the Wolf Lord Berek?' asked Cadmus.

'No, I speak of the whelp, Ragnar!' The portal crackled. Blue bolts of lightning cascaded from the centre, and a large form took shape.

Cadmus took a step back and gripped the hilt of his blade. Though he wouldn't admit it, seeing the image of the huge armoured shape manifest before him put him on his guard. The Chaos Space Marine wasn't truly in the room, he reminded himself, just appeared to speak to him via dark sorcery. Still, Cadmus couldn't escape a feeling of dread in his gut.

'My apologies, Lord Madox,' offered Cadmus.

The huge Chaos Marine sorcerer wore blue armour traced with gold covered with ever-changing sigils of Tzeentch. It was an artifact, a relic of Chaos in its own right, exposed to the power of Tzeentch and the daemons of the warp for untold millennia. Madox's eyeplates burned with a bright yellow-white light, and Cadmus could feel the hatred within this master of the Thousand Sons.

'The Space Wolves destroyed our planet. They betrayed us. Our master, Magnus the Red, attempted to save the Emperor, but he was ignored. Only Horus believed us, and even he did not fully accept the truth! We could have saved the Imperium then, but we will destroy it now! I have walked the surface of Fenris. I have beheld the return of my primarch from the warp. Only one thing has stopped me from being the greatest of the Thousand Sons, that insignificant wolf pup, Ragnar.'

Madox threw his head back, raised his arms, and laughed.

Cadmus was sweating. He had seen hundreds of battles and faced terrifying enemies. He had even barely escaped the Dark Angels on two occasions, but the presence of the Chaos sorcerer chilled his soul.

Madox's voice took on a maniacal tone, and the lightning from the portal struck in tune with his laughter. 'My lord Tzeentch truly is the master of Chaos, the Master of Change, the Master of Magic, and the Almighty God of Fire! Truly, he tests my resilience. Were my adversary a Wolf Lord, or a hero of the Imperium, then my defeats would find excuse, but to face an ignorant warrior has driven me to aspire to greater heights! Thank you, Tzeentch, for Ragnar, for he and he alone has shown me the way to destroy his entire cursed Chapter.'

Laughter responded in a blasphemous cacophony from the portal.

Madox looked directly at Cadmus. 'Now, Fallen, as you said, it is time.'

The Chaos sorcerer raised his arm and fire raced from his fingertips into the ceiling of the bunker, burning purple, blue, indigo, yellow, green and deep red all at once.

'Let the fire in the blood of this world, bring Tzeentch's blessing.'

Cadmus heard shrieking. The sound was soft at first, but soon it echoed from all around him.

'The deaths of the Space Marines must provide fruit. I need more than just their lives; I need their very essence. The children of Tzeentch shall come and they shall reap the souls of their enemies.'

'Lord Madox, what more do you need?' asked Cadmus. 'Have I not given you everything you requested? I have made a war.'

Madox fell quiet, and the shrieking fell to an almost imperceptible scream. 'I wanted more than a war. I wanted bodies. Now, I want gene-seed.'

The gene-seed was the part of every Space Marine that made them what they were. Each gene-seed contained a piece of the DNA of the primarch, the Chapter's founder. When a warrior was chosen to become a Space Marine, the Apothecaries implanted the gene-seed within their body. Other organs would be implanted alongside the gene-seed, which controlled and regulated not only the genetic changes but also the body's acceptance of them.

The gene-seed was the essence of a Space Marine; it was what separated them from ordinary men, far more than their signature power armour or even their faith in the Emperor.

Cadmus suddenly realised that he was just a tool for the Thousand Sons. Everything he had done meant nothing to them. He was merely a pawn in their games. His anger brought courage. He wasn't going to let anyone, not even an ancient evil ten thousand years old, play games with him.

'My lord, I expect you to honour the terms of our agreement,' said Cadmus, 'and if you don't...'

Madox tilted his head and stared directly at the commander, and the protest died in Cadmus's throat. The Fallen felt as if Madox looked into the depths of his soul, as if he knew everything about him. 'I know that you don't wish to finish your threat. Emotion makes you weak. Cadmus, you are not worthy of honour. In that way, you are the same as your former Chapter. I will, however, send allies to you in your time of need,' Madox laughed. 'Now, we have gathered all of our pieces and set the Wolf and the Lion against each other. We must reap our bloody harvest, so we may plant the seeds of destruction for my Lord Tzeentch.'

With a burst of multi-coloured flame, the image of Madox was gone.

Cadmus found himself sweating and trembling. His heart raced in his chest, and he felt the blood burn on his cheeks. The ritual had exhausted him physically and emotionally.

'By Luther's blade,' cursed Cadmus. He walked over to the wall in the darkened room and activated the light. Carefully worked lenses shone into the room from sculpted gargoyles and daemons. Everything about the room had been made in secret to allow this summoning circle to work, just as the sorcerer had requested.

Cadmus glared at the quiet summoning circle. 'Don't trifle with me. I'm not one of your blind cultist pawns,' he muttered to the floor, but he knew that he was the only one listening. He would survive, and one day, there would be a reckoning for all of his enemies.

The commander took a moment to regain his composure. It wouldn't do for the men to see his anger, and he couldn't afford to have his thoughts clouded. He checked his uniform for blood and carefully removed a few incriminating droplets. There was no sign of the lieutenant's body or even his blood in the room. The spell had completely consumed the corpse. Cadmus shuddered.

He activated the door, and then cut the lights. He was worried, even though he knew that everything had gone according to his plan. It was all about time and sequence, one event following another. He had set this in motion and he would see it to the end. He had contacted the Thousand Sons, hadn't he? He was the master manipulator, he reminded himself, but try as he might, he could not dispel his doubts.

Cadmus followed the security corridor past the monitor chamber and the hall to the city complex. The plasteel door at this end of the hall was a duplicate of the other. Two of his loyal men saluted as they maintained their posts. The guards were his people, subservient to his every command.

'Open the door,' he snapped. The guard nearest the control activated it as soon as he dropped the salute. The door slowly slid open and lights activated as Cadmus stepped inside.

The largely empty chamber was nondescript, a storeroom that could easily have been on a thousand planets or even starships throughout the Imperium. The room had one occupant who lay on the ground in the middle of the chamber.

Gabriella lay shackled and bound. She glared up at her captor with hate in her eyes. She looked tired from struggling. It was a pity that she was so dedicated to her house. Despite her lack of classic beauty, Cadmus admired her spirit.

Gabriella had tried in vain to free herself from her bonds, and although she realised that she was probably wasting her strength, she wasn't going to accept any part of this power-hungry officer's plan. 'I felt the presence of Chaos. Tell me, Cadmus, are the dark forces part of your plan as well? Because if they are, you are a bigger fool than I thought.'

Cadmus knelt down over the Navigator and slapped her hard across the face. The small release of anger felt good. 'I promise you, Lady Gabriella, if I die, you'll die as well. Fortunately, I expect that your Space Wolves will show their typical lack of control and spend their energy rending the Dark Angels. While that happens, my men will kill them both. Soon, we will be in a city of the dead, and my allies will put an end to all of this.'

Gabriella smiled; she didn't believe a word of what he said.

ON THE STREETS of Lethe, battle raged between the Dark Angels and the Space Wolves. Both sides fought fiercely against their fellow Space Marines, while the men of Lethe did their best to defend their ruined city. Two ancient champions of the Chapters met on the cratered streets.

The Dark Angels Dreadnought, Arion the Unchallenged, levelled his twin-linked lascannons at his

Space Wolf counterpart, Gymir the Ice-Fisted. The blasts scored a hit, but the Space Wolf war machine took the shots on his arm instead of the sarcophagus on his chest. The glancing strike set a massive Fenrisian wolf pelt ablaze, but failed to disrupt the mind of the entombed Space Marine housed within the venerable Dreadnought's body. The combatants on both sides paused in awe and reverence at the duel unfolding before their eyes.

The Space Wolf Dreadnought kicked aside the remains of a dead Dark Angel as if it were a child's toy and charged, conjuring images in the minds of soldiers on all sides of a sprinting soldier rather than a lumbering mechanical walker. The Dark Angels Dreadnought met the challenge full on, swinging his power fist. Metal clanged on metal like the sounds of a giant forge.

Lieutenant Markham staggered away from the battling Dreadnoughts. He prayed that with the aid of the Space Wolves, House Belisarius would emerge triumphant. Wolf Guard Mikal had contacted the other Imperial Guard units. Markham had been lucky to encounter the Wolf Guard. Word of Cadmus's treason was spreading, but despite that many men would stay loyal to him and assume the rumours were just a Dark Angels trick. Still, the Space Wolves were coordinating the battle. The Dark Angels had adjusted to the challenge and the battle for Lethe was in full swing.

A Leman Russ tank, reinforced with siege armour, drove down a side street. It paused to fire its massive battle cannon at a target that Markham couldn't see. Although the Leman Russ was the main battle tank of the Imperial Guard on countless worlds, the planetary defence force kept few of them on Hyades. The vehicle's size made it difficult to manoeuvre in city streets and in the jungle, yet each one of the tanks received more attention from the tech-priests than the Hellhounds or Chimeras. That was because of the pride that House Belisarius took in the vehicle named for the primarch of their allies, the Space Wolves.

Markham could see the ruins of the city's outer defence wall down the main plaza. Bombardment from the assault had turned it into a mountain of rubble. It was badly breached. Dark shapes crawled through the rubble. If they were some of the defence forces, maybe he could rally them. Commander Cadmus had betrayed him, the Wolfblade and House Belisarius. Markham did not give his loyalty lightly, and something churned in his stomach as the impact of the betrayal struck him. He knew that he was still reeling from the near miss of the Earthshaker cannon earlier, but he felt as if the betrayal was what truly kept his head spinning.

Cadmus had made a mistake. Markham was originally from Catachan, a real deathworld, not some planet where the people hid behind walls and feared the mines more than they feared the plants. He'd find a way to survive and do his duty. He knew that he'd gained some respect from Wolf Guard Mikal when he had demanded a weapon so that he could rejoin the fighting. Markham wasn't going to let a few scrapes, bruises or even a concussion slow him down.

He squinted to see more clearly. The dark shapes that he had spotted moved strangely, and he was sure that there were many more of them than before. Lethe burned from the ongoing war, and with his addled brains, Markham wasn't sure exactly what he was seeing. He wiped his eyes.

The shapes weren't human, they were reptos. Dozens of the creatures were gathering around the breach, all the while the humans on the planet were busy blowing each other to bits. The reptos appeared to be gathering, waiting.

Markham had a vox that he had scavenged from a dead soldier so he could to stay in touch with the Space Wolves. 'Wolf Guard Mikal,' he voxxed. 'I believe we have a problem. The wall has been breached and the reptos have come to scavenge.'

'Lieutenant, what are reptos?' came the reply. Markham heard storm bolter shots echo through the vox.

'The reptos are native creatures from the jungle surrounding Lethe. They've been attacking the mines and anything outside the walls. They are mammalian reptiles,' responded Markham.

Static answered him. Communications were jammed again.

Markham crouched down behind a bit of rubble and took a better look. The reptos shook and convulsed. He was confused. He'd never seen this behaviour. The creatures then poured into the streets, heading to the bodies of Dark Angels. Strangely, they ignored the bodies of the defence forces.

The creatures fell upon their targets, ripping and tearing. Through extreme effort, they found cracks and weak spots in the power armour, and ripped into the dead flesh underneath. Markham shook his head. He hated watching the reptos scavenge and devour any humans, even if the Dark Angels had attacked Hyades.

The reptos were tearing large bloody objects free from the Space Marine bodies. Markham wasn't sure what they were collecting. At first, he thought it might be hearts, but the organs were too large. The reptos gathered in clusters, hissing and snapping at the body parts, as if they were celebrating. Then, they retreated.

All of the reptos moved back to form a semi-circle around a single large member of their species. The large one wore different scaled pelts and held a long staff. The sight fascinated and enthralled Markham. He forgot the sounds of battle behind him, completely oblivious to everything but the scene he was witnessing.

The repto with the staff suddenly ignited, bursting into flame. At first, Markham thought that someone, an infiltrating soldier perhaps, had taken a hand flamer to the beast, but the creature didn't burn with the purifying white fire of promethium. Instead, the flame burned with an unearthly rainbow of colours. As the fire consumed the repto, something even more unexpected took place. Markham cleared his eyes. With the haze of battle he wasn't sure at first that what he saw was real.

Tendrils burst from the body of the flaming creature. Then something covered in mouths and eyes floated out of the fire. The creature was bright blue with streaks of red and pink. It floated above the ground and a nimbus of rainbow fire curled around it. Markham's mind laboured to accept the sight before him. He was a survivor, a man born on a deathworld. He had endured challenges and pain. He had encountered the deadliest predators on planets across the galaxy.

Somehow, he knew that what he saw was not from this galaxy. He felt terror in every fibre of his being.

The reptos gave a shrill greeting sound as one, and handed over their trophies. The abomination took each of them with its tendrils, tenderly grasping them. Then it pulled itself back into the flame and vanished. The reptos spread out, hunting for more trophies, save for one, who picked up the staff from the charred hand of its former owner.

Markham fell on his knees and sobbed a prayer of thanks to the Emperor. The unnameable horror that he had seen was gone. He would not have felt so relieved if he had known that similar scenes were taking place across the city. The harvest had begun.

IN THE PALACE complex, Haegr, Torin, Elijah and Nathaniel searched for Cadmus. Ragnar and Jeremiah were searching together elsewhere, and the other Space Marines assumed that they might be negotiating more details of their alliance without the complications of everyone else's thoughts. The four focused on their search, each one hoping that they would discover the commander first. So far, they had found nothing but bodies, and the lasgun wounds on the bodies coupled with still-secure doors indicated that their killers hadn't been other Dark

Angels. The dead men appeared to have been killed by members of the planetary defence force.

Torin looked over at Haegr after sniffing the air. 'So, lad, your nose can tell us everything else. Where is he? I can't find him.'

Haegr shook his head. 'I'm not sure. There are too many scents.'

'Are you really trying to sniff him out?' asked Elijah. The Dark Angel sounded incredulous. 'I thought that was Space Wolf talk for tracking or something.'

'Young one,' said Nathaniel, 'the Space Wolves are known for their senses.'

'Unfortunately, some of us spend our time trying to track nothing but food,' said Torin.

'What's wrong with that?' questioned Haegr. 'Without my ability to find sustenance, we could die out here if things stay bad. Torin, I think you've gone too long without a good thrashing.'

Haegr had to admit to himself that hearing the banter made him more relaxed. He kept finding scene after scene of death, and he didn't know where Cadmus was. Torin placed his hand on Haegr's shoulder and leaned over to whisper to him in that conspiratorial manner that came so easily to him.

'Brother, are you tracking Cadmus?' he whispered.

'I'm trying,' said Haegr.

'Focus on Gabriella's scent instead. You know it better,' recommended Torin.

Haegr gave his friend a look. He wasn't sure if Torin was implying something or not. Haegr knew that he had a strange feeling for Gabriella, but he told himself it was a sense of protectiveness.

From one of the palace windows, Haegr could see drop-pods descending amidst the fire and smoke of the combat. The Space Wolves had arrived! Just catching sight of the wolf symbol made his blood race, although he felt a sense of disquiet as well. He should be in one of those drop-pods with his battle-brothers. Then, he realised that the symbol belonged to Wolf Lord Berek Thunderfist.

'Impressive, isn't it?' asked Torin. The other Marines were gathered around, momentarily distracted by the scene of drop-pod after drop-pod coming down.

'Look,' said Elijah, pointing out of the window. More Dark Angels drop-pods were descending. The Dark Angels were still coming. The battle was escalating.

They were running out of time.

GABRIELLA STRUGGLED against her bonds as the commander pulled her through dark passage after dark passage. She had lost all sense of time and place. Guards walked behind them, hard-looking men with scars and oddly mixed armour and unique weapons. There were at least six with them, but she couldn't tell if there were more. These were Cadmus's hand-picked troops: men who had followed him to this planet.

She knew that the Wolfblade would come for her. The Space Wolves would not relent until they found her. Cadmus would die for his treason.

Yet she could feel other forces at work. In her mind's eye, colours swirled, vibrant and bright. She could feel the power of Chaos coursing through these dark passages. She saw images of Madox and the Thousand

Sons, just as she had felt them before when Cadmus had contacted them in his ritual. They were coming, and they had something with them, something that they had brought from the warp.

Then, she saw an image that she knew from ancient tapestries and paintings. She saw the Spear of Russ, the artifact that Ragnar had lost. It was in the possession of the Thousand Sons, they must have recovered it from the warp. She knew the story about Ragnar and how the Thousand Sons had nearly opened a gateway between the warp and the physical world, attempting to summon their primarch, Magnus the Red.

Would they succeed this time?

ELEVEN
Dark Angels and Wolfblade Unite

A WAR RAGED in the city of Lethe between the Space Wolves and the Dark Angels. The ten thousand year-old distrust of these two founding members of the Adeptus Astartes was being exploited by the powers of Chaos.

Ragnar and Jeremiah were in unexplored territory. The mixed band of Space Marines was setting out to find Cadmus and bring him to justice, rescue Gabriella, and work out a way to bring this conflict to an end without sacrificing the honour of either of the proud Space Marine Chapters.

Torin, Haegr, Nathaniel and Elijah had just completed their search of the palace. There were no additional signs of Cadmus anywhere to be found. During their search of one of the communication temples they did, however, come across Tech-Priest

Varnus. Varnus was monitoring several communication channels while directing his servitors to areas and equipment that needed to come to the assistance of the Adeptus Mechanicus. The tech-priest accompanied them, walking between Haegr and Torin, his scarlet robes lightly dusting the floor. With the exception of a few minor scraps and some fresh oil stains on his robe, he looked exactly the same as he had when the Wolfblade had first met him.

As the group approached the entrance to the command centre the heavy metal doors slid open as Ragnar and Jeremiah entered the corridor.

'Ragnar, Jeremiah, allow me to introduce Tech-Priest–' Torin began.

'Varnus, it is good to see that you are alive.' Ragnar's surprise and relief were apparent. 'We are in your debt. Had you not opened the blast door, Cadmus's treacherous attempt to destroy us would have succeeded.'

'Indeed, your plight seemed rather perilous. I'm sorry I could not have been of assistance sooner. It had only recently become apparent to me that the governor's forces had been compromised.' There were no emotional inflections in the tech-priest's voice and his mechanically assisted breathing remained eerily rhythmic.

'Compromised is an understatement. Cadmus is undoubtedly in the service of Chaos.'

'Haegr will wipe his Chaos taint from existence,' Haegr promised.

'Yes, Haegr, we will, but first things first,' Ragnar responded.

'What could be more important than cutting out his treacherous heart?' Haegr's words revealed his simplistic perception of the universe.

'I believe that Ragnar is talking about our newly landed brethren who are fighting and dying on the streets of Lethe,' Torin said.

'Perhaps I can be of assistance,' Varnus interrupted. 'Shortly after the Dark Angels began their assault, the Space Wolf patrol fleet commanded by Wolf Lord Berek Thunderfist arrived.' Varnus paused as if checking his facts.

'Yes they were the forces of Thunderfist. After several attempts by him to determine why they had quarantined Hyades, he was forced to engage the Dark Angels, and through a daring ship-to-ship engagement was able to deploy his forces. It was here that I discovered the treachery of Commander Cadmus. His troop deployments were not consistent with defending the city. He had removed his most experienced forces from the city, leaving his less experienced troops defending the brunt of the attack. That, combined with several communications between Cadmus and his storm troopers that I was able to monitor, forced me to take action. I only regret that my actions did not come soon enough.'

'Have you made contact with the Space Wolf landing forces yet?' Ragnar asked.

'No, but I believe that their commander has been successful at contacting some of the loyal Hyades ground forces,' Varnus answered.

'Once the Space Wolves were on the ground they established communication with the loyal factions of

the planetary defence forces. It was through this
alliance that they were able to establish a defensive
perimeter within the city, right around the palace
compound. With the defensive lines firmly established, the allied forces have begun to push back the
Dark Angels,' Varnus concluded.

Ragnar and the rest of the Wolfblade were relieved
to hear that the tide of battle appeared to be swinging
in their direction. Ragnar, however, knew that what
was good news for him and his Wolfblade brothers
was worrying to his new-found allies. The alliance
forged with the Dark Angels kill team was tenuous at
best, and if they were going to bring this conflict to an
end it would be this relationship that would be the
catalyst.

'This madness has to end,' said Ragnar. 'Cadmus has
been pulling the strings from the beginning. Everything that's happened has been according to his
design.'

'That is true, Ragnar, everything except one element:
our alliance! Cadmus could never comprehend that
the Lion and the Wolf would be capable of setting
aside ten thousand years of distrust. It is this alliance
that gives us the advantage,' Jeremiah said.

Ragnar was relieved that Jeremiah's thoughts were
the same as his. However, the Wolfblade's first duty
was to House Belisarius. The information provided by
Varnus left them free to pursue the traitor and rescue
Lady Gabriella.

'Varnus, can you establish communications with the
Spaces Marine forces here on Hyades, and inform
them of Cadmus's treachery? Ragnar asked.

'Yes, I believe that I can,' Varnus replied.

Ragnar hoped that Varnus would be able to use his skills as a tech-priest to establish communication channels with the Space Wolves and the Dark Angels. This could be a useful resource when the time was right.

'Our priority is to locate Cadmus,' Torin exclaimed.

'Yes, but he could be anywhere. In fact, I would be surprised if he was still on the planet at all,' Haegr said.

'No, he's still here. He wants to ensure that his plan works,' Nathaniel added.

'How can you be certain?' Ragnar asked.

The Dark Angels remained silent, exchanging glances between themselves until Jeremiah finally spoke.

'Shortly after our first encounter with you on the palace grounds we were contacted by Interrogator-Chaplain Vargas, who had arrived on board the battle-barge that orbits Hyades. While we were reporting our need for additional time to locate and secure our target, the transmission was interrupted by Cadmus, who we now know to be our quarry. Chaplain Vargas had just agreed to give us the time we needed. However, once the transmission was compromised Cadmus provoked the chaplain into this full-fledged assault. We've been unable to reach the battle-barge since,' Jeremiah concluded.

'Cadmus has gone to great lengths to ensure that these events unfold exactly the way he intends. I find it difficult to believe that he would simply slip away,' Nathaniel added.

'He wouldn't,' Torin agreed.

'Yes. He must still be here on Hyades, but where?' Ragnar asked.

'He would need a place where he could plan events without detection, and free from interruption. That means it would not be within the palace compound,' Varnus concluded.

'How can you be so certain?' Haegr asked.

'The compound is heavily monitored by security surveillance skulls.' Ragnar remembered the command centre's monitors, almost every corridor and room under constant scrutiny.

'Yes,' Varnus confirmed.

'Then he would need to establish his base in a secluded location away from the palace compound,' Jeremiah added.

'The temple,' Haegr said, almost shouting.

The silence of the group was deafening as each member of the Wolfblade reached the same conclusion. Haegr was right – the temple would be the best place to begin their search for the treacherous Cadmus. It was secluded, and out of the way.

'Temple?' Jeremiah asked.

'Upon our arrival on Hyades we conducted a search of the jungle around the city. While there, we came upon an ancient temple. It appeared to be abandoned,' Ragnar explained.

'We just need to find a way to get there without attracting the attention of our brother Space Marines,' Torin explained.

'I think I can help with that,' Elijah said as he walked past the group. Jeremiah looked to Nathaniel who simply shrugged and entered the command centre as well, followed closely by the rest of them.

When they entered the command centre Elijah had pulled several tubes from a plasteel box that rested between the wall and one of the monitoring consoles.

'I saw these when we were in here earlier, I think that they can help.'

Elijah read the label on each tube in turn. 'This one,' he said, pulling the parchment from the tube and unrolling it across the table.

'It's a city map,' Elijah said.

The others watched as Elijah began to trace a path from the jungle to the city walls and on to the palace.

'What are you doing?' Torin asked.

'This is the path we used to gain access to the city,' Jeremiah explained.

'Our insertion went exceptionally well. In fact, I thought at the time that it went too well.' As he continued, Jeremiah pointed out the key locations along the line on the map. 'We teleported in here and made our way through the jungle to the wall here.'

'That's great, but there's a war going on out there.' Haegr's words rang true. There were forces throughout the city: forces that they would have to avoid.

'This is correct. We will need to move undetected if possible. Any contact with either side would spell disaster for our mission,' Nathaniel said.

Varnus looked at the map and then spoke. 'The Dark Angels dropped into the city here, here and here. At first they moved unobstructed towards the palace. Fortunately, the governor's guard report directly to the governor who dispatched them right away, slowing down their advance.'

'I'm impressed. Defence forces going head-to-head against Astartes,' Torin commented.

'That was not their mission. Their numbers were too small to mount an actual defence. Their orders were to harass them, slow them down. With the use of mines and explosives charges they were able to topple several buildings in an attempt to slow their advance on the palace. This gave the governor some time to locate and deploy those forces still loyal to him.'

The Astartes warriors watched and listened as the tech-priest pointed out the most current troop and Marine deployments that he had, committing almost every detail to memory.

'These locations are somewhat out of date but they should give you enough information to move through the city, decreasing your chances of encountering any of the forces engaged on Lethe,' Varnus concluded.

'Again, Varnus, we are in your debt.' Ragnar placed a hand on the tech-priest's shoulder.

'Once you've departed I will attempt to contact both Adeptus Astartes forces and explain the situation to them. May the Emperor and the Machine-God protect all of us.' Varnus bowed and left the command centre.

'Let's get to it then,' Ragnar commanded. 'Torin, go to the Chimera and bring it to the parade grounds, where we first discovered the Dark Angels.'

'I'll go with Torin and Jeremiah, just in case,' Nathaniel said.

'Good idea,' Jeremiah agreed.

'The rest of us will proceed to the armoury to re-supply.'

'The palace armoury? We need bolter rounds not las-gun power cells,' said Elijah.

'Haegr, would you be so kind as to lead us to the armoury where the Wolfblade supplies were housed upon our arrival?'

'It would be my pleasure, Ragnar. Right this way. Fortunately we have to go right past the kitchen. One can not be expected to wage war on an empty stomach.'

Ragnar and the others prepared, re-equipping and re-arming for the journey ahead. Upon their arrival several stowage crates had been offloaded. The Wolfblade were always on the move, supporting and protecting House Belisarius's interests. Since supplies for a contingent of Space Marines were hard to come by on most worlds, the Wolfblade always brought their own. Once the team was ready they left to rendezvous with Torin and Nathaniel.

HAEGR AND ELIJAH were the last to enter the Chimera transport. Elijah moved past the rest towards the front while Haegr took the seats next to the deployment hatch. Chimeras were not designed for Space Marines, especially ones his size.

'I do not know how you expect a man to go to war when all he's had to eat are food packs,' Haegr grumbled.

Torin looked back from the driver's seat. 'What's got Haegr's blood up?'

'We stopped by the kitchen on our way here, and all he could find to eat were food packs,' Elijah said with a grin as he took the tactical seat.

Suspicion and distrust ran through Torin's mind as Elijah sat down, visions of ambush or the Chimera pulling right into a Dark Angels command post flashing in his head. Torin attempted to run a mental checklist of the troop concentrations that Varnus had depicted on the map. He hoped his memory would not fail him.

'I thought I might be able to help with the navigation through the city. I'd hate to round a corner and find we'd entered a Space Wolf command centre,' Elijah said.

'Well said, my friend, we'll keep each other honest,' Torin said with a grin.

'I would hate to have our new alliance severed because I failed in my duties,' Elijah replied with a smile.

Ragnar exchanged a quick glance with Jeremiah. Both had witnessed the exchange. Perhaps there was a chance that they would succeed. With some minor exceptions they were at least setting aside the distrust that stood between their two Chapters. If they could do it then maybe there would be a chance to bring this conflict under control once Gabriella was rescued and Cadmus was dealt with. As the Chimera rolled out Ragnar smiled a slight smile of relief. Haegr simply grunted in disgust.

THE TEAM STOOD at the entrance to the maintenance tunnel where the Dark Angels had first gained entry into Lethe. Sounds of conflict were all around them; explosions and weapons fire from different directions. During their journey several quick direction changes had been needed, but Torin and Elijah worked very well together. Ragnar was relieved that something finally seemed to be going well for them.

Elijah was the first to enter the maintenance tunnel, followed closely by Nathaniel, and then the rest of the group. Haegr was the last one in. Emergency lighting panels illuminated the dull grey rockcrete walls. Elijah moved quietly, until finally reaching the exit door. It still wore the scars from the kill team's creative lock picking techniques.

Elijah slowly opened the door and stepped into the waiting jungle, scanning the immediate surroundings. He moved slowly forwards, trying to get a clear scan. The auspex display screen distorted and blinked out for a split second and then reset and blinked out again. It was still useless.

Nathaniel stood about three metres behind Elijah, visually scanning the surrounding area.

'How does it look, Eli?' Nathaniel asked.

'Hold your position, Nathaniel, the auspex isn't functioning,' Elijah replied.

The rest of the team cautiously stepped into the jungle, fanning out along the wall. There was no kill zone. The jungle grew right up to the walls. Vines and other forms of foliage had even begun to grow up along the wall, covering it with a thick layer of greens and browns. As Ragnar and the other Space Wolves moved into position they exchanged quick glances.

'It must be the heat or the promethium still causing interference,' Elijah said, preoccupied.

Jeremiah and Nathaniel noticed a change in their Space Wolf companions. They were almost frozen in place, eyes locked on the jungle. It was as if they saw something that was not there. 'Put that contraption away Elijah,' Nathaniel ordered.

'Seems to be clea…' A red cloud rose just above Elijah's left shoulder, drizzling red mist on his armour's shoulder pad and the side of his face. The shot spun him around, causing him to lose his footing and fall.

One of their own was down, and the ragtag Adeptus Astartes group reacted instantly. Nathaniel ducked his head and ran towards his fallen comrade while the rest laid down a pattern of suppression fire at their unseen attackers. Ragnar and Jeremiah each broke to opposite flanks while Haegr and Torin stood the middle ground.

Nathaniel moved through the tangle of vines and branches that clogged the jungle floor finally reaching Elijah. He found him lying prone, face down in the dirt. Grabbing his right arm, he spun the younger Marine over onto his back. The round had managed to penetrate the armour at the lower rear section of the shoulder pad, grazing the upper arm. The wound was minor and Elijah was already climbing to his feet.

Branches erupted all around them as the enemy began to fire once again. Firing short controlled bursts they retreated back through the jungle to rejoin their companions.

Once the six Marines were together again, Ragnar activated his internal comm system.

'If we stand here we're just waiting to get shot,' Ragnar declared.

'Then what would you suggest?' Nathaniel asked.

'The best defence is always a good offence. We charge,' Ragnar answered.

'Agreed,' Jeremiah confirmed.

Ragnar slung his boltgun, drew his bolt pistol and sword, thumbed the activation rune as he'd done hundreds of times before, and dived through the dense foliage separating them from their unseen enemies. A bestial howl rose as he charged, the Wolfblade offering their own howl to the battle cry.

The six warriors crashed through the jungle on a head-on collision course. Firing blindly into the barrier of trees and brush in front of them, their swords arched through the air cleanly slicing branches away as they cut a path through the harsh foliage. Ragnar emerged from the jungle onto a path and the scent of Chaos poured into his nostrils. At least they were not facing their fellow Marines.

A ragged, feral-looking guardsman leapt from the jungle slashing wildly at Ragnar, striking the armour of his chest plate, which stopped the attack cold. The clumsy attack reminded the Space Wolf to stay focused and to keep his mind on the events of the here and now. A simple flick of his wrist and a downwards strike imbedded Ragnar's sword deep in the enemy's neck, severing the head from his body.

Members of Cadmus's elite unit of storm troopers poured from the cover of the jungle onto the Space Marines. The remnants of their once-proud uniforms hanging from their bent and twisted bodies were the only indication of who these inhuman beasts had once been. Tooth and claw, talon and horn replaced the once cherished weapons of humanity. Some still carried these weapons but they were now merged with their wielder in an unholy union of flesh and metal.

These creatures were greater in number, fierce, and showed no hint of fear, but they were incredibly outmatched. Undeterred, the storm troopers warriors swarmed over the combined members of the Wolfblade and the Dark Angels.

Haegr's weapon howled from his roundhouse swings, sending the mutated attackers sailing back into the jungle when his hammer struck home. Jeremiah made quick work of the filth surrounding him, his efficiency wasting neither time nor energy. Torin's speed and finesse with a blade allowed him to dance around his opponents, throwing them off-balance. Nathaniel and Elijah fought back-to-back encircled by attackers, using their decades of service together to combine their fighting prowess to overwhelm and confuse. Ragnar, meanwhile, used sheer ferocity to wade into the filth of Chaos.

In a matter of minutes, the Chaos-tainted troopers lay dead on the jungle floor. Ragnar knelt down next to one of the fallen warriors, wondering if this poor soul realised that his misplaced loyalty to Cadmus had led him to this end.

The acrid scent of Chaos nauseated him; the air was heavy with it. When they had first explored the jungle, a few days ago, birds and other indigenous life had been extremely active, now there was nothing. Even the buzz beetles that had constantly harassed them were no longer anywhere to be found.

The Space Marine squad followed Ragnar through the tainted jungle, ignoring the footpath. They simply made their way through the foliage, cutting and slicing through the vines and bushes. Ragnar stopped occasionally to confirm they were heading towards the temple, moving on quickly when he was reassured, for time was of the essence and caution was a luxury that they could no longer afford.

As Ragnar moved through the trees he came across a huge number of tracks, cutting a swathe through the jungle, moving directly towards Lethe. He held up his fist, signalling for the rest to stop.

'What do you have, Ragnar?' Torin asked.

'Fresh repto tracks, hundreds of them, moving towards the city,' Ragnar answered.

'Why should we be so concerned about a bunch of reptiles?' asked Haegr.

'These new forces pose a threat to both the Lion and the Wolf. A new faction is approaching the city,' Jeremiah replied.

'Exactly! The forces in Lethe must be made aware of this new development. We must contact Varnus,' Ragnar said.

SERVITORS SHUFFLED AROUND the command centre, having moved the bodies of Magni and the governor, ready to conduct the necessary repair rituals. Varnus hunched over the comms pulpit. He did not like the new information he had just received. The reptos had been causing work delays for a while on Hyades, and it would appear that they were moving in force on the city. Their objective was still unclear to him, but Ragnar was right, the Space Marines needed to know about the new threat.

The heavy steel doors of the command centre opened with a clang and five Astartes warriors entered,

their ancient armour glittering with a blue-yellow
glow. Spikes like thorns on a vine ran up the sides of
both legs. Horns erupted from the sides of their helmets, curving up and rising high above the green
glowing eye-lenses. These were not Astartes. These
were Thousand Sons Marines.

Three Traitor Marines moved to the body of the
fallen Space Wolf while the other two remained at the
entrance. It was then that Varnus noticed a sixth figure,
standing in the shadows just beyond the entrance,
revealing only a vague silhouette. Terror rose up
within the tech-priest as he faced these ancient enemies of mankind.

'Foolish son of Mars, your time is at an end,'
announced the figure at the rear of the group.

Those words were the last that Varnus would ever
hear as the melta gun superheated his body from the
inside out.

RAGNAR AND THE other Space Marines broke into the
clearing that surrounded the entrance to the temple.
The surrounding area was exactly as he remembered,
the tiered pyramid, faces leering out from the stones.
When they had first found the structure he had
wanted to enter and investigate it. Things might be
different now had he followed his instincts then, but
at the time they'd had other issues to contend with.
He would see to it that he corrected that mistake. Signalling the others, he headed in.

The entrance of the structure was primitive in
design, crudely hewed blocks of stone with mud
used for mortar. The jungle did not intrude here as it

did at the city; it was as if it had simply accepted the structure. The interior floor was hard-packed dirt. They moved through the temple, the blue-green phosphorescent glow from the foliage dimly lighting the winding corridor. Deeper and deeper into the pyramid they descended. The dim light cast shadows across the stones, exaggerating the evil faces with even more vile expressions. Ragnar took point, followed by Jeremiah and the others. Besides the sounds of the Marines walking through the corridors, there was only the sound of the wind that whispered softly.

Ragnar wondered how long the temple had stood here. Had the reptos built this place, or their ancient ancestors? And for how long had they worshipped the gods of Chaos?

As the Space Marines descended into the temple, the light started to change. Eventually, the rough, primitive, construction transformed into a smooth rockcrete corridor, and the natural phosphorescent light was replaced with glow-globes. The hard-packed dirt floor was replaced with the standard textured plasteel plating. The sudden change in the corridor caused the Marines to stop and evaluate their situation.

Torin approached Ragnar, followed closely by Jeremiah. As the three huddled in intense conversation, Haegr, Elijah and Nathaniel took a rear guard position.

'I sense that we're close,' said Ragnar.

'Yes, little brother, I sense it too, but let's not rush in,' Torin replied.

'How can you be sure? This doesn't confirm that Cadmus is here, only that at one point he could have been,' Jeremiah explained.

'You should learn to trust your instincts, Jeremiah,' Torin said.

Concluding their conversation, Ragnar turned and moved down the corridor. Jeremiah signalled Elijah to join him. Ragnar and Elijah moved down opposite sides of the corridor, the rest following behind them. The complex seemed more command centre than bunker. Until this point, the corridor had slowly descended while gently winding. Now it made a ninety-degree turn to the right. Slowly, Ragnar and Elijah approached the corner. Ragnar tested the air, but it was too thick with the ripe stench of Chaos for him to get any kind of a scent trail.

Elijah crouched on the left side of the corridor when Ragnar signalled that there were sentries of some kind around the corner. Acknowledging the information, Elijah reached for his trusted auspex. Then, remembering the attack in the jungle, he decided that his own eyes would be his most useful tools. Leaning out, he saw that the corridor extended for another five metres, ending in a set of double doors. Two storm troopers of Cadmus's elite guard stood on either side of them.

Ragnar looked first at Torin and then to Jeremiah. Both realised exactly what he was thinking. Jeremiah momentarily considered protesting, but then he recalled a ferocious Space Wolf crashing through an Administratum building, tackling him to the ground. It was that ferocity that had halted their incursion. He and Torin nodded their agreement. Ragnar signalled for the charge, grinning as he activated his sword.

Ragnar and Elijah erupted into the corridor, Ragnar's howl filling the air. Both guards were dead before they were able to turn to face their attackers. Without slowing, they crashed into the double doors. Unable to withstand the combined impact of two Space Marines, the doors gave way.

Six of the Emperor's finest warriors poured into the room. Cadmus stood in front of a door on the opposite side of the room, clutching Gabriella by her hair. 'Well, the Wolf and the Lion have joined forces, how unexpected.' The renegade commander growled in disgust, surprised and frustrated.

'It's over, Cadmus. Let her go,' Ragnar shouted.

'I've heard how persistent you can be, mongrel son of a rabid dog, but you have no idea who I am or what I've seen. It's over when I decide it is,' Cadmus said, yanking harder on Gabriella's hair.

Jeremiah slowly manoeuvred himself along the wall, trying to get himself closer to Cadmus, closer to the Fallen. This was his chance, but he would have to move quickly.

Cadmus pointed his pistol at Jeremiah. 'Stop right there, young lion.'

'It's over Cadmus! It's time for you to–' Jeremiah was interrupted as the walls on either side of the commander began to distort. Gabriella started to convulse violently. Blood flowed from her ears and nose, her muffled screams reflecting her pain and terror. Whatever was going on was tearing into her mind.

'Meet my new battle-brothers, young lion,' said Cadmus. 'Now if you will excuse me, it's time for me to depart. I'm sure the interrogator-chaplain will forgive your failure.' The commander released Gabriella and stepped through the door. Suddenly, six Thousand Sons stepped out of the distortion into the room. Unlike the Space Wolves, their armour was not adorned with personal trophies or remembrances from previous battles, the eye of Tzeentch emblazoned across their chest was the only indication of their allegiance. The Chaos Marines stood like a wall between the Space Marines and their quarry.

Ragnar knew instantly that the real masterminds had finally revealed themselves. With a savage howl, he threw himself at the Thousand Sons.

TWELVE
The Real Enemy

CADMUS WAS FURIOUS. The Wolfblade were an enigma. His plan had been perfect; he never made mistakes. When the Space Wolves arrived on their patrol to discover the Dark Angels invasion force, war broke out. The Dark Angels kill team should have joined them in the fight, leaving Ragnar and the other Wolfblade to rescue Gabriella and meet their doom. They should not be working together: the Space Wolves hated the Dark Angels. Apparently, Ragnar was as troublesome as Madox said. He would think on this later, but for now he needed to make his escape.

He reached the back wall, and sliding his hand down along its surface, activated a hidden panel that slid up, revealing a keyed access pad. He entered a pass code.

The panel buzzed its rejection. Cadmus quickly re-entered the code, only for it to be rejected again. He entered the code a third time, this time taking even more care to ensure that he was entering it correctly. Again, the panel buzzed its refusal.

'Running to hide again, Fallen?' The voice seemed to emanate from the walls themselves. Cadmus spun around to see a figure in the corner of the room.

It was Madox, his blue and gold armour shimmering slightly with mystical energies. Spiral horns curved up from his helmet and green light emanated from his eyes. In his right hand he clutched a staff tipped with a glowing orb.

Madox stepped lightly from the shadows.

'I sent the assistance you requested from me, Cadmus, and now you leave my warriors as you left your own battle-brothers all those centuries ago.'

'You don't expect me to believe that you're concerned about a few of your followers do you, Madox?' Cadmus asked, while turning back to the access panel.

'No, you are right. I've been waiting here for you Cadmus,' Madox said.

Again Cadmus tried the access panel, and again it failed to respond. He smashed his fist into the wall in anger.

'The panel no longer works, Cadmus, I've had it disabled,' Madox said.

'I've kept my part of the bargain! I lured the Dark Angels to Hyades! I've orchestrated a war between them and the Space Wolves, and I've even brought the Wolfblade here, as you wanted. Why are you blocking my escape?'

Madox's maniacal chuckle filled the chamber. 'Because Ragnar still lives and as far as you're concerned, I have no further need of you.'

'But we had a bargain! I set all this in motion. You seem to forget, Madox, that without me none of this would have been possible,' Cadmus said, his voice quaking with anger.

'Are you really so naïve that you actually think this all came about because of you? You really believe that all of this was part of your design?' Madox asked.

Cadmus filled with rage. Had he really been a pawn to Chaos? Was he really that easy to manipulate and deceive? He searched his memory for any sign, any clue that he had not been in control of any of it. Drawing his plasma pistol, he stepped towards Madox.

'So, you see the truth of it,' Madox gloated.

'I'm going to kill you,' said Cadmus. Raising his plasma pistol, he pulled the trigger.

'You are truly naïve,' Madox's laughter filled the room as he vanished.

CADMUS'S DEPARTURE LEFT Ragnar and the others squared off with the Thousand Sons. Gabriella lay unconscious on the floor at the back of the room. Crates, boxes and furniture lay strewn around. The Thousand Sons were not noted for their outstanding prowess in hand-to-hand combat, approaching a battle slowly and purposefully, laying down a hail of bolter fire, giving their sorcerers time to win the day. Ragnar guessed the Thousand Sons were merely a delaying tactic to buy the commander time to escape.

With a battle howl, Ragnar and the rest of the team leapt at the Chaos Marines.

Fire sparked off combat weapons as the two sides clashed. Deflecting an attack with his sword, Ragnar crashed into one of the Thousand Sons, driving his shoulder deep into his opponent's abdomen. He had faced this menace before and although not known for their hand-to-hand fighting skill they were stalwart warriors, able to withstand a tremendous amount of damage. As the Thousand Son stepped forwards, Ragnar leapt, stepping on one of the plasteel crates elevating himself above the Chaos Marine. Wedging the point of his sword where his opponent's helmet and neck armour met, he drove it straight down. The Thousand Son buckled and collapsed to the floor and the energy holding him together was released.

Haegr swung his hammer in an upper cut stroke bringing his target off his feet, and dumping him on the ground with a thundering crash. Raising his weapon over his head, he delivered a crushing blow. The helmet of the Thousand Son exploded into hundreds of pieces. The ancient dust that was once the physical form of the Marine poured out onto the rock-crete floor.

Jeremiah bolted for the door that Cadmus had left through moments ago. A Thousand Sons Marine stepped in his path. His chainsword ripped across his chest plate, the force of the attack sending Jeremiah stumbling backwards.

Although quickly regaining his footing, his opponent pressed his advantage, forcing the Dark Angel to retreat, deflecting blow after blow from the Chaos chainsword. The Thousand Son brought his bolt pistol around. Seeing this, Jeremiah deflected the weapon, but this left him exposed, a mistake that was soon exploited as the chainsword crashed down into his shoulder, driving him to his knees.

The Chaos Marine knew he had the advantage and intended to bring the fight to a quick end. As the killing blow came down, Jeremiah reached up, grabbing his opponent's hand, while jabbing his own pistol into his enemy's midsection, firing several rounds. The hollow, lifeless armour fell to the floor.

Torin found himself backed against the wall as one of the Chaos Marines closed on him. Ragnar had warned him that the Thousand Sons were slow, but he didn't think the assessment was entirely accurate. He ducked his head as a chainsword dug into the rock-crete wall. It was the mistake he had been waiting for. Swinging his sword up and around, he sliced clean through his opponent's armour, sending the chainsword and arm greave clanging to the floor. Using the momentum of his attack, Torin tucked into a shoulder roll which brought him up beside and just behind his opponent.

Spinning his sword in his hand, inverting his grip and placing his other hand over the pommel, he spun around, sinking his sword into the joint at the waist of the Chaos Marine's armour. He continued his spin and the sword ripped through the entire side, cleaving the Thousand Son in two.

Nathaniel eliminated his adversary quickly and turned to assist Elijah. As he ran to the aid of his young battle-brother, a Chaos Marine helmet bounced across the floor past him. The Traitor that was facing Elijah slumped to its knees and then collapsed to the floor.

Within a few moments, the empty armour of six Thousand Sons Marines lay inactive and crumpled on the floor of Cadmus's command centre.

Haegr stood at the side of the room, picking up a chest plate, bewildered by the fact that it was empty. Torin, Jeremiah and the other Dark Angels checked the room ensuring that they were safe.

Ragnar leapt to Gabriella's side, removing her gag and bonds. 'Gabriella, are you all right?' he asked.

The Navigator was barely conscious and felt so fragile, nothing like the person he knew. Her face was bruised and swollen. Red stripes of dried blood curved down the side of her face from the corner of her right eye. Fresh blood pooled in her ears.

Slowly, she opened her eyes, but it took her some time to focus properly. 'Ragnar, is Magni alive?' Gabriella asked.

'Do not worry about that now, my lady. We must get you to safety,' said Ragnar, his voice reflecting his concern.

Gabriella started to wipe the blood away from her face, and Ragnar could tell that her faculties were returning. In her eyes he saw the grim determination and confidence that she had always possessed. She looked at Ragnar. 'You must stop Cadmus,' she demanded.

'Once you are safely away from here, my lady. We must get you out,' Ragnar argued.

Gabriella grasped the edge of Ragnar's armour and pulled herself up to a sitting position. 'I will be fine.

Cadmus must be stopped,' she said again, only this time Ragnar knew it was not the request of a delirious woman, but the request of a member of House Belisarius. Gently placing her against the wall, he stood. He was a warrior of the Astartes, a Son of Russ, and he knew what had to be done.

'Torin, see to her wounds. Haegr, cover the door,' Ragnar commanded.

Jeremiah and Nathaniel crossed the room to join Ragnar. Together, the three Space Marines went through the door Cadmus had left by.

As they entered the room beyond they found Cadmus, weapon in hand, staring blankly at a blazing blue-green fire in the corner. He seemed oblivious to the Space Marines' presence. Ragnar took in the Chaos markings that adorned the floor and walls of the room as well as various racks of arcane-looking weapons.

When he saw Jeremiah, Cadmus broke out in laughter.

There was really nothing more for Ragnar to do except honour his oath to Jeremiah. Gabriella was safe with the Wolfblade; his duty was to bring this conflict between the Space Wolves and Dark Angels to an end. 'It's over Jeremiah,' he said. 'I honour my oath to you. Cadmus is yours.'

'Ragnar, I have a message for you from an old acquaintance of yours,' Cadmus said.

'Silence, heretic,' Nathaniel shouted, striking the commander across the face.

Cadmus was defeated, his plan thwarted. What message could he possible have, Ragnar asked himself? He knew better than to listen to the final pleas of a condemned traitor. However, he was still unaware of what Cadmus's true objectives were.

'What could you possibly have to say that I would want to hear, Cadmus?' Ragnar asked.

'I know why you were sent to Terra, and I know of your failure. I know you were sent to the Wolfblade in disgrace for losing the Spear of Russ,' Cadmus said, speaking quietly and with precision.

Jeremiah and Nathaniel exchanged quick glances, unsure of what to make of this information. Jeremiah began to grow concerned. He knew what Cadmus was trying to do. He was trying to divide them, trying to use this information to create a rift between the allies.

'You speak in vague generalities hoping to sound as if you know more than you really do. You speak as someone who is about to be brought to justice and scrambles to find a way out,' Ragnar said.

'That may be, Wolfblade, but I digress; as I said, I have a message for you from and old friend. Madox sends his greetings,' Cadmus said.

Ragnar failed to hide his surprise. He had spoken of the Spear many times while on Hyades. Cadmus's surveillance equipment could have provided him with that information about the Spear of Russ, but how would he know its true name? Logic and reason told him that this was another of Cadmus's attempts to manipulate the situation in his favour, to fracture the fragile alliance between the Space Wolves and the Dark Angels. He needed to proceed carefully.

'How do you know that name?' Ragnar growled.

'As I said, boy, I have much information, but all of it comes at a price.' Confidence grew in Cadmus's voice.

'Ragnar, don't listen to him,' said Jeremiah. 'He is a heretic, a pawn of the Dark Ones.'

'Don't interfere, Dark Angel! Or perhaps you'd like me to discuss other issues. Issues of a more personal nature, perhaps,' Cadmus threatened.

'As I said, Cadmus, how do you know that name,' Ragnar asked again.

'A price Ragnar. You should know that all information has its cost,' Cadmus said, almost gloating.

'Name it, then,' Ragnar demanded.

'A trifle really, not much at all. I just want my life,' said Cadmus, all the fear gone from his voice.

'Tell me what I want to know and your life will be yours,' Ragnar said.

'Ragnar, you swore an oath! Is this how a Son of Russ keeps his word?' Jeremiah asked, stunned.

Ragnar saw the betrayal Jeremiah felt in his eyes and understood his anger. He had given his oath that Cadmus would be his to deal with as he saw fit, but this was a new development. He had to know how Madox fit in to this. Ragnar remembered his first encounter with the Chaos sorcerer. He had never known true evil until that day and never truly understood the scope of the danger that Chaos represented to the Imperium.

The learning machine had taught him of the nature of Chaos and shown him many battles between the forces of the Imperium and Chaos. However, being told what evil is and experiencing it first hand were entirely different. Madox hated everything about the Space Wolves and the Imperium. If he was involved, then everything that had transpired on Hyades had little or nothing to do with House Belisarius, Hyades or its promethium mines. Was that information more important than his oath or his honour?

'If Madox is here then it is imperative that we have all the information, Jeremiah.'

'Ragnar, we had an agreement! I trusted you,' said Jeremiah.

'Then continue to trust me, Jeremiah,' said Ragnar. 'You do not know what Madox is capable of. We must have answers.'

He looked to Jeremiah and then to Nathaniel, trying to determine their course of action. He did not want a conflict with them, since they had earned his respect several times over, but he would have the answers, above all else he would have them.

'Get on with it, Cadmus! What does Madox have to do with what's going on here?' Ragnar demanded.

'He wants you dead, wolf, and once you are dead he intends to destroy the rest of Russ's sons,' Cadmus explained.

'How does he intend to do that and what does Hyades have to do with all this?' Ragnar asked, a growl rising in his voice.

'Hyades is merely a battlefield. He wanted to spark conflict between the Lion and the Wolf. This would give him access to one of the two components he would need, the sacred gene-seed,' Cadmus continued.

'Gene-seed!' The three Marines were horrified. The future of every Chapter of Marines rested in the gene-seed. The most sacred of all things: without it each Chapter would eventually diminish and become extinct.

'I see that got your attention.' Cadmus's voice lowered to a sinister growl.

'You mentioned two components. What's the second?' Ragnar demanded.

Madox hesitated. 'Some kind of ancient relic, a weapon or a device. It was imperative that he have both of these components for the ritual. That much I am sure of,' Cadmus answered.

Ragnar's mind raced back to the day when he had lost the sacred Spear. He saw himself wielding the most cherished of his Chapter's relics. In painstakingly vivid recollection, he witnessed himself throwing the Spear into the portal, striking the giant, one-eyed primarch of the Thousand Sons. Ragnar had forced the evil primarch back into the warp, saving his battle-brothers, but forever losing the Spear! Could Madox have found it? If so, then his failure was even greater than he had thought.

'What artifact is it, and does he have it?' Ragnar asked.

'I'm not sure if he actually has possession of the bauble. If not, I am fairly certain that he knows where to find it,' Cadmus answered with a devious smile, enjoying the effect his words were having on Ragnar.

'So you started this conflict to give Madox access to the gene-seed for use with this unknown artefact for some sort of ritual. To what end?' Ragnar asked.

'A ritual that he is confident will bring about the destruction of the Sons of Russ,' Cadmus explained.

'But why involve the Wolfblade?' Jeremiah asked.

Cadmus pointed at Ragnar. 'Oh, it's not the Wolf-blade he's after, It's Ragnar,' Cadmus replied. 'I told you all I am prepared to. Now it's time for me to leave.'

'Very well, Cadmus, you've kept your word and I in turn will keep mine,' Ragnar said.

Ragnar crossed the room as if clearing the way for Cadmus's departure. Nathaniel and Jeremiah closed ranks, blocking his exit. Jeremiah looked anxiously towards Ragnar, longing to trust his oath. Cadmus stopped, looking puzzled, wondering why he was not being allowed to leave. He looked over his shoulder in Ragnar's direction. 'I've told you all I know. Anything else you will have to find out yourself. You gave me your word that I would be able to leave.'

'Ragnar, I cannot allow him to leave! He has unfinished business with the Dark Angels,' Jeremiah said, controlling his tone, but not his intentions.

'Jeremiah, I gave him my word,' said Ragnar stopping in front of one of the weapons racks on the opposite wall.

'You are not bound to keep your word when it is given to a traitor such as this,' Nathaniel said, compelled to voice his opinion.

'If that were the case then you would be no different than those you call enemies,' Cadmus said.

'Loyal servants of the Emperor cannot choose. They must honour their oaths and follow their masters regardless of the path. I know this better than anyone, and so do you, Son of the Lion,' Cadmus said, sorrow and regret apparent in his words.

'Cadmus is correct, Jeremiah. I have given him my oath. I cannot break my word, just as I am bound to honour my oath to you,' Ragnar said.

'They are in conflict Ragnar,' said Jeremiah.

'Yes, Wolfblade, they would appear to be in conflict,' Cadmus said, spitting the words out like poison.

'Actually, they are not in conflict at all. Jeremiah, I swore to you that Cadmus would be yours to deal with once we had rescued Gabriella,' Ragnar said calmly.

'Yes, and you gave me your word that if I helped you, I'd be free to go,' said Cadmus, the words almost dancing from his lips. He was growing impatient.

'That's not entirely correct,' Ragnar said, pulling a chainsword from the wall. 'I promised you that your life would be yours, and it is.' Ragnar tossed the chainsword to the ground at Cadmus's feet. 'I suggest that you defend it.' Ragnar crossed back across the room past Cadmus, and stopped next to Jeremiah, placing a hand on his shoulder.

'He is yours to do with as you see fit. I'm sure that you will do the right thing,' Ragnar said, before turning and leaving the room.

Jeremiah turned his full attention to Cadmus, who was kneeling to retrieve the sword. For a moment there was fear in his eyes: the fear that someone feels when justice is finally served on them after a lifetime of betrayal. This caused a smile to cross Jeremiah's face. His original mission was to deliver the Fallen to the interrogator-chaplain, but Jeremiah knew that path was no longer possible. Cadmus had lured his battle-brothers, Dark Angel and Space Wolf alike, to their deaths, sacrificing his men to further his own means. Redemption was not possible for the likes of Cadmus. Right or wrong, this was the path that Jeremiah was on.

Drawing his sword, Jeremiah swore to himself that he would see Cadmus dead whatever the consequences.

'So, this is how I will meet my end, killed by the Emperor's lapdogs, on this backwater world, left to rot in this forgotten dungeon.' Scorn dripped from Cadmus's voice as he prepared himself for combat.

'Too good an end for the likes of you,' Nathaniel declared, drawing his sword.

'No, Nathaniel. Leave the room,' ordered Jeremiah. 'Trust me in this. If I fall, keep him from running like the coward that he is.'

Nathaniel wanted to protest but he knew better. He would honour Jeremiah's last order regardless of the price. He nodded, then left the room. He had served with Jeremiah for many years and had unwavering confidence in his skills.

'So, Jeremiah, you intend this to be a single combat: you and I to the death?' Cadmus inquired.

'Absolutely, you and I, single combat, to the death,' Jeremiah answered.

'You know you don't stand a chance. I walked the stars when the Lion himself commanded the legion. I was there when Caliban cracked. Even without my armour you are no match for me.' Cadmus said, gloating.

'You will not leave here victorious, Cadmus, but should I fall this day you will be able to leave here unhindered. My brethren will honour my word in this,' Jeremiah commanded.

Jeremiah knew what he had to do, but Cadmus was right about one thing: he had centuries more experience. Jeremiah would not falter, he couldn't; this evil must be stopped. His faith and determination were all he had. He knew that would be enough.

Jeremiah and Cadmus circled each other in the centre of the chamber. The Dark Angel's heart filled with rage. All he had witnessed on Hyades, all the atrocities were the work of one man, but more than that it was the work of one of the Fallen. The Dark Angels had been paying for the betrayal of the Fallen since the Horus Heresy, and even though Jeremiah was responsible for bringing several members of the Fallen before the interrogator-chaplains, he had never witnessed the corruption of one of the Fallen so closely before.

'You can't beat me, young lion. You haven't got the skills or the experience,' Cadmus said.

'Your arrogance astounds me, Cadmus. You have turned your back on everything you once stood for, on everything you once held dear. Your fate was sealed the moment you stepped foot on Hyades. Neither my skills nor experience will have much effect on the outcome. Your own actions have determined your fate. I am just an instrument of redemption,' Jeremiah said, speaking from his heart.

Cadmus and Jeremiah slowly circled each other around the centre of the chamber. Both warriors were looking for an opening, a sign of weakness that they could exploit. Suddenly, Cadmus swung his sword in an arcing downwards stroke. Jeremiah parried, and then countered. A quick exchange of attacks and parries were exchanged, each combatant measuring the other's skills.

'You speak of betrayal? You speak of things you know nothing about. Should I tell you of betrayal, should I speak to you of turning your back on your brothers,' Cadmus said, goading his opponent.

Jeremiah knew that Cadmus was trying unbalance him and force him to make a mistake. He knew that he must not listen, must not allow himself the luxury of an emotional response. He would not allow himself to be distracted by mere words.

Jeremiah lunged, striking low, trying to catch Cadmus off-guard. Cadmus easily parried the attack, and then turned his parry into an offensive strike at Jeremiah's midsection. He was barely able to parry the attack without putting himself off balance, a fact that Cadmus quickly exploited, as an armoured gauntlet struck Jeremiah squarely in the mouth, knocking him to the ground. Cadmus did not press his advantage, stopping his attack instead to allow Jeremiah to rise to his feet.

Blood trickled from Jeremiah's nose, which he quickly wiped away. 'Keep your lies to yourself Fallen. We are well aware of your treachery. We all bear the burden of your actions. We are the unforgiven, Cadmus, unforgiven for your cowardly actions and for the actions of the rest of the Fallen. It is a burden we will continue to bear until you and all those like you are redeemed.'

Cadmus leapt towards Jeremiah. Their swords clashed and locked at the hilt. The Fallen leaned in, bringing himself face to face with Jeremiah. 'You spit out words like the programmed fool you are, regurgitating the propaganda that the real betrayers of Caliban concocted. We did not betray the Imperium. We did not allow the Emperor to perish,' Cadmus said, his voice full of rage.

Jeremiah had heard all he could take. 'You may not have thought you were a traitor then, Cadmus, but the seeds of treachery can take a long time to take root. You've given in to Chaos. You've abandoned everything, just as your newfound allies have abandoned you. We hunt the Fallen in an attempt to allow them a chance for redemption. You are no longer a Dark Angel. You're not even one of the Fallen any more. You are nothing more than a pawn that Chaos used to lure a disgraced Space Wolf into a trap. You are pathetic. You are beyond redemption and I will hear no more of your lies!'

Jeremiah pushed Cadmus away, allowing his rage to control his actions. He brought his sword around as he spun, an easy parry for the older warrior. However, Jeremiah attacked anew, with blinding speed and fury. Not allowing Cadmus a moment's respite, each attack came quicker and stronger than the last. The Fallen was giving ground, backing up, unable to ward off the flurry of attacks being thrown out by the young Son of the Lion.

Cadmus's footing finally gave way and he fell to one knee, barely able to parry the latest blow, which knocked him off-balance. Jeremiah spun around, thrusting the sword through the abdomen of the Fallen Dark Angel. Blood erupted from Cadmus's mouth.

Jeremiah bent down to stare into the eyes of his adversary, mimicking the Fallen's last offensive move.

'Your time is at an end, betrayer. Confess your sins and be redeemed,' he spat.

'I will confess nothing,' Cadmus said, coughing up blood.

'The betrayal was not mine but that was your beloved primar...' The Fallen's final words would never be heard as Jeremiah's sword tore up through his chest plate, ending Cadmus's life.

THIRTEEN
An Uneasy Peace

THE TWO GROUPS OF Space Marines stood at opposite sides of Cadmus's secret bunker. Both had private reports to make to their superiors and had respectfully stepped away from each other. Since both teams had comms in their helmets that they could use to sub-vocalise, the physical separation was more a matter of propriety than practicality. Gabriella sat on the floor near the Space Wolves, rubbing her wrists where her bonds had cut her flesh. Her ordeal had obviously exhausted her, and she seemed focused on recovering her strength.

'Interrogator-Chaplain Vargas, this is Captain Jeremiah of Kill Team Lion's Pride. The threat was eliminated. Our mission has been accomplished,' Jeremiah said, hoping that the signal would reach the Dark Angels battle-barge far above the planet. The static seemed to have died down on the comms.

Nathaniel and Elijah flanked Jeremiah, waiting for the response and watching their Space Wolf counterparts. The mission was over. All that remained for them to do was to protect their secret.

With one eye on the Dark Angels, Ragnar also made contact with his superior. 'Wolf Lord Berek Thunderfist, this is Ragnar of the Wolfblade. The Dark Angels have completed their mission here and will be leaving soon. There is no reason to continue your attack.'

Torin and Haegr stood quietly, weapons at the ready. The tension hung thick in the air. Both sets of Space Marines hoped that the fighting would end.

Jeremiah moved further away, hoping that he would be far enough from the Space Wolves to avoid being overheard. He didn't want to reveal his Chapter's secrets to their most intense rivals, no matter how honourable they were individually.

'Captain Jeremiah, is the heretic dead?' asked Interrogator-Chaplain Vargas, his voice ringing cold and metallic.

'Yes, my lord.'

'Do you have possession of his remains?' asked Vargas.

'We do, yes.'

'Activate your beacon. A retrieval team will come for you,' ordered Vargas.

'Interrogator-chaplain, may I boldly suggest that we break off the conflict with the Space Wolves?' asked Jeremiah.

'You overextend yourself, captain,' replied Vargas.

The conversation between the Wolfblade and the Wolf lord fared no better.

'Young Ragnar, it is good to hear you.' The booming voice of Berek Thunderfist came over the comm. 'Aye, the battle is nearly over, and we will have these traitors and hang their suits of green armour in the Fang as trophies. Bring about the guns again! Blow them into space, lads!'

Ragnar cringed. He had heard that tone in the Wolf Lord's voice before when he had stood shoulder to shoulder with Berek in battle against Chaos Space Marines. He knew what kind of warrior the Wolf Lord was: he lived for battle, and would never stand down.

'Lord Berek, the commander of the PDF forces was a traitor. Chaos has infested this planet. The Dark Angels only attacked to eliminate that threat. We need to stop the fighting. There's no reason for either side to continue this battle.'

'Ragnar, you know that I wish you were still one of my lads instead of a member of the Wolfblade, but I hope your time on Terra hasn't made you soft,' replied Berek. 'The Dark Angels are still firing, and I'll suffer in the frozen hells of Fenris before I drop my shields or let up, so you had better get them to stop first.'

'I understand,' said Ragnar turning off his comm. He looked over to the Dark Angels, to see if the sensitive part of their conversation was over. Jeremiah nodded and waved Ragnar over, even as Jeremiah continued his conversation.

'Interrogator-chaplain, please hear me out,' said Jeremiah, looking at Ragnar. He knew that Ragnar could not stop the Space Wolves, and in truth, Jeremiah knew that the Wolves were merely defending their territory, no matter how things had escalated. He hoped that the next words he spoke would be inspired by the Lion himself.

'We are in possession of the target, his comm, and his bunker. We have all of his information secure but only because a group of Space Wolves have agreed to a truce with us. If we do not cease hostilities and agree to open negotiations, we will come into conflict with them,' Jeremiah said. Then he looked at Ragnar and added, 'The target put up a hard fight, and we will not be able to hold against the Space Wolves. When we fall, they will have possession of all our target's secrets,' he stated aloud for the benefit of the Space Wolves.

Static crackled over the comm. The Dark Angels and Space Wolves fell silent, waiting for the interrogator-chaplain's response. Ragnar could feel the apprehension as everyone waited for the reply. The only sound came from one of the infernal beetles, floating in the air, oblivious to the moment.

Elijah grabbed the insect in mid-flight and crushed it in his gauntlet. Despite themselves, the six Space Marines grinned.

'It is my decision, Captain Jeremiah of Kill Team Lion's Pride, that we open negotiations. Such an action will be to our advantage. Maintain your truce. Recover what you need. The Lion watches over you.' The metallic voice of Interrogator-Chaplain Vargas made the last blessing sound far more like a threat.

Torin sub-vocalised over his comm to Ragnar. 'Are you sure about leaving this bunker in possession of the Dark Angels?'

Ragnar nodded ever so slightly. He knew Torin would see the answer. They had Gabriella. She was more important than whatever secrets Cadmus held. Besides, Ragnar was sure that Jeremiah would not end his quest against Chaos. To Ragnar's surprise, he trusted the Dark Angels to ceaselessly battle their mutual enemies. Jeremiah wouldn't give up, any more than Ragnar would.

'Our duty is to protect Lady Gabriella. Jeremiah, I trust you and your battle-brothers will take care of this bunker and of Cadmus,' said Ragnar.

Jeremiah looked Ragnar in the eye. So much had happened between them in such a short time. 'You have my respect, Ragnar of the Wolfblade. You and your brothers are men of honour,' he said.

Ragnar nodded. Saying nothing, he, Torin and Haegr turned and left. Ragnar offered Gabriella his arm for support, but she shook her head.

'I can walk, Ragnar,' she said, favouring him with a weak smile.

'My lady, this bunker is out in the jungle, and you might do well to conserve your strength until we've returned to the city,' he offered.

'Very well, you may assist me,' she said, regaining the tone of authority.

The Space Wolves paused to wordlessly exchange salutes with the Dark Angels, although Gabriella did not acknowledge their recent allies. Jeremiah and his men said nothing, and began their search of the bunker for any information left by Cadmus.

'Come! There are lizard-ape creatures that mighty Haegr wishes to add to his legend,' Haegr said, raising his hammer. 'Follow me,' he bellowed and led the way out of Cadmus's secret base.

* * *

INSIDE LETHE, THE battle continued. About halfway between the city centre and the outer walls, Mikal and the Wolf Guard had encountered a squad of Dark Angels. The Dark Angels' weapons were covered in blood and gore, evidence of the many men they had slaughtered since the assault had begun.

Mikal roared as he and the other Wolf Guard fired into the Dark Angels. Seven of their enemy fell as bolter rounds smashed into their ranks. They weren't dead yet, as Space Marines could survive extreme amounts of damage, but they were out of the action. The three remaining Dark Angels reached the ranks of the Wolf Guard, swinging their chainswords and firing their bolt pistols. Mikal licked his fangs. Like most Space Wolves, he preferred dealing with his enemy in hand-to-hand combat.

Chainsword struck ceramite as a Dark Angel thrust at Mikal. The Wolf Guard swung his power fist into the helm of his attacker, disregarding the chainsword strike, trusting that his armour would hold. It did, and the power fist made short work of his opponent's helm.

A shrill cry cut through the air, followed by hissing from all directions. Mikal caught movement in his peripheral vision. New attackers swarmed the Space Marines. Large reptilian humanoids leapt from buildings and rushed into the warriors from all sides.

These new foes stood as tall as the Space Marines. Grey-green scales covered their bodies along with tufts of green, brown and red fur. Their large eyes were yellow with diamond-shaped black pupils. Long fangs and sharp teeth filled their jaws, although they moved more like primates than lizards. Many of them had strange warpaint in red and purple streaked across their bodies. Fearlessly, they launched themselves at the Space Marines.

The attack startled the Wolf Guard, but it did not deter them. No matter the foe, they would fight for their Chapter and the Emperor. If these creatures did not already know enough to fear the Space Wolves, then by the end of the day they would.

Serrated jaws clamped on Mikal's arms, although they had less of an impact than the chainsword had moments before. Mikal threw the creature aside, and blew the guts out of another with his storm bolter. In their power armour, the Space Wolves were nearly impervious to the creatures' blows, but the sheer weight of the attackers' numbers threatened to drag Mikal and the Wolf Guard down.

Mikal redoubled his efforts, giving the wulfen its head and letting the anger and fury within his breast guide him. He was a berserker, slashing and smashing his foes. Mikal tore through tails and teeth, heads and hearts, pushing himself to the limits to overcome his enemies.

The Wolf Guard were hard-pressed. Mikal saw his men pulled down under the horde of aliens to his left and right. They still moved in their armour and he had every hope that they still lived, but the tide of beasts was too much. They could not hold.

The ground shook violently. Mikal didn't notice at first, thinking that it was more explosions. Then screeching started from the horde of creatures. Several hissed and turned to face something down the street.

A large shadow blocked out the sun and one of the beasts fighting Mikal unlocked its jaws and leapt away.

A giant metal claw flung the bodies of three lizard creatures skyward against the smoke- and flame-filled heavens. Mikal felt his blood boil with pride. The shadow belonged to a massive venerable Dreadnought. Towering over the enemy, Gymir the Ice-Fisted reached down to slay them in massive swathes. The mighty Dreadnought had come to the aid of his fellow Space Wolves.

'Die, xenos scum! Face the fury of Fenris,' Gymir boomed through his array of speakers.

Gymir continued to wield his power claw like a scythe, moving it back and forth, and cutting down the creatures in a gory harvest. Bones snapped as the Dreadnought unleashed his might against the beasts. The mere presence of the ancient machine shook the aliens, who stared and hissed at the machine in fear, frustration and rage. Ultimately, fear won out over the other emotions, and the surviving lizards broke off their attack and scattered in all directions. Gymir stood, surrounded by mounds of bodies, looking for more of the creatures to fight. Finding none, he turned with a whirr to face Mikal.

'Are you well, my brothers?' asked Gymir.

'Aye,' answered Mikal.

As the Wolf Guard clambered to their feet and re-formed, Mikal noticed something unusual. The bodies of the Dark Angels lay shredded. Mikal walked over and knelt down beside the body of one of the fallen Marines.

During the attack, some of the creatures had opened up the Space Marine's power armour and dug their claws into his flesh. Mikal felt a chill run through him. Chunks had been dug out of the Dark Angel. Organs had been removed, including the Marine's gene-seed. He checked the other bodies; all of them showed the same signs. The beasts had been collecting the gene-seed of the Emperor's finest.

Mikal looked over at the Wolf Guard and then up to Gymir. 'The creatures stole the Dark Angels' gene-seed,' he roared.

Mikal's comm crackled to life. 'Wolf Guard Mikal, this is Lieutenant Markham. We have reptos entering the city in untold numbers.'

ABOVE THE PLANET, the *Fist of Russ* hung in space and for the moment her guns lay silent. The Dark Angels' fleet backed away from the Space Wolves' ships while Thunderhawks from the planet below docked with their parent vessels.

From his bridge, sitting in his stone command chair, Wolf Lord Berek Thunderfist could not believe his eyes. The battle runes indicated the Dark Angels' retreat, as did the holographic projections of the battle. The Dark Angels were breaking off their attack. The ship's herald called to him, 'M'lord, we are receiving hails from the Dark Angels' battle-barge.'

Berek waited for a moment. He couldn't believe that Ragnar had negotiated something like this. He knew that the young lad had courage to spare and a zeal for battle, but Ragnar wasn't a diplomat unless his time with the Wolfblade had changed him quite a bit.

The Wolf Lord's men held their posts, waiting for orders. They would follow Berek into the Eye of Terror itself if he so commanded. The Wolf Lord stood up. 'Herald, accept the transmission from the Dark Angels.'

The herald touched a rune and two of the carved wolfs' heads opened their jaws to reveal hidden speakers.

A cold metallic voice came over the speaker. 'Space Wolf commander, this is Interrogator-Chaplain Vargas of the *Vinco Redemptor*. We are withdrawing our forces from your planet. We trust that you have the strength to keep Chaos in check, now that you are here in numbers. We have stopped our assaults on your vessels, but be assured, we will defend ourselves if you do not break off your attack immediately.'

Berek cleared his throat and took the comms console. The ship's herald stepped back. 'This is Wolf Lord Berek Thunderfist, interrogator-chaplain. I'm sure you realise that I'm familiar with your Chapter's history of treachery and duplicity.'

'Just as we are familiar with your reputation as ignorant barbarians,' replied Vargas.

'Good,' said Berek baring his fangs. 'Since we understand one another, you are retreating, and you are asking us not to fire upon you. I can understand that, since we've nearly crippled your precious battle-barge and bled you white on the surface. We will stand down. After all, I don't want to leave the Imperium without one of its Chapters of Space Marines, even the Dark Angels, but my men might like to hear you announcing your retreat.'

'I will not rise to your bait, Space Wolf. We will only fire if fired upon. We have accomplished our purpose.

The rest of the mess is yours, Wolf Lord. I also do not wish to leave mankind without several of its defenders, even when they've let their territory be infiltrated by Chaos.'

'Good, so you are retreating,' said Berek.

'We will withdraw once we have retrieved all of our men from the surface,' answered Interrogator-Chaplain Vargas.

The battle in space was over.

THE MEMBERS OF the Wolfblade made their way through Hyades's jungles back towards the city. Ragnar supported Gabriella, while he, Torin and Haegr kept up as fast a pace as they could. Choker vines lashed out at them, and they splattered through swarms of buzzing beetles.

One of the trees tried to trip up Haegr with its roots. The giant Space Wolf swung his hammer around and smashed through the living wood. The entire tree shuddered. 'And don't try that again,' Haegr warned it.

When Torin, Haegr and Ragnar burst from the jungle into the kill zone, several columns of smoke and clouds of dust greeted them. Mounds of broken rockcrete marred the once invincible walls of Lethe. One of the gates hung open. Thunderous explosions echoed from the city. The battle hadn't ended yet.

'We've made it to the city. Now we just need to get through the fighting to the palace and find a shuttle,' said Gabriella. She still looked tired, but she had regained her air of command.

Ragnar's comm crackled to life. 'This is Wolf Lord Berek Thunderfist. Ragnar, lad, if you're out there, answer.'

'This is Ragnar. Have the Dark Angels retreated?' Ragnar was curious since the explosions hadn't stopped.

'They are retreating. I'm impressed, young one. Only one thing prevents us from removing the Dark Angels. The Hyades defence forces keep firing on them. The governor doesn't answer his comm, and well, I know about the commander. Where is Lady Gabriella? Aren't you her bodyguard? I need someone to order the planetary defenders to stand down against the Dark Angels,' the Wolf Lord chuckled. 'Mikal went out onto the battlefield, but I'm having trouble raising him. Do you have Lady Gabriella?'

'Yes, Wolf Lord. She is here with us,' Ragnar replied.

'Wolf Lord Berek Thunderfist is on the comm. He asks you to order the Hyades planetary defence force to stand down against the Dark Angels,' said Ragnar.

Gabriella leaned over to speak into the comm system. 'This is Lady Gabriella of House Belisarius, Wolf Lord Berek Thunderfist. I will immediately give the order to cease hostilities against the Dark Angels.'

'Good to hear your voice, my lady,' said the Wolf Lord. 'We're still ready to defend House Belisarius. I understand that you have a xenos problem on the ground, but I think it's time to start by removing the Dark Angels.'

'House Belisarius will not keep them here. I'm giving the orders now.'

'Aye. Berek Thunderfist, out,' responded the Wolf Lord.

Gabriella adjusted the comm codes. 'Hyades planetary defence forces, this is Lady Gabriella of House

Belisarius. You are ordered to cease hostilities against the invading Dark Angels. They have agreed to withdraw. The Space Wolves will help restore order. Governor Pelias and Commander Cadmus have fallen, and as of this moment, you will take all orders from Wolf Lord Berek Thunderfist or myself. Again, cease all attacks on the Dark Angels immediately.'

'Now, we just need to listen,' said Torin. 'If the guns stop, you did it m'lady. If not, then we're in for a long bout of fighting.'

Without saying anything, the four stood in the kill zone and listened. The regular blasts of the guns slowed, and then stopped. The only sounds Ragnar could hear were servos in the Space Marines' armour and the ever-present buzz of beetles.

'They stopped,' said Ragnar.

'Pity,' said Haegr, 'I would have preferred to thrash the lot of them.'

'Now, we just have to survive the reptos,' said Ragnar, 'and with Berek's company here, we will.'

'Lady Gabriella,' offered Torin, 'let's get you to the House Belisarius shuttle, assuming it's in one piece, and safely off this planet.'

'Finally, Torin has a good idea,' said Haegr.

The four of them clambered over the remnants of a wall and entered the city.

THE WOLFBLADE'S TREK to the city centre revealed the full extent of the devastation. Buildings lay shattered and broken. Craters pockmarked the roads, and the landscape more resembled a volcanic badland than a city. Despite the devastation to the landscape, the real horror came from the number of bodies lying strewn everywhere.

Bodies lay scattered, rotting in the ruins. Some of the corpses wore the colours of the planetary defence force, but far more were civilians. The stench of death and decay burned Ragnar's nostrils. The dead had looks of pain and horror on their faces. Ragnar had a new respect for the terror that Space Marines could inspire in their foes. Lethe had suffered horribly, there was nothing but ruins and flames in all directions. Torin kept pausing and checking his auspex to make certain that they were heading in the proper direction.

'By the Emperor,' said Gabriella, as she stared at the limp body of a child at the edge of a crater, 'what evil guided Cadmus?'

'The worst kind of evil, Gabriella,' said Ragnar, 'Chaos… and not only Chaos, but the work of our worst enemies, the Thousand Sons.'

The mere thought of the Thousand Sons made Ragnar's anger rise within him. Throughout his entire career as a Space Wolf, they had proven to be the most relentless of foes. The legends all spoke of the Thousand Sons as the greatest enemies of the Space Wolves, and Ragnar would vouch for every one of those stories. The passionate rivalry between the Space Wolves and the Dark Angels was a mere shadow of the shared hate between the Space Wolves and the Thousand Sons.

For Ragnar, battling the Thousand Sons was personal. He had served with Berek when he had last fought the Thousand Sons and defeated them using the Spear of Russ. How ironic that he had come face to face with more of that traitor Chapter while Berek's great company fought the Dark Angels both in orbit and on the surface of Hyades.

Still, it was a day of victory. The Dark Angels were leaving, and although they had encountered Chaos Marines, the members of the Wolfblade had defeated them. Cadmus lay dead, his body in possession of the Dark Angels.

The ground shook. Then, it shook again and again... and again. The sound of the explosions kept growing in volume, one after another, after another. A column of white flame burst from the street in front of the Space Wolves. It became a wall of white fire, extending in both directions and rising to nearly thirty metres. The scent of burning promethium was unmistakable.

'Take cover,' yelled Torin.

The next blast threw all of them off their feet, even Haegr. The ground was scalding hot. The explosions weren't like any they had experienced so far in the battle.

Ragnar took cover with the others behind a large still-standing wall with an overhang from what had once been the second floor of a building. Now, it was shelter against a burning rain. He tried to comprehend what was happening. The aerial bombardment had stopped some time ago, what could be causing these explosions?

The smell of promethium was so strong that he wondered if the refineries were blowing up. He could even taste the fuel on his tongue.

The explosions continued in all directions and smoke billowed upwards from cracks in the streets. The blasts were coming from below.

'What is happening?' asked Haegr.

'I'm not sure,' said Gabriella.

'With the smell of promethium everywhere...' started Ragnar.

'The only thing that I can think of is that something in the refineries, the tunnels or the mines has gone terribly wrong,' finished Torin.

Gabriella looked at the members of her Wolfblade, and then settled her gaze on Ragnar. 'We've got to get to the shuttle now,' she said.

'I know. If the promethium has ignited,' said Ragnar, 'we'll cook if we stay here.'

'I see something ahead,' said Haegr. 'Follow me.'

'Be careful,' said Torin.

Ragnar saw Haegr's target. A Chimera sat quietly in the street with its ramp down. The bodies of the men who had once occupied the vehicle lay scattered around the ramp. Bolter holes in the bodies and the distinctive cuts of chainswords indicated that these men had encountered the Dark Angels and things had not gone well.

Torin went to the main hatch, which appeared to have been forced open. He reached down into the driver's compartment and pulled out a charred corpse. 'They killed the drivers too,' he said, scooping out another blackened body and throwing it down to the pavement with a wet thunk. The stench was awful. 'I'll make this thing work. I'm driving. With your permission, m'lady, I believe that this vehicle will allow us to reach the shuttle much more safely,' he said.

'Take us there, Torin. Let's go inside, away from this burning debris,' said Gabriella. Wisps of ash and promethium gently fell from the sky, contrasting with the continuing eruptions.

'You want me to get in one of these, again?' asked Haegr.

'Yes,' said Ragnar. He wanted no delays.

Torin shook his head and climbed into the front of the vehicle. Haegr swore upon the private parts of Fenrisian wolves, but he crouched and angled his way inside.

Static crackled over Ragnar's comm, and he cursed under his breath. He banged his fist against the driver's compartment. 'Torin, I can't get a signal again.'

'I suspect we have interference,' replied Torin.

Ragnar wasn't in the mood for Torin's ability to state the obvious, although he knew his battle-brother faced the task of driving the Chimera through the exploding hell that Lethe had become. He had to think for a moment.

'Torin, what about the Chimera's comm system? Could I access that? Shouldn't it have more signal?' asked Ragnar.

'Try it yourself. There's a comm station right next to your seat,' said Torin.

Ragnar activated the comms on the tank as it rumbled through the debris towards the palace. Gabriella had strapped herself in, but Haegr was fighting with his seat. 'Just how do ogryns ever fit in these things?' he asked.

'Ogryns are smaller than mighty Haegr, I suspect,' said Ragnar, finding the heart to joke. Inside, he prayed to the Emperor to let the comm work. All he received was static.

'By Morkai's Axe,' said Ragnar, 'I can't contact Berek.' He shook the comm, frustrated with the constant signal interference adding to everything else falling apart around them.

A crackle came over the system. Ragnar had a signal. It was weak, but it was a signal nonetheless.

'This is Ragnar to Wolf Lord Berek. Can you hear me?' asked Ragnar.

'This is the *Fist of Russ*, Ragnar, ship's herald here. The Wolf Lord is busy,' came the reply.

The Chimera struck something in one of the roads, bounced, and then got very hot. Haegr cursed again as his head hit the roof of the cramped transport chamber. 'We had better get there soon,' he growled.

'I need to talk to the Wolf Lord. All this isn't just the work of the traitor Cadmus,' said Ragnar.

'This is Berek,' said the voice of the Wolf Lord over the comm. 'Wolfblade Ragnar, the events on the planet below are the work of Chaos. Since you have Lady Gabriella with you, leave the surface of Hyades as soon as you can,'

'Someone ignited the promethium mines,' said Ragnar. 'Everything's exploding.'

'Heh, lad,' said Berek. 'You should see the view from space.'

'What do you mean, my lord?' asked Ragnar.

'The pattern of the burning forms an oval. In fact, it looks like a flaming eye glaring up from the planet, and it's visible from space. I can see it from the observation decks. From your signal, you should be near the centre–'

The comm died. 'In the name of Russ,' said Ragnar. He dropped the comm quietly, taking in the impact of what he had heard.

Gabriella screamed. Light glowed from beneath her headband and she shook violently.

She gurgled something incoherent. Tears streamed down her cheeks and she banged her head against the Chimera's restraints. Ragnar saw her muscles tense. A vein bulged in her neck.

'Gabriella. What's wrong?' asked Ragnar.

'How can we help her?' asked Haegr as Ragnar pulled a med-kit from its storage bin in the back of the Chimera.

Gabriella started hyperventilating.

Ragnar grabbed her hands.

'Hold on, come back to us, your Wolfblade. We're in the Chimera on Lethe.'

Gabriella's breathing slowed and her eyes met Ragnar's. 'Ragnar, something terrible is happening. There are… many disturbances in the warp.'

'Hold on,' shouted Torin from the driver's seat in the front. 'We're heading through a wall of fire.'

Everything became extremely hot and there was a loud bang. The Chimera lurched to the right, sending Haegr flying across into Ragnar. Neither Space Wolf was wearing safety restraints, but fortunately neither of them landed on Gabriella. Torin swore something from the driver's seat in front as he fought for control of the tank.

Another loud bang sent the Chimera lurching back to the left. The two Space Wolves tumbled to the other side of the tank. Gabriella's restraints kept her secure.

'In Russ's name!' said Haegr as Ragnar smashed into him.

Ragnar thought the Chimera had become airborne for a moment, and then a third loud bang reverberated through the vehicle, followed by a metallic grinding. He knew that at the least, the tank had broken multiple tracks. Ragnar smelled oil and the terrible grinding sound continued from the right side of the transport vehicle. With a loud boom, the Chimera shook and jolted from side to side, before coming to a rest with a resounding thud. At least they had stayed upright. Ragnar and Haegr both climbed to their feet.

'Everyone alive back there? Sorry about that – driving conditions are rather poor at the moment,' snarled Torin.

Ragnar ignored Torin for the moment. 'Gabriella, are you all right?' he asked. He looked at her bloodshot eyes and immediately realised it wasn't one of the brightest questions that he had ever asked.

Gabriella managed a smile, as she seemed to notice what a stupid question it was.

'Mighty Haegr is getting out,' announced Haegr. He pushed open the rear access ramp. Stepping outside, he drew his hammer.

Ragnar took a moment to examine Gabriella for additional injuries. Once he was confident that she was relatively unharmed, he joined Haegr.

Reptos swarmed all around them, leaping and running as explosions went off in all directions. There were hundreds of them, milling around in a frenzied mass. One of the creatures paused to stare at the Space Wolves. As if given a silent signal, the others stopped as well, and then the mass of creatures turned their heads as one to glare at the Space Wolves.

Showing their fangs and hissing, they advanced on the Space Wolves, their previous panic apparently forgotten.

'Hah,' said Haegr, clapping Ragnar's shoulder and raising his hammer. 'Lad, the two of us have them outnumbered.'

FOURTEEN
The True Enemy

SURROUNDED BY REPTOS, Ragnar and Haegr took the only course of action that made any sense at all: they charged.

Ragnar remembered when his squad of Blood Claws had dropped in the wrong location on Garm and had been overrun by hundreds of Garmites. Only the actions of his old friend Sven and their fallen sergeant Hakon had saved him that day. Then, he had fought like a man possessed; now it was time to do so again. He just wished he had a heavy weapon to provide some covering fire.

Haegr swung his thunder hammer around, scattering reptos with the force of the blow. The huge warrior seemed almost inhuman, as if he were a miniature Dreadnought rather than a man. Bodies of reptos flew into the air and the hammer boomed like its namesake. A spray of flesh, scales, bone and blood erupted with each swing and Haegr laughed.

Where Haegr used large strokes to scatter the enemy before him, Ragnar leapt into a knot of the creatures. His blade sliced through bodies, sending blood running into the streets. One clamped its jaws on his sword arm, so he took his bolt pistol and put a shot into its skull. He flung the corpse off his arm into the midsection of two others and finished them both with shots. Without hesitating, Ragnar spun around, swinging his sword in a deadly arc that took down two more that were attacking him from behind.

He slammed a repto with the front of his bolt pistol and then fired. The round ripped through the first creature and blew a hole out of the back of the second. Claws raked at his armour, trying to find a weakness. Ragnar felt the scrapes and scratches and the impact of the blows threatened to unbalance him. If he fell, they would win by sheer weight of numbers, but he wouldn't let that happen.

He looked to Haegr. In one hand the giant still held his hammer, but with the other, he swung a repto by its tail. He slammed the creature back and forth into its brothers as if it were a reptilian blackjack. The repto screamed and its brethren hesitated, uncertain how to react to Haegr's improvised weapon. Taking advantage of the moment, Ragnar sprang into the air, flipping over some would-be attackers and crossing to Haegr.

Haegr smashed the street with his lizard flail again and again. The creature was just a sack of skin now, barely holding its remains inside.

Torin dived out of the driver's hatch of the Chimera, firing shots from his bolter as he moved. With a blade in one hand, he expertly decapitated the closest repto, as he maintained his firing. Another repto sprang high into the air at Torin, but the Space Wolf's reflexes allowed him to sidestep the creature's pounce and bring his blade around in a downwards stroke that severed the beast's spinal cord.

All three Space Wolves moved towards each other, forming a circle of blades and bolter fire. The frenzied mass of reptos lost member after member, but it seemed they would never stop coming. Then, the knot of alien beasts was gone. The Space Wolves had broken the horde. The survivors turned tail and disappeared into the smoke of the burning city.

Gabriella walked down the ramp of the Chimera. She had a slight limp, but still managed to hold herself tall. She cradled a lasgun in her arms, and she had a med-kit slung over her shoulder. 'I shot a few on the other side of the Chimera,' she said, looking at the ruined tracks of the vehicle. 'How far are we from the shuttle hangar in the main city complex?'

Torin took an auspex from his belt, while Ragnar and Haegr instinctively checked the area for more signs of immediate danger. 'We're less than five hundred metres from the city centre. Despite the interference, I can still pick up on the signals from the palace. It's this way, follow me,' said Torin. 'We'll have to walk the rest of the way.'

BEREK WAS STANDING on the bridge of the *Fist of Russ*, glaring down at the surface of Hyades, with Morgrim, his skald, standing beside him. The face of the Wolf Lord was contorted with rage at the sight of an eye burning on the planet below.

'Curse the Dark Angels for their arrogance,' he snarled. 'Bring us around. What damage have we suffered?'

An Iron Priest, one of the Space Wolves' own Techmarines, stood on the bridge, alongside the many Fenrisian warriors assigned as crew. A huge servo-arm shifted on his back and he held a massive thunder hammer with many wolf tails hanging from it, a sign of worth over his many years of service. 'My lord, the battle has drained many of the ship's spirits. The strength of the generators is spent. The proper rites and rituals are replenishing their energy, but for now, providing shields and engines is the extent of their ability. To restore them would take time.'

'Restore the spirits as quickly as you can. I trust in the rites and rituals of my Iron Priest,' Berek said, flexing his power fist for emphasis.

'My lord, I am picking up some strange signals,' said Hroth. 'I'm detecting ships at the edge of Hyades's space.'

'More Dark Angels?' asked Berek. 'Do they ever stand ready to interfere in our business?'

'No, my lord, these are not Imperial vessels...' Hroth's expression hardened. 'Wolf Lord, a Chaos fleet approaches!'

The guide touched the activation runes of the holographic projector. The Dark Angels ships moving to the edge of the display appeared green, while the Hyades defence patrol and the Space Wolf vessels showed blue. Flickering red shapes indicated the incoming enemy ships.

'Give me a tactical report,' growled the Wolf Lord.

'The fleet appears to be composed of a number of cruisers, escort ships and one larger vessel, a Styx-class heavy cruiser,' replied Hroth.

'Let's hope we didn't cripple that Dark Angels' battle-barge too badly, lads,' snarled Berek. 'We'll need her guns. Herald, open a channel to the Dark Angels. Iron Priest, how long until the generator spirits have their strength renewed? Has Mikal reported on withdrawing from Hyades? I want my Thunderhawks back and my men ready to board the enemy vessels.'

Berek considered the tactical possibilities. Most Imperial strategists would say that the Chaos fleet should split, sending half their force to one side of the Imperial vessels and half to the other and trap them in the middle. It would be a good strategy, considering the range and armaments of the Chaos ships, and it might work.

These Chaos ships must have known about the battle between the Space Wolves and the Dark Angels to be ready to take advantage of them so quickly. Analysing the tactics of his enemies, he determined that they would soon close for the attack, bringing their guns to bear and attempting to board his ships. After all, they had a battered Space Wolf fleet in their sights.

'A large number of Chaos fighters have launched and are forming up ahead of the main cruisers,' announced Hroth. 'I believe that they are meant to screen the cruisers from our guns and shoot down any Thunderhawks we launch, m'lord.'

'I suspect you are correct, Hroth. Alert the fleet to be ready for the enemy to close directly with us,' said the Wolf Lord. 'Iron Priest, see if the spirits can find us a bit more essence. I will need all our weapons for this battle.'

'Of course, m'lord. I will oversee the libations and rituals on the generators myself.' The Iron Priest strode off the bridge past the banners and carved wolf heads.

'Half of the Thunderhawks have returned to the ship,' announced the ship's herald.

'Where's my channel to the Dark Angels?' demanded Berek.

'I have them now, Lord Berek,' responded the herald.

The *Vinco Redemptor* had moved down towards Hyades, nearly touching the atmosphere. On the holographic display, several Thunderhawks were docking with the Dark Angels' battle-barge. The Dark Angels were pulling all of their troops back.

'Interrogator-Chaplain Vargas, this is Wolf Lord Berek Thunderfist. I hope that you and your men are ready to defend the Imperium from an actual enemy,' said Berek.

'Wolf Lord Berek Thunderfist, this is Interrogator-Chaplain Vargas. We have agreed to withdraw and withdraw we shall. The enemy has numbers and both of our fleets are weary. We are currently receiving the last of our vessels. Hyades is lost to us. We shall return with the wrath of the Lion at the appropriate time.' Interrogator-Chaplain Vargas's voice was metallic and inhuman, which Berek felt matched Vargas's heart.

'Get out of the system, and don't worry, we won't need you watching our backs. You've done enough damage. This isn't over,' snarled Berek.

The last green blips representing Thunderhawk gunships disappeared as they touched the holographic image of the *Vinco Redemptor*. The Dark Angels' withdrawal was complete.

'It is over. May the Emperor watch over you if you decide to throw away your lives defending this corrupt planet,' said the Dark Angel commander.

'We understand about defending a man's homeworld,' retorted Berek.

He cut the channel on the interrogator-chaplain, hoping to annoy the Dark Angels by having the last word. The Dark Angels' lack of compassion and lack of apparent desire to defend the Imperium annoyed him deeply. Berek hoped that Vargas would catch the reference to losing a home world and take it as he meant it, as a reminder that the Dark Angels had failed to defend their own world during the Horus Heresy.

'All the ships fire with full guns,' commanded Berek. 'Let's blow through the Chaos fighter screens quickly and cripple those Chaos cruisers before the Styx joins the fray.'

Even as Berek gave the order, he could see the cloud of red blips on the holographic display descending on the blue ones.

THROUGH THE HAZE of promethium smoke, Ragnar could see the palace. The structure was burning, like everything else, although the banner of House

Belisarius still waved. Five ogryns stood in front of the palace, the same ones that the Wolfblade had fought earlier. They looked relatively untouched from the day's events. Ragnar couldn't believe that the monstrous mutants were still on guard. The abhumans hadn't appeared to notice the Space Wolves' approach due to the smoke all around them.

Haegr readied his thunder hammer. Torin calmly unsheathed his sword and raised his bolt pistol. Ragnar stepped in front of Gabriella. He didn't want to take a chance on the ogryns' ripper guns shredding her. He would protect her with his armoured body if need be.

As the Space Marines approached, the ogryns finally spotted them. The huge mutants leered down at the Space Wolves and readied their guns more as clubs than shooting weapons. The largest of them roared and flexed his huge arms. If he meant to intimidate the Space Wolves, then he failed.

'Wait,' said Torin, 'they aren't firing,'

'So?' Ragnar and Haegr responded as one.

'Don't you see? They are obeying orders. In their simple way, they are doing what they were ordered to do, guard the palace,' said Torin.

'And we need to enter the palace, Torin, so we need to kill them,' said Ragnar.

'Wait,' said Gabriella, 'if they are so devoutly following orders, maybe they would follow new orders.'

'My thoughts exactly,' said Torin.

Gabriella stepped in front of Ragnar and addressed the ogryns. 'I am Lady Gabriella of House Belisarius. Commander Cadmus is dead. I am in charge. Go fight the reptos. Kill them all.'

Ragnar exchanged looks with Torin. Gabriella folded her arms across her chest. The ogryns tilted their heads from side to side as if they were trying to understand.

'Yes, lady,' said the lead ogryn. 'Bring you dead ape-lizards.'

Gabriella pointed back the way the Space Wolves had come. 'That way,' she prompted.

The ogryns nodded, and then the five abhumans charged off into the smoke and flame with their ripper guns at the ready, never glancing back. Ragnar watched them disappear in the promethium haze.

Gabriella touched her temple and winced. Ragnar could see her forehead wrinkle around her headband. Her third eye was active. There was psychic activity somewhere, disturbances in the warp. It was straining Gabriella. Ragnar wondered how much of a curse these psyker gifts were. For a moment, he gave a fleeting thought back to Lars, a fey touched youth who had been part of his first pack. The youth had always suffered from haunted visions before giving his life for the Imperium. Ragnar thought Gabriella was stronger than Lars had been, despite the fact that she was no Space Wolf. Still, whatever was happening was taking a greater and greater toll on her.

'What is it?' asked Torin.

'An ancient evil approaches. We need to get off the planet and join up with the Space Wolf fleet. Then we can worry about defeating the enemy,' said Gabriella.

ON THE BRIDGE of the *Fist of Russ*, Berek cursed. 'By the blood of Russ! Those cowards,' shouted the Wolf Lord.

The Dark Angels vessels were fleeing the engagement. They had accomplished their task, ruined Hyades's defences, damaged the Space Wolf fleet, and now they were leaving. Berek had hoped that his final taunt about defending a home world would have changed their minds, but it wasn't so.

The Chaos fleet was closing in on the Space Wolves and its fighter screen had already arrived. Guns blazed across the battle-barge as it shot down dozens of small enemy craft. A Chaos fighter crashed against the hull of the *Fist of Russ*. Two Chaos cruisers closed the kilometres quickly, readying their broadside guns. The screen of Chaos escorts was scattered space dust, but they had fulfilled their mission. Nothing would stop the enemy cruisers from bringing their big guns to bear.

Berek turned to his skald. 'Horgrim, make sure that a Thunderhawk is ready for me. If Mikal's back from the surface, get my Wolf Guard, if not, I want Krom's Grey Hunters. I'm going to give these Chaos bastards a taste of the Thunderfist.'

'Yes, Wolf Lord.' Horgrim knew that Berek wanted this task completed immediately, otherwise he wouldn't have given it to his most trusted advisor.

Berek knew if he could fire the Nova cannon without completely draining the ship, the *Fist of Russ* had a chance. If they could take out one cruiser with a single shot, and that's all that they'd have, then they could board the other while the Iron Priests strengthened the ship's spirits. He wouldn't concern himself about the other vessels. The powerful engines of the Chaos cruisers had put them further forwards than the rest of their fleet. If the Space Wolves could deal with this threat, then they would have time to figure out the rest.

'The Iron Priest reports that we have enough power for the Nova cannon, my lord,' shouted the ship's guide with unabashed enthusiasm.

'Excellent,' said Berek, smiling. 'We'll only have time for one shot with it before they close. Horgrim, have my Thunderhawk wait.'

The *Fist of Russ* shuddered as the spirits of the Nova cannon drew all available power. Berek watched the lights dim across the bridge, growing dark in the wolfs' heads. He could see the glow from the engines of the escorts and Thunderhawk gunships streaking around his ship like the auroras of Fenris. Russ was with them. 'Fire!' he ordered.

The beam exploded out from the prow of the *Fist of Russ*. It felt as if the legendary Firewolf itself had opened its maw and unleashed the fury of every volcano on Fenris as one.

'Lord Berek, the spirits of the Nova cannon have drawn too much power in their zeal,' said the voice of the Iron Priest.

Warning runes glared red across the bridge. The hull of the *Fist of Russ* roared. Berek clenched his teeth and raised his power fist.

The beam struck home against the Chaos cruiser, spearing it through and erupting from the other side to continue tearing through space. The holographic display showed the blast continuing unabated, glancing another distant cruiser, but all eyes on the bridge focused on the main target. The enemy ship shivered, and was replaced for an instant by a new sun in the

Hyades system. As the light faded, there was nothing left.

Cheers came from the officers and crew of the *Fist of Russ*. Several men pumped their fists and more than a few threw back their heads to howl.

Berek shouted, 'Let's go and show those treacherous spawn how warriors of Fenris fight! To the Thunder-hawks!'

THE SURVIVING MEMBERS of the Wolfblade and Gabriella had arrived at the shuttle hangar in the heart of the Imperial palace. Once they had passed the ogryns, they had fought through minimal opposition, just a few planetary defence forces holding to a mis-guided loyalty to the now-dead Cadmus.

Torin activated the locks to the hangar doors. The inside of the hangar was stacked with supplies and a few servitors went about their duties. The House Belis-arius shuttle sat, remarkably unscathed, in the centre of the hangar. Her hatches were closed, indicating that the crew was on board and that they had taken the proper defensive stance. The lights on the shuttle acti-vated as the Space Wolves and Gabriella entered. Russ be praised, thought Ragnar.

They had barely taken three steps when the speakers on the shuttle crackled to life. 'Lady Gabriella, Wolf-blade, behind you!'

'What? Who would dare,' asked Haegr, apparently forgetful of the traitors, xenos and Chaos Space Marines on Hyades.

Clad in glittering blue and gold armour, nine Chaos Space Marines had entered the open hangar doors. Each one wore his own heraldry, but each of them had the symbol of Tzeentch emblazoned upon his power armour. The power of the Chaos god infected the warriors, causing their armour to glow with faint tongues of fire. Ragnar could feel the hate of ten thousand years burning in them. Every one was a potential match for a Wolfblade. One among them wore a glittering cape and had a tall spiked helm. A blue flame wrapped itself around his left gauntlet.

The Chaos Marine sorcerer gestured, raising the blue flame towards the ceiling. A voice came from the fire itself.

'We would dare.'

The silky mocking voice echoed in Ragnar's soul. He'd know that voice anywhere. It was Madox, the same Chaos Marine who had assaulted Fenris, the mastermind behind the theft of the Spear of Russ and the one who had nearly killed Ragnar's best friend, Sven.

'Madox,' shouted Ragnar.

'As always, Ragnar Blackmane, it is good to be recognised. Alas, I shall not have the luxury of killing you personally, but we must all make some sacrifices.'

The Chaos Marines aimed their bolters at the Space Wolves. Gabriella dived for cover behind some supply crates, holding onto her lasgun. Ragnar felt his blood run cold for an instant, but he was shocked out of any hesitation by his battle-brother, Haegr.

Haegr shouted, 'Hah! They didn't account for you and Ragnar, Torin. There are barely enough of them for me.' Then the giant bellowed and charged.

Torin readied his bolter and growled softly.

For once, Ragnar agreed with Haegr; all they could do was fight. 'For Fenris,' he yelled, and joined Haegr's charge.

FIFTEEN
Escape to Fenris

NINE CHAOS SPACE Marines, including a sorcerer, confronted Ragnar, Torin and Haegr in the shuttle hangar. The crew of the shuttle had activated their ship's systems in preparation for launch, but the Space Wolves wouldn't be able to board unless they stopped the Chaos Space Marines first.

Haegr charged the enemy with a tremendous roar. Though hardened from thousands of years of combat, even the Chaos Space Marines appeared taken aback by the giant Space Wolf's charge. For a moment, they hesitated as Haegr closed with them.

Three of the Chaos warriors swung their bolters at Haegr. Ragnar heard shrieks come from the Chaos bolter rounds as they burned through the air, smashing into the Space Wolf. Ragnar heard the crack of power armour, yet Haegr had reached full speed and the force of the shots wouldn't slow him. Three more of the Thousand Sons commenced firing on Haegr.

Perhaps the real reason for their hesitation was that they hadn't decided how best to kill the giant Space Marine.

Looking at the Thousand Sons, Ragnar did not see them as much as feel the emotions they radiated. Their ornate gold and lapis lazuli armour evoked racial memories of the most ancient of humanity's gods with its ancient shapes and markings. Daemonic forms twisted and melted on the polished surfaces of the metal. Ragnar saw the hate burn inside them as they mercilessly fired at Haegr.

Ragnar knew this foe was a full-fledged sorcerer; not as powerful as Madox, but truly an enemy to be reckoned with. Ragnar and Torin didn't wait. The last two members of the Wolfblade drew their weapons and charged. Ragnar's runeblade glowed as he closed with the enemy. Torin thumbed the activation rune on his blade.

The sorcerer gestured at his attackers. Ragnar saw a flash, and a bolt of dark energy lifted him into the air and threw him backwards as if he was merely a child's toy. Instinctively, he twisted and came down in a crouch. Torin was not as agile as his battle-brother and landed hard on his shoulder.

The shuttle's engines roared as they started up. The defence forces of House Belisarius appeared as the shuttle's ramp lowered. The men held lasguns at the ready, but they didn't fire at the Chaos Space Marines. Haegr was almost in the midst of the enemy, and they wouldn't chance shooting one of their own. Gabriella saw the ramp open and made a dash towards the shuttle, from her cover behind a crate.

Haegr had reached the Chaos Space Marines. 'You face the mighty Haegr,' he shouted, swinging his hammer into the large helm of a Thousand Son. The hammer struck with a loud echoing boom, and the Chaos Marine crashed backwards. Flickering flames escaped from the hammer-sized hole in the Chaos Marine's armour. The creatures facing them were dead spirits haunting the shells of their ancient armour.

Ragnar howled and charged at the sorcerer. The Chaos Marines levelled their bolters at him. Their shots struck with deadly accuracy, but Ragnar broke off his straight-line charge to roll, and then leap, making himself a moving target. Ragnar was powerful, but his reflexes had always been his greatest physical asset.

Torin braced himself and opened fire with his bolter, drawing the enemy's attention. Shot after shot struck the enemy squad. Unfortunately, their arcane armour held, but Ragnar knew that Torin had bought him just enough of a respite. He would be in their ranks in a second.

The sorcerer intoned a phrase in a strange tongue and another bolt of dark magic raced from his hands. Ragnar dodged to his left, but the bolt followed him. The Space Wolf howled in pain as the arcane energy threw him back into a pile of crates, knocking him off his feet. Spots danced in front of his eyes and pain came from each place a bolter round had struck him. He clutched a refuelling line as he tried to pull himself to his feet.

Torin tried to duck the return fire from the Thousand Sons, but they had numbers. Possessing a skill that matched the Space Wolves, they blasted Torin. Haegr had three fighting him. Although they could not match the giant Space Wolf's strength or his skill with the hammer, they were still formidable adversaries. Haegr was breathing heavily and the hammer was swinging slowly and wildly. He was being pushed back, and the enemy were gaining the advantage.

Anger raged within Ragnar's heart. The wolf in his soul howled and he joined in chorus; his pack needed him. He threw himself at the sorcerer and the Thousand Sons. This time, Ragnar reached the sorcerer and thrust his blade through the Thousand Sons helm, breaking through ancient ceramite and arcane protections to jut out of the back of the Chaos Space Marine's helmet.

Ragnar roared and took his blade to the next Chaos Marine. The ancient warrior raised his bolter in an attempt to parry, but Ragnar sliced through the gun. Ghostly smoke came from the ruined bolter. On the down stroke, Ragnar brought up his other arm and levelled his foe with two point-blank bolt pistol shots.

Then, a mighty blow cracked Ragnar on the back of the head, dropping him to the ground.

The sorcerer's other guard stood over Ragnar and fired his bolter into the Space Wolf's back. Ragnar heard his armour's backpack crack and felt the shot through his spine. Ragnar's genetically altered hearts pounded as his enhanced physique raced to repair the damage.

Ragnar rolled from his stomach to his wounded back and kicked up into the Thousand Son. The Chaos Marine fell back, nearly losing his balance. Somehow, Ragnar got back to his feet and brought his sword up into his foe's abdomen.

Flames flared within the helm of the Thousand Son. Even as the Chaos Marine's essence was leaking out of his armour, he reached for Ragnar's throat, impaling himself further on the blade. 'Madox will be pleased with your death,' his foe grated.

'Go to hell,' said Ragnar, placing his bolt pistol squarely on his opponent's forehead and pulling the trigger.

The Chaos Marine fell limp on the end of Ragnar's blade.

Ragnar realised that he had killed three of their foe in the last few seconds. He took an instant to assess the battle. Haegr stood near him and had felled another in addition to his first kill. Haegr swayed and Ragnar wondered how much longer he could stand. Torin was on the ground, slightly closer to the shuttle, struggling to get to his feet. The odds were almost even, four Chaos Space Marines against three Space Wolves, and despite Ragnar's wounds, he knew that victory was in their grasp.

The body of the sorcerer rose from the hangar floor, pulled as if by invisible strings. Blue flames wreathed the sorcerer's gauntlets. The hair rose on Ragnar's neck and his eyes widened as the lifeless body raised its hands.

Reality shuddered. Fire burst forth from the armour and Ragnar brought his arm up to shield his face. He heard insane laughing echo from all sides and a sickly sweet scent filled his nostrils.

Something started to materialise in the middle of the chamber. A creature floated in the air, drifting on nonexistent winds. Its flesh was blue and pink with one colour replacing the other. Tendrils sprang from bubbling twisting flesh and flailed towards the Space Wolves.

A wave of horror and revulsion swept over Ragnar and he raised his sword defiantly. If this was the end, he would go out like a true Space Wolf. He threw his head back and howled for as long and loud as he could, until his cry drowned out the laughter of the daemon.

When he lowered his head, he heard an answering howl, one with a mechanical undertone. With a huge crash, the wall of the hangar bay cracked. Large rents appeared in the rockcrete. Suddenly, a large section fell inwards, crumbling to dust.

Gymir the Ice-Fisted, venerable Dreadnought of the Thunderfist great company, howled once again as he strode into the hangar. *Russ takes care of his own,* thought Ragnar, *and we take care of his enemies!*

The ground shook with each step of the towering Dreadnought. Behind the mighty one, Space Wolves, members of Berek's great company, rushed in. It was an entrance worthy of a song.

The sight of the ancient Dreadnought and the arrival of so many battle-brothers inspired Ragnar. Chanting a prayer to Russ, he charged into the daemon with renewed vigour. He slashed with his blade to his left and right, transforming himself into a whirlwind of mayhem and destruction. Tentacles flew through the air, spraying black ichor everywhere.

'Ragnar Blackmane,' shouted Mikal, as he and his fellow Space Wolves followed the Dreadnought into the hangar. Ragnar had saved Mikal and the Wolf Lord once on a space hulk, and Mikal had always sought an opportunity to repay him.

Ragnar forgot himself for a moment and glanced over at Mikal. With preternatural speed, a tentacle grasped his sword arm and another wrapped itself around his neck. One of the dismembered limbs snaked across the floor and wrapped itself around Ragnar's leg. He spat at the daemon as he tried to loosen its hold on his neck with his free hand.

'For Russ!' boomed Gymir. The great Dreadnought swung a massive power fist full into the central mass of the daemon. Energy cascaded from the power fist and the daemon's tendrils snapped away from Ragnar as the creature looked to its own defence.

One of the Chaos Space Marines knocked the thunder hammer from Haegr's grasp, while a second attempted to slice through his power armour with a chainsword. Sparks flew, but they had seized their advantage too late. Two Grey Hunters engaged the Thousand Sons, swinging axes and firing bolters into their foes at close range. The Chaos Space Marines turned their attention from Haegr to their new attackers.

Mikal and three other Space Wolves tackled the two Chaos Space Marines attacking Torin and with a howl, the four of them charged into the enemy. Mikal smashed one of the Chaos Marines with a power fist, tearing a gaping hole in his armour. A shrieking exhalation of smoke and fire came from the rent, leaving only empty armour.

The second Thousand Son brought his chainsword up to defend himself against the first Grey Hunter who reached him. With a skilful parry, the Chaos Marine not only blocked the Space Wolf's attack, but disarmed him as well. A bolter shot to the chest dropped the first Grey Hunter, even as the second sprang upon his foe.

This Space Wolf seemed fresher and more determined, toppling the Thousand Son. The two engaged in brutal combat, rolling on the hangar floor, each trying to gain the upper hand and make a lethal blow. In the end, the blade of the Grey Hunter claimed the Thousand Son, finding enough of a weakness in a joint to sever the helm.

The Grey Hunters attacking Haegr's foes seemed evenly matched by the Thousand Sons. The Chaos Marines were unrelenting in their attacks as if they could not feel pain or fatigue, while the Grey Hunters' blows became weaker after the initial charge. Haegr reclaimed his thunder hammer and rose again. He swung it into the back of one of the ancient warriors. With a loud boom, the Chaos Space Marine's backpack shattered in a burst of gold and lapis lazuli. The Chaos Marine fell, not to rise again.

Ragnar tried to regain his feet as he watched the final moments of the battle. A Grey Hunter took a double-bladed axe in one hand and slashed through the last standing member of the Thousand Sons. Gymir the Ice-Fisted had locked both power fists against the central mass of the daemon. The thing from the warp lashed tendril after tendril around the mechanical body of the entombed Space Marine, but the horror held no terror for one who had faced death. Strange warp fire leapt in an aura around the daemon, but Gymir held firm. Then the Dreadnought forced his arms apart, tearing the daemon into pieces. The lights in the hangar bay flickered and a terrible screaming began, but was cut short. Nothing was left of the daemon, and the Dreadnought stood triumphant.

The fight was over and the Space Wolves stayed on guard for a moment before allowing themselves a respite. Haegr leaned against his hammer, standing over his fallen enemies and recovering his strength. Lady Gabriella examined Torin's wounds, and House Belisarius's men formed a semi-circle around her. The other Space Wolves moved together, gathering around waiting for orders. As for Ragnar, he could feel the world spinning as he walked over to the shuttle and Lady Gabriella.

Mikal's voice seemed distant, 'Blackmane! How many other members of the Wolfblade do you have?'

Ragnar was exhausted. 'As far as I know, we are the last three Wolfblade on the planet. I believe that the others are dead.'

'Lady Gabriella, I have orders from the Wolf Lord to return to the *Fist of Russ* immediately. Your shuttle looks large enough for us. Does its cargo bay have room enough for a Dreadnought?' asked Mikal.

Gabriella looked to the men of House Belisarius. They nodded affirmatively. The shuttle had extra cargo space to deliver supplies to Belisarius's custodial holdings. 'We're ready to take you to the Wolf Lord,' she said.

THE SHUTTLE STREAMED skyward, its wings touching the licking flames from the towering columns of fire bursting from beneath Lethe. Ragnar knew that he would not return for a long time, if ever. He glanced back towards the city from the viewport.

'By Russ,' he cursed. It was as Wolf Lord Berek had described it – the fiery explosions traced an eye of flame across the devastated city. Anger mixed with superstitious fear inside him. What type of ritual demanded a symbol so vast? Ragnar shook his head, tearing his eyes away from the foul symbol.

Ragnar's superhuman healing had allowed him to recover from most of his wounds from the battle. Haegr and Torin both sat quietly, Torin with his eyes closed. Ragnar had not realised just how many bolter shells his battle-brothers had taken. To his credit, Torin made no noise, instead he focused inwards, willing his wounds to close. Ragnar knew that his brothers would be ready for battle again soon.

He looked over at Mikal and the other Space Wolves. They all showed signs of the combat, but Ragnar could feel their desire to join their Wolf Lord in space. They had fought in countless battles and they would fight in countless more.

Compared to these warriors, Ragnar thought the Wolfblade looked out of place. Torin's well-manicured moustache and disparate awards seemed foppish. Haegr looked like a horribly out of shape rotund caricature of a Space Wolf. Yet, they were

Ragnar's battle-brothers with a prowess that he would never have guessed at on a first glance. He wondered how he looked. Moreover, he wondered what Berek's men thought of him.

He had been a member of Berek Thunderfist's great company when he had lost the Spear of Russ. Had he brought shame on the company? How could he not have? Ragnar wondered if his former brothers cursed his name. These men would not give him any sign, and he knew that Mikal Stenmark had never cared for him.

Mikal looked over at Ragnar. 'We will arrive at the *Fist of Russ* and disembark to join the ship-to-ship fighting.' Ragnar's heart leapt, he would be fighting alongside the Space Wolves. Mikal continued, 'You and the Wolfblade will wait aboard this shuttle for further orders. I suspect you'll return to the *Wings of Belisarius*. Don't worry. We will deal with this Chaos incursion.' Ragnar's heart sank at first, and then anger and frustration rose in his chest.

Lady Gabriella entered from the cockpit and strapped herself into one of the seats. She was paler than usual, but she had recovered her grace and inner strength. She turned to Mikal. 'We have a problem. I have spoken to the Navigator on the *Fist of Russ*. Unusual turbulence in the warp has blinded the astropaths. We cannot send word of what has happened to Fenris.'

The shuttle made a hard turn into a cloud of silent explosions. They dived towards the *Fist of Russ*. Ragnar thought he could feel the ship turning as it approached the landing bay.

The Wolf Guard checked their weapons. They nodded to each other in acknowledgement and Ragnar could see the exchange of grins. They were ready for battle. Ragnar longed to be one of them.

The shuttle landed fast and hard in the hangar bay. The landing gear screeched against the deck of the *Fist of Russ*. Sparks shot across the viewports. Ragnar heard the cargo hold doors drop, and he felt Gymir the Ice-Fisted lumber out of the shuttle.

The other Space Wolves immediately released their restraints and followed suit. Mikal paused and gave Ragnar a last look. 'Rough battle down there, Blackmane. You have a gift for finding trouble. May the Emperor watch over you,' he said and without another word, Mikal left.

Ragnar wondered what his words meant, but he was tired of pondering such things.

'Lady Gabriella, the Wolf Lord wishes to speak to you,' said the pilot. Gabriella unstrapped herself and walked up to the front of the shuttle. With his sharpened senses, Ragnar could hear Gabriella's half of the conversation.

'Yes, Wolf Lord. I would be honoured to deliver word of this incident to Fenris,' she said. 'Pilot, take us to our cruiser, the *Wings of Belisarius*. Wolf Lord Berek has entrusted us to deliver news of this battle to the Great Wolf. Let the *Wings of Belisarius* know that we must traverse the warp to Fenris.'

Within moments, the shuttle left the hangar of the *Fist of Russ*, bound for the *Wings of Belisarius*.

WITHIN MINUTES, THE shuttle docked with the *Wings of Belisarius*. The cruiser was warp-capable, and it had a fair complement of guns, although it was hardly a match for the powerful vessels of the Space Wolf fleet. Ragnar knew that they were being left out of the battle, sent to Fenris because Wolf Lord Berek Thunderfist felt that the Wolfblade couldn't help him defeat the Chaos fleet. What angered Ragnar most was that he knew that the Wolf Lord was right.

The members of the Wolfblade and the crew of the shuttle disembarked swiftly. The servitors in the hangar had already begun securing the shuttle for the larger ship's warp travel. There was no time to waste. Gabriella was already on the comm to the bridge.

'Captain, we are aboard and we will be strapped in as quickly as possible. Once we are secure, we shouldn't waste any time. We need to reach Fenris as quickly as we can,' she said.

'Haegr will once again return to Fenris. Let the gods themselves tremble in their halls,' bellowed Haegr.

A beetle flew out from under Ragnar's shoulder pad as the group left the hangar for one of the main corridors to the restraining couches. Ragnar crushed it against the wall. 'We're done with Hyades.'

'Brilliant holiday idea,' offered Haegr cheerfully, but Ragnar wasn't smiling.

Torin waved his hand over the activation runes for the door to one of the ship's transport chambers. He stepped back to let Gabriella enter the room first with enough of a flourish for Ragnar to be certain that he had fully recovered.

'Captain, we're ready,' announced Gabriella over her comm. She sat down and pulled the restraints. The others hurried to do the same.

'Activate restraints and harnesses. Prepare to enter the warp,' came the command from the ship's speakers.

Gabriella looked over at Ragnar. 'I'm sorry. You served with them before the Wolfblade,' she said.

'Sorry about what?' asked Ragnar as he finished adjusting his restraints.

'There are too many Chaos ships. They won't survive,' she stated flatly.

Ragnar set his jaw. 'They are Space Wolves.'

Before Gabriella could respond, reality folded in on itself and the colours of the room lengthened and shifted. Ragnar lost all sense of space and time. The *Wings of Belisarius* had entered the warp.

FROM THE OBSERVATION window on the bridge of the *Fist of Russ*, Wolf Lord Berek Thunderfist watched the attackers come for them. Waves of enemy attack craft swarmed out of the bays of the Styx cruiser. Like monstrous bats, they covered space, blocking the light of the sun and blotting out the stars. Berek knew that it was time to find his place in the sagas, but, by Russ, they would remember him and his men for this day!

The cloud of death descended towards the Space Wolves. Berek cursed under his breath. The men of his great company had outdone themselves. They had fought the Dark Angels to a standstill and yet they had found the heart to destroy far more of the

Thousand Sons than any tactician would have deemed possible.

Berek remembered the run through the Chaos cruiser. Ah! Those were the experiences that made a man's blood burn with life. They had killed her mutant crew and detonated her power core. Two Chaos cruisers had fallen to the *Fist of Russ*. Now, the Styx cruiser came at them, and they limped through space, badly damaged. Berek knew that the hull of the Space Wolf vessel wouldn't hold for much longer. 'Come on you treacherous bastards! Come and destroy us if you can,' he said waving his power fist at the enemy.

'My lord, Lady Gabriella and the *Wings of Belisarius* have made it into the warp,' reported the ship's guide.

'All is not lost. She'll get word to Logan Grimnar,' the Wolf Lord said, and then continued to shout at the Styx. 'Burn in hell, you traitors!'

Then, as if it was intimidated by the cursing of the Wolf Lord, the wave of enemy bombers and fighters wavered and turned, breaking up and retreating towards the Styx.

'What in the name of the Gates of Morkai?' asked Berek.

The Dark Angels battle-barge suddenly filled the view screens on the *Fist of Russ*. The *Vinco Redemptor* opened up on the Styx with all of her guns, beams of energy illuminating the void with holy fury. A myriad of smaller Dark Angels vessels erupted from behind the mighty battle-barge, guns blazing.

The Dark Angels were back. Dark Angel escorts flew in behind the remaining Chaos ships sending ravening blasts of white-hot energy into the hulls of the enemy vessels. The *Vinco Redemptor* showed no mercy as it launched barrage after barrage into the Styx. Large sections of the Chaos cruiser glowed and exploded into molten fragments.

The Astartes were victorious. Berek raised his fist and his heart pumped wildly.

'Wolf Lord Berek, incoming transmission,' reported comms.

Interrogator-Chaplain Vargas appeared. 'Wolf Lord Berek Thunderfist, I offer my congratulations and praise for your efforts and for those of your men. Your distractions allowed us time to repair and flank the enemy. The Lion will be victorious this day. Praise to the Emperor!' His voice retained a metallic ring.

'Praise to the Emperor! You abandoned us! You fled and left us to do the fighting,' shouted Berek, as anger replaced the feeling of victory. 'You said that you were leaving!'

'We could not speak the truth over open channels, Wolf Lord. We are a proud Chapter just as you are. We always intended to flank them. I will grant you this: we never expected to discover that you destroyed so many. Our praise to you, Wolf Lord. Now, let both our Chapters fight as brothers against this foe and let Chaos be destroyed.'

Berek nodded. 'Let Chaos be destroyed.'

The transmission ended. Berek didn't trust the Dark Angels, but thanks to them, they would win the day.

'Engines, get us full power,' ordered the Wolf Lord. Berek turned on the ship's full comms. 'The Dark Angels have decided to join the fray. Let's remind them who won this battle. For Fenris! For Russ! For the Emperor!'

Berek could hear the cheering of his men fill the *Fist of Russ*.

SIXTEEN
Return to Fenris

THE *Wings of Belisarius* had traversed the warp to Fenris, making the journey to Fenris in good time. Upon entering orbit, Gabriella and the surviving members of the Wolfblade had boarded the same shuttle that had taken them to Hyades. Now, they rode the vehicle to Fenris. The foursome sat quietly, Gabriella beside Ragnar, who stared out of a viewport, with Haegr and Torin seated further down on the same side at another viewport. The Space Wolves all longed to see their homeworld.

Ragnar gazed out at the planet below. He was almost home. He could see the raging seas and the mountainous icebergs surging with the waves, great white shapes rocking back and forth. Storm clouds crackled with lightning, voicing their power with peals of thunder, and a wall of weather threatened to shroud the surface of the planet. Fenris was a harsh world, a cold and bitter place where only the strong survived, but most of all it was home.

He struggled to avoid shaking from the emotions he felt. He knew that he had thought a great deal of home, brooded on it in fact, but he hadn't expected to feel this strong a reaction. He shook his head, and then grinned with exultation. Finally, he was returning to the Fang.

'Aye, I know how you feel, lad,' said Haegr. 'Nothing stirs a warrior's heart like a return home. Now, poor Torin who was completely corrupted by civilisation, he's in for a bit of misery.'

Torin looked over. 'I harbour strong feelings for Fenris as well. It's the homeworld of our Chapter. Beyond that, I can't feel too sentimental over endless winters, krakens, and a harsh life filled with nothing but battle and cold. Still, I understand why my brother Ragnar loves Fenris so much, and well, as for you, I expect you'll be the cause of decades of starvation once you find the Fang's pantries.'

'Hah, it'll just make the rest of the Wolves tougher, weed out the frail and weak,' responded Haegr.

Ragnar could almost taste the Fenrisian ale and hear the stories of the grizzled veterans concerning battles against the ork, the eldar and Chaos. He had stories that he wanted to tell too, stories about fighting cultists, Imperial assassins, Dark Angels and Thousand Sons. He couldn't wait to see his old friends, especially Sven and the old Wolf Priest, Ranek. Sven had been with Ragnar since his choosing and was a member of Ragnar's first claw, a bonded group of Blood Claws. Ranek had chosen

Ragnar as a warrior, and although he trained hundreds of Space Wolves, Ranek had the ability to make him feel as though he were the only Space Wolf that Ranek had ever recruited.

The Fang came into view. It was the eternal fortress of the Space Wolves, the greatest mountain on all of Fenris, a spike of rock and ice so high that it pierced the sky. It dwarfed the other mountains surrounding it, and its peak even rose above the oncoming storm clouds. The warriors of Fenris viewed the Fang with superstitious awe as the home of gods. In some ways, they were right; compared to ordinary men, the Space Wolves might as well be gods. Unlike other Chapters though, the Space Wolves had never forgotten that they had once also been men.

Ragnar felt a chill race along his spine and spread outwards to cross his body. The Fang still inspired awe in his heart, and he knew that no matter what the future held, how many battles he fought or where he travelled, the Fang would always affect him this way. For him, it represented the heart of the Space Wolves and their desire to fight for their ideals against all mankind's enemies.

Excitement mixed with dread in his gut. He was still an exile. This was a temporary visit. Seeing his friends would be bittersweet indeed, because he would have to leave again. Ragnar wanted to watch the Fang for the entire descent, but he thought that seemed like the action of a young Blood Claw and Ragnar knew that he should wait like the others.

Ragnar looked over at Gabriella, who turned her head to look away. Had she been looking at him?

Ragnar realised that Gabriella had seemed quiet and reserved since her rescue, especially around him.

'Gabriella, is something bothering you?' Ragnar whispered, although he knew that Haegr and Torin could both hear.

Gabriella met Ragnar's eyes. 'Yes, I had a vision on Hyades.'

'What was it?' he asked.

'I'm not exactly sure. It was many things, colours, shapes and images. It's hard to know what was real and what was delusion,' she whispered, 'but I think I saw a great spear, perhaps the Spear of Russ.'

'What?' asked Ragnar. His hearts nearly burst from his body. 'Tell me. I have to know'

'I don't know much, Ragnar. I think that I saw the Thousand Sons with the Spear of Russ, but there were so many other images that I can't be certain. It happened when I was in the bunker in the Chaos temple. I don't know whether it was a real vision, it may just have been a hallucination. Perhaps it was a scene from the past, but I felt like the Thousand Sons had retrieved the Spear from the warp. As I said, I'm not sure, but I know how you feel about it. I just thought I should mention it. I'll speak to the Great Wolf and the Rune Priests and see if they think it's real.' Gabriella turned away.

'I have to find it. We have to have the chance to bring it back. That's my chance,' said Ragnar.

The shuttle suddenly angled, making its final descent into the hangar of the Fang. The shadow of the mountain fell over the craft, darkening the viewports.

'Ho! Enough talk,' said Haegr. The shuttle decelerated and Ragnar saw the mighty sculpted wolves that stood guard over the hangar. A large emblem of the Great Wolf marked the side of the hangar. This was Logan Grimnar's territory. The shuttle soared into the hangar and then he heard the crunch of landing gear on ice.

'We've landed. We are home, brothers,' said Haegr.

As the four walked out onto the icy surface of Fenris, Torin took Ragnar's arm and pulled him aside. 'Brother, listen to me and listen well. Both Haegr and I overhead what Gabriella said to you, our ears are too sharp for small quarters. Let Gabriella speak to Logan Grimnar. Don't speak of the Spear of Russ yourself. Trust the Great Wolf.'

Ragnar swallowed. His friend was probably right. Torin understood politics. If there was any justice in the galaxy, Ragnar would get his chance, and if any leader was just, it was Logan Grimnar.

Ragnar felt chills as he walked out of the hangar into the halls of the Fang with his Wolfblade brothers, following Gabriella. The imposing majesty and strength in the rock gave this hallowed ground an indescribable feeling. Other Space Wolves walked all around, along with the human warriors who dedicated their lives to serving the Chapter. It had been a long time since he had seen so many of his fellows. The Fang was where his life as a Space Wolf had started and it was his home.

Ranek, the ancient Wolf Priest, stood in the centre of the great passage, awaiting them. 'Wolfblade Ragnar, let me see you,' he said.

Ragnar immediately came to attention.

Clad in black power armour, the Wolf Priest wore a cape made from the pelt of a massive Fenrisian wolf. Like all Space Wolves, he wore teeth and wolf tails along with runes and wolf skulls as per his station. He was a large man, grey and dominating, old and strong like the mountain of the Fang itself. His fangs protruded like tusks and his beard was so grey and fine that it evoked comparisons to the colour of snow at twilight.

Ranek's glacial blue and piercing eyes studied Ragnar, assessing him. He felt as if the Wolf Priest knew everything that had transpired in his life since he had joined the Wolfblade.

'Lady Gabriella, may I have a moment with this member of your Wolfblade?' asked Ranek.

'As you wish, Wolf Priest Ranek,' she answered. Ragnar thought that he saw a hint of a smile in her eyes. Gabriella, Haegr and Torin continued into the Fang, leaving Ragnar behind.

The old Wolf Priest sized up Ragnar, pacing around him with a stern eye. Ragnar stood to attention, feeling as nervous as he ever did under the watchful eye of the Wolf Priest. How long ago it seemed that Ranek had taken him to be reborn as a Space Wolf. Indeed, to Ragnar, it seemed long ago that Ranek had seen him, before the judgement that led to his exile. 'You look good, laddie. Your time in the Wolfblade has helped you. Do you still feel like just a bodyguard?'

'No, I... I've learnt quite a bit,' Ragnar said, momentarily surprised at Ranek's observations, but then, he realised that he had changed and Wolf Priests were known for their abilities to look into the hearts of men.

Ranek raised a bushy eyebrow. 'I see judgement and wisdom in your eyes to go with that fire in your heart. You'll need it.'

'Need it? For what?' asked Ragnar.

'To defend the Imperium and Fenris, as you were chosen to do. Join your battle-brothers. I want to hear your report on Hyades as well. We'll speak more later.' Ranek clapped Ragnar's shoulder, held his eyes for a moment, and then strode off towards a group of bellowing Blood Claws.

Ragnar hurried to rejoin the Wolfblade. Torin was grinning and Haegr looked slightly annoyed as they paced respectfully behind Gabriella.

'He was not,' said Haegr.

'Aye, that he was,' retorted Torin.

'What are you talking about?' asked Ragnar.

'We saw some new Blood Claws,' answered Torin, 'and one of them was larger than Haegr, except perhaps in the belly,' Torin chuckled.

'There is no Space Wolf larger than mighty Haegr. Don't you agree, Ragnar?' asked Haegr.

Ragnar laughed. The banter and kinship of his battle-brothers gave him relief. 'Well, not that I've seen.'

'See, Torin? That settles the matter,' said Haegr. 'Later, I'll give you a good thrashing. Maybe it'll put some sense back into your head.'

As they approached the Hall of the Great Wolf, the members of the Wolfblade fell into silence.

Lady Gabriella led her champions into the hall of Logan Grimnar. Great stone-carved wolfs' heads looked down upon them. Ice coating parts of the walls of the cavernous hall made it seem like a deep cave, yet the banners and heraldry proclaimed that this was the hall of the greatest of lords. Advisors and warriors of the Chapter stood silently around the chamber, almost forming an honour guard, yet at the same time appearing as impassive as statues, as if they were part of the mountain itself.

The Great Wolf sat on the wolf throne, two Fenrisian wolves sitting quietly on either side. Even these massive beasts were humbled by the presence of their master. Logan Grimnar was the heart of the Fang, impassive and old beyond reckoning, yet as strong as the world. He rested a gauntleted hand on a double-headed frostaxe. He had a hardened face, craggy like the rocks and worn, yet strong, stronger than that of any man Ragnar had ever met. His beard framed his face like the ice on the sides of the Fang.

Ragnar took a deep breath and made sure to keep his eyes on the Great Wolf. He would not show fear or cowardice in front of his Chapter Master.

Gabriella knelt before the master of the Wolf Lords, as did the members of the Wolfblade in a proper show of respect.

'Lady Gabriella of House Belisarius, what tidings do you bring?' asked Logan Grimnar.

Gabriella rose to speak, and Ragnar, Torin and Haegr followed suit. Gabriella seemed like a thin dark shadow in the massive hall of the Wolf Lord.

'I bring ill tidings, Great Wolf. The capital of the planet Hyades was overrun by Chaos, and there was conflict as well with the Dark Angels. Our House was betrayed from within and the forces of the Thousand Sons are responsible for the deaths of many of my people including many noble Space Wolves.'

He replied, 'Tell me everything.'

Ragnar listened as Gabriella recounted the events on Hyades. He noticed that she emphasised the heroics of the Wolfblade, although she told the truth. One did not lie to the Great Wolf.

Gabriella finished with her revelation, 'There is more as well. I had a vision on Hyades. I believe that in my vision, I saw the Spear of Russ in the possession of the Thousand Sons.'

Although Ragnar did not hear a noise, he felt a collective gasp come from the assembled advisors. Such news could cause even the unwavering to waver.

'I believe that it may be possible that the Thousand Sons will once again attempt to draw Magnus the Red from the warp back into Imperial space,' she concluded.

Logan Grimnar remained impassive. Silence filled the chamber. The quiet lasted an eternity for Ragnar. It took every ounce of his self-control not to shout an oath to Leman Russ and the Emperor before the Great Wolf himself, that he would find and return the Spear of Russ. Still, he kept his tongue, but at that moment, he looked into the eyes of the mighty Wolf Lord and made the oath in his heart.

Ragnar thought that Logan Grimnar nodded, ever so slightly.

The doors to the great hall opened and a messenger came in, running swiftly. He went over to Logan Grimnar and whispered something to the Great Wolf.

Ragnar had a sudden feeling of déjà vu. At his last meeting with Logan Grimnar, a messenger had also interrupted to bring word of the death of Gabriella's father, the Great Wolf's old friend, Skander.

'Good news coupled with more grim tidings,' announced the Great Wolf. 'Berek Thunderfist and his fleet have returned battle-worn from Hyades, but the astropaths have reported attacks on many worlds. The Thousand Sons have launched an offensive, unforeseen in recent centuries against planets protected by our Chapter. Our enemies have declared war, and boldly, but we will rise to the challenge. There will be a council of war. Lady Gabriella, you and the Wolfblade may go. I will call upon you later.'

Gabriella knelt before the Chapter Master of the Space Wolves and departed with the Wolfblade following behind.

FOR THE NEXT several hours, Ragnar volunteered to spend his time guarding Lady Gabriella's chambers. He wanted the time to brood and think. Gabriella had wanted to sleep. Haegr had needed food, Torin looked as if he wished to explore so Ragnar decided to volunteer for the first shift of guard duty.

Ragnar wanted to recover the Spear of Russ. He knew that it should satisfy him if the Chapter found it, but he wanted to have a chance to restore his honour and he felt that it was his responsibility. He had lost it. He had been exiled and he wanted the chance to set things right.

After a several hours, Torin came up to him. 'Still on guard, brother?' he asked

'Aye,' said Ragnar, 'she still rests.'

'Well, Haegr will be eating a few more krakens before we see him again,' Torin said, shaking his head. 'I hope that the Chapter's stores will recover.'

Ragnar just looked at him.

'Brother,' said Torin, 'you have a great deal on your mind, but you can't change any of it. You look tense. I knew there was a problem when you didn't argue with Haegr or myself about guard duty and volunteered. Let me relieve you. Besides, someone important is in the observation chamber near the hangars, wanting to speak with you.'

'Who?' asked Ragnar.

'I think it best that you find out yourself. You'll know soon enough,' said Torin.

'Thank you, Torin. I'm on my way,' Ragnar said, slapping his fellow Space Wolf's shoulder. He walked quickly, and then broke into a jog as he headed to the observation chamber.

Someone wanted to speak to him. Ragnar wondered who it could be. Ranek, perhaps, wanting to give him advice?

Ragnar opened the stone doors, marked with Logan Grimnar's dancing wolf crest. The chamber looked out over the hangars, and from its vantage point, an observer could watch the Thunderhawks and shuttles arriving and departing. The panoramic view of Fenris seen through floor to ceiling panels was impressive. He could see the lesser mountains under the shadow of the Fang with their icecaps and forests, and the dark shadows of deep valleys. Far off, he could even make out the stormy oceans and a few of the distant islands as well as the mighty icebergs that floated on the cold seas.

Ragnar saw a Space Wolf standing by the viewing window. 'I've come as quickly as I could,' he blurted out, before he even took a good look at whoever was waiting for him.

'Well, not bad for someone as slow as you.' Ragnar instantly recognised the voice of Sven, his long-time friend. He smiled at the sound of the voice. Sven had been with Ragnar since the beginning. They had been chosen at the same time from the battlefields of Fenris. It had been so many years ago that Ragnar had lost count. They had survived initiation together, both confronting their personal struggles with the wulfen. They had seen many battles and were made members of the same claw. Sven had been with him when the Spear was lost, fighting alongside him against the Thousand Sons and the Sorcerer, Madox. Sven had lost a hand that day and more. The hellblade that had wounded him had cut deep.

Sven's hair was now silvery grey and his face far more lined than it should be. He reached out to Ragnar. Sven was more than a friend. He was a battle-brother, and closer to Ragnar than anyone else in the galaxy.

'Ragnar,' Sven said, grabbing him in a bear hug. 'It's good to see you. I had hoped to make planetfall on Hyades and find you.'

'Sven!' Ragnar returned the bear hug.

The two men broke their embrace and smiled at one another, but Ragnar knew that Sven could tell that something was wrong.

'Don't look so excited to see me,' said Sven.

Ragnar shook his head. 'I'm sorry, it's just…'

Sven held up his hand. 'I know, my brother. The Thousand Sons are back, and last time, you jammed the Spear of Russ into the eye of their primarch and got made into a Wolfblade. You know how I feel, especially about Madox. When I see him again, I'm going to take my blade and thrust it straight up his…'

'I remember,' said Ragnar, grinning. 'It is good to see you, Sven.' He gave Sven a hearty clasp.

'I can't believe that you have been living the soft life on Blessed Terra,' said Sven.

'You'd be surprised at life on Terra. Besides, what happened after we left Hyades?' asked Ragnar.

It was Sven's turn to grow quiet. 'The Dark Angels showed up and helped us finish the battle. We drove the Chaos fleet back, but we had to abandon Hyades. We had too much damage to stay there, and the Dark Angels left little in the way of facilities in the system to repair our ships. I think the future of Hyades is no longer ours to determine.'

The two friends exchanged a meaningful look. Word of what had happened on Hyades would reach the Imperium… and the Inquisition.

'While you were on guard duty, we finished a major briefing. The Thousand Sons have attacked across the sector. Some of the Wolf Lords got hit hard. Even as we speak, battle rages on,' said Sven. 'I suspect that you would have been invited if you weren't assigned to guard Lady Gabriella.'

'I see that the two of you are once again attempting to chart the future of the galaxy. Sven, you are needed with your company. Go,' said a deep voice.

Ragnar and Sven both jumped, startled, and reached for their weapons, before they realised that it was Ranek. Despite their senses, neither Ragnar nor Sven had noticed the Wolf Priest enter the chamber. Ragnar wondered how long he had been there.

'Of course,' Sven said removing his hand from his bolter. 'Good to see you again, Ragnar. Hope Terra hasn't made you too soft.' Sven clapped Ragnar's shoulder and left the chamber.

Ragnar came to attention, as he always did under Ranek's eye.

The Wolf Priest waited until the door closed before he spoke. 'The Thousand Sons have attacked us on all sides. Even now, we are looking for help wherever we can find it. The Wolfblade will be needed. The alliance between the Space Wolves and House Belisarius works both ways.'

'Laddie, you look as if you lost Hyades to the Thousand Sons. I have some terrible news for you. We lost a city on Hyades, not the planet, and it wasn't just you, but our entire Chapter, and we may be on the verge of losing much more. Ready yourself for your duties in the fight, wherever they may take you.'

'Yes, of course,' Ragnar said, taking a deep breath. Whatever he did, he would help his Chapter.

A gleam shone in the old man's eyes. 'Besides, I hear that there's a wolf around who stuck the primarch of the Thousand Sons in the eye.'

Ragnar grinned and to his surprise, Ranek grinned back. 'Go back to your duties,' said the Wolf Priest.

Ragnar nodded and left, heading back to Torin. When he arrived, the older Wolfblade stood at

Gabriella's door, straightening his moustache. Ragnar had a strange feeling his friend knew everything that had transpired.

'So, everything went well, I take it?' asked Torin.

'Indeed,' said Ragnar. 'Thank you. I'll take over guard duty again.'

'No need,' said Torin. 'Get yourself some food. I'll call if I need you.'

Ragnar decided to take his friend's advice and get something to eat. As he walked through the halls, the impact of the Fang and of Fenris struck him again. He was glad to be home. He made his way through the ice and rock-hewn corridors to the great hall, where he had enjoyed several feasts as a Blood Claw.

When Ragnar entered the great hall, he was astounded to see Berek Thunderfist's company. They were his friends and battle-brothers, and he had fought alongside them against the Thousand Sons. Many of them had fresh scars. Others wore gleaming cybernetics, a sure sign of their newness. A few also carried Dark Angels helms, obvious trophies. Ragnar felt strange to see so many who knew him so well. They knew of the Spear of Russ, and they had been on Hyades.

Ragnar saw Haegr, sitting alone at the other end of the hall. He paused, wondering if the others would recognise him. He wondered if they hated him as a disgrace to the company, if any of them would even acknowledge him. He was who he was, and he couldn't change the past.

He decided to make his way towards his giant battle-brother and the debris that Haegr had left on the table. As he walked, he thought about Magni and the young Wolfblade's last words.

Halfway across the room, he was noticed. Several Space Wolves stood up as he went towards Haegr. Ragnar felt the eyes and the stares. He remained focused on Haegr, who seemed to be the only person in the room oblivious to his presence. Haegr was too busy devouring a huge joint of meat and drinking a keg of Fenrisian ale, apparently at the same time.

'Ragnar,' shouted a Grey Hunter. Ragnar stopped and turned.

'To our battle-brother Ragnar! May he have another chance to drive a spear into the eye of Magnus the Red.'

'To your health, little brother.'

'It hasn't been the same without you.'

Suddenly, the voices came from all sides and so did the cheers. Then, a number of Space Wolves were all around him, attempting to commiserate for his assignment to the Wolfblade, asking about his part in the battle on Hyades, wishing him well, and hoping that he'd get a chance to get back at the Thousand Sons. It all seemed overwhelming and wonderful all at once. His battle-brothers knew the truth.

Ragnar was home. Someone thrust a drink into his hand and he gulped it down. It was the best-tasting ale he had ever had. 'To Berek's great company!' he shouted.

Cheers of agreement followed. 'When are you rejoining us?' yelled a Space Wolf. 'You should be there when we drive the Thousand Sons into the warp.'

'Ho!' roared Haegr, before belching loudly.

Haegr pushed his way through the crowd. 'Hands off, he's a Wolfblade now.' Ragnar could tell by the way that Haegr was swaying that the giant had drunk too much, even for him.

Haegr clapped Ragnar's shoulder.

'I am a Wolfblade,' announced Ragnar, 'but I will always be the battle-brother of any member of Berek Thunderfist's great company.'

There was a loud cheering and then, much drinking.

SEVENTEEN
Councils of War

LOGAN GRIMNAR STOOD at the window looking out over the mountains of Asaheim. His grey hair flowed like a mane, blending with the wolf pelt cloak he wore, making it hard to tell one from the other. This was the tallest tower in the Fang, and he often found himself here at times like this. Looking out over the mountain ranges of Asaheim brought him focus. He was the Chapter Master of the Space Wolves. He'd been the Great Wolf for several centuries, so long in fact that he was sometimes referred to as the Old Wolf. He sometimes found that title humorous for it was only at times like this that he actually felt old.

The Thousand Sons, the Space Wolves' ancient hated nemesis, were once again wreaking destruction and mayhem within Space Wolf-controlled space, on a scale that had not been seen since their assault on the Fang, many years ago. The actions on Hyades were just one of a series of events that were unfolding; several worlds were under siege.

Logan knew the Thousand Sons all too well. They did not just initiate random assaults, mindless violence, or kill for the sake of killing. He wondered if the Sons of Magnus might be hiding their true intentions within several attacks. Perhaps a mastermind among them had devised a terrifying scheme. Maybe they were hoping to spread the Space Wolves so thin that their true objective would go unnoticed until it was too late. Dealing with the Thousand Sons was always problematic.

Logan pondered the challenges that lay before his Chapter and his battle-brothers. Upon hearing of the attacks he had instructed the Rune Priests to consult the runes in an attempt to unravel the mystery of Thousand Sons' true intentions. He had called on his available Wolf Lords to seek the advice of their veteran leadership. He had even woken one of the mighty Dreadnoughts to hear the wisdom of the ancient one. This information was imperative to allow him and his Wolf Lords to develop a cohesive plan of action and bring the incursion of the Thousand Sons to an abrupt halt.

The door to the Great Wolf's chamber slid open and Rune Priest Aldrek entered the room, accompanied by Ranek and two other Rune Priests. Grimnar stood gazing out of the window with his back to them, apparently oblivious to their presence. The four priests stood perfectly silent, waiting for the Great Wolf to acknowledge them before daring to speak.

Several minutes passed before Aldrek took a breath as he prepared to interrupt the Great Wolf's concentration.

'Yes, Aldrek, I know you are here. You've consulted the runes, I take it?' Grimnar asked.

'We have, Great Wolf,' Aldrek said.

'What do they tell you?' Logan took a deep breath and slowly turned to face the priests.

'The news is grave, Great Wolf, far worse than we first thought. The runes suggest that the Thousand Sons have recovered the Spear of Russ, and the signs indicate that they will attempt far more than they did in the past.' Dread filled Aldrek's voice as he continued.

Aldrek left unspoken the fact that when the Thousand Sons had last possessed the Spear of Russ they had attempted to summon their primarch, Magnus the Red from the warp. All of the Space Wolves had heard the tale of that battle.

'The runes show that the ritual they are attempting could bring about the destruction of Fenris and the entire Space Wolf Chapter!'

WITHIN HOURS, THE leadership of the Space Wolves had gathered in the Great Hall of the Fang at the command of the Great Wolf. Five Wolf Lords, each a leader of one of the Chapter's great companies, sat at an oval table, carved from rare woods. A large circular stone tablet hung at one end, the grand annulus with the symbols of each great company. Dominating them all was the rampant wolf, symbol of Logan Grimnar. The Great Wolf sat on a throne of stone, directly below his crest. Behind each of the Wolf Lords stood a small retinue of Wolf Guard, hand-picked warriors from their companies, chosen to serve as the Wolf Lord's personal guard.

Other advisors and personages, such as Lady Gabriella of House Belisarius, held seats or stood behind the Wolf Guards. They included many Wolf Priests, Iron Priests and Rune Priests, the spiritual, technological and psychic advisors to their leaders.

Like the grand annulus, the table within the great hall depicted the symbols of each great company, each one having an assigned position. Several of those positions were empty, representing the severity of the situation facing the Space Wolves. It was not uncommon for a number of the great companies to be away from the Fang, on various missions, conducting Chapter business, however this time their absence indicated another threat within Fenrisian-protected space.

Logan Grimnar listened intently to Wolf Lord Berek's report on the events that had taken place on Hyades. Slowly stroking his beard, the Old Wolf had deep concentration etched on his face as he contemplated the course before the Space Wolves.

Logan rose to his feet and walked around the table, arms crossed. All eyes followed the Great Wolf as he paced across the room.

'The Thousand Sons manipulated us into fighting the Dark Angels and vice versa. This is not an isolated incident. On Gere, a Chaos uprising has destroyed valuable factories. Across the worlds we protect, numerous threats have arisen. Each one seems random, with no connection to the others, but we all suspect that this isn't coincidence. We are at a dangerous crossroads, my Wolf Lords.' The Great Wolf walked back to his seat. 'We have other indicators as well. Rune Lord Aldrek will explain further.'

Aldrek bowed to the Great Wolf and stepped forwards.

'Wolf Lords, at the behest of Lord Grimnar, I have gathered many Rune Priests and consulted the runes, interpreting the portents. The signs are disturbing. Dark castings indicate a terrible threat and show signs that the Chapter may be in even more danger than we imagined. We believe that the Thousand Sons may be seeking a powerful artifact, but we cannot be certain what and why. What we do know is that the runes indicate a threat to the Chapter as strongly as they ever have,' Aldrek finished.

'Iron Priest Rorik,' commanded the Great Wolf.

Holding a massive thunder hammer as the sign of his station, a large Iron Priest strode before the assembled lords. 'Wolf Lords, at the behest of Lord Grimnar, I have analysed the worlds attacked so far, along with others of my order and many of them held valuable resources. The Chaos Marines have attacked our production abilities, and although they have done nothing that we cannot rebuild, they have weakened our ability to maintain our production. We are not well-positioned for a protracted conflict.'

'Finally, Wolf Priest Ranek,' said the Great Wolf.

'I bring grim tidings indeed. In the battles that have unfolded in this conflict, we have harvested few gene-seed from our fallen battle-brothers. Although the number of gene-seed lost is small, every one is a precious gift from our primarch, Leman Russ and a terrible loss. Without them, we cannot recruit battle-brothers to replace those lost in battle.' Ranek stepped back.

Logan Grimnar stood once again, and this time he raised the double-bladed Axe of Morkai. 'The attacks have begun, and I believe that these random events are a prelude to the true ambitions of the Thousand Sons. I need every one of you, and every one of your men, to meet this threat. What you have not been told is this, and this information will not leave this hall without my leave: we have reason to believe that the Thousand Sons may have recovered the Spear of Russ from the warp. Each of you knows what the Thousand Sons attempted the last time they possessed the relic. You will find out the truth and discover the enemy's plans and intentions, as well as defending your assigned regions of space.'

Skalds entered the great hall, placing a scrolled parchment on the table in front of each of the Wolf Lords.

'The scrolls you've just been given detail the assign-ments for each of your great companies,' said the Great Wolf. 'We cannot let our personal ambitions cloud our judgement. We each must do what must be done. Now go and prepare your Wolves, for once again the Sons of Russ must cleanse the galaxy of the wretched Thousand Sons, just as Russ the Wolf Father did when he led our brothers to Prospero to destroy Magnus himself.'

A howl of agreement rose within the hall, as Wolf Lords and their Wolf Guards raised their weapons in salute to the Great Wolf. The howl continued even as they began to leave the great hall.

As Gabriella rose from her seat, Rune Lord Aldrek approached her. 'Lady Gabriella, might we have a few more minutes of your time?' Aldrek asked, gesturing towards the Great Wolf.

'Of course, Lord Aldrek,' Gabriella said, moving down the table to stand near the Great Wolf.

As Aldrek took his place beside the Logan Grimnar, Grimnar leaned forwards and rested his arms on the table. 'Lady Gabriella our situation is dire, and our forces are spread thin.'

'Great Wolf, how may House Belisarius be of assistance?' Gabriella asked, her concern genuine. She had lived on Fenris and she valued the ancient alliance with the Space Wolves and the services of the Wolfblade.

'It pleases this old warrior to hear the sincerity in your words, Lady Gabriella, again proving the wisdom of our ancestors in the forging of this alliance. I will need all the Space Wolves that we have to investigate and battle this threat. Although their numbers are few, the members of the Wolfblade have shown their abilities on Terra and on Hyades. I require their aid in unravelling this threat.'

'Great Wolf, House Belisarius and the Wolfblade are at your service.'

RAGNAR AWOKE WITH a start, and for an instant he did not recognise the group bunks in the guest chambers of the Fang. Then the blur that was the night before coalesced in his mind with images of toasts, song and heroic stories of battle. He felt as if he was sitting in

the learning machine again as the images of last
night's events poured through his mind. There were
also the strangest images of Haegr entering some kind
of bizarre eating contest. It had been a long time since
Ragnar had consumed that much Fenrisian ale. A
Space Marine's physiology was designed to resist
almost any kind of toxin or poison, however, ale from
Fenris was a different story entirely.

Standing up he looked around for Haegr and Torin,
but they were nowhere to be found. He walked across
the room, until his legs became a little wobbly, forcing
him to take a seat. In all his recollections of Fenris, his
reminiscences of the Fang, he hadn't remembered the
ale being so potent. Placing his elbows on his knees, he
rested his forehead in his hands.

He leaned back in the chair and started to laugh. He
was so happy to be back in the Fang, even though he
knew it would not last. Soon he and his battle-brothers
would be at war again, but right at this moment he was
pleased to be home.

The door to the sleeping quarters opened and Haegr
entered the room. 'Have you been drinking all night,
Ragnar? Why are you laughing?' Haegr looked puzzled.

Ragnar was amazed at the resilience of his fellow
Space Wolf. He knew that Haegr had consumed much
more ale than he had, but here he was this morning
completely free of the effects. Ragnar stood up, not
about to allow Haegr to see him in his true condition.

'Good day, Haegr,' Ragnar greeted his friend.

'Ragnar, the Great Wolf summoned all of his Wolf
Lords into the great hall. They've been in there for
hours,' Haegr informed Ragnar. 'They should have just

finished. I thought you'd like to see if we can find out what's happening.'

'Give me a moment,' Ragnar said. He dressed quickly, and found that the ritual of putting on his power armour helped to clear his head.

Ragnar and Haegr entered the corridor, heading towards the great hall. Ragnar hoped that there would be a need for the Wolfblade. With so many systems under siege, Ragnar felt that every Space Wolf would be needed.

As they rounded the corner of one of the stone corridors, they saw Torin striding in their direction. As Torin approached, Ragnar wondered if his rebirth as a Space Wolf had an unseen flaw, because here was another of his battle-brothers who seemed to have no ill-effects from the night before.

'Greetings, Torin,' Haegr said. 'Ragnar and I are going to the great hall to find out what's happened, unless you already know?'

'I'll join you and make sure you don't get into too many fights. Meanwhile, I have special instructions for Ragnar. Our brother here needs to see Wolf Priest Ranek in his chambers. The old priest asked to speak to you once the meeting ended.'

'Very well, I'll catch up with you later,' Ragnar said, quickening his pace and heading down the corridor to the Wolf Priest's chambers.

As soon as Ragnar was out of earshot, Haegr turned to Torin. 'What's the story, Torin?'

'I'm not sure, old friend, but whatever it is I fear that things will never be the same,' Torin replied.

* * *

ONCE HE GOT out of sight of the other members of the Wolfblade, Ragnar stepped up his pace. Although he tried not to seem like he was an overly enthusiastic Blood Claw running through the Fang, he was failing miserably in his attempt. He couldn't help but move quickly, as his mind was running through the possibilities of why his old mentor might have summoned him.

Things were very confusing for Ragnar. Since his interrogation of Cadmus on Hyades, where Cadmus had mentioned the use of an ancient artifact by Madox, he had thought that it might be the Spear of Russ. Then with Gabriella's visions, he felt that his hopes might be affirmed. His excitement was matched only by his dread. If Madox was using the Spear of Russ again, that meant he would be responsible for more than the loss of the holy artifact, he would have given the Thousand Sons a deadly weapon.

These scenarios dominated Ragnar's thoughts as he moved through the corridors of the Fang. He wanted to have the opportunity to redeem himself by recovering the Spear.

If the Thousand Sons had the Spear then maybe he had made a mistake using the weapon against Magnus. He had always told himself that he had made the decision in the moment and if called upon to make that decision again he would do so. Now, doubt crept into his mind, and doubt was the most deadly enemy of the warrior.

Ragnar chided himself silently. This was idle speculation, and he knew that his thoughts were getting away from him. Besides, the most important thing was the defence of the Chapter and the Imperium. That was his first duty, and he would live with his decision as long as he continued to serve the Emperor. There was a reason that the Wolf Priest wished to see him, and he would find out in a moment.

Ragnar weaved and sidestepped his way through the busy traffic of the Fang as skalds and servitors went to perform their required duties in this time of war. Finally, he entered the corridor leading to Ranek's chamber. He slowed his pace. Now that he was almost at the meeting, he hesitated, not really sure if he wanted to hear what Ranek had to say.

Rage filled Ragnar's heart, rage at his constant feelings of doubt. He was a Son of Russ and he would face his destiny, whatever it might be. Pausing for a moment, he cleared his mind, forcing himself to accept his actions for what they were. He would do whatever was required of him, but this self-doubt and desire for redemption needed to be set aside. His honour was not more important than his duty.

Large wolf skulls hung on the door to Ranek's chamber. Ragnar knocked and waited, calming himself and focusing. He was ready to meet with Ranek.

The Wolf Priest pulled open the door. 'Ragnar, thank you for coming so quickly,' Ranek said, stepping aside to allow Ragnar to enter. His quarters were sparse, exactly what one would expect for the living area of a Wolf Priest of Russ.

'It is my pleasure, Wolf Priest. How may I be of service?'

'It is actually I who may be of service to you.' Ranek walked across the room and sat down, gesturing for

Ragnar to sit in the chair opposite him. Ragnar hesitated for a moment, and then sat.

'I'm not sure what you mean, Lord Ranek,' Ragnar said, confused.

'When you left here, Ragnar, you left under a cloud of political turmoil, with the Chapter split by your decision in regards to the Spear of Russ,' Ranek began. 'It was a decision that I and many others agreed with, a decision based on the choice of evils. Had you chosen otherwise then I believe that you and your brothers would be dead and the Imperium would have been plunged into war once again as the Thousand Sons invaded.' Ranek paused for a moment.

'Since your return from Hyades, Rune Lord Aldrek and his priests have deciphered their runes, and the Wolf Lords have studied the tactics and strategies of the Chaos Space Marines. They suspect that the Thousand Sons have a terrible plan for all of us.'

'Ranek, I understand the severity of the situation, and I would ask for your forgiveness for the bluntness of this question–'

Ranek anticipated Ragnar's question, interrupting him with the answer. 'Yes, Ragnar, the runes imply that the Thousand Sons have found the Spear of Russ. With the sacred artifact, combined with the holy gene-seed harvested on Hyades, we suspect that they plan on conducting a massive ritual that might somehow bring about the destruction of the Sons of Russ.'

Excitement and dread filled Ragnar's heart. In that moment he discovered clarity, clarity of mind that he had never known. He knew what must be done. The events that were unfolding were events that were directly tied to his actions, not just the loss of the Spear, but his actions prior to that as well. He had thwarted the Chaos Sorcerer Madox on two separate occasions. Madox's plot was as much about Ragnar as it was about the Space Wolves. His hatred of Ragnar was at the heart of his plan. That was why Cadmus lured the Wolfblade to Hyades. Ragnar knew that it fell to him to bring this situation to an end, regardless of the cost. Ragnar would stop Madox, redemption or not. It was his destiny.

'Lord Ranek, you know my heart better than anyone. You know that I will do whatever is asked of me. Madox is at the heart of this plan, and the Spear of Russ may be in their hands because of my actions. It falls to me to bring this situation to an end,' Ragnar said, meeting Ranek's gaze, without flinching.

'The Great Wolf made that decision earlier today Ragnar, and he asked Lady Gabriella for the services of Wolfblade. But, know this, what I have told you about the Spear of Russ is known only to a few and with the leave of the Great Wolf. Do not speak of it, save to Lady Gabriella, a Wolf Lord, myself or the Great Wolf himself. He bade me to tell you. He felt you deserved to know,' Ranek said beginning to smile. 'You've grown, Ragnar. I asked you here with the intention of guiding you through the turmoil that I had assumed these events would have thrown you into. However, it would appear that you are no longer the impetuous young warrior that I once knew.'

Ranek rose from his seat, extending his hand to Ragnar, who grasped his forearm in a warrior's handshake. Ranek's pride showed even on his hard face.

'Now, Son of Russ, go and fulfil your destiny.'

Ragnar left Ranek's chamber for the guest quarters he and the Wolfblade had been assigned. There was no longer any doubt in his heart, no question of where he belonged. Everything he had accomplished, every decision, his every failure had led him to this moment. For the first time in a long time, Ragnar's destiny was clear and he would face that destiny as a Space Wolf.

EPILOGUE

THE WAR FOR Corinthus V was nearly over. One more victory and the Space Wolves would break the power of the Night Lords. Yet the war had gone on for one day more than the Space Wolves had expected. With victory in their grasp in a battle on the streets of Saint Harman, Tor, a member of the Wolf Guard, had led his fellow Space Marines into an ambush meant to draw out the Wolf Lord and decapitate the great company. The strength and skill of the Space Wolves had allowed them to emerge defeated but unbowed. Based on information gathered by Space Wolf scouts, Ragnar Blackmane was ready to turn the tables on the forces of Chaos. This time, the main attack by the Space Wolves would provide a diversion, while Tor would get the chance to redeem himself in an assault against a Chaos sorcerer, possibly the leader of these renegades.

Wolf Lord Ragnar Blackmane paced back and forth in front of his men, as they readied themselves for an offensive into Saint Harman. The members of his force waited just outside the Administratum sector, the city's heart, the same sector of the city where the Wolf Lord had been ambushed only the day before.

Ragnar wanted to give the order to attack. He was ready to seize victory over the traitors and the souls who slavishly followed them, but he knew that timing would be critical. He had to wait until he received the signal that Tor was in place.

WITHIN THE FETID and rusted sewer tunnels beneath Saint Harman, over a kilometre away from the Wolf Lord, Tor led a group of Grey Hunters as they followed two Space Wolf scouts. A powerful sorcerer among the Chaos Space Marines had planned a ritual to open a portal into the warp. According to the scouts, the blasphemous servants of Chaos had chosen the Cathedral of Saint Harman, the city's namesake, as the site of their unholy ceremony.

Tor clenched and unclenched his fist. His Wolf Lord had chosen him from his Wolf Guard to lead this strike, while the rest of the Space Wolves provided a distraction. The day before, Tor had led his pack into an ambush and drawn another pack with him. He had nearly lost his life and had cost his Chapter a few of their great warriors, but Ragnar had chosen him, regardless. For that, Tor was thankful.

He felt responsible for what had happened, and he longed for a chance to restore his honour and make amends. Ragnar had taken him aside before dawn and explained the plan. Tor and a hand-picked group of Grey Hunters would interrupt the Chaos ritual and slay the sorcerer responsible. To provide cover, the Space Wolves would conduct a massive assault, hopefully drawing away as many of the enemy as possible. Tor was surprised that after his failure the Wolf Lord would select him, but one look in Ragnar's eyes and Tor knew that the Wolf Lord understood exactly how he felt. Tor would not fail.

The older scout, Hoskuld, raised his hand for Tor and his men to halt. The squad hesitated in the acrid dimly-lit sewers. Tor could hear the water dripping from leaking pipes and even in the dim light, he could see the colours of contaminants swirling in the water where he and his men stood.

Hoskuld indicated a set of metal rungs leading to a large grate to the street above. 'The alley next to the cathedral,' he whispered. With that, the scouts turned their backs on Tor and his men and jogged off into the deepening shadows of the sewers. Tor knew that they would find their own positions to support the assault.

It was time. Tor activated his comm and signalled to Ragnar, before deactivating it again. The attack would begin, and the rest would be up to him and his pack.

RAGNAR'S COMM BUZZED, and then went silent. Just as he had previously instructed, Tor had simply signalled, and then cut his comm. There was no need to risk the enemy intercepting their messages. The time to launch the attack had come.

Ragnar activated his comm, speaking to all of his Wolf Guard, save Tor, who were scattered throughout the force. 'Move out! The time has come!'

A soft chorus of howls began from one end of the Space Wolf force, and then raced to the other as each pack joined in. Ragnar enjoyed the sound and he could feel the excitement in his veins. There would be nothing subtle about this attack. The Wolf Lord wanted the Night Lords to know he was coming, and he counted on the fact that in their arrogance, the Chaos Space Marines would see the howls as the foolish bravado of a mob of barbarians, rather than realise this entire attack was a distraction.

Packs of Grey Hunters, Blood Claws and a team of Long Fangs made their way into the rockcrete and plasteel canyons of Saint Harman fanning out into different streets. Each group moved carefully, checking for booby traps and ambushes.

A pack of ten Blood Claws escorted the Wolf Lord. Ragnar's push through the street came with its own mobile cover. A tank, the Predator Annihilator *Wolf's Rage*, led the way, with a modified bulldozer blade fused to its front hull, allowing it to push through the debris-filled street. The tank's lascannons gave the *Wolf's Rage* the firepower to deal with almost any enemy. The vehicle was at a disadvantage in the narrow city streets, but Ragnar had chosen the vehicle and its crew because he knew that the threat they posed would draw attention.

The Night Lords didn't disappoint Ragnar. The front blade of the predator struck a large chunk of rock, and then a melta-bomb detonated, incinerating the blade and sending a spray of hot metal across the front of the tank. Ragnar and the Blood Claws threw themselves to the ground, instinctively going for cover. Their instincts proved correct as bolter fire rained down from the windows of two buildings on each side of the street ahead of them.

'Everyone, follow me,' Ragnar ordered the Blood Claws on his comm. He got off the pavement and immediately broke into a full run, racing past the damaged tank into the building on his left. The only way to eliminate the enemy would be to carve them out of their holes. Skulls of long-dead scribes and bureaucrats stared blankly from the rockcrete facing of the building. Ragnar joked to himself that they had retained their personalities in death.

Bolter rounds ricocheted off Ragnar's power armour, pelting him like hail. He took a grenade from his belt and threw it on the run at the main doors to the building. They were large and darkened with a yellow Imperial eagle emblazoned upon them, which made a perfect target. The krak grenade blew the doors to pieces.

Within seconds, Ragnar and the Blood Claws entered the smoke left behind by the doors and found cover in the building. Now, Ragnar had to lead his men up and find the foe. He hit his comm. 'This is the Wolf Lord. My pack has engaged the enemy.'

Tor and his men had waited for over half an hour in the sewer tunnel since giving the signal. He looked over at Jarl, one of the most experienced Grey Hunters, a warrior best known for his service against orks. Jarl wore a strand of ork fangs as a trophy, in addition to a necklace with a single wolf tooth. He rested a large axe on one shoulder and held his bolter one-handed. 'We're ready, sir, if the time is right,' Jarl said.

Tor realised that he had been looking to Jarl for consent to start the assault, but that wasn't Jarl's decision to make, it was his. Tor knew this was another reason why Ragnar had chosen him. Tor could make sound decisions and he needed to do so again before he let yesterday's events creep into his brain and make him doubt himself. 'The time is right. Let's move, quickly and quietly. We make sure the ritual is starting before we reveal ourselves.'

Tor grabbed the rungs and climbed up to the metal grate. He carefully opened the grate and stepped into an alley between two buildings. The alley was dark, the only light coming from the street visible at one end of the alley. Tor could hear the distant echoes of bolter shots and explosions. He raised his bolter and stealthily moved towards the street.

When he reached the end of the alley, he peered out. His augmented eyes adjusted to the low light just as the eyes of a nocturnal predator would, but he didn't need any enhanced vision to see. The alley opened to a street that ran into a main square in front of the cathedral. The giant religious edifice rose triumphantly above all of the surrounding buildings. Though he was about one hundred metres from the cathedral, the signs of heresy were unmistakable.

A large fountain in front of the cathedral was lit up, shining lights on a statue of Saint Harman, who appeared as an elderly monk, having devoted every waking breath to his devotion to the Emperor. Someone had chipped the face off the statue, leaving it to appear as an empty robe, and instead of clean water, the fountain was filled with blood. Just looking at the building, Tor felt something was very wrong, as if the beast within him could sense the unnatural events that the scouts had assured him were happening there.

A faint greenish light appeared for a moment from the cathedral's front windows. There could be no question in Tor's mind. It was time to set matters right and, defeat the enemy.

'Let's move around the perimeter of the square, keep to as much cover as possible and make your way to the left side of the cathedral. We may be able to find an entrance besides the front,' he said.

Like true wolves of Fenris, the Grey Hunters stalked through the shadows and made their way along the edge of the square. If they were detected, the enemy gave no sign. Twice more, the greenish glow came from the cathedral.

The pack reached the outer wall of the cathedral and made its way around the side of the building. A modest door rested in an alcove on the side of the titanic structure, and a carved image of Saint Harman stood untouched over the door. 'The Emperor protects,' said Tor.

As Tor paused to reflect on the Emperor, he caught a faint scent from behind the door, the smell of sulphur and oils. It instantly made him think of the Chaos Marines from the previous day. Waving his men away, he readied his bolter.

He gave the door a hard kick, smashing it inwards and then whirled away.

A Night Lord blasted gouts of flame out of the door. In his ornate armour, the light of the flame reflected and burned all the brighter. The Traitor Marine advanced without a word, his flamer held ready to incinerate his target.

Tor had avoided the worst of the blast. He threw himself into the passage with no cover, trusting that his power armour and natural speed would provide enough protection. He activated his power sword, sending energy cascading from the hilt, without losing a step of his charge. Before the Night Lord could raise his weapon to fire again, the power sword sliced through the barrel. Tor jammed the blade into his foe, piercing his power armour and leaving him thrashing on the end of the sword. With a solid jerk, he pulled the weapon free and led his men up a staircase, and he hoped, into the main sanctuary.

RAGNAR LED THE Blood Claws up a battered flight of stairs as they raced to the upper floors of the building used by the Night Lords to fire down on the street. Ragnar took the stairs three at a time. He looked forward to running a few traitors through with his runeblade. A door at the top of the stairs marked this as the fifth floor of the building dedicated to the memory of the scribe Leonardus.

The door fell forwards and the servants of Chaos threw grenades down at the Space Wolves. Ragnar could see two of his foes, both Night Lords. They were tall warriors, even for Space Marines, made taller still by large horns jutting from their helms. 'Grenade!' shouted Ragnar as he continued forwards. The sudden attack had momentarily surprised Ragnar and all he could do was keep charging.

The first Night Lord drew a chainsword and interposed himself on the stairs in front of Ragnar. He showed no fear and no hesitation. With his off-hand, he ripped a large pouch off his belt and threw it at the Wolf Lord. This time Ragnar was ready, lashing out at the makeshift missile with his runeblade, and slashing open the pouch to reveal the bloodied helm of a Space Wolf.

'Look upon your fate, dog of the Emperor,' the Night Lord snarled then thrust at Ragnar with his whirring chainsword. Ragnar regained his wits and parried the blade with his own.

Behind him, the other Night Lord readied his bolter, looking for a clean shot at Ragnar.

These were worthy foes, thought Ragnar. In a moment, they had seized the initiative and blocked the stairs, enabling them to fight the Space Wolves one at a time, while the rest of their squad made ready for battle or made their escape. He decided that he had had enough of the Night Lords.

With a sweep of his blade and a howl, the Wolf Lord slashed through the chainsword, rendering it useless, and then raised his bolter to the helm of the Night Lord and squeezed the trigger. Round after round impacted the head of the Chaos Space Marine, blowing large holes in his skull.

Ragnar wasted no time, tossing the body of the first Night Lord aside. The second one mercilessly opened up on the Space Wolf with a torrent of bolter rounds. Ragnar growled and threw himself into the enemy. He took the large man off his feet, and then sat up to give himself enough room to plunge the runeblade into the Chaos Marine's gut.

The Night Lord glared at Ragnar even as he lay dying. Ragnar could feel the anger and disgust this traitor held in his heart for the Imperium, a hatred so great that he had sold his soul to Chaos. The Night Lord writhed, but reached for the grenades on his belt. Ragnar saw the move and pinned his foe's wrist to the ground with the barrel of his bolter and then pulled the trigger, blowing his foe's hand off.

With his final chance to kill the Wolf Lord gone, the light in the Night Lord's eyeplates dimmed, and his ghost left him, taking his hatred with it.

The Blood Claws rushed up around Ragnar and into a long corridor. Ragnar's men seemed relatively unscathed from the grenade attack. 'Find any more of them that you can, each of these foes costs the enemy dearly.'

Soon, the Night Lords would try something desperate. Ragnar could hear distant artillery echo from outside. He hadn't ordered artillery bombardment. If anything, Ragnar was hoping to keep the city as intact as possible. If the forces of Chaos had any artillery, then it would be precious indeed.

A Night Lord dropped out of an air vent at the end of the hall and began firing. The Blood Claws saw him and howled. Then they charged like starving wolves having sighted their prey. By the time Ragnar stood, the axes and blades of the Blood Claws had struck the

Night Lord in dozens of places. He fell and the Blood Claws continued to reduce him to nearly unrecognisable gore.

Then, a blast shook the building. The Night Lords were willing to fire on their own men in order to kill their enemies. Ragnar looked down at the tall Night Lord he had dismembered and killed. In the remaining hand, the warrior clutched a comm. The attempt to reach the grenade had been a distraction. He might have signalled the enemy to strike the building with their ordinance.

'We need to get out, now!' shouted Ragnar. He hoped that Tor would be successful and soon.

Tor RACED UP a flight of stairs in the darkened stone Cathedral of Saint Harman, hoping that he had chosen wisely and found a way to the ritual site. Nine Grey Hunters followed their Wolf Guard, ready to complete their mission. The sight before them made all of them take pause.

The entire inner sanctuary of the cathedral had been gutted. Pews were thrown asunder, blood had been poured on the sacred stones of the floor, statues had been toppled and praises to the Gods of Chaos had been written on the walls, proclaiming their power. A billowing emerald bonfire roared between collapsed pews, and robed heretics stood with their arms spread at the edges of the flames, chanting in a strange undulating tongue.

A figure in a horned helm and long blood-red robes led them. Pale veined long-fingered hands extended from his sleeves, and as he gestured, the chanters changed their words and pitch, as if he was some sinister maestro conducting a choir of blasphemy. The flames also reacted to his every gesture, and Tor knew that this man was the sorcerer.

Then, there were the Chaos Space Marines.

Eight Night Lords held positions around the room, standing in four pairs with rubble nearby providing easy cover. Each one of the ancient Chaos Marines had his own distinctive armour, but all of them shared the same look. Spikes and blades designed to inspire fear doubled as practical weapons, while belts of ammunition were strung over their chests. The Night Lords were hard fighters and each individual was prepared to hold out against terrible odds. They showed no hesitation when the Space Wolves arrived, although Tor was certain that they must have surprised their enemy. They raised their bolters at the Space Wolves in well-drilled unison.

Tor knew what he needed to do. The Night Lords would be content to engage the Space Wolves in a firefight until the ritual brought something unholy from the warp to finish them off. Tor wasn't about to wait for that to happen. It was time to charge.

Bolter rounds crashed into the Grey Hunters as they charged. The Night Lords mercilessly fired shots as fast as their bolters allowed. Tor felt the rounds battering his power armour, but he clenched his teeth and focused on the sorcerer – his objective.

A Night Lord leapt over a crumbling statue and launched himself at Tor, realising that the Wolf Guard intended to kill the sorcerer. Circular chainblades spun on the Chaos Marine's armour, and he leapt at

Tor, thrusting the blades forwards to slash through the Space Wolf's armour and then his flesh and bone. He moved with a speed that rivalled Tor's own.

Tor paused to bring up his power sword to defend himself, but even as he began, he knew that he would be too slow. Fortunately for him, Space Wolves ran in packs. Although Jarl was a step behind Tor, the Grey Hunter had been watching for an attack. He threw his body up as a shield and the Night Lord crashed into Jarl instead of Tor. Sparks flew as the Night Lord's chainblades ripped into Jarl's power armour. The decorated veteran with his ork trophies roared rather than screamed from the pain as he wrestled with the foe.

Tor turned back to the sorcerer. He would not let Jarl's effort go for naught. The mage gestured at Tor, breaking the ritual as he did so. Immediately, the emerald flame flickered and died. The monks screamed as one, while bolts of power flashed from the sorcerer's fingertips at Tor.

Ozone and brimstone mixed in the air as the bolts crashed into Tor. He felt all of his hearts seize up at once, and suddenly he couldn't breathe. He kept moving as if he were an automaton. The sorcerer clenched his fists and as he did, Tor's chest tightened. The Space Wolf's eyesight dimmed and his ears rang. He thought to himself that no matter what, even if it meant death, he would reach the sorcerer and complete his mission. He would justify Ragnar's faith in him. He had been given a chance to redeem himself and nothing, not even the dark magics of Chaos would prevent him from succeeding.

The Chaos sorcerer gazed at the Wolf Guard, and although his eyesight blurred, the Space Wolf glared back. The Space Marine's reaction surprised the sorcerer, and Tor watched the malicious confidence leave the robed figure. As it did, Tor almost felt his strength return. He closed the gap between them.

One of the monks tried to intervene, much as Jarl had gone to Tor's aid, but even half-blind and in agony, Tor still possessed enough strength to lash out with his power sword and cut down his blocker.

The energy flickered on the Chaos sorcerer's fingers. Tor couldn't tell if his foe said anything – the rushing in his ears was too great – but there was no longer any distance to cross. The sorcerer broke the spell and attempted to draw a blade to defend himself.

Breath flowed back into Tor's lungs and his hearts pounded. His sight instantly improved and the rushing in his ears faded. Instead of pausing to cherish the return of his senses and breathe, Tor brought his power sword up into the body of the sorcerer. Mystic robes, flesh and bone couldn't stop the stroke as Tor cut the sorcerer in half. The monks screamed again as one and then fell, like marionettes suddenly without strings.

The Night Lords redoubled their attacks against the Space Wolves. They had failed to protect the sorcerer and the Chaos Marines knew that only death would satisfy their Dark Gods. Tor felt power fill his body. He had completed the mission for the Wolf Lord. He activated his comm quickly. 'Wolf Lord, the deed is done,' he said and without waiting for a response, leapt to the aid of his fellow Space Wolves.

RAGNAR AND THE Blood Claws had escaped the building where the ambushers had lain in wait for them, but only moments before artillery fire rained down upon it. The bolter fire had stopped on the street and, cautiously, the Wolf Lord led his men forwards.

The Wolf Lord's comm crackled to life, 'Wolf Lord, the deed is done,' said Tor, triumph filling his voice.

'Well done,' said Ragnar, although he heard the sounds of battle on the other end of the comm. Still, he knew the battle would be over soon. Without the sorcerer, the Night Lords wouldn't have access to their daemonic allies and their material resources were too little for them to continue to hold out. Ragnar knew the enemy would have to retreat with whatever forces they had left.

Ranulf came running through a cross street with a pack of men. 'Hail, Wolf Lord! The foe appears to be in full retreat.'

'Good, that's how it was supposed to happen. Well done. Give me a moment, Ranulf.'

Ragnar opened a comm channel to Hoskuld, the old Space Wolf scout. 'Tor succeeded. Go ahead and help him.'

'Aye, Wolf Lord, we're there to back him up,' said Hoskuld.

Ranulf looked over at his Wolf Lord. Quietly, he asked, 'Why didn't you just have the scouts try to kill the sorcerer?'

Ragnar placed his hand on Ranulf's wide shoulder, 'Because, I'll need Tor's spirit on the next planet. He deserved a chance to take responsibility. It'll make him a better warrior.'

After a moment, Ragnar added, 'It worked for me.'

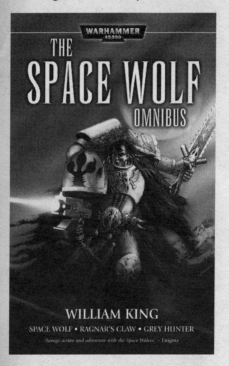

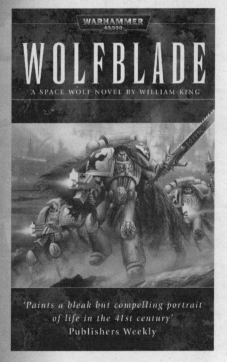

GHOSTS